Destiny Never Sleeps
Quest of the Two Queens

About the Authors

Bernadette Thompson Martin

I've often been asked who I am, and what makes me tick. Well, I'm not anyone special — I'm simply a person with something 'special' to give. Writing is a gift, not only to me, but also to the many people who will come to enjoy what I've penned.

My background is rather humble. I was born in Philadelphia, Pennsylvania and raised in the small New Jersey city of Millville. All that I am, I owe to my Mom. She not only nurtured my body, but my heart, soul, and mind. Her teachings shaped and polished a child's active imagination.

In 2007, my husband Ken and I left the Sunshine state and moved to the sleepy, quaint town of Cottageville, South Carolina. At long last, I sat down, gathered my tattered hatbox full of a lifetime of notes, and gave birth to the novel of my fantasies.

The story line began to take form at a *very* young age. Over the years, both it and I have grown expeditiously. Had I not endured the many wonderful and bizarre experiences of life, this novel would be unable to reach the level of realism and uniqueness it presents. Writing is my world, my dream — my destiny.

Jeannie Faulkner Barber

I'm a diehard Texan. Born and raised in Marshall, I now live in the East Texas piney woods of Kilgore with my wonderful husband, Monte. We have three grown sons, Joe Bryan, Adam, and Garry. They and their wives have blessed us with nine beautiful grandchildren who we love and adore. Monte and I share our home with our 'daughter', a black and tan mini-dachshund, Holley, who has us *very* well trained.

"How 'bout them Cowboys?" Yep … I'm a true blue Dallas Cowboys fan. During game time, I can be found glued to the television. My mood depends on if they win or lose the game … poor Monte.

There are *two* passions in my life: writing and drag racing. I drive my own racecar, 'Connie', a 1981 white Monte Carlo with pink racing stripes. Monte and I even met at the dragstrip. The fun thing is I've won more trophies and cash at the pulse-pounding sport than he has, but still have his love and admiration. He *is* my beloved hero and Crew Chief.

Presently, I work for the Overton-New London Chamber of Commerce as Office Manager and Executive Vice President. I'm also a member and officer of the East Texas Writers Association (ETWA), the North East Texas Writers Organization (NETWO), and a 2007 & 2011 Award Winner of NaNoWriMo.

Now, you have some insight about these two chirpy blondes, from two dynamic states, who combined their talents, but have never met face to face — **YET!**

Destiny Never Sleeps
Quest of the Two Queens

by

Bernadette Thompson Martin
&
Jeannie Faulkner Barber

Published by
Desert Coyote Productions
Longview, Texas

Library of Congress Control Number: 2012947865
EAN-13: 978-0-9859379-1-1
ISBN-10: 0-9859379-1-2

Typeset in 12pt Garamond
Printed in the U.S.A.
First edition 2012

We dedicate this novel
to all those who dare to dream.
Wondrous miracles can happen
if you only believe.

ঌ৩৩ঌ

To Helen Castor — *our special guardian Angel*.

Acknowledgments

Bernadette:

To my husband Ken, who patiently endured many late night dinner's. Thank you for your support and encouragement in this ambitious quest.

Thank you to my wonderful friends Bruce, Ray, and Peppy who have stood beside me since childhood. You have always been my inspiration.

I wish to thank my Mom, who not only encouraged a child's active imagination, but instilled courtly virtues. I also wish to thank my Dad who opened my eyes to nature and revealed its wholesome beauty. I owe the very heart and soul of my foundation to these incredible parents.

Thank you to Ms. Pat Witt, my high school teacher who recognized unrealized talent and unknowingly nudged me down a path I may have never found.

And thank you Jeannie for being my co-author, and more importantly, my friend.

అంగా

Jeannie:

To my husband Monte, thank you for always being my rock — you allow me to be me without any inhibitions. I love you, sweetheart.

To the rest of my family, especially my awesome grandkids, regardless of your age, continue to reach for the brass ring that leads to your goals, even if it is a *fantasy*!

And of course, I will always be appreciative to my co-author, Bernie who is more like a sister. Thank you for the 'invitation' to exist in Bowlandria with you.

&~CஜCஐ~ᰥ

We both wish to acknowledge some *very special* friends:

Thank you Richard Turner (www.richardturnerart.com) for our fabulous cover. Your artistic creativity completely captured our vision. We look forward to working with you on the next book in this series.

A super sincere thank you to Joe M. Jones for the mesmerizing back cover photo. Our 'ride' on Junar could not have taken place without the aide of your special talent.

Also, thank you Don A. Martinez, Editor and Publisher of Desert Coyote Productions, Inc. Your dedicated efforts have made our dream come true.

&~CஜCஐ~ᰥ

We invite you to enter our realm by visiting our website at www.destinyneversleeps.com.

For information and purchase of Jeannie's solo mystery novel, **Taste of Fire**, go to Amazon, Barnes & Noble, Kindle, Nook, or www.jeanniebarber.com.

You can also visit our blogs:
www.bernadette-thompson-martin.blogspot.com
www.jeanniefaulknerbarber.blogspot.com.

Contents

Destiny Never Sleeps
Quest of the Two Queens

Chapter 1
Life's Golden Dream

The great beast, awakened from a deathless sleep, peered into the dim obscurity of his cavernous tomb through ageless rage-filled eyes. Centuries had passed since Ios ventured from the confines of this watery prison. At last, his ancient chains of banishment were unfastened. Bit by bit, the Titan's grotesque body uncoiled and undulated into the crystal clarity of the tepid ocean waters in search of prey. Ravenous, the few morsels engulfed did little to satisfy a gluttonous appetite.

Suddenly, a familiar shadow above seized his attention, igniting an insatiable thirst for blood. He raced toward the cruiser and erupted from beneath liquid swells with the intensity of an undersea missile. Ios whirled around and attacked with wild ferocity. Within seconds, the seaworthy hull was reduced to diminutive splinters.

The forceful assault hurled five hapless victims into the water. One by one, he devoured the screaming members of the family until the scarlet-stained sea fell silent. All vestiges of the yacht, and its innocent occupants, would become another statistic of those who appear to vanish within the *dreaded triangle*. A voracious hunger now appeased, the monstrous servant headed off to the great abyss where a vile new mistress awaited.

சுஇஜ சுஇஜ

The violent summer squall hammered a torrent of raindrops against the prodigious plate-glass window. "If

1

this weather continues, our little sea voyage will surely be postponed." Kat leaned back in the frumpish green chair, drew a deep breath, and stared trance-like into the chaotic night sky. The serenity of the darkened hotel room provided blissful comfort to a mind inundated by a cornucopia of lifetime remembrances. She did not suspect an unfathomable, preordained journey would soon materialize or knew the specter of death lurked in nearby shadows.

Now in her late sixties, Kathleen Alexis Tate continued to present an attractive appearance. Long, silky black hair was cropped short and tinted blonde … a vain attempt to conceal the obnoxious progression of gray. The continual onslaught of arthritis deformed delicate fingers and robbed a body of youthful agility. Skin, once unblemished, was now sallow and wrinkled, while the unavoidable progression of weight disfigured a statuesque frame. Only those unique, exquisite golden eyes remained untouched by the devastation of time.

Being of sturdy Irish descent, she was a precocious child and outdoorsy much like her father, Patrick. He was a stout and rugged yet somewhat handsome man, the complete opposite of his showy and genteel city-born wife, Madeleine.

Kat learned to respect and appreciate nature through her dad. The warm days of summer provided the open-air duo with boundless adventures, but none more pleasurable than peaceful horseback rides along fragrant Wisteria-draped wooded trails. However, the blissful days would come to a sudden end when autumn arrived, and Patrick's fancies turned to hunting. This activity wasn't in the gentle girl's chemistry. She found it unbearable to watch a hapless animal slaughtered — much less cause their demise.

Her trek through the past continued as a long buried memory caused a composed pulse to race. Visions of Tom, the true love of her life, flooded a distressed mind like an unstoppable tidal wave. Kat's teen years overflowed with casual, carefree dates. A serious relationship was an unthought-of venture, until the night she gazed into the mesmeric brown eyes of Tom, the man who would forever possess her heart. The attraction was instantaneous and exploded into an incomparable love. However, the unforeseen intervention of destiny would lead them down far different paths.

Two weeks after graduation, Tom joined the Navy. He desired to escape their loathsome hick town and experience the sophistication of the cosmopolitan world.

Kat did not share this enthusiasm and brushed it off as meaningless chatter. *I don't understand why anyone would want to leave this place. We live among sincere, down-to-earth country folk where the way of life is simple and pure.*

A week prior to embarkation, Tom proposed, but Kat gave an unexplained, icy rejection as the unwelcome brutality of fate transformed a dream into a living nightmare.

"I can't believe I was so blasted wrong about you," he yelled. "You've played with my heart like a child's puppet. Well baby doll, the strings have just been severed, and this stupid dummy's outta here."

Fingers trembled as she touched his arm. "I don't know why I said no. Please Tom, give me a moment to sort things out in my mind."

"Give you time? For what? More childish nonsense? It's obvious you don't love me, Kat, or you wouldn't hesitate to say yes. No more fun and games, I've had it. It's over. This slob has bigger and better fish to fry." He yanked his arm from her grasp and turned to leave.

"Tom, wait," her voice resonated sorrow, but the desperate plea fell on deaf ears.

The handsome young man paused at the doorway and glanced back.

She hoped to see a touch of pity in his rich brown eyes, but instead they flashed with fierce emotion.

"Have a miserable life, you deceitful little witch." A violent slam of the door made the room shudder as he stormed out.

The venomous words were a deathblow ... her spirit shattered. In time, the heartache would fade, but never the love she held.

Eventually, a lucrative job promotion whisked her off to Miami, Florida. There she would meet the man who would become her husband.

Bill was tall, tan, handsome, and muscular. His white-blond hair, deep green eyes, and an infectious smile were heart-stopping.

Life in the tropical environment brought days of bliss, but for Kat the nightmare surfaced again.

A week before their thirty-fifth anniversary, Bill was involved in a horrible auto accident on his way home from a fishing trip in Key West. For several days he laid in a coma. Day and night Kat remained at his side praying her words would bring him back, but they did not. He would never awaken.

Once again, she faced catastrophic heartbreak. Only three years had passed since cancer claimed the life of her mother. A short time later, distraught over the death of his beloved wife, Patrick also went to his grave. Now, Bill was gone.

Unable to cope alone, Kat placed a call to lifelong friends, Randy, Tippy, and Jay. She desperately needed the boundless degree of consolation only they could provide. The following morning, all three arrived in Miami.

The day after Bill's memorial, Randy appeared to sense Kat's loneliness. "Look kiddo, we have more acres than we can use. Why not move back to South Carolina with me and Jay. If privacy's an issue, put a dang house anywhere you want on the property. It doesn't matter to us, just come home."

Jay shared a palatial Victorian farmhouse with Randy, nestled on three hundred and fifty-five acres in the fertile South Carolina lowcountry. Both were accomplished riders, so they transformed the old, abandoned property into a magnificent horse ranch.

After a few months of mourning, Kat accepted the offer and settled into a comfortable new dwelling located in a secluded area of the luxuriant farm. The peaceful stillness it provided soothed tattered nerves and healed a tormented soul. She felt uplifted and content with the thought of this being her final abode.

The sharp pierce of a car backfiring snatched her from thoughts of the past. She rose, walked to the hotel room window, and looked out. Ominous clouds began to part, and silvery beacons of moonlight crept through. "Shoot, looks like we'll set sail at daybreak after all. Well, at least my Bill will at long last be laid to rest."

A glance at the insignificant box that held the ashes of her beloved spouse caused emotions to boil with rage. *What wrong have I committed for life to treat me so cruelly. This world has finally staked claim to every person I've ever loved.* Tears erupted as months of pent-up frustration burst forth like a powerful wind. "I wish I could find another place, a magical land, where there was no death or grief. I hate this world. I hate it!" She spun around, snatched a brown ginger-jar lamp from a nearby table, and hurled it against the wall.

The strident commotion brought Kat's companions to her room. Crumpled in a mound by the window, she sobbed into folded arms.

Randy hurried over and embraced her. "Go ahead Kat, let it all out. You've earned the right. I know tomorrow's gonna be rough, but together we'll get through it. We're here for ya kiddo and not about to leave."

Tippy plopped down alongside and caressed Kat's hands. "Dang right, we all love you. *Nothing* on this earth will *ever* separate us."

Kat looked up, wiped away the tears, and forced a smile in gratitude. Without their unselfish support, the despicable task ahead would be impossible to carry out.

Jay lumbered in last, aided by the sturdy hand-carved wooden cane used to support unsteady, decimated knees. "Hey dudes, let's have no more of this boo-hooing tonight. What say we lighten things up a little with a smidgen of Jay's special remedy?" A devilish smile crossed his face as he held up a bottle of rum.

None were avid drinkers, but tonight a good hefty stiff one was in order. Within moments, the room's thick cloud of tension evaporated as the anesthetic effects of the alcohol took hold.

Randy eased down into a faded maroon wing-backed chair. "What would you all say to a little R&R? I can arrange a couple additional days on the boat lease, and we could head on over to the Islands afterward. A bit of fun might just be what the doctor ordered. Shall we go for it kiddo?"

Kat thought it was an excellent idea and nodded in agreement.

Jay nudged Tippy in the side. "Well old girl, looks like we're going on a little cruise. It's not the Queen Mary, but it floats. At least I hope it does."

"I'm starting to get a tad nervous, Jay. You know I've never liked boats and dread going out on the water, *especially* in the ocean. I can't seem to throw off this horrific sense something terrible is about to happen, and we won't come back."

"Dang gum it girl, will you get off that kick. Only thing you need to worry about out there is me, so just drop it. You can be such a party-pooper at times."

Later, the trio grew weary, said good night to Kat, and retired to their rooms.

ജ‍ൠ   ജ‍ൠ

Randy called the marina and extended the lease, then checked the weather report. "Looks like tomorrow will be a mighty fine day ... sunny with a chance of showers. Maybe with a bit of luck we'll see a rainbow — a doggone big one. That should put a smile on Kat's face." He yawned and switched off the light. A timeless phrase came to mind: *Be careful what you wish for because you may not like what you get.* Confident there was little to go wrong, he chuckled at the worrisome thought, rolled over, and fell fast asleep. However, the innocent proverb would prove prophetic. Tomorrow's venture would be *far* from ordinary.

ജ‍ൠ   ജ‍ൠ

7

Sheets fluttered as Kat tossed and turned. Her overtired eyes felt like two fiery embers. The night before granted little sleep, and it appeared tonight would be a repeat performance. Unable to achieve rest, she walked to the sink and splashed some cool water on a tear-swollen face. The aged image in the mirror caused a heave of disgust. Only yesterday, she was a young, pretty girl, full of life. Now, time had erased all evidence of youth. A perky oval face sagged. Wrinkled eyelids drooped over listless amber eyes, and sexy, plump lips grew thin. "This old age garbage is for the birds. I look like some creepy hag. I swear the next person who tells me how wonderful these *golden years* are, I'm gonna slap them simple." She thought of her three friends and how each were now mere shadows of what they once were.

In younger days, Randy was almost beyond handsome. A tall muscular body, covered by flawless sun-kissed skin, was topped by a head of thick, wavy black hair. Prominent indigo-blue eyes complimented an incomparable masculine face. Contagious happiness surrounded him prior to the premature death of his wife, Sandy. He was never quite the same after cancer took her life. As always, he would laugh and joke, but the special spark in his eyes vanished, and Kat wondered if it would ever return.

She recalled when Jay first met Randy. It was in elementary school. The two boys immediately formed a strong, dedicated bond of friendship. Although small and stocky in stature, he presented a well-proportioned, debonair appearance. Short, dark brown hair and effervescent coffee-colored eyes complimented a radiant smile. Always prepared to perform his funniness at the drop of a hat, every second around this natural born

8

clown and jokester seemed like a day at the circus. It was unbearable to watch the happy-go-lucky man wither away in loneliness after his wife Mary was killed — the innocent victim of a drunk driver.

Randy, also widowed and lonely, suggested he and Jay pool resources and buy a place to share. Months passed before they stumbled upon the dilapidated old farm. Restoration required was enormous, but the difficult task provided a plethora of consolation.

Visions of a youthful Tippy now marched into Kat's thoughts. She was of Scandinavian heritage, with shoulder length flaxen hair, electric sky-blue eyes, and an enviable curvaceous body.

Although given the name Tyra at birth, most friends called her Tippy due to an unbelievable aptitude for clumsiness. Bouncy, charismatic, and full of life, she was the type of person everyone enjoyed being around. The eventual marriage to Jim, a mirthful and enlivened man, produced two sons who later surrounded the ecstatic woman with several grandchildren. Family was, and remained, the most important factor in her life. Not only was Tippy an exceptional wife and mother, but also an incomparable true friend.

Reveries vanished as an avalanche of water overflowed from the sink and nipped at Kat's toes. She grabbed towels to mop up and mumbled in sarcastic irritation, "Blast it. I hate this nonsense. My feet are swollen, my back hurts, my kidneys are weak, my mind is gone, and I can't see worth a ding without these stupid contacts. They can take these *golden years* and shove 'em."

She shuffled into the bedroom, sat on the edge of the bed, and sighed in awe at the remarkable beauty of dawn. Twilight now surrendered to daybreak, as vibrant shades of pink, gold, red, and lavender dotted the sky in a magnificent display. *Well, there's no use trying to sleep now.* A rap at the door caused her to jump. Once again, time had become lost in a daydream.

"Kat," Randy yelled. "Snap to it girl. Time's a wastin'."

"Oh hold your britches on. I'm almost ready." The bold-faced lie brought a pinkish glow to pallid cheeks. She hurried to dress, gave her hair a quick brush, and in a few minutes joined everyone in the hall — Bill's ashes in hand.

"Let's get this show on the road. Got these bum legs of mine a movin' and ain't about to stop 'em now." Jay appeared to be in a jovial frame of mind as he hobbled toward the elevator.

Kat knew a number of old football injuries limited every movement, but although in constant and severe pain, he never complained. To control diabetes and heart disease, a stringent diet eliminated the majority of tasty goodies he loved, adding more misery. His pill case resembled a miniature pharmacy, but survival was impossible without the medications. Nevertheless, Jay remained the life of the party and a treasured friend.

As the elevator doors opened, providence prevailed. A wide concrete walkway to the dock stood less than ten feet away. The four strolled past a long line of vessels and soon spotted the brilliant white hull of the Charger, a flashy 54-foot sportfisherman. Her graceful sheer lines and magnificent flared bow were impressive. A copious teak deck led into the luxurious salon, which provided all the comforts of home.

Tippy's voice cracked somewhat as she spoke, the obvious result of escalating apprehensions, "Y'all know the legends of the 'Devil's Triangle' are justifiably renowned. I sure hope our little *pleasure trip* doesn't add to its mystery."

Randy scowled, drew a breath, and snappishly tossed his gear aboard. "I think we've heard enough of this doom and gloom stuff, Tip. Nothing is gonna happen out there. The cabin's open y'all, so make yourselves comfortable. I have to go check in, but will be right back."

Jay stood at attention on the deck, stuck out his tongue, and saluted as Randy hurried off. "Arrrrr … aye, aye Cap'n, ya miserable, old bilge-suckin' son of a seadog."

Tippy and Kat almost doubled over in laugher at the hilarious antics. Some things never change, and Jay continued to remain the clown.

Within moments, Randy returned and leaped on board, his voice energized, "Okay you guys, we're clear to shove off. Let's see what this baby has to offer." The Charger was a seaman's dream, and they all chuckled at his eagerness to take command of the wheel. He bounded up the ladder to the fly bridge and turned the ignition key. The powerful twin diesels sprung to life like a pair of tiger cubs. Jay threw off the lines and Randy eased her out of the slip. The Charger glided through the rolling swells of the jetty, and as they passed the last channel buoy, Randy smiled, throttled up, and headed for open water.

Unbeknownst to the naive group, their destination would be a world apart from the one anticipated.

The rising sun inched higher on the horizon, and the flawless dawn sky turned a resplendent shade of blue as the onset of a glorious day began. A salty breeze filled the air and danced upon the oceans unruffled surface.

The two girls tossed their things inside the salon and hurried out to soak up a few welcome rays.

Jay slowly climbed to the bridge where he proceeded to ask a myriad of questions about this and that and its use.

Kat could not help overhear and drew a deep breath. *Randy, I sure hope your patience holds out.*

As the Charger was brought up to running speed, its slick hull sliced through the waves like a sharp hot blade in butter. "Hey guys, since we're well out to sea now, I'm gonna set the autopilot, kick back, and enjoy the ride." The huge grin on his face made it obvious to the others he was delighted to be the skipper of this incredible vessel.

The steady hum of the diesels, together with the sedating sway of the boat, quickly rocked Kat to sleep. It felt as though mere seconds had passed when she was awakened by the sudden silence of the engines. Startled, her mind swathed in a perplexed fog, she looked around, confused and unable to focus through bloodshot eyes. "W-what's going on?"

Randy, who had come down from the fly bridge, stood alongside her chair and spoke in a soft, gentle manner, "Kat, we're over three miles out ... it's time to put Bill to rest."

The sight of the tiny container he held sent a jolt of nauseating revulsion through her body. "Please Randy, spread them for me. I c-can't do it. I don't have the strength." Uncontrollable tears tumbled to the deck.

Randy opened the box in revered silence, leaned over the rail, and lowered it near the sea. From out of nowhere, a ghostlike wisp of air brushed his hand and coaxed the cremated remains from the cardboard urn.

12

For a split second, the gray powdery ashes hovered in the air like a stray cloud, then began their descent and floated to the surface as though guided by the wings of an angel. "It's over, Kat — Bill's home."

She stared at the empty carton and was astonished to feel an odd rush of relief. Randy predicted this final act would provide the necessary closure, and he was correct. Kat took his hand and peered into joyless eyes. "I'm sorry. I couldn't do it myself. I just couldn't."

"No need to apologize, kiddo. I understand. It's never easy to let go of those we love," he replied.

Kat knew the statement was valid. Death was by no means a stranger to him.

The burial at sea had been quick, yet traumatic. All four friends now stood in silence with bowed heads, as each bid farewell to an endeared companion in their own special way.

"Good-bye, Bill. I'll always remember and love you," Kat whispered.

Randy returned to the bridge, fired up the engines, and headed for the open sea.

A great weight was lifted and pent up tensions eased. They were in good spirits, returned to their normal, playful selves, but from this point on *nothing* would ever be normal.

The farther out the boat traveled the more beautiful the tranquil ocean became, turning deep cobalt blue as the depth of the sky reflected in the waters clarity. So far, it had been a splendid day, but the unpredictable was about to surface.

Randy yawned and lazily scanned the horizon. "Well I'll be a son-of-a-gun. Hey Kat, get your fanny up here. I

13

believe this sucker's made an appearance just for you, kid. Now is this a perfect day or what?"

Kat leaped from the chair and rocketed up the ladder steps. "Wow!" Dead ahead were the bright-banded arches of a colossal rainbow. Although quite beautiful, the sight made her skin prickle. "Randy, there's something strange about this thing."

"Strange? Have you gone bats? I'm thinkin' the only weird thing out here is *you*."

"Well I know what a rainbow is, Mr. Smarty-pants, but isn't it odd for one to appear when there's no rain. Look around. The sky's clear as a bell, not a cloud in sight, so how's this possible?"

Randy took the boat out of gear and let it drift. The pair noticed an eerie stillness of the radio and an erratic spin of the compass. He reached for the mic, and a sound of panic was detected in his voice, "Miami Coast Guard, this is the vessel Charger requesting a radio check." Moments passed without a reply. "Miami Coast Guard, this is the vessel Charger requesting a radio check. Please come in." Fingers trembled as he switched channels, but received no response. He grabbed the portable GPS, the one device that could not fail, and his face blanched white. "This is impossible, Kat." The humdrum voyage had grown dangerous. "Like it or not, I'm going back. We've lost all our electronics, and I don't know why. Maybe it's your stinking rainbow." The harsh words stung a tender heart and showed clearly on her face. "Dang my nasty mouth. I'm sorry and didn't mean to take it out on you like that, but something is radically wrong about all this. We need to book out of here this instant."

All of a sudden, Kat was besieged by a strange sensation, as though the rainbow beckoned to her. "No," she yelled. "We have to keep going."

"You don't get it, Kat. We're in deep trouble. I'm sorry, but we're going back."

"Why are you in such a state, Randy? It's only a harmless rainbow. We'll probably find out the equipment failure is due to something stupid like a blown fuse or broken wire. Besides, we're a lot closer to the Islands than Miami."

It *was* true. They were only about twenty miles from Freeport. "Well, you have a valid point. I'm gonna try the Bahamas and see if I can get someone on the horn." As before, all they heard was an unnatural static. He tossed the mic to the floor in frustration and drew a deep breath. "I give up. You win this round, kid. We'll keep going. Once we dock, I'll call the leasing office and arrange to get the Charger fixed. Looks like we're gonna spend a few days ashore and have some fun in the sun."

As the sturdy sportfisherman moved forward, it sped through the water with the velocity of a thoroughbred. "I really have a bad feeling in the pit of my stomach, Kat. This apparition's not normal. A rainbow is only a prismatic reflection and ought to move away as we progress, yet this one appears to draw closer. Everything about it's unnatural. The ocean and sky should be visible under the arches, not that endless tunnel of black emptiness ahead. Throw a fit if you like, but this baby's turning around." Unsteady hands spun the wheel and tried to bring the Charger about, but the craft would not respond. "Feels like the wheel's frozen." He slammed the controls into neutral, only to find them unresponsive as the vessel continued the trek forward.

15

Randy directed Jay and Tippy, who were alone on the deck below, to don their life jackets and go into the cabin.

"What's wrong?" Tippy screamed.

Randy swallowed hard. "Kinda looks as though we're in for some rough weather, and it might be safer for you two inside."

"You're lying. I knew something like this would happen. We're going to die." She began to sob.

Jay tried to calm her. "Look, Randy knows what he's doing, and we need to do as he asks. Come on old girl, let's go." He took an arm and escorted her into the salon.

Tippy shivered and sunk down on the plush sofa beside Jay while tears poured from terrified eyes. "I'm not ready to die and don't want to leave my family, not this way."

Huddled together, they waited for whatever was to come.

Randy looked into Kat's zombie-like amber eyes. "What's going on with you? Why aren't you frightened?"

She touched his shoulder in reassurance. "The rainbow hasn't been sent to hurt us. This is how it's meant to be. Don't worry. We're going to be fine, I promise."

Every possible maneuver proved futile. Randy and Kat stood side-by-side on the bridge in total helplessness, while a mysterious, unseen force pulled the Charger toward the awaiting multihued doorway. There would be no earthly deviation from this inescapable course — for it had been set by Destiny.

Chapter 2
This Isn't Kansas

Two tiny gnomes scurried down the long corridor toward the opulent tower room. Gleek and Pudge were in charge of the Castle grounds and magnificent gardens. Breathless, they knocked and entered.

Sight of the petite duo brightened the exquisite face of Queen Adera. "Good day, my dear ones. How delightful it is to see you. Several chores of utmost importance require your exceptional handiwork."

"Of course, Your Highness," replied the pair of high-pitched voices in chorus. "It is indeed a pleasure to do whatever you desire ... a true pleasure."

Gleek was about three foot high, had a round jolly face, cute pug nose, and twinkling brown eyes. A long, bushy white beard all but covered a stout belly, while thin, snowy wisps of hair peeked out from the sides of his large pointed red hat. Black trousers, neatly tucked inside brown suede boots, were topped by a crisp powder-blue knee-length tunic.

Pudge, a rosy-cheeked, brown-eyed, bouncy bundle of animation, stood two inches shorter. Long straw-colored braids, trimmed with tiny red bows, protruded from under a hat similar to Gleek's. Covering the properly tucked white peasant blouse was a quaint red vest. Atop an ankle-length green and gold argyle-print skirt was a starched white apron. On her feet were tiny satin slippers with an upright curled point on each tip.

"Gleek, your distinctive talents make our gardens the loveliest in the region, but today I ask an added touch of magic be applied to the small west courtyard. Dear sweet Pudge, will you kindly fill every vase in the Castle with copious bundles of your most fragrant flowers."

"Oh yes, Your Highness, yes. We will start at once, at once," the two replied in unison. After an inelegant, polite bow to the Sovereign, they whirled around and dashed from the room. The antics caused Adera to giggle.

"Pardon the intrusion, Your Majesty, you requested my presence." The stately nymph bowed her head in respect as she entered the room. Bagi was tall with floor length cardinal-red curly hair, delicate pointed ears, and large seductive eyes that glistened like two exquisite emeralds. Full rose-red lips and a dainty button nose complimented a sun-kissed, oval face. Her voice was soft and gentle, yet possessed a sense of aloofness and extreme intelligence. She wore a lace trimmed, billowy crimson velvet gown, while a wreath of dainty roses and daisies adorned her head. Bagi was the embodiment of natural physical beauty … young, charming, and graceful.

"Yes, dear friend. New guests shall arrive soon, which necessitates your services. My carriage has been made ready and awaits you."

"I will leave immediately, Majesty."

"Without a doubt, your usual competence will apply to this mission. However, I have an additional, rather unorthodox, request to make. Please send word to McLachen and ask he join you at the beach."

The nymph wrinkled her brow. "I do not understand. The great stallion has never before accompanied me to greet arrivals."

"These visitors are unlike any we have encountered in the past. If my presumptions are correct, one will enter who shall be of great interest to him."

"All shall be handled as you desire." Bagi bowed cordially and exited.

Adera strolled to the voluminous, gothic tower room window and gazed out over her beloved kingdom. In the distance, she noticed a familiar green speck dart across the flamboyant blue sky, and her lips forced a faint smile. Mellow rays of morning light drifted over the land and awakened the nearby village. Knowledge of imminent new voyagers electrified the air with excitement.

"And so at last it begins." A veil of sadness engulfed the gentle Queen, and concern clouded celestial turquoise eyes. She knew another would also enter, an unwelcome creature, controlled by a vixen determined to destroy her and the realm. The ancient foretold time of evil had arrived.

℘∝ ℘∝

The ocean was serene, not a ripple upon its surface. Suddenly, it erupted with savage violence and tossed the sea-worthy boat around like a tiny wooden toothpick.

Kat could hear the labored sound of the engines as they struggled to stay alive and wondered how much more they would take. Her nerves continued to mount. "Perhaps you were right, Randy. Maybe we should have turned around."

"Well it's too late now. We're stuck in this mess. The choice is no longer ours to make."

The brute force from a monstrous wave slammed hard against the hull, almost tossing the twosome from the fly bridge.

19

"You better go join Jay and Tippy in the cabin before you get thrown overboard, Kat. I have enough on my mind and don't need to worry about you on top of everything else. So move it girl. Get your butt downstairs," Randy barked.

"Are you crazy? If I try to climb down the ladder now I'll get washed over for sure. No way, bucko. I'm staying right here." The words no sooner left her mouth when another colossal wave struck and nearly broached the vessel. Kat's body began to tremble, and her voice quivered from fright, "I … I don't understand. Why is the ocean so rough? It's as though we're in the middle of a hurricane yet there's no wind or rain."

The strange calmness she experienced only a short time ago was replaced by unadulterated terror. A torrent of seawater from the massive waves tumbled over the sides and began to flood the deck.

"Beat's me, kiddo. None of this makes a lick of sense. You better slip on a life jacket. I don't know how much longer the boat can take this kind of abuse. The bilge pumps are about to quit, and with all of this water pouring in, I'm afraid it will be the end of the Charger."

She grimaced and clutched his arm. "Have you ever known a rainbow to cause a phenomenon like this?"

"No. A common rainbow is harmless. I don't know what in the dickens this thing is, but it's not a rainbow. Look, we're about to enter a pipeline of nothingness."

She glanced up and screamed as a jab of panic struck a blow to her heart. "What? That's not possible."

Randy snatched the radio mic from its holder and hurried to place a distress call. "Mayday, Mayday, this is the vessel Charger. We're twenty miles due west of

Freeport and taking on water. We request immediate assistance — Mayday."

The call went unanswered.

Within seconds, the ill-fated boat entered the unnatural arches and became engulfed by a multitude of vibrant colors.

Once inside, the air grew still, and a spine-chilling calm overtook the sea. The vessel shuddered as the engines died, and it was brought to a sudden halt. The Charger sat motionless, surrounded by colorful light of unbelievable brightness.

Static from the electrified air prickled Kat's skin, and her head throbbed from intense pressure. A downward glance brought a gasp. The blue water of the Atlantic Ocean was becoming visible through the Charger's semi-transparent hull.

"Randy, what's happening to the boat?" She turned to find him in a clump on the deck of the bridge, lifeless.

The buzz in her head was unbearable and movement agonizingly difficult. Kat fought to remain conscious. She struggled to reach the ladder, climb down, and crawl to the cabin. Inside, lying side by side on the floor was Tippy and Jay. "This is my fault. What have I done?" Strength at last diminished, she succumbed and drifted into blank darkness.

One by one, the four friends began to regain consciousness.

Kat raised her head and tried to look around, but couldn't focus.

Randy staggered to his feet. "Is everyone all right?"

"Sort of," Kat replied. "I don't know about anyone else, but I feel like a wet noodle and can't see worth a darn. Everything is blurry."

Jay mumbled somewhat as he got up, "Where the blazes are we, and where the heck are you two? I can't see a confounded thing except a bunch of fuzzy outlines."

Randy touched his eye. "Well, one contact is gone, so may as well ditch the other." He blinked a few times and gasped. "What the …? Kat, are your contacts still in place?"

"Yeah, I can't believe they didn't fall out. Hey, I'm not wet either. Guess we didn't go into the water."

"Hah. If you think that's incredible, kiddo, wait 'til you remove those contacts."

She obeyed. "Jiminy danged crickets! My 20/20's returned."

Jay followed the lead of the other two and let out a whoop of excitement. "Dudes, my eyesight's back, too. I can see as clear as the day I was born. Awesome."

"Holy kee-rap," Randy exclaimed. "This has to be some sort of hallucination. All of us are … uh … young again."

The four friends stood in silence and stared at each other.

They now appeared to be in their early twenties and all signs of old age removed.

Tippy teetered on wobbly legs and let out a bloodcurdling scream. "I knew this would happen. I just knew it. Don't any of you morons understand why we look this way? We're dead."

Randy took hold of her shoulders, his voice calm but stern, "No Tip, we're not dead. I don't understand what's happened, but I'm sure there's a perfectly normal explanation."

"Duh. Do you seriously think all this is *normal*, genius? We have to be in some sort of afterlife. For someone supposedly so intelligent, you can sure act stupid at times."

Jay cleared his throat. "Uh dudes, I hate to interrupt such a tender moment, but can ya'll tell me just what the blazes we're standing on?"

The others glanced down at the hardened expanse of sapphire. There was no hint of the Charger in sight, only its four passengers, who stood upon an eerie, frozen sea.

"Look, I don't know any more than the rest of you, but think its time to make for that shoreline ahead. After our toes are planted on solid soil, the discussion can continue," Randy advised.

As the friends sprinted in the direction of the uncharacteristic beach, a gargantuan, black shadow slithered beneath their feet in the ocean's icy depths.

"Hey, is that a woman over there?" Tippy pointed.

Bagi's hair and gown fluttered in the gentle breeze as she stood near the water's edge. Once the group touched land, the poised nymph approached — a hand outstretched in welcome. "Good afternoon. I am Bagi and extend sincere greetings. We know who you are and anticipated your arrival."

Randy's face turned brick red. "What? How did we get here, and just *who* is the *we* you refer to?"

"All will be explained in due time. I shall escort you to the Castle. There, rest and refreshments may be obtained."

"Oh no, missy, I'm afraid that lily-livered explanation is not acceptable. Tell us right here and now what this is all about, or we're not budging one inch." Randy stomped a foot.

"I am sorry, but must insist you come with me. I shall try to disclose what I know as we travel. The carriage waits."

Bewildered, fatigued, and unsure, the group gave in and followed her.

The unmistakable sound of hoof-beats in the surf caused everyone to turn and draw a breath of disbelief. A magnificent, ebony-coated Andalusian stallion galloped toward them. Strong legs pounded against the wet, silvery sand, while an extensive black mane and tail fluttered in the wind.

Kat was mesmerized by the sheer elegance of this animal and stood in awed silence. The great horse paused, nickered, and arched a thick muscular neck, then pranced over to her. She affectionately cradled the suede-like muzzle in her hand and felt comforted by the warmth of his breath which reassured her they were alive.

Bagi strolled over and stood next to the noble beast. "It appears McLachen has come to greet you, mistress Kat, which is indeed a rare privilege. He seldom finds favor with any human. Nevertheless, we must put this moment aside and be underway. Our trip is long, and you are most likely weary from today's ordeal."

Kat pulled herself away from the splendid stallion, walked over to Tippy, and took her hand. "Come on y'all, we need to do as the lady says. I don't know about the rest of you, but I feel as though every drop of energy has been drained from my body."

Randy and Jay nodded in agreement, joined the two girls, and with great reluctance followed Bagi to the forest's edge.

A grand carriage, parked in the shadow of a tall oak, waited. The open wooden vehicle was white with graceful fluid lines and plush red velvet seats. Harnessed to it were four black extremely large incomparable horses.

"Whoa dudes, aren't these Shires?"

"Yeah, I think they are, Jay," Randy replied as he eyed the gigantic creatures.

The animals were massive, standing a good 18 hands high with a powerful muscular build and large heads supported by thick, graceful necks. Long wisps of white hair covered the enormous hooves like fine silk feathers, and although giants, the brown, wide-set eyes projected an unruffled docile expression. The impressive fine-grained leather harness was black and shiny. Engraved silver rosettes peppered the bridles and chest bands.

As the group climbed aboard the exquisite carriage, the driver turned and greeted them in a dignified baritone voice with a Jamaican accent undertone, "Good day. I am Relar, Queen Adera's personal driver, and these are not common Shires, my lads. We call them Thunder Hooves."

Although vintage, the coachman's attire was elegant. Relar, a handsome dark-skinned man of medium height, had short black hair, deep brown eyes, and appeared more than capable of handling the reins of these brawny steeds.

The tufted seats were a welcomed comfort to the fatigued group as they settled down. Kat eased in between Randy and Tippy, while Jay sat opposite them with the peculiar redhead at his side.

Bagi spoke in a detached, authoritative manner, "The Thunder Hooves possess unmeasured speed and shall pull us along at a blistering pace. However, I believe you will find the journey to be a smooth and pleasant one."

A snap from the coachman's whip brought the horses to life, and they were underway, McLachen cantering alongside.

Tippy, who had not uttered a word since they came ashore, leaned forward. "Miss Bagi, are ... are we ... dead?"

"No madam. You are alive."

Randy's voice was harsh and aggressive, "Okay lady, enough. If we're not in some sort of purgatory, tell us where the blazes we are, *now.*"

The demure nymph fidgeted as she replied, "Out of courtesy I shall offer some explanation, but understand, it is not my duty to make clear the realm. You are in the Kingdom of Bowlandria and have been brought into our world by the Great Force. We do not question why you have entered, but be assured there is a reason. Queen Adera will soon explain everything in explicit detail."

Kat's insatiable curiosity surfaced. "Whoa, this place has a Queen?"

"Yes, mistress. Adera is a great, gentle Queen and loved by all who reside in this land." Bagi's emerald eyes were aglow with obvious admiration.

Eventual emergence from the forest revealed resplendent meadows from horizon to horizon. Flowers of lavender, yellow, and red dotted the gentle sun-streaked slopes, and infused the tepid air with provocative scents.

The clamor of the giant hooves sounded like distant thunder as they pounded against the stone covered path.

Kat noticed Randy's puckered lips and knew he was still annoyed. She reached over and squeezed his hand. "I know patience has never been a virtue you possess, but please try to be a little more tolerant. I'm sure the answers

26

will come soon enough. At least we're all together, safe, and alive. For heaven's sake, will you try to relax? This place is remarkable."

"Remarkable? Did your brains fall out somewhere along the line? The most fundamental issue happens to be our safety. Yet, in your warped mind, our welfare isn't a vital concern. Hey y'all, Kat thinks it's more important for us to sit back, take in the sights, and enjoy the ride. Now isn't that sweet of her?" The verbal attack was loud and sarcastic, but sight of her distressed face tempered the cantankerous outburst. "I'm sorry, kiddo." He put an arm around her shoulder. "I can be such an inconsiderate jerk at times. If it will make you feel better, I'll try to act with more restraint, but won't promise how long it'll last."

The carriage ride continued and passed through several polychromatic valleys each more spectacular than the last. Colorful birds fluttered about in the high safety of the tall hardwoods, while plentiful herds of deer grazed nonchalantly in nearby meadows, undaunted by the carriage as it swept by.

At last, Randy broke the silence, "You claim we're not dead, Miss Bagi, but if that's the case, why are we young again?"

The nymph's buttery complexion sparkled in the sunlight. "When you entered our realm, the wondrous gift of eternal youth was bestowed upon you."

Randy frowned. "How's *that* possible?"

"I am unable to answer. However, Queen Adera will put to rest all apprehensions."

"Yo, dudes. I never realized 'til now, but there's not a lick of pain in my body. I'd almost forgotten what it's like not to hurt. Man, I could really get used to this." Jay chuckled and slapped his knee.

Kat noticed Randy cast a displeased look and leaned in close to him. "Will you please try to lighten up? I don't know about you, but I sure appreciate the return of our youth. I'm sorry, but old age sucked. Take a gander at Jay. Doesn't it do your heart good to see him free of pain after suffering so many years in agony?"

"You're right, kid. I need to shut my big mouth and deal with things. I'm a tad ashamed of myself, but truly didn't notice y'all had changed at first. Pretty weird, huh?"

Kat smiled and replied, her voice calm and supportive, "Not at all, Randy. We've always seen each other this way. You've never changed to me, not really, and neither has Jay or Tippy. Our hearts allow our eyes to see each other as we were."

She looked over at Tippy, who sat alongside. All vestiges of age had vanished. Silken blonde hair draped delicate shoulders and firmness returned to a slim body.

"Why are you staring at me, Kat? What's wrong? Do I look goofy or something?"

"No Tip, you look perfect."

"This can't be real, Kat. It's just not possible. Are you positive we're not dead?" A reassuring pat on the hand brought a smile to the frightened girl's face.

Jay shouted out as the Castle came into view, "Holy crapola. That's one dang big piece of real estate. Y'all might want to cast a glance at what sits over yonder."

Heads turned, and for a moment, the lifelong companions were rendered speechless by a building of such breathtaking magnitude. The pretentious granite block structure, perched atop a high plateau, was visible for miles. A spectacular roof, covered with weathered slate tiles, enhanced the ancient appearance. Atop the

28

elegant formation were fabulous turrets, and radiant white spires towered so high they seemed to touch the sky.

"I'm sure glad we're almost there 'cause my stomach's growling like a cornered bobcat," Jay bellowed as he rubbed his belly. "Sure hope this joint has some grub behind those walls. I'm so hungry right now I could eat a horse."

"I beg your pardon, Sir, but I do not wish to be considered a meal. I would not insult you by stating I would eat a man," McLachen replied in a rather indignant tone.

Jay's jaw dropped and eyes widened. "Whoa. Did y'all hear that? This horse just talked. I mean he actually talked, you know speak, spoke, whatever you want to call it. Dudes, I don't think we're in Kansas anymore."

Bagi giggled. "Our McLachen does indeed speak. He is only one of the many magical creatures who reside in Bowlandria."

Kat looked at Bagi with skepticism. "This is a joke, right?"

"No madam, it is the truth. Many incredible life forms reside in our realm, and all are indeed spectacular. I am certain you will encounter them in time."

Randy perked up and scooted to the edge of his seat. "Well Miss Bagi, at last you've mentioned something of interest. Kat and I have always been fascinated by magic and so-called mystical creatures. Perhaps your world isn't such a nasty place after all and might be somewhat intriguing to explore. Until we leave for home, that is."

Kat was oblivious to the conversation — her mind had become transfixed on the onyx stallion that galloped alongside and the unorthodox fact he could speak. *I must get to know this remarkable creature. It feels as though I'm caught up in a dream, but I know I'm awake.* She had felt the same sense of peace when they first encountered the rainbow. Now, it seemed perfectly natural for them to be here.

As they approached the grand entrance to the Castle, the robust steeds were slowed to a walk. The sound was almost deafening as their colossal hooves pounded against the ancient wooden planks of an impressive drawbridge. Below, in water clear as ice, fiery-orange fish darted in and out of the lime-green grass.

The clank of the titanic horseshoes upon the brown cobblestones ricocheted off the sides of the monolithic stonewalls as they entered into an immoderate circular courtyard. A splendiferous fountain stood in the center. Gushers of misty water sprayed from the heads of bronze dolphins and tumbled gently into a hand-hammered copper bowl.

Finally, the carriage came to a halt in front of two voluminous, weighty oak doors.

The nymph appeared aloof as she exited the carriage, forced a smile, and motioned toward the opulent entrance. "Please, come this way. The Queen awaits your arrival."

"I'm sure glad she's going first 'cause I sure as shoot wouldn't want to open those hummers," Jay joked. He let out a whoop, leaped from the carriage, and sprinted up the king-size steps like a chirpy schoolboy.

"Wow, he must really be starved. Guess we better hurry before he eats all the chow." Randy chuckled as he tried to catch up with his high-spirited friend.

"I'm famished, too," Tippy replied. "I swear I could eat a ho — I mean a big turkey." She peered over at McLachen and corrected herself.

Kat did not join her friends, but walked to the extraordinary stallion, unable to suppress budding curiosity for another second. She spoke with caution so as not to offend him, "You actually talk, McLachen?"

"Yes, My Lady," he replied in a soft, genteel voice. "I vocalize as easily as you."

The fascination between the two was incredible, almost prophetic.

Kat reached up and stroked his head. "I hope we'll get the opportunity to know each other better, McLachen, and perhaps develop a friendship."

"I believe we shall indeed become close friends, My Lady. I sense the bond has already begun. You have much gentleness in your golden eyes, and I feel great love in your heart. Now, you must go with your companions to eat and rest. There will be time for us another day." He turned and strolled off.

He's right. I am hungry and exhausted. She had eaten very little over the past two days and sleep was more than overdue. Kat ran to join her friends as they approached the gigantic doors.

Bagi uttered a phrase in an unfamiliar language, and the aged wood creaked eerily as the Herculean barriers mysteriously swung open and granted passageway.

Chapter 3
The Fantasy of it All

Overwhelmed, Kat's eyes probed every inch of the wondrous space. "It's almost beyond my mind's comprehension."

Randy turned at a snail's pace and gazed openmouthed. "That's an understatement, kiddo."

The Great Hall was a monumental, and rather impressive, piece of architecture. Shiny rose-colored marble floor tiles were set in a diamond pattern accentuated by an ornamental border of luminous green jade. A lavish chandelier of gold, silver, and crystal dangled from the center of the spectacular pointed arched ceiling. Ornate columns of gold, crowned by engraved capitals of white marble, supported sophisticated walnut beams. Near the entrance wall was an immense fireplace capped by an artistic mantel of ivory inlaid with pink and blue lapis.

Many frescos of prestigious quality hung from the smooth beige plaster walls. An enormous cathedral-style window, framed by luxurious hunter-green velvet draperies, all but encompassed the entire back wall. In close proximity was a grand staircase — its delicate carved banister the unmistakable handiwork of master craftsmen.

The doorways, edged by festooned colonnettes, were topped with cornices of intricate designs. In the center of the room stood a resplendent alabaster angel with wings so skillfully carved one might expect to see her fly off the pedestal upon which she stood.

"Please, make yourselves comfortable. I must notify the Queen of your arrival." Bagi bid a subdued, yet polite, goodbye and hastened off.

The four companions began to stroll around the room, their bodies dwarfed by its enormity.

Jay sauntered over to an antique, mahogany chair and patted the cushy, mint-green satin seat. "Yo dudes, think we dare sit in one of these? I'm beat and my fanny needs a rest."

"Well, I personally don't give a hoot one way or the other. If they don't like it, that's tough. This weary butt is gonna park itself." Tippy let out a sigh as she eased into one of the posh amply stuffed pieces. "Say, these buggers are pretty comfortable."

Within seconds, the rest followed her lead, plopped down, and sat in quiet observance.

ഇരു   ഇരു

Adera paced the study floor in nervous anticipation and whirled around to face the door as it creaked open.

Bagi entered. "I have returned, Majesty. Your guests wait in the Great Hall."

"You have performed well, my dear friend. Thank you. Were any problems encountered?"

"I fear many questions will be asked. Randy is most inpatient and demands immediate answers. Tippy appears frightened and concerned about her mortality. Jay is a bit peculiar, but remains more or less composed."

"What of the girl called Kat?" Adera inquired.

"This one's actions confuse me. She is not the slightest bit upset, but in high spirits. A rather inexplicable connection took place between her and

33

McLachen. I have never before witnessed the great stallion take to an individual in such a manner."

"It is a good sign — a *very* good sign. At last, she returns home, and the *prophecy* shall be fulfilled. Come Bagi, it is time to welcome our guests."

ಬಂಧ ಬಂಧ

The sound of footsteps from above made the four travelers spring from their seats and turn toward the staircase.

Bagi was the first to descend followed by a vision of sheer beauty. Adera glided down the broad steps as though supported by an invisible cloud.

Tippy gasped. "Oh my stars … she's beautiful."

"Girl, I don't believe words exist to describe her," Randy whispered.

Kat noticed his eyes were riveted on this figure of enchantment as she drew close.

Adera paused at the bottom of the staircase and smiled. Honey-blonde hair hung like wavy ringlets of spun gold. A buttery complexion, unsurpassed delicate features, mesmeric turquoise eyes, and plump pink lips, completed the embodiment of pure feminine perfection. She was perhaps twenty, medium height, slim, and admirably proportioned. The medieval-style white silk gown had a bodice of elegant gold brocade inset with a modest collection of semi-precious stones. On her head rested a golden crown embellished with emeralds, rubies, and pearls secured in place by diamond-embedded silver leaves.

"Welcome. I am Adera, Queen of Bowlandria. You have endured a most difficult journey and are no doubt tired and hungry. Please, join me in the drawing room. Refreshments have been prepared." She motioned to the

34

tiered half-moon steps on the far side of the room, her voice soft and melodious.

"Thank you, Ader — I mean Your Majesty," Randy stammered.

His awkward demeanor caused Kat to snicker. She knew none of them had ever met royalty before. *Wow, one glance from this lady and he's meek as a puppy. Is it possible she might tame the wild beast in him?*

Adera led them through an arched doorway into the adjacent room. Although smaller, it equaled the Great Hall's elegance.

Masterful painted woodland scenes covered the vaulted ceiling, while colorful murals and grand tapestries adorned the honeydew-peach walls. Soft candlelight, from a gold filigree chandelier, bounced off the polished terra cotta floor tiles and added to the hospitable atmosphere. Scattered around the room were numerous pieces of antique furnishings. The sharp crackle of fiery embers from a massive earthen fireplace added to the ambiance. A bounty of aromatic food and frosty pitchers of wine were placed on a hefty marble-top table in the center of the room.

"I trust this meal will suffice for now." Adera smiled, walked to a nearby sofa, and with great poise, sat down.

Jay and Tippy rushed to the table, quickly filled a plate with the inviting morsels then headed for a secluded corner.

Randy did not join them, but instead approached Adera. "Forgive my anxiety, Your Majesty, but I can't eat until some questions are answered."

"Please, take note. I prefer the informal address of Adera within the isolated confines of the Castle. I understand a tremendous ordeal has been suffered and now answers sought. I vow all concerns *will* be properly addressed. For the moment, hunger must be satisfied, followed by rest. Tomorrow, when you are refreshed, we shall talk."

"Look Adera, we've been brought here against our will, wherever this is, and don't understand a lick of it. Poor Tippy over there thinks she's dead. Our minds are in hyper-drive, lady. We need answers."

Adera's demeanor appeared unaffected by his assault. "I promise to reveal all you desire to know, however, I insist you do as I have requested."

Randy put his head down and drew a deep breath. "I can see it's pointless to continue this one-sided conversation. For now, I'll play the part of a good little boy and do as *Mommy* directs. What other choice do I have? Good night, *Your Highness*." He turned away and joined Kat at the table.

"Forget the chow, I'm here for the booze, kiddo." He grabbed a pitcher and proceeded to pour a rather sizable glass. "Say, this is a mighty fine brew. I don't believe I've ever tasted wine quite like it, but I guarantee I'm gonna indulge in a lot more before the night is over."

"Will you please try to settle down and relax?" Kat took his hand and snickered. "Adera seems sincere, so let it be. I'm sure she'll resolve our fears tomorrow. Besides, I don't know about you, but this minute my feeble mind couldn't comprehend a thing she'd say anyhow."

"You win this round. However, you can bet your sweet bippy I'll be up bright and early to get what I want come dawn." He gave her a friendly pat on the back then joined Jay and Tippy.

Kat nibbled on a few tasty tidbits, put down the plate, and strolled over to Adera. "May I sit and talk with you a moment?" She felt an odd familiarity to the charismatic monarch as though they had met before.

Although Adera appeared young, a sense of aged wisdom surrounded her. "Of course, Kat, your company is most welcome."

"I apologize for the way Randy acted a few minutes ago. This whole fiasco has traumatized him beyond words. In general, he's very sweet and has a heart as big as Texas."

"His actions are understandable, Kat. No more need be said." Turquoise eyes cast a fleeting look at the half-empty plate left on the table's edge. "I noticed you ate very little. Was the food disagreeable?"

"Oh my stars no, the whole lot is scrumptious. In fact, if I wasn't so dang blasted tired, I could really pig out on this stuff." Kat's unsophisticated outburst brought a rose-colored blush to her cheeks and a laugh to the Queen.

"My sweet girl, do not feel obliged to act so proper around me. I pray we shall grow close in time."

"I'd like that as well and believe the others will feel the same once they calm down." Kat fought back a yawn.

Adera glanced at Tippy who had nodded off. Randy and Jay were not far from doing the same. "The hour is late and sleep overdue."

A slight wave of her hand brought immediate response, and a tall stately man entered the room. "This is Jerome. He will light the way to prepared quarters. All requirements have been taken into consideration, but should the necessity arise for a particular item, simply pull the sash alongside the fireplace. Your needs will be addressed without a moment's delay. Now, I shall leave you and retire as well."

Kat smiled. "Thank you, Adera. Your generosity and kindness are appreciated. Good night."

"Pleasant dreams, Kat, and to each of you." She rose and hastened from the room.

Jerome spoke in a deep monotone voice as boney fingers pointed at a secluded archway across the room. "If you would be so kind as to follow me, we shall be underway." The gangly butler led the group through a labyrinth of corridors.

"I don't know about you dudes, but sure glad he's in the lead. I'm over stuffed, somewhat drunk, and tired as an old tom cat after a night out on the prowl." Jay yawned. "For all I care, they could take me to the barn and let me sleep on a mound of hay ... uh, unsoiled hay that is."

Soon, they arrived at the first room, which Jerome announced was for Jay. "Okay guys, guess these are my digs. See y'all later. Don't let the bedbugs bite." He laughed, rushed inside, and slammed the door.

The next room was Randy's. Before entering, he blew the girls a kiss.

Tippy gave Kat an odd glance as they approached the next two bulky doors. "I suppose these are for us."

"That is correct, madam Tippy." The genteel butler turned the patina-encrusted knob and waited for her to enter.

"I hate to be a pain, Jerome, but do you suppose I could bunk in with Kat? I'm not comfortable with the thought of being alone in this strange place. It scares the dickens out of me."

"Of course, madam. I will make the proper arrangements without delay."

Kat hated to sound offensive, but felt the need to spend time alone. She wanted to muddle over the events of the day and was not in the mood for company. "Listen, Tip, why not give your room a try first. I'm only right next door. If you start to feel afraid, just come over."

"I suppose you're right, Kat. I'm not a little kid anymore and need to show some backbone. Thanks. I'll see ya tomorrow."

"Try to get a good night's sleep. Now don't forget, I'll be right here if you need me. Sweet dreams, Tip." Kat breathed a sigh of relief. *She'll be fine once she settles in. It's all a tad overwhelming, even for me.*

"This is your room, mistress Kat. Good night."

"Thanks, Jerome. Good night." She watched until the inelegant man disappeared from sight and the hall fell into darkness. As the door eased shut, she turned and caught sight of the overgenerous quarters. "Holy crickets, I don't believe my eyes."

The spacious room looked as though it had been fashioned from the pages of a fairy tale book. Exquisite sconces cast a friendly warm glow upon the diffused bisque-colored walls. The ghost-white marble floor had a shine reminiscent of mother of pearl covered in part by a massive forest-green oriental rug. Two enormous crystal chandeliers illuminated an oval mural painted in the center of the vaulted ceiling.

A full-length stained glass window, flanked on each side by two smaller panels, enhanced a far wall. Placed in a nearby corner was a breathtaking bed. An elegant golden frame, carved in the shape of a shell, held the round mattress like a delicate pearl. Yards of billowy ivory silk, hung from an elaborate bed crown, flowed alongside the gold filigree and diamond-dust headboard. Upholstered in rich deep green and gold velvet, the furniture added serenity. Scattered about were extraordinary crystal vases of fragrant scarlet roses.

Kat spun around in slow motion as a fatigued mind strained to absorb the wonder of it all. Curious, she darted into the adjacent room and screeched to a halt at the doorway, mouth agape.

The bathroom was even more spectacular. Candlelight, from a suspended chandelier, danced around the hunter-green marble walls and floor. Columns of jade, garlanded in silver and gold, supported countless graceful arches of white stone. A spectacular bath was placed in front of the gilt-framed mirror that encompassed the entire back wall. At the base of the raised platform sat a pair of life-size porcelain swans. Two cloth covered steps led to an oversized tub, which had a golden dolphin at each end.

Kat blinked in wonderment and chuckled. "Well, I felt tired, but am sure as shoot awake now." She reentered the bedroom, walked across to the mysterious panels on a far wall, and flung open the frosted glass doors. Sight of the unexpected small courtyard, shadowed by silvery rays of moonlight, took her breath. "Oh!" A showy profusion of stars illuminated the black velvet night sky like an array of fine cut diamonds.

She stepped onto the gray flagstone path and looked around in disbelief. In the center stood a small fountain encircled by granite benches. A tranquil babble of water trickled gracefully from the backs of brass doves.

Refreshed by the cool night breeze, Kat sat alone in this secluded piece of paradise.

Randy shattered the fantasy spell by a sudden appearance. "I can't sleep either. Been one dilly of a day, huh? I'm wound up tighter than a ticked off rattlesnake."

Anxious to know about his quarters, she blurted out a barrage of questions. "How's your room? Is it nice and big? Is your bathroom massive? What color is it?"

He laughed at her exuberance. "Whoa girl, slow down. Yes, my room is incredible, and that's a meager description. I almost need a map just to go to the bathroom which is monstrous. It's kinda masculine … black, gold, and red. How 'bout yours?"

"Oh Randy, I never knew such luxuries existed. Sure hope my clumsiness doesn't surface. I wouldn't want to break any of these valuable pieces. As for my bathroom, well let's just say it boggles the mind. I almost hate to use it." She blushed.

Randy let out a loud, robust whoop. "Well girly, you darn well better make proper use of the facilities, or you're gonna have one heck of a smelly problem."

"Shhh, you'll wake the others. In fact, you'll wake the whole dang castle, loud mouth."

"Aw, who cares, Kat? I seriously doubt they're anymore asleep than we are."

"Well, I'll bet Tip's awake. The poor thing didn't want to stay alone at first, but then agreed to give it a try. I am a little concerned though because our friend has never liked to use anyone's stuff but her own, almost to the point of obsession. Let's hope she sleeps in the bed and doesn't curl up on the floor somewhere."

They looked at each other a moment, then burst out in explosive laughter.

"Can you picture Jay in these digs, kid? If he has a tub similar to ours, that nitwit will think it's a mini pool and probably take a dip. Talk about a sight to see — Jay the whale in a goldfish bowl."

The spirited chat continued for at least another hour.

Kat was delighted to see Randy act more like his old self. *Old self, now that's a laugh and a half. He's as young and handsome as ever.* She put a hand on his shoulder. "Feel a little better now?"

"Yeah, I suppose so. Doesn't any of this frighten you? It does me. Take our appearance, for example. We're not just young again, but look *exactly* as we did in our early twenties. Then there's this palace and the talking horse. It's a bit too weird for my blood."

"I don't understand things any more than you, but it is what it is, so let's take one step at a time. Okay?"

"You're right, kiddo. At least we're all safe and together. Say, that Adera chick is really some kinda looker."

"Randy, that's disrespectful. Adera's a Queen and shouldn't be referred to as a common 'looker'." She scowled and slapped at him.

He chuckled and jumped out of reach. "Well, she is, but if you insist, I'll try to act more like a gentleman. Let me restate the tasteless remark. Adera's one dynamite, good-looking broad. How's that suit ya?"

"Darn you, cut it out. You can be such a twit at times. Show a little class for once in your bleak life."

Randy yawned and stretched his arms overhead. "I don't know about you girl, but think I'm ready to call it a night and try to catch some Z's." He rose, gave her a brotherly kiss on the cheek, and left.

Alone, she pondered the incomprehensible events. Although tired, rest eluded her, thanks to an overactive mind.

A voice from behind broke the serenity. "I find the night strangely charming at times, although many fear it. You do not rest, I see. Is there a problem?"

Kat shot to her feet, let out a squeal, and turned. "Adera, you scared the be-jeepers out of me. Unless you want this garden fertilized, I'd suggest you don't ever do that again. As for your question, no, I can't sleep. Guess I'm way too wound up."

"Perhaps this might help. I often listen to it when rest avoids me." The Queen handed Kat a peculiar object, old in appearance. It was cylindrical, crystal, with a gold-hinged top engraved with strange symbols.

"It's so unusual and quite beautiful, but I don't understand how a glass jar can make me sleep."

Adera gave a wispy laugh as she lifted the lid. A tinkling melody began to play. "It is a music box, Kat … my most cherished possession. Someone very close to my heart presented it to me many years ago. I believe the gentle medley will help you sleep as it has done for me on many occasions."

Kat was spellbound by the haunting tune. "Thank you, but I can't accept this Adera. It's much too valuable and precious."

"I have no requirement for the soothing magic this night and insist you make use of it to gain rest. You may return it to me in the morning." She placed the antique instrument in Kat's hands and wrapped her fingers around the delicate casing. "Pleasant dreams, my sweet one. Sleep well." Adera smiled, gave Kat a tender stroke on the cheek, then vanished into the shadowy darkness.

Kat shrugged. *Well, if you insist Adera. I'll try anything once. My poor body aches for sleep.*

43

Back in her room, she set the music box on a small table next to the bed and sauntered into the bathroom. "Randy's right, we're stuck here, so may as well take advantage of these accommodations. I certainly could use a bit of cleaning up."

Water flowed from the two dolphins and filled the pewter tub in short order. She lowered her tattered body into the warm reparative water. Almost immediately, tension-drenched muscles began to relax and uncoil.

After a long soak, she felt refreshed. Folded on the ledge beside her was a thick cotton towel. *This is odd. I know that wasn't there when I got in. Well, on second thought, perhaps it might have been. I'm so tired I don't know what's up or down right now.* She rose from the water and caught a glimpse of herself in the mirrored wall. The grotesque image of an age-ravished woman had now been replaced by one of youthful loveliness. Gone were the loathsome signs of advanced maturity. Her body, no longer a pudgy balloon of disgusting flesh and cellulite, was now thin and willowy, covered in firm, smooth skin. Silky waist-long, coal black strands had replaced thin, dull hair.

Kat twirled around and admired the reflection. "Now, *this* is what I call a body." She not only looked good, but also felt good and welcomed the miraculous transformation. *Who in their right mind wouldn't want to be young again?*

A faint giggle broke her thoughts. She spun around to see who was there only to discover the room empty. "Either I'm more tired than I realize, or I've gone bonkers."

Modestly wrapped in the comfy towel, Kat withdrew to the bedroom in hopes some nightwear might be obtained. The large corner wardrobe revealed a colorful assortment of garments. A full-length, pale pink silk nightgown caught her eye, the exact type she fancied, and it fit as though made exclusively for her.

She walked to the shell-shaped bed and noticed the covers pulled back, ready to enter. "What the heck? I know darn well these things were untouched before. This is ridiculous. I'm so blasted tired my mind is playing stupid games. Better get some rest before I go insane."

The fine-loomed cotton sheets felt like woven air, and a cushy mattress cradled her body.

Without a doubt, tomorrow would shed some light on where they were and how all this came to be. She desired to learn more about Bowlandria and wondered if there were any other inhabitants. *I can't explain it, but I really love this place. It feels as though I've come home. Only that's impossible because I've never been here before.*

She glanced at the tiny music box and lifted the lid. At once, the enchanted melody engulfed the room. Within minutes, eyelids grew heavy as the magic of the melodious sound drew her mind into the wondrous world of dreams — pleasant dreams.

One by one, a mysterious unseen force snuffed out each candle and allowed the serenity of obscure slumber to enter the room. From the base of the bed, out of earshot, came a faint sigh.

Chapter 4
Rooms of Splendor

A rapid series of knocks echoed off the deserted corridor walls. "Hey sleepyhead, rise and shine. It's me, Tip. Get up."

"All right, hold your britches." Half asleep, and resentful of the abrupt intrusion, Kat threw off the tangle of linens and leaped out of bed. Unaccustomed to the raised platform, she tumbled head over heels onto the hard marble floor. "Blast it." An attempt to focus through confused, bloodshot eyes revealed this was not her familiar, snug little bedroom in South Carolina.

Tippy again pounded on the door. "Come on, Kat, open up. I'm out here in just a robe."

Kat stood, rubbed newly bruised knees, and stumbled to the door. "Where are we?"

"Are you going mental on me? We came to this stupid place yesterday. Don't you remember? What's wrong with you?"

"Sorry, my brain's a little numb. What time is it?"

Tippy checked her wrist and smirked. "Sure beats me. This piece of junk watch hasn't worked since the whole fiasco began. All I know is the sun's up, and its daylight. Other than that, your guess is as good as mine."

Kat closed the door and looked around. Illuminated by the brightness of day, she gasped at the grandeur. An array of miniature rainbows twirled in animated playfulness around the walls as radiant shafts of sunlight flowed through the large window and refracted off the chandelier's crystal prisms.

"Holy smokes lady, these fancy-dancy accommodations are awesome. Say, what's over yonder?" Before Kat could reply, Tippy darted into the adjacent room. "Whoa, this is some outhouse. How the blazes are we supposed to do our business in such a pretty place? Mine's a tad smaller, but the bed, well let me tell you, it is pure obscene luxury. At first, I was plum scared out of my wits to touch a single thing and darn near slept on the floor. Y'all know how I hate sleeping in anyone else's bed but my own. Shoot, I must be the only person alive who takes her own linens and pillows to a hotel. Anyhow, I decided the marble floor was too darn hard to suit this little old country girl, so said, dog it, let them pitch a hissie fit. If things get soiled, they get soiled. I didn't ask to come here, so as far as I'm concerned it's their problem, not mine."

Surprised at Tippy's attitude, Kat laughed. The quiet, reserved young woman had become a full-blown chatterbox. *It appears prior qualms have diminished — thanks to a decent night's sleep. Sure hope the good mood isn't short lived.*

Kat hobbled to the sink and splashed water on her face. "Oh, that feels much better."

"Where did you get the nightgown, Kat? I didn't have one, so slept in my undies."

"I found it in the wardrobe last night, along with a whole slew of clothes. I'm almost afraid to ask, but where did you get the robe?"

"The darn thing was draped over the foot of the bed this morning. To be honest, I'm grateful and don't give two hoots where it came from or who put it there because all my clothes have disappeared."

47

A quick glance across the room brought a puzzled look to Kat's face. "Dang, looks like we're in the same boat. Mine are also missing. There's some mighty odd goings on around this joint." She saw Tippy's expression change and worried the words had ignited dormant fears. "Aw, pay no attention to my silly old prattle. Somebody probably picked them up during the night to wash the stinky things."

They strolled to the hefty wardrobe and flung open the doors. Tippy gasped. "Wow. Do you suppose any of these garments will fit?"

"I sure hope so, or we're gonna be in a lick of trouble. All that stands between our birthday suits and the world is my nightgown and your robe."

Out of habit, Kat cast a glance at her watch. "Darn. I wish these would work. I hate not knowing what time it is. I suppose we should dress and check on the guys."

"Oh rats, I plum forgot about those two. Let's go." Tippy headed toward the door.

"Slow down, girl. We're a tad underdressed, and I imagine they are as well. Let's find something to wear before we're *all* embarrassed. I'll bet the guys are ticked off to beat the band. Sure would love to be a fly on the wall in their rooms. Can't you just see those clowns cussing like sailors while they ransack the joint in their skivvies — or worse, without any?"

A moment passed before the the two girls burst into laughter.

"I don't know about you, Tip, but I could really use a good cup of coffee right about now. My head is about to split."

"Duh, no wonder it feels like someone whacked me in the skull with a baseball bat. You suppose they have any here?"

"Sure as shoot hope so, or they're gonna have a pair of mean old mountain lions on their hands." Kat giggled, turned, and began to fumble through the array of clothes. "Can you believe all this stuff? There's every style in here from medieval times to the present, all in pristine condition. I've never seen such finery. Where on earth do you suppose they came from?"

"Beats the daylights out of me, but we shouldn't look a gift horse in the mouth." Tippy chuckled at first, but quickly turned serious. "Do you suppose these items came from other guests who were once here? Maybe these people took their belongings before they killed them. You have to admit, it's a plausible scenario."

"Get that evil thought out of your mind right this second. I'm sure there's a logical and harmless explanation. So knock it off before you blow a gasket."

The sudden aroma of fresh brewed coffee seized their attention. Nearby, on a small marble table, sat a steaming white china pot and two demitasse cups.

Kat looked around and scratched her head, feeling somewhat agitated by these strange occurrences. "This is the final straw. What the devil's going on? That table was empty a second ago, and I'll be dinged if I saw anyone come in this room," she huffed.

"I know it might sound ridiculous, Kat, but do you suppose all we have to do is ask for something and it will magically appear? We *did* wish for coffee, and bingo, it materialized." Tippy snapped her fingers. "I truthfully don't care one way or the other right now. It smells great, and I'm thirsty."

49

They rushed over, sat down, and eagerly poured a cup of the aromatic liquid caffeine.

Kat took a sip, exhaled, and eased back in the chair. "Oh my stars, this tastes wonderful. I'm mighty thankful for this eye-opening brew, but baffled. It's spooky how things just pop up around here. Last night for instance, I decided a nice hot bath might provide some relaxation, but stupid me forgot to grab a towel before I got in. However, when I went to get out, there was one placed alongside the tub. Then when I came in to go to bed, I found the quilt and sheets turned down. A bit weird, huh?"

"Sure is. I found my covers the same way. That's actually what made me get in. Figured since it was already messed up, what the heck, I may as well use it. You suppose this old palace is haunted? I'm beginning to get the heebie-jeebies."

"Sorry, Tip. As usual, I failed to think before I opened my big mouth. I'm positive there's nothing to be afraid of and am more curious than scared. When we see Adera today, we'll ask about it. Bet we'll find out there's a perfectly logical explanation for all this. In the meantime, I'm going to slip into these clothes. Why don't you trot on over to your room and do the same. I'll be over in a few minutes, and then we'll go check on our knucklehead friends."

After Tippy left, Kat dressed and was delighted to find the chosen white jeans and navy blouse fit perfectly. Tousled locks were given a quick brush, and she started off, but screeched to a halt by the sitting table. The empty pot and dirty cups had been removed. A glance at the bed caused her to draw a breath. It had been made. "What sort of magic is this? Hello? Is anyone in here?" She scanned the room, but it appeared empty. "Maybe the darn place *is* haunted. Sure hope Adera can shed some light on the subject."

Unable to resolve the mysteries, Kat shrugged it off and headed out. She barely knocked at Tippy's door before it flung open.

"It's about time you got here." Tippy beamed and twirled around. "Check out my dynamite outfit. It's like we have our own personal garment store, and girl, every single piece fits like a glove."

Kat laughed at the exuberance of her friend and entered the smaller, yet equally spectacular suite. "Okay, come clean. Did you truly sleep in that big canopy bed?"

"I most certainly did, and it's super comfortable. Even the pillows are perfect. If this is any indication of how royalty lives, they can bring it on."

"Say Tip, did you make the bed this morning?"

"Nope, sure didn't. I hurried over to see you first thing and never paid a lick of attention to it. When I returned, it had been tidied up. Oh shoot, was I supposed to do that?"

"Of course not you silly goose." Kat tried to hide the anxiety with a chuckle, but felt uneasy about the unexplained and abnormal deeds. *How are these being accomplished without any visual means? Well, I can't explain it, so why fret over the small stuff.* "Have you opened those double doors?"

Tippy turned and glanced at the two frosted panels. "Well raise my rent — I hadn't noticed them. Where do you suppose they lead?"

"Come with me, my lady. Wait till you see what's behind curtain number two." The twin doors were opened and the lovely garden revealed.

51

Uncloaked by the clearness of day, they viewed a vast green meadow that stretched far beyond the garden wall. In the distance, a great herd of horses grazed in carefree leisure on the thick lime-green grass. Clusters of brilliant peacocks strutted along the sides ... their magnificent tail feathers spread in proud display as they gave off an eerie cry. It was a wonderful, unexpected sight for both girls.

"What an incredible garden, Kat. I had no idea it was here." Tippy spun in a circle.

"I couldn't sleep, so prowled around and found it. Randy joined me a short time later. We sat in the moonlight and shot the breeze for awhile."

Tippy giggled. "Oh? Just exactly what did you two do by the light of the silvery moon, spoon?"

Kat blinked in disbelief. She knew the words were spoken in jest, but felt a bit irritated. "I swear you sound just like Jay. Think it's near time we separated you two. Randy and I talked, that's all. Don't try to write any more into it. You know he's like a brother to me and always has been. What a brat you are."

Tippy dropped her gaze. "I'm sorry ... shouldn't have made such a tasteless remark, but couldn't help myself. Sure have to admit he looks mighty fine now. Even I could be tempted. Why the dickens didn't the two of you come get me?"

"We were gonna, but figured you were asleep and didn't want to interrupt the needed rest. It's a miracle you didn't hear us. Randy was in rare form and rather loud."

"Nope, it was quiet as a tomb. I probably wasn't asleep though. My mind wouldn't allow it. Kat, tell me the truth. Do you think we'll get back home?"

"Gee Tip, I don't rightly know, but if there's a way to get back, you can be assured this bunch will find it."

"I hope so. It's only been a few hours, and I already miss Jim and the kids. That man might be a pain in the pa-toot sometimes, but I do love him. The thought of never seeing my family again is almost more than I can bear. It's been said laughter is a stronger medicine than tears, so I dried my eyes and put on a smile. Surprisingly, the phony jubilation has eased the ache a bit."

The two girls conversed for nearly an hour. Tears were shed and laughs shared, but most of all, their saddened hearts were soothed by the love of friendship.

"I'm sure the guys must be up and about by now. What say we go check on them?" Kat went to the one set of doors she knew led to Randy's room and knocked, while Tippy hollered for him to get up.

Wrapped in a towel, he threw open the doors and roared at them, his voice flustered, "Will ya knock off the noise? Have you both gone nuts?"

Undaunted by his aggression, Tippy spoke in a cheerful manner, "Randy, come join us. It's such a beautiful morning. Wait 'til you see all the horses."

"What in the blue blazes are you rambling about, girl? There's no way a horse would fit in that tiny garden."

Kat chuckled. "They're not in the garden, you moron, but in the prettiest meadow I've ever seen. It was hidden by the darkness last night, but boy you can see it now. Snap to it, buster, and meet us by the fountain. We'll go get Jay."

"Hold on just a doggone minute, you two brainiacs. My clothes are gone, and I sure as shoot can't go around like this. Where did you get those duds, and how can I get some?"

Kat never broke stride and snickered as she yelled, "Look in your wardrobe, dummy."

Jay greeted the energetic girls with a cheek-to-cheek smile. He was dressed and had obviously located every necessity. "It's about time. I was beginning to wonder if you two were still with us."

Tippy tugged at his arm, her voice alive, "Come see our garden. It's gorgeous. Wait 'til you see all the horses and the peacocks. Hurry it up, Jay."

"Kat, what have you done to our girl? Whoa, slow down a second, Tip. What on earth are you talking about?" He chuckled.

"The horses and peacocks, oh, just come see for your self, dimwit." She pulled him into the airy courtyard.

"Looks like you never checked behind the doors either." Kat pointed.

"Nope, was busy scouting out the rest of the digs, and boy are they some kinda fine. Folks here sure know how to put you up for the night — and to think I was about to settle for a parcel of stinky hay in the barn."

Tippy ran ahead and stood in front of the ivy-covered stone wall. "Ta-dah. Is this a scene right off a postcard or what?" She gestured at the meadow.

Moments later, Randy, now properly dressed, opened his doors and stepped into the garden.

Jay turned and greeted him with a big grin. "Hey, there's my buddy. How'd ya sleep last night?"

"Don't rightly know, Jay — had my eyes closed." He strolled over and joined the group. "Well, I'll be danged. You girls weren't kidding, were ya? There was no way Kat or I could have seen past our noses in the pitch-black darkness. We had no idea what was outside that wall."

Kat looked at Jay and could see the devilish wheels start to turn. *Oh crap. Now you've gone and done it, Randy.*

He'll take advantage of your stupid comment and have a rousing good time.

"Back it up just a dang-blasted minute. Did I hear right? This is starting to get *very* interesting. Mind telling us what the blazes you two youngins were doin' out here all alone in the middle of the night?"

"Knock it off, bonehead," Kat replied in a rather stern voice. "You're as bad as Tippy. All we did was sit and talk. Nothing happened, nada, zilch-o. Case closed."

Randy started to laugh and put his arm around her. "Now fess up, kiddo, you know that's not the whole truth."

She pulled from him, eyes ablaze in hopelessness. "You guys are rotten to the core. Well, I can dish it out as easy as you can. The truth is … Randy and I had a jolly good roll in the turf. We shared passionate kisses, pulled our bodies lustfully close, and it felt pretty darn good. On top of it all, we were buck naked to boot, and that's because *all* of our stupid clothes had disappeared. There, turkeys — satisfied?"

Her three friends stared at each other and bit a lip, but laughter erupted. Although the evening had been innocent, the playful banter continued.

"Randy, do you suppose there might be a stable located somewhere around here?" Kat hoped the change of subject would put a halt to the foolish brouhaha.

"Might be, why? What's going through that pee brain of yours?"

"Maybe if we ask Adera in a polite nice way, hint, hint, she might arrange for us to take a little ride. I'd love to explore this place while we're here. If it's half as nice as the meadow, we're in for a real treat."

Jay nudged Randy in the side. "I sure wouldn't object to a brisk ride in the country. These legs have kept me out of the saddle way too long, but they're like new again, and I feel pretty darn good. It's been decades since I've felt so pain free, and baby, this old boy is ready to rock 'n roll."

Kat glanced at her girlfriend, who stood void of expression. "Tip, it's not necessary to put another worry wrinkle on that pretty brow. We all grew up together and know how you fear riding. You're not obliged to go with us. I'm sure Adera will help you find a means to occupy the time while we're out."

Tippy exhaled. "Thanks y'all. It's not that I dislike the animals, but if I rode with you, at some point I'd wind up on the ground. Sorry, but it doesn't sound like fun to me."

"It would definitely be creepy if you ever stayed aboard a horse, Tip." Randy chuckled and gave her chin a gentle touch. "Okay, sweet cakes, let's see a grin on that face. We'll ask if it's possible to use a carriage one day so you can also view the countryside."

Jay rubbed his belly. "On a different note, any of you dudes hungry?"

Randy put a hand on his friend's shoulder. "I swear, Jay, you're a bottomless pit, but matter of fact, I am hungry."

The foursome walked from the courtyard and entered the long, narrow hallway.

Jay scratched his head and looked around. "How the heck do we get out of here? I was dog-tired last night and didn't pay a lick of attention. All I did was follow that big dude. Figured one of you would take notice, so why tax my enormous brain."

Randy grunted. "You are one unique piece of work, buddy. If I'm correct, the entrance to the room we were in last night is this way." The group immediately fell in behind their appointed leader.

"Well, cork the jug," Jay exclaimed as they emerged into the drawing room. "The ole pathfinder's done it again. Now, all he needs to do is find us some chow."

Kat slinked up beside Randy. She leaned in close to his ear and expressed a soft, yet somewhat sarcastic, bit of advice, "Why don't you go pull the sash alongside the fireplace McGenius? Adera told us to use it if we needed assistance."

He returned a quick sideways look, sauntered over, and gave the golden tasseled rope a gentle tug. "Well, I didn't hear a gong go off. Guess this one's out of order. Got any more brilliant suggestions, Kat?"

A bit out of breath, the petite, chubby woman dashed into the room. "Yes sir? How may I help you?" Her round, plain face displayed a jovial expression.

"Uh, my name is Kat. We're all new here and a bit hungry. Could you please tell us where we might go to have some breakfast?"

"Yes, of course, mistress. I will escort you to the dining hall where the Queen waits. Come this way, dears."

Randy rushed up alongside Kat and nudged her. "Ah-ha, Adera waits, huh? These peepers can't wait to check out that fine looking dame again." He laughed as Kat returned a scowl of disapproval. "Aw, what's the matter? Afraid I might embarrass you again? Well, set your mind at ease. The only thing I'm interested in from that lady, are answers. Let's pray she's a woman of her word."

The maid led the way through a maze of corridors to the grand dining room. At the head of an elegant inlaid wooden table sat the Queen. She looked up and smiled. "Good day. Please, come and sit. I shall have breakfast served. I presume you are famished."

"I don't know about these other dudes, but I'm starving," Jay shouted.

Adera waved a hand. Without hesitation, the food was presented.

The four companions filled their plates and ate voraciously. Hunger appeased, concerns began to be voiced.

"I promised to reveal all today, and it is now the proper time. Please join me in the drawing room." Adera rose and motioned them to follow.

As they left, Kat looked back, shocked to see most of the dishes cleared. *What the heck is going on? Again, I didn't see or hear anyone. Well, at least I know the one big question I want answered.*

Chapter 5
The Doorway

Illuminated by mellow shafts of sunlight, the atmosphere in the drawing room was pleasant and comfortable. Unsure of how the anticipated session would unfold, Kat frowned and whispered to Randy, "Remember, you promised to be nice."

He smirked and brushed by.

She noticed his eyes follow Adera as she walked to a lime-green brocade sofa and sat.

"Please, gather chairs gentlemen and place them in a semi-circle so we may converse more intimately." Daylight flattered the noble Queen. Turquoise eyes beamed and blonde locks cascaded down her back like a golden waterfall.

Words unspoken, Jay and Randy did as instructed. One by one, the four friends took a seat.

"I trust each of you have had sufficient time to gather your thoughts. Who would like to begin?"

Randy held a list they assembled earlier and spoke first, "Adera, could you please tell us where we are?"

"You have entered into another realm. Our land has no specific title. This particular Kingdom is called Bowlandria."

Randy looked at Kat and gritted his teeth. "Bagi more or less told us the same thing and said the details would be left to you. It's obvious this is another realm, but where is it? Are we still on earth, dead, or in some kinda purgatory?"

"You are quite alive and on earth. The realm resides in another dimension. It runs parallel to your world, obstructed from sight by time. The expansive technology is complicated, and I admit it even confuses me."

Jay perked up. "Are you serious? A parallel time continuum has never been proven to exist and is only theoretical conjecture. I'm by no stretch of the imagination a rocket scientist, but am intrigued by this information."

Kat fidgeted in the seat, uneasy at the vague explanation. "Excuse me, Adera, but is it possible for us to return home?"

The noble Sovereign lowered her eyes and drew a deep breath. "I cannot, nor will not, say it is impossible, but since the passing of my father, no one has ever returned."

Tippy put a death grip on Kat's arm. "If what you say is true, then aren't we in essence dead?"

Randy leaned forward and interrupted, "Hold that thought a second, Tip. Adera, if this place lies in another time band, explain how we got here? All I remember is being pulled through that darn silly rainbow."

"Correct. It was not what it seemed, but in actuality is an ancient doorway into this world."

Adera's answers only led to more questions. Parallel time was an object of fiction — an unfounded term used only in movies or novels.

"Forgive me, but my brain finds it difficult to deal with the reality of this existence." Randy sat up straight. "Why were we brought here? Did *you* open the portal?"

"No, it was not I. A mysterious, unseen, and powerful force is in control. The doorway will only open when it feels there is a need for one to enter. Most were destined to arrive, while others would have met a premature death had the portal not intervened. Why the four of you were brought into this realm, I cannot say."

Tippy scowled. "Pardon me for being blunt, but if we can't return home to our families, we have no existence. Oh sure, we're alive, or so you tell us, but that's garbage." Her voice grew loud and irate as a gusher of tears began to flow. "We're not dead in a physical sense. We can eat, drink, talk, and breathe, but emotionally we're deceased. I didn't ask for this, not one putrid ounce of it. You, your wretched castle, and this make believe fantasyland can sail to the moon for all I care. I want to return to South Carolina where I belong, and I want to go now."

Kat jumped up and embraced her friend's quaking body. "Go ahead, Tip, let it all out. You've held it in long enough. Everything will be fine, you'll see. Somehow or other, we'll get back home. I promise."

Adera cleared her throat. "Your anguish, mistress, is understandable, but if you recall, I stated it was not impossible to return. An act of unselfish valor will reverse the portal and thus grant passage to the other world, or so it has been written. The procedure, known only to my father, was explicitly documented within the pages of an ancient manuscript. However, it vanished prior to his infinite slumber and remains lost. I must also warn, the necessary courageous act may be more than one is willing to undertake. It will not be simple and could result in your unfortunate demise."

"My family means more to me than life itself." Tippy lifted her head from Kat's shoulder and wiped the tears. "I don't care about the danger and will do whatever it takes to get home. Without them, I'm already dead."

Randy kissed Tippy on the cheek then turned to Adera. "This realm appears void of any problems, so how are we supposed to perform an act of valor? We're not children Adera and far from stupid. Why not come clean and knock off the riddles. The way I see it, unless some hideous incident materializes, and we get the pleasure to obliterate it for you, we're stuck here."

"There's a solemn expression on your face, Adera," Kat interjected. "Is there something you haven't told us?"

The Queen nodded. "I hoped for the present time to spare you from this disclosure, but you leave me no choice. As you entered, a monstrous evil followed in the waters below your feet. This creature is not only fearsome, but also lethal. Perhaps it is the reason you have been brought into our time, and through its defeat is how you shall return."

Jay bolted up, hands in the air. "Ah. Now, the real nitty-gritty of it all comes to the surface. What is this mysterious entity, or is that another of your secrets? I didn't see anything enter with us."

"No, you did not. Since the day of the portal's creation, evil is forbidden to enter. However, the force has a negligible effect within the watery depths of the great abyss, and thus granted access to this fiend."

Eyes ablaze, Randy shot to his feet and lashed out, "What kind of warped game are you playing here, lady? You knew about this all along and apparently did not intend to tell us. If we hadn't prodded you on, none of this would have surfaced 'til it jumped up and bit us square in the butt. Either come clean, or leave us alone. We're not your royal play toys."

"Randy! Knock it off right now. Chill out and give her a chance to explain." Kat latched onto his arm, her face inches from his.

He glared back, but she was not about to yield. They stared at each other for several seconds until he relented and returned to his seat. "I — I apologize, Your Highness, and didn't mean to be so rude."

Adera's pink lips curled upward, and she touched his hand. "I understand and am not offended. You have every right to feel as you do."

"Since this is all out in the open now, Your Majesty, may I ask what this *evil* is?" Kat raised an eyebrow.

"We believe it to be the creature Ios, but have not received confirmation at the present moment. When a definitive answer is supplied, you will be advised at once. There shall be no further secrets."

Jay spoke up, "Let me get this straight in my wooden noggin. If we somehow help you destroy the 'evil thingy' without getting ourselves killed in the process, it might be possible for us to return home. *If* we're still alive, that is. Correct?"

"Yes, Master Jay. Your statement is correct."

Playfully, he slapped his hands together. "Hot dang — bring it on, baby girl. Let's get this show on the road. We'll take care of your problem and make fast work of it, right dudes? Then we can all get the blazes out of this joint and head back home."

Randy and Tippy nodded in agreement.

In hopes no one would notice a lack of response, Kat changed the subject, "Adera, can you explain how this realm came to be and how you got here?"

"I would be honored to do so. It began around the dawn of humankind. My ancestors journeyed to this planet from a distant star system. They desired to witness mankind in its most primitive state. All were brilliant scientists who possessed consummate knowledge of interplanetary travel and time transgression."

"Alas, the vessel, and most of its instruments, became damaged beyond repair as it entered your atmosphere. The complexity of time and space made it impossible for the home world to locate them, and the crew became stranded on earth."

She paused, as though gathering thoughts. "In this dominion, those remarkable beings were called Travelers. However, due to extraordinary powers of the mind and boundless wisdom, humanity inappropriately titled them ancient gods and goddesses."

"As the years and humans progressed, these entities were forgotten. During a time of great turbulence, the continuum was created as a refuge. None wished the corruption of your race to enter and closed off your world from this realm. The rainbow is but one of many cleverly disguised doorways. Many times, it appears as a mist or cloud. Our time band has remained invisible … unknown to all humans for eons and shall remain so until the end of days."

A light twinkled in the depths of her blue-green eyes. "Although ageless, members of this alien culture, such as my father, grew weary and elected to rest. I am his direct descendant and appointed caretaker of the realm. The great force guides me in this difficult task. Our land is vast, more so than your entire continent. Bowlandria is the most significant of *all* kingdoms, for it is where the portal opens. Though the populace refers to me as Queen, I am not of royal blood as those in your time."

"Holy leapin' lizards," Kat exclaimed. "Mythological tales of the gods always fascinated me. Now, I find out these beings existed … and we're in the presence of a real goddess. It's incredible. You mentioned the portal force acts as a guide. Does it speak to you?"

"No, it does not vocalize, but speaks in a manner more as a thought. At times, it will enlighten me with vague bits of information about arrivals, as it did with the four of you. In my study rests an orb. When the portal is activated, it lights and begins to pulsate. The closer they draw near, the brighter it glows."

Kat inched so close to the edge of the chair she nearly tumbled. "It almost sounds as though our arrival wasn't a random act."

"I suspect you were chosen. Most *are* selected, and perhaps this has always been your fate. One seldom knows what path we are to follow … for destiny never sleeps."

Randy shook his head and drew a breath. "Okay, one last thing, and we'll get off this particular subject for a while. I don't think my old gray matter will absorb much more. Does the portal only open in the Atlantic, or can it transport people here from anywhere?"

"It has the unique ability to open anywhere in your world and transport the favored ones directly to Bowlandria. Throughout time, residents from around the globe have entered."

Jay spoke up, "I'm a tad bit curious how the dickens you made us young again. Now don't get me wrong, Your Highness, 'cause I sure as shoot like what you've done. It feels pretty dang good." He chuckled and made a comical face.

Randy chimed in, "Good point. I'm curious about this transformation myself. Thanks buddy."

"Your youthful restoration is a gift from the Elves. They presented it to us many centuries ago. All living creatures that cross the threshold are instantly returned to the prime of his or her life for as long as they choose."

"Whoa, hold the horses, Nelly," Randy bellowed. "Did you say *Elves?*"

Adera began to giggle. "Yes, that is correct. They were among the first residents to arrive. I have been told stories of a great, terrible war, which took place in your world eons ago. When it was over, the Elves' time among man ended. Many creatures discarded by your world now reside in our land, where all are revered and welcomed."

Kat looked at Randy with an expression of disbelief. "You said there are many more creatures? Exactly what kind are we talking about?"

"Well, there are Unicorns. We have three — a stallion, a mare, and their adorable new colt. They are truly beautiful and quite magical."

"That's not possible. Unicorns don't exist." Kat shrugged.

"Oh but it is possible, and they do exist in *this* world. Perhaps one day you will meet them as you travel about."

Randy's voice was enthusiastic, "So, we're at liberty to roam around?"

"Yes. You are guests … not prisoners. The realm is a picturesque place, and you may find the wondrous sights it has to offer most enjoyable. This palace, for example, is rather unique in itself and worthy of exploration."

Adera's answers relaxed the atmosphere. Many questions lingered, but all were presented in a more lighthearted manner. Even Tippy's expression reverted to a somewhat pleasant one, though she remained quiet.

"We noticed several horses in the meadow earlier. Would it be possible to wrangle up a few so we can prowl around? I'm anxious to get back in the saddle since these broken old limbs of mine are working again." Jay wore a huge smile, his eyes alert.

"Utilize our steeds anytime you so desire. What particular type would you prefer?"

"We're not particular, Your Highness. It could be a Mustang, Clydesdale, or plug, makes no never-mind to us." Jay slapped his knee.

A mischievous grin formed, and Adera snickered. "You misunderstand, Sir Jay. I inquired what *type* of horse, not breed. We have many unusual kinds here."

"You mean like McLachen?" Kat inquired. "A talking horse is far from a common animal."

"McLachen is a Bayard, and the only one of his kind left. He is indeed matchless, but there are other species. Flying horses, for example."

Randy edged to the tip of the chair. "Okay Lady, now you have my full attention. There are flying horses here?"

"Yes. These magnificent creatures could no longer exist in your world and teetered on the brink of extinction. Several were brought to us, and I am pleased to say we now have a rather extensive herd."

Kat squirmed, excited. "Holy crickets — this place is awesome. I'm in love with it." A startling sensation brought her exuberance to an abrupt halt. It was as though Adera's voice spoke to her mind. *I am pleased you feel such love for Bowlandria my sweet girl, for you are the destined one.* Kat returned a puzzled glance to the haunting eyes fixed on her.

"You mentioned several other humans. Do they live in the Castle?" Randy's words dissolved Adera's trance.

"No. I would relish the companionship, but all have chosen homes of their own throughout the land, and I respect the wishes. A few live a great distance away, but most reside in nearby villages."

"Well, I can't speak for anyone else, but I wanna stay put. It's so beautiful."

Tippy jumped up and jerked Kat to her feet. "We're not staying, so get that out of your fat head, right now," she barked.

"I'm sorry, Tip. I meant to say while we're here and didn't mean it to sound so permanent." Kat hoped to mask the deceptive lie, for she had already decided to remain. The only future for her back home would be the certainty of death. If the others elected to return, that is how it would be. To avoid further conflict, the subject was again changed, "Adera, I have a question, and it bugs the tar out of me. Things sort of appear and disappear. What's going on?"

"The tasks in question were performed by our Brownies. They are quite efficient."

Jay wrinkled his brow. "What in the sam hill is a Brownie? Are they like those little Girl Scouts back home?"

Adera giggled in a kittenish manner. "Brownies are tiny, distant relatives of Elves. They are magical, harmless creatures, whose greatest pleasure in life is to care for those who reside within the Castle. Most times, they remain invisible and complete chores faster than the human eye can comprehend. On rare occasions, however, they may show themselves to someone they trust and admire or to one who has a childlike mind."

"Hey Jay, you oughta see a bunch of them."

"Ha ha, very funny Randy," Jay replied. "This might sound corny, Adera, but are they all, uh, girls? I'd sorta feel embarrassed if one saw me naked or something."

At first, the others joked about his concern, but smiles quickly turned serious.

"You may rest easy. We have both sexes. The males attend to Jay and Randy, while the females attend to Tippy and Kat."

"Whew, that's a relief." Jay wiped his forehead as though soaked in sweat. "I look pretty darn good now and wouldn't want to break their poor little hearts."

Randy rapped Jay on the back. "Oh, give it a rest you warped clown. You won't break any hearts with this bod — maybe cause a few deaths from laughter."

"Adera, did the Brownies make our clothes?" A hint of blush crept upon Tippy's face.

"All garments are Elf tailored. Nearly everything in this land has been fabricated by one of their proficient artisans."

The timid girl beamed. "I've never had clothes fit so well. How did they know what size we wore? I for one was a little heavier before we arrived."

Jay laughed so hard tears began to roll. "I can't stand it, this is too blasted funny, Tip. You were a *little* heavier? Give me a break. Is that like a whale being a little heavier than a guppy? Baby doll, Bigfoot would have been lost in those old duds."

The four companions began to joke and tease each other. Even the inexpressive Queen was brought to laughter by the group's innocent banter.

"Pardon the intrusion, Your Highness. I have brought refreshments," Jerome announced in a distinctive monotone voice. He carried a large platter over to the center table and set it down. "Is there anything more you require?"

"No, that will be all. Thank you." Adera bit her lip. "I really must compose my dignity."

The clown surfaced and Jay began to mimic the pan-faced butler. "Please partake of the goodies, my Lords and Ladies, before I devour every bite."

"You are such a jokester, Jay. No one has ever caused me to laugh so." Adera stroked him lightly on the cheek.

Everyone was in a good mood as they headed to the table.

Kat filled a plate, turned, and saw Adera cast a discreet glance at Randy. A moment later, he strolled over and sat down alongside the blushing Sovereign. *Hmmm, this is interesting.* She already suspected his attraction to the lovely Queen. After all, the young man's restored good looks could not be denied nor Adera's beauty. Logic dictated they would naturally attract one another.

After Kat finished her meal, she scanned the room. A large tapestry, hung on the far back wall, caught her attention. She walked over to get a better look at the remarkable print and sensed an odd familiarity. In front of a colorful wooded scene was a young woman with one foot placed on the bloodied head of a creature, her sword raised in triumph.

"You appear captivated by the most celebrated of our tapestries, Kat."

"It's so unusual, Adera. This might sound preposterous, but the girl reminds me of myself. Our features are almost identical, including the weird colored eyes. At a distance, it looks pretty, but up close it's quite grotesque and feels somewhat sinister."

"This hallowed masterpiece is the representation of a long foretold prophecy. It *is* astonishing how you and she are similar in appearance."

A perplexed frown shrouded Kat's face. "What prophecy?"

The Queen leaned close and spoke low, "For the moment, let us keep it to ourselves. I shall tell you in due time. Your companions have had quite enough for today, would you not agree? I promised not to withhold further secrets, and I shall abide by my word."

"You're right. It could upset them again, and I don't want to cause more unnecessary grief. Can you at least give me a hint and tell me if it's bad or good?"

Adera gazed into amber eyes. "The measure is equal. Now, I shall say no more at this time."

The haunting print tantalized Kat's senses. *Could I have dreamt of this at some point? What's so secretive about their prophecy? How is it possible for the young woman in this ancient tapestry to look so much like me? Who is she?*

Chapter 6
The Ride

The flawless cornflower-blue midday sky beckoned to Kat and her companions. Interrogation of the Queen had receded, and a desire to explore the mysterious land expressed.

"I shall arrange an escort to the stables. Choose whatever steed you prefer, and it will be made ready." Adera peered out the window. "It is a lovely day."

"A lively romp across the meadow would sure hit the spot. Maybe it'll bounce off a few pounds. I'm stuffed." Jay puffed out his stomach so it appeared bigger than normal.

Randy looked at him and snickered. "Cut it out, you idiot. Adera's gonna believe we're a bunch of uncivilized buffoons."

"I do not think of you in such a manner and find his jest rather delightful. It has long been said laughter is good for the soul. Ages have passed since I have felt so lighthearted. May you never change from the witty person you are, Jay."

Kat began to giggle at her two friends. She sat back, rested folded arms on her chest, and watched this enjoyable tennis match of words.

"Oh boy, you've gone and done it now. He'll never stop the tomfoolery, and it will probably get worse." Randy jokingly thumped Jay's back. "Do you ride, Adera?"

The question caused her to hesitate before she spoke. "I — I do ride, but have not sat a horse in quite some time."

Randy smiled coyly. "Well, perhaps we might convince you to join us."

Jay cast a sheepish grin at Kat.

She returned the look with a frown and shook her head no.

However, the discreet warning was disregarded. The notorious cutup made a comical face, stuck out his tongue, and turned from her glare.

"Thank you for the invitation, Randy, however, many projects require my attention, and I must decline. No ... on second thought, I *shall* join you. Idle pleasures have been denied for far too long."

Kat inched over to Jay. "If you utter so much as one word out of line, I will knock you from here to the moon."

Eyes danced with mischief as Jay stepped out of reach. "I'm sure we'll all find this ride a *lot* more stimulating with you along, Your Highness."

Tippy nudged Kat, her face taught. "I don't want to go, but hate to offend the Queen. Have any suggestions?" The wink of an amber eye and gentle pat on the hand brought a slight smile.

"Adera, Tippy's never been one to ride and really doesn't care to join us. Will it be all right if she remains here while we're gone?"

"Why yes, of course. What is your preferred interest, Tippy?"

"My real passion is reading. I adore a great novel. Love stories are my favorite."

"Bor — ing," Jay whispered to Kat as he passed behind.

She flashed an irate glance. "Zip it, you nitwit."

"What an excellent choice, Tippy. I also share this passion. Our library holds a rather impressive collection. Some are rare volumes, exclusive to this realm. I am confident you shall find what you seek. If you are ready, someone will lead you there at once." The Queen walked to the doorway and snapped her fingers.

Tippy mouthed a silent 'thank you' to Kat and exhaled as a bubbly dark-skinned maid entered. "Come and get me when y'all get back. Have fun."

Adera turned to the others. "We should change into proper riding apparel. You will find the necessary garments in your rooms. I shall meet you here in about half an hour, if that is acceptable?"

"That's fine and dandy with us. We'll be back in a jiffy with bells on our toes." Randy's eyes were radiant.

The three companions snaked along the maze of hallways toward their quarters.

Jay spoke up and wiggled like a girl, "Adera, my lovely goddess, I'll be back in a jiffy wearing only bells just for your viewing pleasure."

Kat slapped him on the back, but it proved useless.

The jokester had emerged. "Oh, my Queen, said the big bad Randy, what lovely lips you have. Slap me a big old wet one, Adera."

Randy halted, spun around, and stuck his face in Jay's. "Knock it off, you Neanderthal, before I fill that big mouth of yours with something you won't appreciate, like my fist. Adera's a lady. I'm only trying to show some good manners, which you obviously know nothing about. Besides, what the blazes is it to you if I think she's nice

74

looking. It's none of your stinking business, so butt out, you overgrown, overweight, blockheaded nincompoop."

Jay's smirk turned to an expression of shock. He stammered an apology. "I'm sorry, dude. I — I was only foolin' around. Shoot buddy, you know I'd be thrilled to see you find someone. I didn't mean to uncork your bottle like this. Honest, dude."

"You're a real mental case at times. After all these years, ya think I'd be accustomed to the nonsense." Randy glared straight-faced. "Heed these words, Jay. Lay off Adera and me, or next time you'll be spitting teeth, got it — *Dude?*"

Kat remained quiet as her eyes traveled back and forth between the two. *Whew, that was close, but I think Jay got the idea. Maybe now he'll leave Randy alone.*

Void of further conversation, the trio continued to their designated rooms.

"Get going you two. Meet me out here in ten minutes." Randy darted inside and slammed the door.

Jay stood in his doorway and beckoned, "Psst, hey Kat. Is Randy really taken with Adera? I'm not sure if he's jerking my chain or serious."

"Yeah, I do think he's attracted to her. Better watch your P's and Q's, Jay, or you might lose a friend."

"Man. I really screwed up, didn't I? No wonder he was so ripped. I should have listened to you instead of making a fool of myself."

Kat revealed her observations, then took hold of his hands, and spoke with soft firmness, "Look nit-wit, Randy loves you like a brother. That will *never* change. However, he's lived in loneliness for a very long time. If someone can bring a glint of happiness into his life, then so be it. From now on, be careful, and don't make any more stupid remarks about them, okay?"

He leaned forward and planted a kiss on her cheek. "Thanks Kat, you're a good friend. I'll try to keep my feet on the floor and out of my big mouth."

"Way to go, Jay. Now hurry up and get dressed before we're left behind."

"Okay, gotcha. I'm gone."

In a mad scramble to get ready, she dashed into her room. Draped over the foot of the bed was everything she required. "Wow. These things had to be supplied by the Brownies, but how the dickens did they know? Hello. Is anyone here?" A faint giggle answered the question. "Thank you for the wonderful clothes, my little invisible friends. Maybe later you'll reveal yourselves, but not right at this moment. I'm in a super hurry." She dressed, grabbed the black, buttery soft boots, and pulled them on as she stumbled out the door.

The two guys arrived a mere second later, and all headed for the drawing room. They entered and were soon joined by the Queen who looked incredible in an exquisite black suede riding habit.

Kat noticed Randy's ear-to-ear smile indicating a long dormant fire had been ignited.

A brief return glance at the handsome young man caused Adera's face to flush. "Ready?"

Jay quipped a lame imitation of a cowpoke, "Darn toot'n ma'am. Just lead me to the old corral, and we'll get this wagon train a rollin."

Adera snickered and motioned to follow. "I have taken the liberty and notified our stable master to make ready four horses. This will save time and allow us to enjoy a longer ride."

76

The stables, located a short distance behind the Castle, were elegant and massive structures. Four magnificent white Arabians, each saddled and secured to the hitching posts, awaited the riders.

"I trust these will suffice, but should you prefer a different mount, chose another, and it shall be made ready."

"Are you serious? These critters are fantastic," Jay bubbled. "Which one is mine?"

"Whatever steed you desire ... the choice is yours." Adera walked to one, grabbed the reins, and ascended onto the rich leather saddle. Each followed her lead, and within moments, they were underway.

The enlivened feel of a spirited beast brought shouts of bliss, as the four riders loped across the colorful meadow. Spread before them were rolling hillsides of multihued green grass dotted with blood-red poppies and pert white daisies.

Slightly winded, the frisky Arabians were slowed to a walk. This rested the horses and allowed the group a moment to converse.

At the edge of the valley, the pathway narrowed slightly, and they entered a dense forest. Massive trees formed a leafy tunnel, while gentle beams of sunlight peered through the branches and sprinkled the ground with translucent rays of liquid gold.

Adera glowed. "This is but one of our many great forests and home to my favorite creatures."

Jay looked at Kat and grimaced. "Not sure I like the sound of this *creature* stuff. Kind of makes me nervous."

"Yeah, know what you mean. Sure hope they're friendly." Kat chuckled.

The rhythmic plod of the fiery steeds enhanced the dreamy tranquility of the ride. A blanket of rich moss, speckled with an abundance of tiny yellow buttercups, sloped up the side of the stone path and caressed mighty trunks. A temperate breeze seemed to whisper hello as they passed beneath the lofty emerald boughs. Perched high above, a diverse assortment of birds serenaded the group with unique melodies, while deer, rabbits, and squirrels scampered about in aimless play.

They traveled on and admired the spectacular sights. However, from the darkness of the underbrush, a grotesque pair of crimson eyes followed their movement.

Kat felt an icy prickle on the back of her neck, as if the very hand of death touched her. She turned, but saw nothing, so shrugged it off as a mindless delusion.

Slowly, the abomination retreated, and the monolithic body slithered into shadowed obscurity.

Adera and Randy rode side-by-side and chatted. "I have been absent from this land far too long and almost forgotten how breathtaking it is. Now, if my mind remembers the way, I shall take you to a place few mortals have ever visited." A wide, bulky wooden bridge, arched over a softly animated bubbling stream, came into view. "Ah, there it is," she exclaimed, reining her horse in its direction.

The sound of the high stepping hooves against the age-worn planks echoed as the group crossed the structure and entered a small knoll. In the distance, the thunderous roar of a waterfall grew louder as they proceeded.

Adera motioned. "A pristine freshwater pond lies ahead. There, we may refresh the horses and ourselves."

"That's fine with me. I could use a break." Randy rubbed his legs and stretched.

Around the next bend, an indescribable vision appeared and each rider gasped. A lavish meadow surrounded the crystal blue lagoon water. Boundless exotic flowers saturated the area with collective sweet scents. Three majestic waterfalls cascaded in graceful splendor from atop a colossal wall of stone into the utopian pond below. An eerie cloud of white mist rose toward the heavens with angelic grace.

"The beauty of this place is beyond belief. It's as though we've left earth and entered an enchanted fairyland." Randy dismounted and led his horse to the water's edge for a drink.

"You just said a mouthful, buddy," Jay replied. "It's enough to render me speechless."

"What? Jay's speechless? We *must* be out of this world," Kat teased.

The horses were unsaddled and turned loose to graze upon the sweet grass, which provided a comfortable mat for the riders.

Kat laid back, relaxed by the scenery's ambiance. The snap of a branch off to the side pulled her head from the clouds. She sat up and looked around, but did not see anything. Suddenly, two celestial figures emerged from the tall bushes. "Oh my stars, I — I don't believe it. Randy, look — Unicorns."

Adera rose and spoke softly to the elegant mare and colt, "Good afternoon, Adel. I see you have brought little Wister to visit with us."

Kat leaped to her feet and dashed to Randy and Jay. Each, wide-eyed in disbelief, stared at the romanticized vision before them.

An iridescent white coat covered delicate frames and from their chins hung a goat-like beard. The mare appeared guarded as china-blue eyes sized up these unfamiliar visitors. A lengthy mane of ivory curls fluttered in the soft breeze. From the center of her head protruded a brilliant golden horn. However, due to his young age, the colt possessed only a small nub. Around their necks hung an ornamental band inset with gold roses and oversized sapphires.

"Holy cow, Adera, you sure as shoot weren't kidding. I can't believe they truly exist." Randy put an arm around the Queen and gave a hearty hug, but just as quickly released his grip. "I am so sorry. Guess the sight of these creatures overwhelmed me more than I realized."

A hint of pink tinted her cheeks. "You need not apologize. They have been known to cause such an effect. Perhaps Adel will allow us to approach. If you are pure of heart, which I believe you to be, they will show no fear." She strolled slowly over to the mare and stroked the velvety arched neck. "Come my friends, Adel welcomes your visit."

Kat, Jay, and Randy advanced cautiously, but there was no apparent sign of retreat from the Unicorns. Soon, all stood face-to-face with two extraordinary figures of legend.

"They are the most breathtaking creatures I've ever seen," Kat exclaimed. The mare nickered and nuzzled her hand as though pleased by the compliment. "Do they also talk?"

"Unfortunately, they do not, Kat," Adera replied. "That unique talent resides only with McLachen. However, they do understand what you say and will react. I believe Adel is thanking you for the kind words."

Randy lightly stroked the mare's head. "You and your colt are truly beautiful, Adel. I've read of these marvels all my life, but never thought I would actually see one, let alone touch it. This is just incredible."

Kat scanned the area, eyes wide with anticipation. "Where's the stallion?"

Adera turned and pointed up to a nearby ridge.

Overlooking the group stood the great Unicorn … his prodigious golden horn glistened in the bright sunlight. He was quite large and even more magnificent than the other two.

The Queen bowed slightly before she spoke, "Nalay, my dear friend, I have brought guests. Will you join us?"

The stallion reared, then turned, and within seconds stood alongside the mare and colt.

"Wow. That was fast. I barely saw him move." Jay scratched his head.

Adera let out a slight chuckle. "Yes, Master Jay, their speed is truly inconceivable. I am pleased to introduce Nalay, King of the Unicorns."

The noble stallion held his distance and eyed the three strangers. He then strolled to Kat, folded one leg under the massive body, and reverently bowed in greeting.

For a short time, Kat stood in silent awe, but gasped as the stallion raised his head. She felt a strange magic emanate from the pair of spellbinding blue eyes and penetrate deep into her soul.

"It appears someone is quite taken with you, Kat," Adera announced, a puzzled expression in her eyes. "This is indeed a rare occurrance, for Nalay will seldom approach anyone. To have a Unicorn bow as he has done is to be blessed by the most mystical of all creatures."

81

"Your gallant gesture overwhelms me, great Nalay." Kat lovingly reached to pet the stallion. "I am very pleased to meet you and your remarkable family."

"Unicorns are gifted with incredible wisdom," Adera said, her voice proud. "They are wonderfully magical creatures and possess many remarkable powers. It is said they find the purity of unselfish love irresistible, for only such love may reach into the depths of their hearts."

Randy cleared his throat and pointed to the fading horizon. "Ahm, excuse me, I hate to break this up and really don't want to leave, but perhaps we better start back. It's getting late and will be dark soon."

Adera's eyes widened as she glanced at the dusky sky. "How careless of me, you are correct. We must return immediately."

Although reluctant to leave, Kat knew it was unwise to stay. "Thank you for the visit, Nalay. I do hope to come again some time."

The stallion tossed his lengthy mane and nodded. He then whinnied and led his family into the dark seclusion of the forest from where they had ventured.

Randy quickly gathered the horses, and all four mounted. Once across the bridge, they broke into a gallop in a challenging effort to beat the retreating sun.

Suddenly, Kat pulled up her horse, which nearly caused Jay to crash into her.

"What in the dang blasted blazes are you doing, Kat?" He fought to bring the startled mount under control. "Are you totally nuts? We could have been killed."

Randy and Adera heard the commotion and hurried back to them.

"I'm sorry, it was an accident." Panic filled Kat's voice, "Jay, I just saw a horrible pair of monstrous red eyes over there in the underbrush. Let me tell you, the mere sight of them actually made the hair on the back of my neck stand up. I felt a similar sensation on our way to the lagoon, but thought it was only my stupid imagination going haywire again."

There was a touch of fear detected in the Queen's voice as she asked Kat to specifically describe the sighting.

"I don't know what it was, Adera. All I saw were those two terrifying, red eyes. I've never felt fear like that before in my life."

Adera and Randy glanced at each other then scanned the landscape. Their nervous demeanor told Kat something was very wrong. The horses seemed to sense fear as well and were difficult to control.

"We better get movin'." Randy's brow furrowed. "Is the Castle much farther, Adera?"

"No, it is not. I believe it is time we see how swift these horses can travel. We must return at once."

"Okay you two, what's going on?" Jay snapped. "Is what she saw dangerous? That is, *if* she actually saw anything at all. You know how Kat's imagination runs amuck."

"Well thank you Lord Know-It-All," Kat yelled. "I'm telling you I saw something, and if you don't believe me that's your problem. Would you prefer I offer an introduction? You can be such a twit."

Adera's face turned pale as her stern voice interrupted, "Enough. This is neither the time nor the place for the two of you to squabble. The sun will soon disappear. We must return before nightfall. Devoid of light to illuminate the land, travel becomes precarious."

Kat frowned at her with a look of skepticism.

"Knock it off," Randy shouted. "What Adera says is true. It might be difficult, if not impossible, to find our way back at night. So cut it out, and let's get going. We'll discuss this later." He reined his horse in the direction of the Castle and gave it a gentle kick.

Without hesitation, the others followed and galloped off.

The legs of the fleet-footed Arabians were like delicate pistons as they pounded the earth. Soon, the outline of the stables came into view.

"Thank goodness you are back and safe. Lateness of the hour caused great concern." The horse master took the reins of the winded horses from each rider.

"You and your dumb imagination," Jay bellowed at Kat. "We were having a super time 'til that idiotic mind of yours ruined it."

"Hey, you big overgrown baboon, don't you dare talk to me like that unless you want a red nose to go with your warped clown personality. I'm telling you, I really saw something." She stomped her foot and scowled. "Believe what you want. It *wasn't* my imagination."

"Yeah, yeah, yeah, tell me another story," he barked and strutted off.

Randy looked at Adera and shrugged. "Don't pay any attention to those two. Their anger will fade away as fast as it flared up. It's nothing new." He took her arm as they walked to the Castle.

Once safely inside, all four proceeded to the library. They found Tippy snuggled up in a large old overstuffed chair immersed in a novel. "Hey, you're back. Y'all have a good time?"

Kat and Jay rushed over, pulled up chairs, and with robust enthusiasm began to tell about their ride and what they had seen. As predicted, the vicious spat was already forgotten.

ഇറ്റ   ഇറ്റ

Randy stood alongside Adera in the doorway and stared at the floor in deep thought. "May I have a word with you in private?" He motioned toward the isolation of the hallway. "I don't think we fooled anyone. Kat *did* see something, including the alarmed look on our faces."

Adera pulled him farther out of sight to avoid being overheard. "I cannot be sure, for I did not witness the vision, but I believe Kat may have caught a glimpse of the vile creature we briefly spoke of."

He took hold of a trembling hand and touched her taut face. "It's all right, my Queen, I'm as concerned as you," his voice soft and reassuring.

"Please try to understand, Randy, I could not bear to spoil Kat and Jay's afternoon with the revelation of this beast."

"Hey, don't let it get to you. Your actions were perfectly justified. I'm just happy you thought to confide in me."

She drew a long, deep breath. "Before I can disclose my true fears, I must consult with someone more knowledgeable. I suspect what Kat saw were the unholy eyes of the Titan, Ios, who has apparently come ashore. I am sorry to appear vague, but at the moment I do not have the proper answers." A solitary tear rolled down her porcelain cheek.

He felt a tug at his heart and tenderly wiped the salty droplet away. "Everything's going to be fine. Nothing happened, and we're all safe. Now, let's dry those tears."

"My heart overflows with gratitude, Randy. It is a relief to share my knowledge of this terror. I truly did not believe it would surface so soon and hoped we had additional time."

"You shocked the daylights out of me when you expressed these concerns during our ride. I can't tell you how happy that makes me. It sure helps not being stuck in the dark. Now all we have to do is figure out what to tell Kat. I have no doubt she's going to pick my brain later."

Adera smiled. "I shall leave this matter to your discretion and trust you will disclose to her what you feel she should know."

He nodded in agreement, gave her a quick hug, and they re-entered the library.

ജഇ   ജഇ

Kat and Jay had not broken stride, and the vigorous conversation continued.

"I mean to tell you, Tip, these horses were awesome," Jay went on. "I thought our buggers back home were swift, but girl, they're nags compared to these spunky critters. You should have gone with us. Shoot, as fast as we were going, you wouldn't have had time to think about the pain when you fell off."

"Thanks a bunch, knucklehead," she chuckled. "So, you actually saw real live Unicorns? Are you serious, or is this just another notorious prank?"

"Honest, Tip. This isn't one his dumb jokes. They were magnificent," Kat bubbled.

"Sure wish I had seen them, but *not* at the expense of riding one of those animals. Actually, I've enjoyed a rather pleasant afternoon myself — *boring* as it might seem to you, Jay."

"Oh crap, you heard what I said?" He winced.

She patted his knee. "Anyone within ten thousand feet could have heard you, Motor Mouth. This library is incredible. I've never seen such a fabulous collection of books. I found one old volume that's jam packed with some darn interesting bits of information."

Kat's eyes brightened. "I'm glad the day went well for you, Tip. I enjoy flippin' the pages of a good novel now and then myself. Of course, unlike some primitive slobs we know, I can read."

They were all laughing when Adera and Randy walked up. Kat glanced at Adera and noticed her puffy, reddened eyes. *Oh please, don't tell me you said something to upset her, Randy. Darn it, you promised.*

"I would imagine you are all hungry, especially Sir Jay," Adera announced. "We should return to our rooms to refresh and change into something a bit, uh, cleaner. I shall inform Cook to serve dinner in one hour."

"Gee, now that you mention it, I sure could use a bite to eat. I can't even remember the last time a sliver of food touched these poor lips of mine." Jay's statement caused the entire group to burst into roaring laughter.

"As fast as you gobble things down, buddy, I seriously doubt anything has ever had time to touch your lips," Randy joked. "I don't know what we're gonna do with this guy — he's a bottomless pit."

Moments later, the companions and the Queen headed for their respective quarters.

"Hey Randy, what were you and Adera talking about in the hallway … not that it's any of my business. I don't want to sound like I'm being nosey again." Jay held up both hands.

"Aw, it wasn't anything important. I thanked her for the use of the horses and the awesome visit with the Unicorns. Really was nice of her."

"Man, I'm glad you thought to say thanks. In all the excitement, it plum slipped my mind. Sure has been a long time since I could ride like that. Although, I hate to admit it, but a couple parts are beginning to feel the after effects." Jay rubbed his buttocks.

ഇരു ഇരു

After making himself presentable, Randy strolled out into the garden and stared into nothingness. Absorbed in thought, he failed to notice Kat saunter up.

"Daydreaming?" She giggled at his startled reaction.

"Nah, just enjoying the gorgeous sunset." He hoped to avoid any probing questions.

"Yeah, it's nice, but a sunset wouldn't cause such deep thought. Could it be something about those red eyes I said I saw?"

Her statement told him the gig was up. "Well, it could be, but Adera assured me it was nothing to worry about."

"I saw you and Adera gape at each other. Can't fool me Randy — we've been friends far too long. I think she asked you not to say anything to me. If that's true, the devil himself couldn't drag it out. So, I'll drop it … for now." She smiled coyly. "Starting to like Adera?"

He turned and looked at her, as the heat rose in his face. "Yeah, a wee bit, but nothing serious. I just think she's a real looker, that's all."

ഇരു ഇരു

Before Kat closed her garden doors, she peered into the meadow. *Those eyes were not a figment of my imagination.* Tiny goosebumps erupted. *Wonder if they have something to do with that prophecy. I've got to get Adera alone and find out what it's all about.*

She tossed the thought aside, hurried to dress, and soon joined her friends who waited in the hallway.

After enjoying the scrumptious dinner Cook prepared, they adjourned to the drawing room and spent the remainder of the evening chatting about the day.

Later, tormented by the vision, Kat was unable to sleep. She felt strangely involved. *Surely Randy wouldn't hold back if there was any real danger.* "I'm just going to put it out of my mind and get a good night's rest." Exhausted, she rolled over and nodded off to sleep.

An eerie, hushed tranquility drifted over the kingdom as the moon graced a starlit evening sky. However, peace would not come to several luckless residents. The ghostly darkness of night would deliver terrifying death as the evil leviathan searched the land for innocent prey.

Chapter 7
Inside Castle Walls

Daylight beacons flowed through the large gothic window and stirred Kat to the dawn of a new day. In a futile attempt to shield her eyes from the meddlesome beams, she buried her head deep into the lofty pillow.

Events of the prior day remained fresh in her mind. Adera had answered every question asked and quelled most apprehensions. However, the ordeal with those hideous eyes lingered, and Kat feared the answer.

Fully awake, she pulled herself from the comfort of the cozy bed, strolled to the small settee, and sat down. "I could sure use a nice hot cup of coffee." She hoped the announcement would allow her to witness its delivery.

Within seconds, a china pot and cups appeared. Although diligent, she did not see a thing. *Wow, they're quick little suckers. Adera said they move faster than the human eye could comprehend, but had no idea it was quite this fast.*

"Hello, little Brownies. Are you still in the room with me? I was told you sometimes appear and would love to meet the party responsible for my great care." From behind came two sharp snaps. She turned and drew a breath of joyous exclamation. "There you are … good morning. I'm pleased you've elected to show yourselves."

The two tiny ladies huddled so close they almost appeared as one. Each stood about a foot high with sharp pointed ears and large doe-like eyes. Short-cropped hair framed a pixie face and each wore a frame-flattering

90

wispy dress. An introduction came in a pleasant high-pitched voice, "Good day, mistress Kat. I am Hoki, and this is Meon. We hope our service to you has been adequate."

Kat beamed at the sight of her two caretakers. She towered above them, so decided to lessen the imposing stance and lowered herself to the floor. To her dismay, both grabbed hold of each other and quickly backed off. "Please, don't be afraid. I won't hurt you. I'd like to be your friend. As for the service being adequate, well, I think you outperform any other Brownies in the entire Castle."

"Thank you for the gracious words, mistress. We find it pleasurable to pamper you and shall enjoy doing so in the future." The pair loosened their grip from each other, but remained cautious.

Hoki stated, "We were chosen from all the others to assist. Each night Meon resides with Tippy, while I remain with you. It is our task to keep guard throughout the evening."

"I had no idea we were watched over in such a manner. From now on, I'll dang well rest better knowing you're here. May I ask where you sleep?"

"Most times we curl up on a settee, but there are occasions when we sleep on a floor pillow placed at the base of the bed," Meon replied.

"What? Well, that arrangement is coming to a screeching halt right now," Kat declared. "From this minute on, I insist you sleep on the bed with me, Hoki, and if not, I'll be highly insulted. Tippy will feel the same, Meon. Have you revealed yourselves to her as well?"

"No mistress, we have not. In truth, we have never appeared to *any* human before. However, unlike others we have encountered, there seems to be an aura of kindness around you.

"Perhaps you might grant me a favor later this afternoon and also show yourselves to Tippy. Not only will it deliver a great deal of pleasure, but help alleviate her phobia of being alone at night."

"As a rule we do not make our presence known, mistress, but for you, we will make an exception," Hoki replied.

"Excellent. Now, I'd like to enjoy a bit of this tasty coffee you have brought, then dress and join my friends. They surely must be up and about."

"Oh yes, they have all risen. Mistress Tippy has been awake for over an hour," Meon replied as a faint blush crept upon her delicate face. "She is a most pleasant human, and what a lovely voice she has. We take great pleasure listening to her sing as she putters about."

Kat sipped the coffee and talked more with the delightful creatures. Finally, she excused herself, bathed, changed into the clothes Hoki laid out, and hurried off to join the others and the Queen for breakfast.

"Have you given any thought toward today's activities?" Adera inquired after the morning meal was finished.

"We haven't really talked about it yet," Randy said. "Anyone have a suggestion?"

"I can't believe I'm going to admit this, but after yesterday, I don't feel much like riding today. Seems my butt and my muscles are a bit on the tender side," Jay smirked. "Either that dang horse was a lot broader than he seemed, or I'm more out of shape than I thought."

Tippy pushed her chair from the table. "If y'all don't mind, I'd like to get back to this old book I found. It's really spiked my interest."

"Whatever you want to do is fine with us," Kat replied. "So what's up with this mysterious book? You started to tell us about it yesterday, but we rattled on incessantly about our adventure and didn't allow a word in edgewise. Sorry. We can be so rotten self-centered at times."

"That's okay." Tippy chuckled. "I understand. It's plain to see y'all had a bit more excitement than I did." She held up a tattered tome. "Adera, know anything about this nameless volume?"

The Queen's expression appeared puzzled. "I have no knowledge of this particular text, my dear. It may be possible you have located the fabled manuscript written by my ancestors, and I would be most anxious to view the pages as well. Since it had never surfaced, I presumed it to be a fictitious fabrication."

Tippy winced. "Well, the thing was kinda found by sheer accident. I spotted a novel I wanted to read. Of course, the darn bugger had to be on the top shelf. I climbed on a chair to reach for it, but slipped and grabbed onto the bookcase to keep from falling. Unfortunately, my weight caused the structure to tilt, and this dusty, ragged book fell to the floor. I thought it looked a bit odd since all the others were in such pristine condition. I started to flip through the pages and realized this text possessed a wealth of information. For instance, did you know that dragon scales, ground into a fine powder and glued to the surface of a shield, can make it nearly impenetrable?"

"No Tip, don't think we knew that," Randy teased. "Sorry to break this news flash, kid, but the task might prove a tad difficult since we don't happen to have a dragon handy."

"Don't be such a donkey's butt, Randy," she snorted. "Some of this stuff might help us return home. Adera, a few pages speak of the portal, but I don't understand what it all means. However, one paragraph specifically mentions its reversal. So take *that*, Randy, and pull it over your bonehead."

He laughed and gave her a squeeze. "I'm sorry, Tip, and honestly don't know what gets into me at times. Maybe your clumsiness has finally paid off and this is just the tool we need to get us back."

Jay made a comical face. "Well slap my head and call me silly. Seems I owe you a big apology, old girl, and give you full permission to boot me straight in the derriere. On second thought, mind holdin' off a few days 'til my gluteus maximus feels better?"

She laughed and gave him a playful shove. "Don't sweat the small stuff, jar brain. I'll hold off — for now. Without a doubt, you'll pull another stunt before long that will warrant a good swift butt kick. For now though, all I care to do is get back to the library and read more."

After a lengthy discussion, Kat, Randy, and Jay announced they preferred to explore the Castle.

Adera heaved a sigh. "I am most pleased you have each decided to remain within our walls today. Fearsome tragedies occurred during the night, and it will prove safer to linger on home grounds."

"What occurrences?" Kat exclaimed. "Do they have something to do with what I saw yesterday?"

"Yes, dear one, it grieves me to say they may be related. Several sheep were savagely killed in the valley as were some of our precious horses."

"Oh my stars in heaven, please tell me one of them was not McLachen," Kat screeched.

"No. He is without harm, but six others we brutally slaughtered. Several guests shall join us this evening for dinner. Afterward, we will gather to discuss what has transpired. Now, there are matters that require my immediate attention, and I must bid good day."

Jay's face reddened. "Yikes Kat, guess I especially owe you an apology. I honestly thought your imagination ran amuck again, but boy was I dead wrong, uh, no pun intended. What do you suppose you saw?"

"My goodness, Jay, so many apologies today … I'm not sure we can handle this," Kat joked. "Like Tip, I'll save my kick for another time. On a serious note, I haven't a clue what it might have been. All I saw were two hideous red eyes. I mean to tell you, they would scare the skin off a lizard. Well, whatever they belong to, I'd say it's obviously vicious. I feel bad for those poor animals. How awful. "

"Hey you two, let's not ponder on this junk and ruin our day. Adera said we're out of harm's way as long as we stay on these grounds. What say we explore this joint and try to have a pleasant afternoon," Randy advised.

"You got it," Kat replied. "Well, where should we start the tour? This place is a virtual maze of rooms."

"Doesn't matter one iota to me," Jay said. "You lead the way, Randy, and we'll follow. Then if we get lost it'll be your fault, and you can take the kick in the derrière."

"Thanks Jay, you're all heart." Randy chuckled. "I suppose the most logical place to start would be the

Great Hall. Let's go." He motioned them to follow, and soon the three adventurers entered the grand room.

Kat pointed to a far wall. "Hey, I wonder what's through that entryway where those suits of armor are standing guard."

"Dunno," Randy replied. "Your guess is as good as mine, kiddo. Let's check it out."

They passed through the doorway and found it opened into a somewhat smaller chamber, yet appeared as equally extravagant. Several musical instruments were strategically placed around the parameter. The most eye-catching feature, however, was the magnificent golden harp which stood alone in the center.

"I think it's fair to say this is the music room," Kat said as her voice reverberated off the walls.

Randy tapped on top of the shiny black baby grand piano and ran a finger across the ivory keys. "Yeah, I believe you're right. The acoustics in here are amazing."

Jay yelled, "Yo dudes, there's an entrance to another room hidden behind this big old rug." He flipped the dusty tapestry aside and quickly disappeared through the tiny archway.

"Don't go in there, Jay. Dang it, will you wait. Aw crap, now we have to chase after him and will probably get lost in the process." Randy snatched Kat's arm, and they raced after their capricious friend.

The three continued their adventurous trek. At last, they came to a red door with a carved inscription … KITCHEN.

"Holy bazookas," Jay shouted as he rushed in. "Check out the size of this joint. I plum believe I've died and gone to chow heaven."

Several large wood burning stoves stood alone in the center of the room. Speckled granite-topped preparation counters, dotted with elaborate white china washbasins, lined the outer perimeter. Stately silver chandeliers hung in random from the vaulted ceiling, as fiery light reflected off the ivory tiled floor and polished beige stone walls.

"So, I see ya have found me kitchen," came a hearty voice. A large plump woman entered through the side doorway and spoke with a distinctive brogue.

"We were just roaming around and hope we haven't intruded," Randy apologized.

"No, not a 'tall, me darlins, tis a grand pleasure ta meet ya three it tis. Visitors rarely come down here, and it's a welcome sight ya are indeed."

Eyes twinkled as she scanned the three of them, but appeared to brighten even more when they caught sight of Jay. "Now don't be tellin me that himself has come ta raid me kitchen? By the look of things, I would say ya must be the ever starvin Jay I've been hearin so much about." She mischievously poked him in the stomach with a large silver ladle.

"Ouch, yeah, I suppose that would be me." He frowned and tightened his lips.

"The name me sweet mother gave ta me is Margaret Mary, but most around here call me Cook, as ya should be doin as well. In case ya might be wanderin, I'm a wee bit Irish and proud ta say that I am."

They found Cook to be a pleasurable, jolly soul. She showed off the kitchen, clearly prideful of every inch of it. After the tour, the three thanked her and bid good-bye, saying they understood the dining event would require her full attention.

"Aye, twill be a bustle of activity in a short time. Sorry ya couldn't meet me staff, but I sent them ta gather goods for me planned menu. Nice of ya to stop by and hope ya will come again for a wee visit, especially you Jay me darlin." She gave off a robust laugh and winked as the group left.

Their investigation of the splendid structure continued through the great labyrinth of passageways. Each room encountered was more ostentatious than the last.

"I have to admit this is some pad." Randy looked around, open-mouthed. "If there was such a thing as a fairy tale castle, this one would take all the ribbons."

"Well, in actuality, it *is* one." Kat gestured at the surroundings. "We didn't think Unicorns existed either and found out that wasn't true."

"She's right," Jay agreed. "There's things here that ought not be real and yet are. No telling who, or what, we'll see tonight. Have any idea who's coming?"

"Not a solitary clue, buddy. Adera never made mentioned of anyone. We'll just have to wait and see."

Out of habit, Kat glanced at her watch. "Randy, what time do you think it is?"

"Beats me, kiddo, probably early afternoon, I guess."

"Do you two guys think we dare go upstairs?"

"*Certainly*," Randy replied with a chuckle. "Adera gave us free rein of the joint."

They hurried back to the Great Hall and climbed the graceful staircase to the second floor. An open door led to a long corridor. Lining both walls were gilt-framed paintings of unfamiliar men and women.

Kat sauntered along in wide-eyed wonderment. "Do you suppose these could be portraits of Adera's ancestors, Randy?"

98

"That's a good possibility. The beauty of these ladies is incredible, much like Adera, and to say the men are merely handsome would be a gross injustice."

The group ambled down the lengthy passage and stopped at each fresco to study it.

Kat paused in front of a blank spot on the wall and ran her finger across the stained plaster. *I wonder what hung here.*

At the end of the hall, they discovered an elaborate door.

Kat tugged at the pair's sleeves. "Hey guys, I don't think we should enter this room."

Jay chuckled at her forewarning and twisted an ornate golden knob. The unlocked carved-wooden door creaked eerily as it opened.

"Oh crap. I told you guys we shouldn't come in here. This is Adera's personal sanctuary. We need to leave, right now." Kat turned, but was halted by Randy's firm grip on her waistband.

"Just hold your britches. This is perfect. Look, I'm not saying we should invade her privacy, but let's take a few minutes to browse around. We might uncover some valuable information."

"I don't approve of this one little bit. We wouldn't like someone snooping around *our* rooms. There are things sacred to a woman, moreover, a Queen."

"Kat, if Adera didn't want us to come in here, the dang door would have been locked. So, cool your knickers and look around."

"Hey, love birds," Jay yelled from across the room. "Take a gander at this gizmo. It must be that orb doohickey she spoke about."

Nestled on a silver pedestal was a large, iridescent crystal globe. Randy touched it and jumped back. "Whoa, talk about weird. Kat, get over here and feel this thing."

She gingerly placed a finger on the mysterious orb, screeched, and jerked back her hand. "Holy smokes! It feels like water, but my finger's perfectly dry."

"I told you it was weird. Wonder what other tidbits this room holds. Check out that archway. Maybe it leads to the ladies boudoir."

"Stay the heck out." Kat stomped a foot. "That's off limits. I don't give a hoot if this door was unlocked or not, stay the blazes away from her bedroom. Think it's time to go."

"Okay, okay, don't get your panties in a bind. Jay, remind me not to bring this wet blanket along next time."

Kat glowered. "Let's get the dickens out of here and find Tippy. We've been gone quite a while. I'm sure she's ready to put down that book by now."

"Yeah, suppose you're right. I'll come visit some other time. Who knows, might even get a *personal* tour." Randy nudged her as he brushed by.

They gave the space one last glance, eased the door closed, and headed for the library.

"Stumble across anything interesting, oh studious one?" Jay declared as the three sauntered in.

Tippy looked up and smiled. "Sure did. It took a while, but found several references about reversing the portal, and it *is* possible. Don't know about y'all, but that little snippet of information makes me feel better."

Jay let out a whoop of laughter and slapped the side of his leg. "Well knock me down and grease my fanny with butter. Good thing we brought you along, old girl. On a serious note though, I have to admit it scares the bejeepers out of me to think we'll have to risk our lives and fight in order to get home."

Randy placed a hand on Jay's shoulder. "It's a cold hard fact, buddy, but if that's what it takes, then that's what we'll do. Right, Kat?"

"If you say so," she replied solemnly. "Sorry to change the subject, but we should think about getting ready for dinner. I doubt this will be an *informal* event."

Before Kat could close her bedroom door, she was pushed aside as Tippy rushed in. "I need help, Kat. I'm lousy with this dress up stuff and don't have a clue what to wear."

"Don't worry, girlfriend. Everything you need will be laid out for you. Dang, almost forgot. I have something remarkable to show you. Now, this might startle you at first, but you need to trust me. Hoki, what should I wear tonight?"

Tippy scrunched her face. "Girl, you have finally lost it."

Kat laughed and pointed to the dress neatly draped across the foot of her bed.

"Wha — how the blazes did that get there, and who the dickens is Hoki?"

"She's one of our Brownie attendants. Hoki is assigned to me, and Meon cares for you. Feel up to meeting them?"

"You've seen and talked to these beings?" Tippy exclaimed.

"Yep, sure have, and they're amazing. Okay, my little friends, it's show time."

Tippy beamed as the elusive servants magically appeared and were properly introduced. "Bless my heart, Kat, they're downright precious."

101

As predicted, the timid girl breathed a sigh of relief to know she was not alone in the evenings and insisted the tiny sprite reside on her bed.

"I will go prepare your clothes for this evening, mistress Tippy," Meon squeaked, then disappeared with the snap of a finger.

Tippy jumped and looked around. "Whoa, that was fast. Guess I'd better hurry to my room. Dang blast it, wish we knew what time it was. This is driving me nuts."

Hoki stepped up. "I believe your time telling apparatus works now. It often takes a day or so for them to function."

Tippy shot a glance at her wrist. "Well I'll be — it works. How 'bout yours, Kat?"

"Yep, tickin' like a clock."

After Tippy left, Kat walked to the bed and gasped at the cocktail length dress laid out for her. Copious yards of billowy ivory chiffon flowed from an empire waist, topped by a lavish gold brocade bodice beaded with dangling teardrops of crystal and silver.

"Holy crickets, Hoki, this is one dynamite outfit. Thanks."

"The garment should flatter you in every way, mistress. I am happy you are pleased with my choice," the shy Brownie muttered.

Kat bathed, braided her raven locks to one side, and applied a touch of makeup. When finished, she peered into the mirror. *After forty years of looking old, I'd almost forgotten what it's like to be this pretty.*

Pleased, she strolled into the garden to wait for everyone else. Almost immediately, the two guys made an appearance, followed by Tippy, who looked remarkable in the midnight-blue velvet dress Meon chose.

"Wow, you two babes are gorgeous." Randy wore a broad smile.

Jay walked up to Tippy and held out a hand. "You sure as shoot are. Why, you look so good, old girl, I don't mind being your escort after all."

"Thanks a bunch, you pompous clown." She laughed and placed her hand in his.

"Tonight should prove to be quite interesting," Kat said. "I can't wait to meet our mysterious guests."

In a gallant gesture, Randy extended an arm. "Shall we journey to the dining room, Kat?"

"Yeah, I guess its time. Speaking of time, have you guys checked your watches? They should work now."

Jay let out a whoop. "Hey, they do. Now, we'll know what time it is to do whatever it is we find to do wherever that's at."

Randy shook his head and chuckled. "Ladies, don't *even* try to make sense of what he just said. Buddy, you really amaze me at times. I swear you don't have both oars in the water."

As they entered the dining hall, all four stopped and peered around.

The spacious room had been magnificently transformed. Lavish garlands of white and red roses were artfully strung from the grand ceiling and walls. Elegant centerpieces adorned the white linen covered table, set with blue patterned white china, delicate crystal goblets, and fine silverware.

All eyes turned as the Queen entered in a striking powder-blue gown that shimmered and sparkled as though woven from pure starlight. Her hair, pulled back on the sides, cascaded down her back like wavy locks of melted honey. The crown she wore was indescribably

103

elegant — set so thick with diamonds, the gold was barely visible beneath the luminous jewels.

"Okay Randy, *now* tell me Adera is just a looker," Kat whispered.

His eyes danced with fire. "No, I can't say such a thing tonight," he whispered back. "She's a vision beyond words."

Deep turquoise eyes glittered like faceted gemstones as she walked to them. "Good evening."

Randy bowed politely. "You look *spectacular*, Your Highness."

A slight blush graced her cheeks. "What a lovely compliment, Randy. I hoped my appearance would be found pleasing and am touched by such gracious words. Our guests should begin to arrive any moment. Most are rather anxious to meet each of you. There will be a unique mixture of humans, as well as non-humans, and I believe you will find each rather remarkable in their own particular way."

Kat's thoughts of the world from where they came were erased as if by magic. She winced as a pang of apprehension caused her stomach to flip. *What is affecting me so?*

Chapter 8
Enlightening

In the clear depths of the crystal sea, watchful eyes of three mermaid princesses peered over the top of a massive coral-encrusted formation. Every subject in the watery kingdom, including their father, King Legar, had been captured by the black-hearted sorceress, Nimue. They alone managed to escape and now risked their lives to spy for Adera. Taking great care not to be discovered, the three crept closer to witness their father's torment.

The loathsome body of the hideous serpent nuzzled Nimue, who tauntingly hovered in front of the cave of imprisonment. "Ah, my faithful servant has returned. I can see by the bulging stomach you feasted well last evening." She stroked the creature's head and gave off a wicked laugh.

King Legar yelled angrily, "Ios should never have been brought back from his eternal sleep. He is a ruthless creature and belongs in the distant cave where I exiled him centuries ago. Why are you doing these things, Nimue? What has turned your heart to stone? My people committed no crime. Release them, and do with me what you please, but let them go. I beg you."

"Me, bargain with you? What a pompous blowfish. You can offer nothing but your life, and I already control that fate. As for your people, I will enjoy watching my precious pets feed on them one by one. It is well known sharks favor Mer-people as a delicacy."

"No, I beseech you, please spare them," he pleaded. "They are innocent and have done nothing to deserve this horror."

Her eyes blazed as she grabbed hold of the bars and shrieked, "Innocent? These treacherous subjects refuse to follow me, their Queen. Instead, they remain loyal to Adera, and I shall not tolerate such behavior. Their actions seal their fate. I assure you, they will be punished, particularly your traitorous daughters. These three renegades shall pay dearly for being disloyal. My sharks are to dine upon them first. It will be delightful to watch them be torn apart, bite by savage bite, while you, my darling husband, witness their destruction."

"How could anyone choose to follow such a despicable Queen? Be warned, my vile wife, you shall soon suffer the wrath of Adera. I pray she will be as merciless with your life as you are with others."

The evil sea witch threw her head back and cackled. "Your precious Adera is no longer a threat to me. My powers are strong. I relish the day her lifeless body hangs from the Castle gates, and the stench of her rotting flesh permeates throughout the land. Soon, all will bow to me as their Queen, not only in this realm, but in the other as well. Humans are such weak, mindless beings and can easily be controlled. I alone shall *rule* the earth."

Legar shook the bars. "No, it is forbidden! You cannot interfere with the other world."

"Forbidden? I think not. Nothing, or no one, can suppress my powers. I shall sweep happiness and laughter from both worlds as easily as one whisks dust from a floor."

The mighty King hung his head as hope faded. His eyes glared as he watched her swim into blue infinity. "My heart fills with hatred for you, Nimue. I pray a champion will arise, one capable of eliminating your wickedness."

Slowly, the princesses eased away and swam to safety.

Romey, the youngest of the three, looked at her sisters. "We must get word to Queen Adera. Nimue is completely out of control. You are the oldest, Maris. Use the amulet and take this information to her."

"No, I cannot leave you both alone. There is much danger, and I fear for your lives. You heard Nimue. We are being hunted." White-blue eyes began to fill and concern clouded her ivory face.

"You must go to Queen Adera or all will be lost, and our people destroyed ... Father as well," Romey pleaded. "Do not worry. For the moment, we are safe. Please Maris, take the amulet and hurry to the Castle. Now go, sister, quickly."

ഇരു   ഇരു

The light of the day had retreated, and the large chandeliers now cast a warm glow around the spacious banquet hall. One by one, the guests began to arrive. In short time, the empty room filled.

Adera strolled over to Kat escorted by a very handsome, regal man with peculiar pointed ears. He was somewhat Scandinavian in appearance with long ivory-blonde hair, pale skin, refined features, and flamboyant sapphire eyes. The ice-blue silk tunic he wore covered white leggings, which were tucked into fine black leather boots. An ornamental band of platinum rested upon his forehead, and an immoderate diamond ring swathed a long, delicate index finger.

"Kat, I would like to introduce a dear friend, Merneos, King of the Elf city of Durmeleigh."

107

"I am delighted we meet at last," he said melodiously. "You are as lovely as described."

Kat felt an uncontrollable rush of blood flow into her face. Unfamiliar with the customary protocol to address such nobility, she stammered, "I — I'm happy to meet you, your Maj — Highness. Tha — thanks for such a generous compliment." She struggled to gain composure and not give the impression of being an unsophisticated buffoon.

Prior to another word being uttered, an eye-catching, exotic Elf woman joined them. She was tall and slender with luminous moon-kissed skin. Willowy strands of waist-long platinum tresses outlined an incomparable face enhanced by distant, aquamarine eyes. Large bell sleeves adorned her radiant snow-white gown cut from an unusual material that moved like loomed mist. An ornate silver filigree sash encircled the lady's waist and continued down the front of the impressive gown.

Merneos took her hand and smiled. "It gives me great pleasure to present Nirage. She is a particularly gifted Elf sorceress, and I am embarrassed to admit, wisest of us all."

The charismatic Elf bowed her head in a gesture of respect. Blushed lips curled faintly as she looked into the intense eyes of the King. "You flatter me, My Lord." Her gaze turned. "This coveted arrival is met with much joy, Kat. We hope in time you will grow to admire Bowlandria as we do."

"I'm sure I will," Kat replied. "Strange as it may sound, this land has already ensnared my heart."

A robust voice heralded the arrival of a vivacious young female who burst into the room with the force of a hurricane. "Sorry I'm late gang, but had a bit of a problem with Knox. Poor thing's still a little shaky on landings."

Merneos viewed this new guest with a furrowed brow. "If you will excuse us, Kat, I believe Nirage and I have taken enough of your time."

She gave a slight bow. "It was a delight to meet both of you. Your Highness, is it permissible for outsiders such as myself to visit your city? It must be a wonder to see."

"Our picturesque kingdom *is* unique. You and your companions may visit whenever you choose, which *could* be sooner than anticipated." The King offered an arm to Nirage, bid a good evening to all, and strolled off.

Kat was fascinated by these wondrous beings. "Wow, they're remarkable. Is Nirage sort of like a wizard or something? I'm not really sure what it is she does."

Adera explained how Nirage acted more like an advisor to the King than an actual sorceress, but was capable of boundless magic. She was very old and possessed immeasurable wisdom. The gift of divination allowed her to foresee the future, a talent Adera confessed to employ on occasion.

"Come, Kat. Allow me to introduce someone you will find enjoyable. Be forewarned, she is an exuberant character and very full of life. They approached a woman who was actively talking to a group of men. Adera walked up and cleared her throat. "Excuse me dear, there is someone I would like you to meet."

"Good evening. Thanks for inviting me, Your Majesty. I must say the room is spectacular tonight, and the guests are unbelievable."

She was young, slim, and on the tall side, with a long slender neck. Short mousy-blonde hair bordered a plain, but attractive freckled face. Gray eyes danced, and there was a slight tomboyish mannerism about her. Unlike everyone else, she was not dressed in typical formal attire, yet the clothes seem to match the extravert personality. She wore camel-brown tailored trousers, a long-sleeved paisley blouse tied at the neck with a contrasting silk scarf, and dark-brown leather loafers.

"Hi there, I'm Meeley. My guess is you're the celebrated Kat we've all heard about, right?" She spoke in a cheerful whispery drawl.

"Uh, yeah, I suppose that's me, but I certainly didn't realize I was so well known." Kat chuckled.

The effervescent girl let out a hearty laugh and gave Kat a friendly rap on the back which nearly knocked the wind out of her. "That's a good one. I think I'm gonna like you."

Adera choked back a giggle. "Kat, if you have no objections, I shall leave you in the company of Meeley. There are many introductions yet to be made."

"Not a problem. I *think* I'm in good hands." She drew a deep breath and crossed her fingers.

"Let's grab a couple chairs so we can sit and chit-chat better." Before a reply could be made, Meeley dashed off to retrieve the objects.

The conversation with this free spirit was invigorating, and Kat could feel a bond of friendship begin to form.

"How are you coping with things? Was a bit of a shocker when you first arrived, wasn't it? I know it sure rattled my brains."

Kat nodded. "You better believe it. We were just on a casual cruise to the Islands when we encountered this strange rainbow. Somehow, it transported us here. Our youthful transformation really blew my mind. Then we met McLachen, the talking horse, followed by a visit with the Unicorns. I'm kinda reeling from all this."

A puzzled expression appeared on Meeley's face. "I've never met McLachen. You say he's a talking horse? That's pretty snazzy. Wow. Here all this time I thought Knox was the most unique thing in this place."

Kat looked at her inquisitively. "Who's Knox?"

Meeley roared. "Let's just say he's my *pet* and leave it at that." She motioned for Kat to draw close and spoke low, "You're not going to believe a lot of things you see in this realm. There are people and creatures here that will literally knock your smelly socks off. Don't get me wrong, there's nothing to hurt you or anything like that, just stuff you might struggle to comprehend. After all these years, I'm still amazed by what I come across at times. Say, who's that handsome bloke over there, the one by the fireplace talking to Charlie?"

"Oh, that's my friend, Jay. Would you like to meet him? Uh, by the way, who's Charlie?"

Meeley bounced to her feet and dashed off.

"Dang, I swear that girl is spring loaded."

The conversation halted as the two girls stormed up to the guys.

Kat caught her breath and apologized, "I'm sorry for the intrusion. Jay, this is Meeley, and she's *rather* anxious to meet you."

The jolly girl grabbed hold of his hand and shook it with great enthusiasm. "Darn right I wanted to meet you. I'd be nuts to ignore such a good looking guy."

At first Jay stood motionless, his mouth agape. Finally, he wrenched his hand free from the iron grip of Meeley. "Kat, this is Charlie. He and his squadron came here during the last world war. Equipment failure caused them to get lost during a routine training mission out of Ft. Lauderdale. The planes were about out of gas, and the mission seemed doomed. Suddenly, a heavy fog surrounded them. Next thing they knew, they arrived in Bowlandria."

"It's nice to meet you, Charlie. Sure is a little comforting to know there are other humans here. So, you were a pilot? I suppose you really miss flying."

Charlie laughed, but quickly composed himself and apologized, "Sorry for the outburst. You see, we still fly. Meeley's probably the best one of us all. You do know she was also an aviator and somewhat of a legend in her own time."

"No, I didn't. Meeley never mentioned anything about being a pilot." Kat was dumbfounded by this incredible disclosure.

"It's really nothing. I soloed across the Atlantic a few times, but in those days it was kind of a big deal, especially for a woman. Darn near bit the bullet while on one of my foolhardy adventures in the South Pacific. Thankfully, I was rescued by the rainbow force."

Jay scratched his head. "You guys have planes? I didn't think such things existed in this realm."

"They don't, in fact, there's nothing mechanical here. However, I can assure you we often take to the air." Charlie winked.

Impatient, Kat drew a deep breath. "Why don't you two just tell us what the dickens you're talking about before we die from curiosity?"

"Nah, it's going to be more fun to show you. I wouldn't want to ruin the surprise." Meeley gave off a fiendish cackle.

"Okay, I can see it's completely useless to try and prod anything from you two. Guess if we're going to have the-you-know-what scared out of us, we'll just have to keep a roll of toilet paper handy." Jay chuckled.

The tinkle of a crystal bell announced dinner was about to be served. Once everyone settled into their designated seats, the staff began to serve the succulent feast Cook had prepared. Chilled wine filled every glass, while stupendous platters of ambrosial delicacies were placed before the eager guests. The arrival of decadent desserts signaled the consummation of the festive banquet.

After allowing sufficient time to digest the meal, Adera requested everyone gather in the drawing room.

Startled by the unexpected placement of a hand on her shoulder, Kat twitched. She spun around and peered into the face of a towering, ruggedly handsome man.

A chest long beard of cocoa-brown matched his bedraggled shoulder length hair. He was dressed in elegant robes of rich amethyst velvet, trimmed in silver embroidery, which draped downward from square shoulders. Devilishly twinkling eyes were such a deep shade of midnight-blue they appeared black. "May I escort you to the appointed area, dear Lady?" His voice was soft and courtly.

"I suppose that would be fine." She placed a hand on the chivalrous arm offered.

"It seems I have failed to properly introduce myself," he said as they walked. "My name is Ambrose, though most refer to me as Merlin."

Shocked by this incredible disclosure, Kat nearly stumbled and screeched to a halt. "Forgive me if this sounds rude, but are you *the* Merlin of human folklore?"

"Yes Madam, we are one and the same. I am sorry my title causes such distress. That was far from my intent."

"No, I'm the one who should apologize. Your salutation sort of unhinged my brain. It was very rude of me."

Merlin grinned and patted her hand. "It does seem the mention of my name has such an effect on people, and quite often I must say. How do you like our little world, Kat?"

"It's unusual, but I'm beginning to actually like it here. Unfortunately, I don't think my friends share this enthusiasm. They can't wait to return home. I have mixed feelings about it and right now don't know if I want to go back. Everything I've seen is like something out of a dream."

Kat rambled on and on as they traveled to the drawing room where the duo continued a lively conversation. She found Merlin's stories enthralling — his knowledge remarkable.

"Can you really do magic, or was that simply an old wives tale?"

"Yes, I am indeed charmed, but I seldom have use for such frivolities in this land of peace and harmony."

"I can't believe I'm standing here talking to the one and only Merlin, in the flesh. Do you realize you're a legend in our world? The stories date back for centuries. What an honor it is to meet the greatest of all wizards. I feel rather humble in your presence."

"Oh no, Madam, it is I who should feel humble before you. My purported status is due to many unfounded tales, but you cannot believe all you have heard. I fear they hold little truth. However, to find I am considered the greatest of all wizards is delightful. It has always been my utmost ambition to be titled as such."

"Merlin, may I ask what is it you do here? Are you like the court wizard or divine enchanter?"

The great conjurer smiled brightly. "I merely enjoy life and do whatever I please. Many ages ago, I arrived with my beloved sister and two others. Our time in the other world had grown dangerous. Wizards were being hunted or worse — killed. Powers, once revered by Kings, were now considered evil. All who possessed similar talents became known as creatures of darkness. Some were indeed evil, but most of my kind remained peaceful, harmless beings. Refuge in this realm provided an escape from persecution. Adera and I grew close and remain dedicated friends to this very day. She and I share a mutual memory."

He paused and cleared his throat. "Eventually, I became bored. Our wise, noble Queen sensed my unhappiness and graciously offered the task of tending to our herd of winged horses. I was appreciative and accepted in an instant. Now I am most content. They are fascinating creatures. It is a pleasure beyond words to view the heavens seated upon the back of such a celebrated animal. You must try it one day. I am confident you will find it exhilarating."

Kat's face glowed with excitement. "So it's true. Flying horses really exist. In answer to your invitation, you better believe I accept. Is it difficult to ride one?"

"Not at all. The Elves created special saddles for them, as well as magnificent bridles forged from the purest gold. It is not so different from riding a common horse, only you are no longer earth bound. Their powerful wings allow one to rocket through the sky at tremendous speed."

"Well Mr. Ambrose, you have a date. The first chance I get, I'll give it a try. How will I find you?"

"When you are ready, speak to Adera. She will have you brought to our stable. We do not keep the winged herd with the other horses. The two species do not mingle well. My personal mount is a fabulous chestnut stallion I call Kiv."

"What a coincidence. When I was a little girl I had a horse, a chestnut. I can't tell you how often I used to imagine he could fly. I hope we'll soon get a chance to see them and go for a ride."

"I believe it will be very soon, my dearest Lady, for you, and your friends. Our herd has grown quite large, and there are several fine mounts to choose from, each more magnificent than the next. I do not wish to change the subject, and please forgive my forwardness, but I must say Kat, you have the most intriguing and beautiful eyes I have ever viewed."

Scarlet seared her cheeks.

Merlin frowned. "By the expression you wear, I fear my words have greatly offended you, madam."

"Sorry, you've said nothing wrong. It's sort of a touchy subject with me. I've always been self-conscious of my eyes and consider them more of a curse than anything else. All my life, I've been teased about their weird amber color. It's a little difficult to accept a compliment about something that's brought me embarrassment and shame. Maybe one day I'll feel different. I hope you can understand."

He gently cupped her hands in his. "Your eyes are indeed like two fine pieces of Amber. I could not think of

116

a more accurate description, but the unique hue is not what intrigues me. Within their depths reside great compassion and love, a quality few possess. My dear, never again be ashamed of your eyes, for they should be envied."

Kat could not stop blushing, but accepted his words of wisdom and noble compliment graciously. She felt relieved when Adera and Randy walked over to join them. Anxious to see Randy's expression, she quickly introduced the wizard.

"Mer — lin?" he stammered. "You're r-real?"

"He sure as shoot is, Randy. Kind of rattles your brain a bit at first, but his name has that effect on people." Kat glanced mischievously at the great sorcerer and both burst into laughter.

Adera slowly ran a finger across Merlin's cheek. "Since the day of his arrival, this kind man has been my closest companion. Our hearts, and souls, intertwine."

"Yes Adera, our memories are splendid, but regrettably, they are infused with a tormenting loathsomeness."

"We shall not reminiscence of that event, and let it be long forgotten, Merlin." The tone of her voice changed … her expression solemn.

Merlin stared at the Queen, his eyes soulless. "This night we are obligated to speak of that unholy incident. I know the intense grief it will produce. Like you, I do not cherish the thought, but the choice is no longer ours to make. Sadly, it must be done."

Adera glowered at him, and Kat could see her body tremble. "I have long struggled to erase these particular memories from my consciousness. They pierce my heart with such boundless hatred. Forgive me, old friend, you are right. I must lay aside my feelings and properly attend to the appointed task. Tonight, the fetid name must pass from my lips, and I shall speak of her evil ways. The time draws near."

Kat looked at Randy, confused by the unexplained banter, and whispered, "What in tarnation is going on? I feel odd standing here."

"Know what you mean, kiddo." He squeezed her hand. "Uh, Your Highness, I don't mean to butt in, but perhaps Kat and I should leave you two alone."

The Queen turned toward the pair. Engrossed in the exchange with Merlin, she obviously ignored their presence. "I am sorry to have exposed you to this deplorable conversation. It was wrong, and I ask your forgiveness."

Kat and Randy excused themselves and hurried off to find Jay and Tippy.

As they walked away, Kat glanced back at Adera. An overwhelming sense of impending doom shot through her body like a bolt of lightening. *I'm far from being a clairvoyant, but feel the truth regarding a clandestine event is about to surface. I have no idea what it is, but know I am inevitably involved.*

Chapter 9
__Revelation__

As the night progressed, the clamor of voices filled the great drawing room. Kat and Randy stood by the massive earthen fireplace engrossed in conversation.

Jay waved his hands and yelled, "Hey dudes, Tippy and I are over here. Come join us."

The duo walked up, and Jay grabbed Randy's arm. "Not sure if you've been introduced to these two, buddy. This is Meeley and Charlie."

"Sorry to say I haven't had the pleasure, Jay. Nice to know y'all." He extended a hand in friendship.

Kat bit the inside of her lower lip to stifle a snigger. *I'm curious to see how Randy handles this disclosure — should be quite interesting.*

Jay explained how and when the pilots arrived. "Charlie claims they all still fly, but won't reveal what they use, dude. It's kind of a big secret."

"Is this nut case telling the truth?" Randy cocked his left eyebrow. "I'm a bit dumbfounded. Mind explaining?"

"Oh, we found a way." A sheepish grin formed on Charlie's face. "You should see Meeley up there. This babe can out maneuver any of us."

Randy did a double take. "You fly, Meeley?"

She let out a whoop. "Certainly do. Can't keep a good woman out of the sky, now can you?"

119

"I don't get it. If there aren't any planes here, what the blue blazes y'all fly … *brooms?*" Randy sounded a bit sarcastic.

Charlie cast Meeley a playful wink. "Sorry pal, we shouldn't tease you like this. I hate to disappoint you guys, but the only use we have for brooms around this joint are to sweep our floors. When we take to the air, we use the flying horses."

Meeley nudged him in the side and gave a quirky look. "Well, not *all* of us sit aboard one of those smelly beasts. I prefer Knox."

Kat, Jay, Randy, and Tippy looked at each other and shrugged.

Unable to contain the intensifying curiosity a second longer, Kat spoke up, "Okay, I'll bite, Meeley. What the dickens is a Knox?"

"Oh, he's just my little green flying machine," she replied in a nonchalant manner. "I'll introduce you tomorrow if you like. Looks like we'll all be around come morning. Seems some sort of problem popped up, so Adera advised everyone to stay the night. Truth be told, your first encounter with Knox would be best done in broad daylight."

Charlie laughed. "Just make sure you all take along some clean drawers. A good pair of running shoes wouldn't hurt either."

"I just might hold you to that invitation, Meeley. Can't speak for the rest, but I'd like to see what this so called *green thingy* of yours is." A corner of Randy's lip curled upward. "Charlie, you mentioned flying horses? Were you serious or just clowning around?"

"Trust me, it's not a joke, Randy. The guys and I take them up for a spin several times a week. They're a bit tricky to ride until you get the hang of it. I do okay, but can't hold a candle to Howell and Edward over there. I swear those two aces have learned to maneuver their horses better than they can walk."

Several taps on a crystal goblet brought the room to silence. Adera began to speak, "May I have everyone's attention? I would like to apologize for such an impromptu gathering and convey my gratitude for your unquestionable attendance." Fluid eyes scanned the room. "A series of violent attacks occurred within the kingdom last evening which necessitates our immediate attention. Accommodations have been prepared. Regrettably, the night is no longer safe. An evil has fallen upon the land, and I am saddened to say it will bring war."

Heads turned and eyes darted about. The assembly stood motionless and silent, their faces sheathed in a myriad of emotions. The cheerfulness of the evening vanished, and an unsettled atmosphere began to sweep over the room.

King Merneos rose, as his masterful voice pierced the stillness, "Long ago, our kind entered this realm to escape the ruthlessness of the other world. We do not approve of war or the violence it entails. However, heed my word. No Elf will *ever* cower nor run from impending doom. We now offer our allegiance, Queen Adera and shall fight by your side to destroy the impiety. May we assume the prophecy has at last come to surface, and *she* is in control of the Titan?"

Randy looked wide-eyed. "What do you suppose this is all about? Not a single word he said made a lick of sense to me. Did it to any of you?"

The entire group nodded no, except Kat. *Apparently, I'm part of the few who has some prior knowledge of the prophecy. Dang it, I didn't get the chance to speak to Adera about it yet. I only know of its existence, but nothing of the content. However, King Merneos appears more than informed, and his statement alluded to the fact a war is eminent. One item in particular seems to unnerve everyone ... the mention of some Titan. Even the valiant King sounded fearful.*

Kat exhaled in a futile attempt to hide rapidly surfacing emotions. *Could this creature be the so-called 'evil' Adera mentioned?* Her heart raced and insides quivered as fear and anxiety grabbed hold. Every muscle and bone begged to flee. She sensed an unwelcome involvement, but knew the only choice was to sit and wait for the inevitable.

A glance at the tapestry sent a shot of fear through her heart as though pierced by a flaming iron. Little doubt remained. The girl, so masterly woven in the fabric, was *indeed* a representation of her. The colorful threads signaled she would soon encounter an incomprehensible and horrifying danger. A combination of worry and fright flooded the golden yellow eyes. *I'm so scared. Oh dear Lord, what does fate hold for us. Why is all this happening?*

Charlie's voice penetrated the aberrant quietness, "Excuse me, Adera, but would you please explain to the rest of us what you and King Merneos are talking about? I, for one, am clueless."

The Queen nodded then searched the room until her gaze at last fell on Kat. "It is time everyone understands what is to be. No power on earth can alter the events that have now been set in motion. I will try to explain everything in simplified detail so each mind will be free of any confusion. For many years, I have avoided these ignoble thoughts from the past, for they hold an abundance of painful memories. At last, the time has arrived when they must be fully addressed so you are aware of what terror we shall *all* soon face."

A vexed expression shrouded Kat's face. She felt the impending words would not be welcomed and furtively peered at Tippy, who huddled close to Jay, her right arm wrapped tightly around his left. It was more than obvious fear had emphatically overtaken her.

"This story unfolds many centuries ago when our dear friend Merlin arrived. With him came his equally talented sister, Ganieda, a handsome and gifted protégé, Tanas, and another, whose wicked intentions were shrouded by deceit — the sorceress, Nimue. It is she who is the controlling energy behind the detestable occurrences we have encountered."

Kat flinched as a stout man with mousy blonde hair leaped to his feet.

A finger pointed toward the wizard. "It seems all of this was brought on us by Merlin. I say, since he's the one at fault, let him clean up the mess and be done with it."

Turquoise eyes flashed, and Adera spun around to face the antagonist. The swiftness of the action caused the young man to fall back into his chair. A mellow voice cracked with obvious irritation, "Unless you wish to feel the brunt of my ire, let no one say or think such absurdities again. Merlin is blameless and merely an innocent victim ... deceived by a ruthless heart and a treacherous plan. Nimue is not only magically strong, but possesses an enormous wealth of seduction. This evil talent has been conveniently used throughout the years on many unsuspecting males. In order to obtain inconceivable knowledge, Merlin was bewitched. Once her artfulness matured, he was no longer an equal. During a moment of passion, Nimue turned on the unsuspecting tutor."

The Queen swallowed hard before continuing, "Using the newfound magic to confine him, she forced the immobilized wizard to watch while she viciously tortured and killed his beloved sister, Ganieda. Tanas attacked the witch in a desperate attempt to rid the land of her wickedness. It was a valiant endeavor, but his meager talents had little effect against such intense powers, and she savagely killed him as well." She paused and cleared her throat. "My attempt to save them failed. I shall never forget the sight of the broken and blood-drenched bodies that lay silent at my feet or the tears that flowed from our great wizard's eyes."

Gasps rumbled around the room. Adera's revelation was a nightmarish story of incredible sadness.

All eyes turned toward the somber conjuror who sat in the corner, head hung low.

Merneos walked over and placed a hand on Merlin's shoulder. "I have long known of Nimue and her sadistic ways, but had no knowledge of the personal anguish you endured, my old friend. It is indeed a tragic tale and reinforces our resolve to destroy this loathsome imitation of a woman."

"Thank you, Merneos. Your empathy is most appreciated." Merlin slowly stood. "Memories of that day continue to deliver great sadness. My sister was not only beautiful of body, but a kind, gentle soul, incapable of inflicting injury upon any creature. The echoes of her screams will haunt my mind to the end of time. However, there is more to this tale. I am not the only one who suffered agony at the hand of this depraved creature. I am sorry, Adera, but the entire story must at last be unveiled so all fully understand the extent of Nimue's sinfulness. You know I would gladly endure all the pains of the earth rather than allow you to bear one moment of grief, but the truth can no longer be avoided."

Adera turned her head as pent-up emotions surfaced.

Merlin wiped a falling tear from a creamy cheek. "Feelings for my protégé, Tanas, were like those of a brother, but could not hold light to the love Adera felt for him. He was to become her future husband."

Many rose from their seats and sounds of exclamation were heard.

A flood of eyes fell upon the Queen as Merlin continued, "First, Nimue restrained Adera by magic then savagely murdered Tanas. A morbid cackle of delight spewed from the witch's mouth as she slowly ran a sharp blade across his throat, spattering a stream of warm blood upon the gown of his captive sweetheart. Our enraged Queen struggled and at last overcame the spell, vowing revenge for these senseless murders. In fear of retaliation, the witch fled to the sea, but before Adera could reach her, Nimue transformed into a shark and escaped into the shadowy depths of the abyss. There, she remains in banishment. Yet, her inhuman ways continue. An army of filth has been resurrected. She now prepares to attack the realm, and I suspect make an attempt on both our lives."

Adera's face was taut. For several minutes, she did not look up, but kept her stare fixed on the floor.

Sight of the distressed Queen, looking at the burnished tiles as though they would render some form of consolation, tore at Kat's heartstrings. Uncontrollable tears flowed in sympathy. The mere thought of this gentle woman being forced to witness the death of her beloved and view the slain body that lay dead at her feet, her gown awash with his blood, caused a shudder.

The entire room grew quiet as a tomb.

Kat leaned over to Randy who sat still, his gaze fixed on Adera. "Some story, isn't it? By the look on everyone's face, I'd say they are about as stunned as we are. I swear, the hatred for Nimue is so blasted thick in this room you can actually feel it. They sure as shoot know how to drop a bomb around this place."

Suddenly, the unearthly silence broke as Jerome burst in. "Majesty, there is an unfamiliar maiden in the hall who requests an audience. She wishes to speak to you at once."

Adera's voice was strained, the tone agitated, "Now is not the time for such nonsense, Jerome. Go away." She looked at him, blinked, and drew a deep breath. "Wait. I apologize. My demeanor was inappropriate. Tell me the maiden's name and the nature of this untimely visit."

"She says her name is Maris, Your Highness."

Adera leaped to her feet. "Maris! Show her in at once."

The gangly butler hurried from the room and promptly returned followed by a shapely, petite girl.

Waist long, brown hair billowed around a scantly clothed trembling body. Enchantment seemed to radiate all around this exotic maiden. Her ivory skin had a luminescent quality, as though coated with pearl dust. Breathless, she rushed forward, her gait awkward. "Queen Adera, we are in grave danger. It was crucial I risk coming. I have much to report."

"Dear sweet Maris, please sit and rest. Your legs are not yet strong. What has caused such panic?" With subtle

126

gentleness, Adera took the girl's arm and led her to a nearby sofa.

"It is Nimue. Oh Adera, she is out of her mind. My people are in such terrible peril. They have all been imprisoned. She plans to feed them to the sharks — soon."

Adera glowered at Merneos and Merlin, her nostrils flared in obvious anger.

Maris paused and drew a breath. "Nimue has amassed legions of devilish fiends to do her bidding, even more than anticipated. Not only does she plot to conquer and destroy this realm, killing all who stand in her way, but now intends to invade the other world as well. She seeks divine supremacy over the entire earth and will stop at nothing until the desired quest is realized. Her powers have become boundless … even stronger than perceived. Never have I witnessed such sordid evilness."

"This cannot be allowed," Merneos bellowed. "It is forbidden for anyone in our realm to interfere with the other world. Peace is no longer a viable option, Adera. The only conceivable path is to forthwith engage her unholy army in battle. Nimue's corrupt actions have at last sealed her fate. She must *now* be eradicated at all costs. King Legar is a kind, gentle monarch and an honored friend. Tell me, Maris, your father and sisters, are they safe?"

"No, Lord Merneos. For the moment, Father is not in imminent danger, but my two sisters are being hunted as we speak. I very much fear for their lives. Nimue possesses Father's Trident and now controls all creatures who occupy the sea. Our waters are no longer secure. The Sea Queen's spies are everywhere, and the sharks relentlessly search for us. The past several days we have obtained little rest or nourishment."

Adera addressed Merlin, "I believe you know what is needed. Do not linger."

He nodded and rushed out of the room.

Jay cast a sideways glance at Randy. "What in the world's going on, and who the blazes is King Legar?"

"I have no idea, but Adera certainly appears upset," Randy replied. "Merlin ran outta here like he sat on a hill of fire ants. Its obvious King Merneos knows this girl. From what little I can gather, she and her family live in the ocean. I'm as lost about all of this as you, buddy, and can't rightly give you an answer."

Everyone in the room had risen to their feet. A murmur began to spread and grow louder as the guests viewed Adera and Maris.

The Queen slowly rose. "My friends, an explanation is in order. Once again, I have acted improperly and ask forgiveness. Allow me to introduce Princess Maris. Her father, King Legar, is the royal sovereign of the Mer-people who reside in the great Abyss."

"Holy crap, she's a mermaid!" Jay's outburst caused all to turn and gawk. "Uh, I'm sorry Adera. I apologize to you and to the Princess. It just sorta slipped out of my big unethical mouth."

"Can you believe this, Kat?" Tippy whispered. "It certainly explains why she's such an eye-catcher. Even her voice is mesmerizing. It sounds as though she sings her words. I never believed the seamen's yarns. Kinda figured they were drunken hallucinations. Sure busted that thought all to blazes, like everything else here. Wonder how she got legs?"

"I don't know, but apparently she hasn't had them long. Poor little thing can barely walk. I certainly have to agree with you. Everything about her is almost hypnotic. Check out the guys. They're one hundred percent gaga." The two girls began to snicker under their breath. "I swear, Tip, about the time I think nothing else can surprise me in this land, something else happens."

Charlie stepped forward from the crowd. "Excuse me, Your Highness, but from what I've gathered, it appears we lay on the brink of war. My fellow compatriots asked me to speak on their behalf. We humans hold a strong belief in freedom and justice. These values have long been the driving force that keeps us united. Tyranny is not acceptable to my race. To overcome such atrocities in our world, we have entered into many battles … fought many wars throughout time. My men and I were deprived the opportunity to fight for our country. We would feel honored to defend Bowlandria and proudly stand by your side." Charlie held his head high and raised a clenched fist in the air.

Residents cried out in agreement. Vows of their allegiance to Bowlandria, and its Queen, resounded around the room.

Adera peered at her guests through misty eyes and smiled as she sank down upon the sofa alongside Maris.

Merlin, who had been away only minutes, returned in time to witness this touching gesture. He approached the Queen, paused, then knelt on bended knee and caressed her hand. "Adera, my dear friend, I pledge body and soul to bring about the final destruction of Nimue. I dedicate my life so it may end hers."

His noble words caused the room to erupt in thunderous applause.

The Queen placed a hand on top of his. "Merlin, this time you and I will unite and succeed. Together, we will fight as one to rid the earth of this contemptible, depraved being." She raised her head. "My friends, I am numb with emotion. You have delivered immeasurable joy in a moment of tremendous sadness. Words cannot express my gratitude for such outstanding devotion. I shall do all within my power to render you free of harm. There will be many dark days ahead, but with your aid and passionate loyalty, we shall prevail. Our conjoined efforts will send this foul creature back to the depths of hell where she belongs."

Once again, the room burst into spirited cheers. The air quickly filled with boisterous yammering as everyone began discussing all that had occurred and been said.

☙☙ ☙☙

Adera drew very close to Maris so as not to be overheard. "Merlin anticipated this event and prepared these tokens in advance. They will allow your sisters to obtain legs and provide escape." She discreetly placed two small talismans into the mermaid's delicate hand.

"You must hurry back to them, but take care. Use extreme caution. My carriage shall offer transport to the sea where it will await your return. The three of you shall remain within these grounds until your home is once again safe. Do not fear, my sweet child. We will free your father *and* your people. No harm shall befall them." Adera hugged the brave little mermaid as she rose to leave.

Maris smiled, kissed Adera and Merlin on the cheek then hurried from the room.

"May we now continue with our previous concerns, Your Majesty?" Nirage spoke in a tranquil and dignified manner. "What of the prophecy? Has the chosen one been advised of her role in this yet?"

Adera heaved a sigh. *I must regain my composure. I hoped to delay this joyless task a time longer. With events unraveling so rapidly, little choice is left. Please, forgive me.*

ഓര   ഓര

Kat, nestled between Jay and Tippy, felt her stomach lurch as Adera approached.

The Queen reached for her hand. "Will you kindly join me in front of the tapestry we once viewed?"

Fear shot through the apprehensive girl like a hot dagger. "Why, I know what it looks like." One hand recoiled while the other clung to Jay's arm.

"What the devil's going on?" Tippy asked.

"I don't know, kitten, and I'm not so sure I want to either," he replied. "Apparently, it has something to do with that wall-hanging, and I have a sneaky suspicion we're not about to get an art lesson."

Kat finally relented and was led toward the site of the timeless masterpiece. As she and the Queen walked away, a glance over her shoulder exposed the confusion in her friends' eyes.

"You and I have stood here before, Kat. At that time, you questioned the meaning of this tapestry and the prophecy. I wished to offer a more gentle explanation, but fate does not always grant us the luxury of choice."

"Yeah, yeah, I understand we have no control over fate, but what's this all about, and why does it involve me?" Kat replied, irritated. "Look Adera, I'm just a plain old country girl from South Carolina and couldn't possibly play a role in your prophecy junk. This is ridiculous and nothing more than a stupid coincidence."

131

"It is no coincidence, dear one. You are here because *this* has been your destiny — since birth. When you look at the tapestry, does it not appear familiar to you?"

Kat's heart raced as she gazed upon the eerie presentation. Immediately, she knew the Queen's statement was correct.

Adera turned to the crowd. "In the time of my ancestors, a riddle emerged foretelling of these terrible days. I shall now disclose to all present what it declares and why there is little doubt Kat is the one of whom it speaks."

> *The creature shall swim when the twin comets fly,*
> *entering unseen below the sea and the sky.*
> *From the land of the Eagle arrives one like a dove,*
> *with boldness of mind and a heart filled with love.*
> *She will have eyes of gold, hair like night,*
> *and compassion for all, this daughter of light.*
> *In a battle of death, these rivals shall meet,*
> *as one obtains conquest, the other defeat.*

The death-like silence was interrupted by the Elf King, "Adera, have you forgotten something?"

"I have *not*, Merneos — there is *nothing* more to tell." Adera's stern reply caused the noble sovereign to frown.

೮ಾೞ   ೮ಾೞ

Randy's bewildered eyes darted between the two sovereigns.

"Can you believe this dung?" Anger rang in Jay's voice. "Sure sounds like a lot of bunk to me. I think they're pulling our leg and using Kat as a scapegoat for their stupid war. She's no more a part of that bull than I am."

Randy grimaced. "Sorry, buddy, but believe you're wrong this time. Check out the girl on that tapestry. It's a

132

mirror image of Kat. Unfortunately, prophecies have been known to come true, even in our world. I'm afraid she's in this head over heels."

Tippy fidgeted. "We can't just sit back and let them use her like a cheap piece of bait. Dang it, Randy, you're the one with the brains. Think of something."

"Easy Tip, we're not about to abandon Kat. Actually, this confrontation might turn out to be our ticket home. Besides, from what I've heard tonight, Nimue sounds like a real witch with a capital B. To tell you the truth, I might enjoy a chance to pop her a good one."

Jay slapped the side of his leg. "Well dude, count me in. I certainly wouldn't mind taking a punch at the old bat either. Are you with us, Tip old girl?"

"Have you two gone and lost your wits? Considering the fact none of us has had a lick of combat training and are void of any magical talents, how the dickens can we help? All we would do is get in the way … or killed. Wait just a doggone second, my book might hold the solution."

"Blast it, Tippy, now's not the time to think about reading a stupid book," Jay snorted.

"Oh really, you non-attentive donkey, the *stupid book* holds a wealth of valuable information and could save our miserable lives. So, put that in you pipe and smoke it."

Randy pushed his way in between them. "Will you two cut it out? Tip, if there's something useful in those pages then bring it on, baby girl. We need all the help we can muster. Look, I know you're both upset, but this isn't the time for us to bicker. For Kat's sake, we need to stick together. She's in serious trouble, guys."

From across the room, Adera's voice boomed like distant thunder as she spoke, "I understand what shock this revelation delivers and am not without empathy, Kat. Please remember, you now dwell in a land of magic. I promise we shall take enormous measures to maintain your safety. Nimue is not to be your concern. Only Merlin and I possess the power to destroy her. That task will be left entirely to us. Your destiny is to confront the beast who is under her control. His name is Ios. I cannot lie ... the very sight of him is enough to affright any being, mortal or immortal."

"Well that's certainly a comfort, Adera. Mind telling me a bit more about Ios, or is that another thing I'm supposed to guess."

"He is the last Titan, a ghastly, vile creature," King Merneos announced as he strolled up. "Ios is Lord of the Sea Serpents."

Kat's face drained, her voice prickled with fierceness, "Adera, please tell me this creature isn't some sort of snake. If it is, I can tell you right now our discussion is over. Count me out. I've always been terrified of snakes. How can you expect me to face such a thing when even a picture of one gives me the willies? I'm serious. I can't, and won't fight it — not if it's a snake. You demand too much of me. It's not fair. I didn't ask for this, none of it. To blazes with your stupid prophecy. Just leave me alone." Kat ran sobbing from the room.

Randy started to go after her, but was brought to an abrupt halt by Tippy's firm grip. "You stay put and find out what you can. Meeley and I will go after her. I'm sorry Randy, but right now she needs the comfort of another female. Kat, hold up," Tippy yelled as she and Meeley rushed to their friend and disappeared into the darkened corridor.

The air in the drawing room was abuzz with aimless chatter. Some discussed how they would fight, while others pondered over their abilities to engage Nimue's army. Eventually, most guests drew weary and soon retired to their quarters.

A select group was requested to remain behind for a private discussion. When the room had at last emptied, only Randy, Jay, Charlie, Merneos, and Merlin remained with Adera.

"I sense you are deeply concerned about Kat," Adera said. "I am equally distressed. In a short course of time, I have grown to love her as one would a sister."

Randy was cordial with his reply, "Thanks, Adera. That means a lot to us. However, I'm afraid caring for someone isn't going to save her. We're far from cowards, but we're not soldiers either. Tippy's right. Without the necessary skills, how can we offer any help?"

Adera smiled. "I thought perhaps these concerns would prey on your minds. That is precisely why I asked you stay. Would you do me the honor of divulging our plan, Merneos?"

"It is rather uncomplicated," the noble Elf replied, his voice unemotional. "You and your friends, as well as several others, will be brought to Durmeleigh to be trained for combat by my most commendable warriors. As I stated earlier, we disapprove of war, but beyond our tranquility resides skilled warriors. To face them, is to face death. We shall prepare you both physically and mentally, molding you into formidable combatants. When we are finished, there will be none who would not gladly fight alongside you."

"My help will be given as well," Merlin interjected. "I have already prepared multiple spells. After applied, they will allow your weapons to become devastatingly accurate — even when you are not. I have also devised an element of surprise for Nimue, one she will not suspect. That is where you come in, Charlie. Would you and your men agree to wage battle from the air?"

Charlie's face lit up. "Ingenious, Merlin, an aerial assault. You're talking of course about attacking from above on our flying horses. It's brilliant, and without a doubt, my men will eagerly jump at the opportunity. You fly with us all the time and know how skilled they've become. We'll still need some training of course, especially in the use of weapons while soaring through the air. I presume we'll be armed with bows?"

"Yes, indeed so," Merlin replied. "Nimue will not anticipate such an onslaught. It should give us the edge we desperately require. All riders will be trained by the Elves' best archers, and we shall attack with deadly force."

"Well, you can certainly count on us." Charlie gave a double thumb's up. "Merlin's Marauders will do our share."

"Adera, I know Kat said she won't fight, but I've known her all my life. When the chips are down, I guarantee she'll be there for you." Randy's brow furrowed. "However, I have to say in all fairness, she wasn't kidding about her fear of snakes. Our girl has always been terrified of them. Merlin, is there anything you could conjure up to get her over this phobia?"

The wizard laughed. "You must have read my mind, dear lad. Indeed there is." A tiny bottle of clear liquid was offered. "This potion will temporarily eliminate the apprehensions. I would suggest she partakes of it as soon as possible to be totally effective. Would you be willing to discretely add this to her drink? I assure you, it is safe. She will not sense the elixir has been given."

Randy peered at the insignificant container. "That's really a rotten thing to do, but I understand it's best for her and everyone else concerned. It shouldn't be a problem to sneak it into her morning coffee."

"Then it is settled." Adera rose from her chair. "Tomorrow afternoon, we will all journey to Durmeleigh. At that time, you shall begin to train. I suggest we try to gain rest, for I fear the coming days shall be difficult. The quest at hand shall not be easy, but I see great strength within each of you. I am confident we shall achieve success and eradicate this malignancy. Sleep well, my friends." She bid everyone good night and left, followed by Merlin and Merneos.

"Dudes, don't know about you, but it feels like I've been run over by a bus — twice." Jay chuckled. "I suppose we should do like the lady suggested and try to get some shut eye, although I seriously doubt anyone will sleep after the bombshell we had dropped on us tonight."

"Well, we can at least try, old buddy." Randy patted Jay on the back then cast a quirky glance at Charlie ... Merlin's Marauders?"

"Hey it fits." Charlie laughed. "Think you'll better understand the expression once you get to see the guys in action. I'll bet you a dime to a dollar we travel via the flying horses. Durmeleigh is an arduous distance from here, but easily accessible by air. Perhaps tomorrow we'll find out just how well you two can sit a horse."

Laughter echoed down the stony hallways as the three guys headed toward their rooms and actively chatted as they ambled along.

At long last, the day of hardship ended, and the Castle drifted into a peaceful silence — a stillness that flowed across the land like a breath of doom.

Chapter 10
Knox

Kat paced the iridescent marble floor, her mind tortured. Relentless, the odious revelation played through like an old movie. She glanced at Tippy and Meeley, who lay outstretched on the bed fast asleep. Hint of a smile crept on her face. *There's no way I could have made it through last night without the unselfish kindness of your friendships. You two gave me strength when I had none.*

Concerned any movement might stir them, she tiptoed out to the garden. *Perhaps the fresh morning air will furnish a bit of revitalization.*

In the ghostly luminosity of sunup, the landscape took on an almost pious atmosphere. Beads of dew glistened on the dense leafy grass like flickering sequins. *How can a place of such boundless, serene beauty be fraught with impending destruction?* She buried her head in both hands and surrendered to suppressed emotions.

A velvety voice infringed upon the morning's hush, "My Lady, why do you weep?"

Startled, she whirled around and blinked to clear blurred eyes. "McLachen." She dashed to the great stallion, embraced his neck, and sobbed into the thick mane. "I'm so glad you're here. I don't know what to do. They want me to fight something I haven't the courage to face. How can I help when I'm so fearful of this creature?"

"My Lady, you need not fear. Within your heart resides a powerful force, a strength I believe is not yet

139

realized. I am aware of what has been asked of you. It is indeed a frightful chore. However, you greatly misunderstand Queen Adera. Had she thought you incapable to achieve the specified task, it would not have been presented."

Kat peeled her head from the ebony tresses and looked into the unruffled brown eyes of the magnificent horse. An unexpected calm began to encase her tense body as the sensation of relief inundated an exhausted mind.

"Do not worry, My Lady. I shall not allow harm to befall you. Until this filth is eradicated, I will remain by your side to ensure your wellbeing."

"No McLachen, promise you'll stay out of this. Please, do as I ask. It would be unbearable if something were to happen to you. This obligation has been appointed to me, *only* to me." Kat gently stroked his head as she spoke.

"My Lady, I cannot imagine a greater honor than to act as your mount in the forthcoming battle. Our friendship is deep-seated … our unity resolute. The abomination shall be vanquished from the earth and peace restored. I do this of my own accord and hold no trepidation. Your selfless love and devotion shall act as my shield. It will protect me from injury. Now, do not waste further speech. My decision is firm."

She kissed the suede-like charcoal muzzle of the great stallion. *Have it your way, McLachen, at least for now. I realize no words will discourage you once your mind is set, but somehow I will keep you from this conflict. You, more than any other, must remain safe. From the moment our eyes met, I felt a bond form, one more powerful than the camaraderie between my human friends. Sorry, but you are not going to war with me.*

140

Her thoughts trailed into words. "If you insist, McLachen, you may be my noble steed in battle. Although, I have to say it might feel kinda weird to sit astride my best friend." She giggled at the comment, self-assured her words were simply a bold-faced lie.

The great horse threw back his head and whinnied as though laughing in reply to her statement. "In truth, I do not relish the idea of a saddle upon my back. They are most uncomfortable contraptions. However, I will gladly tolerate such a contrivance for you."

"What? I won't hear of putting you through such torture. I can ride just as well bareback as I can with a saddle. That, my dear McLachen, is *my* final word on this particular subject."

He snorted. "If that is what you wish, My Lady, I shall not object. Now, I shall bid you good day and attend to my family. They must be led to safety."

"Whoa. Hold it, buster. Let's back it up a little. Did I hear you say your *family*?" Kat exclaimed.

"I do indeed have a family. My mate is Darcy. We have at last been blessed with a little colt. He is called Chendar ... a combined play on our names. It was uncertain if he would possess my Bayard talents, but only yesterday he belligerently told his mother no, vocalizing as clearly as we now speak."

"Dang McLachen, this is one mind-boggling news flash. Guess we can no longer consider you the last of your breed, can we?"

Kat listened as a proud McLachen spoke of his family. When finished, he excused himself, bowed politely then trotted off, his long mane flying wildly about his head as usual.

141

The conversation with McLachen had somewhat eased her angst. However, his remarkable disclosure reinforced her determination to keep him out of danger. She would speak to Adera. Surely the Queen would not allow the stallion to enter the battle. He must remain safe. That was definite.

Kat strolled back into the bedroom and noticed the two girls begin to stir. "Hey lazy bones, 'bout time you got up."

Tippy yawned and stretched. "Morning girlfriend, what time is it?"

"Time to rise and shine, sleepy heads." She rushed over, leaped on the bed, and nestled between the pair.

"How long have you all been awake?" Meeley rubbed the sleep from her classic gray eyes. "You catch any rest, Kat?"

"I'm afraid not, Meeley. Just came in from outside and had a nice long chat with McLachen. This might sound bonkers, but the conversation eased a bit of my apprehension. Can't say I feel one hundred percent okay, but do feel better."

An unexpected pounding at the door brought the three to their feet.

Kat cracked open the door and peered out.

"Good morning, Miss Sunshine. Is the coffee ready yet?" Randy planted a little kiss on her cheek as he entered. "If y'all don't mind, thought I'd join you dolls for a quick wake me up drink?"

"Well, aren't you the bright chipper one. Guess one of us got some shut-eye." Kat snickered. "I suppose we can tolerate your presence for at least one cup o' Joe. Say, how come you're up so early?"

Randy chuckled. "You can't possibly be serious? I doubt anyone in this joint got a wink of sleep last night, me included. They sure know how to liven up a dull party. It was rough going there for a while. How ya feel this morning, kiddo? "

"A tad better, thanks to McLachen. Randy, he told me he has a mate and a new colt. Can you believe it?"

"No way — you're joshing. He's a Pop? Who would have ever guessed? See, it's just like I've always said … whenever you hear bad news, it seems good news is not far behind. Everything will work itself out." He gave her a hearty hug.

All heads turned as the aroma of freshly brewed coffee filled the room.

Kat started to bolt for the table, but was yanked back by Randy's firm grip. "Chill it, girl. Allow me to be your personal server today. You just go sit your butt down, okay?"

An expression of puzzlement formed on her face. "Who are you, and what did you do with Randy?"

"Oh, you're just a barrel of laughs. Much more of that nonsense and you can get your own drink," he replied as he hurried off. Within seconds he returned.

Kat looked up and smiled as Randy handed her the steaming cup. "Here ya go missy, just how you like it, hot and sweet. Oh wait! Merlin wanted me to try this new additive he whipped up last night. Said it would enhance the coffee's flavor. You may as well get poisoned along with me." Before she could utter a word, he emptied the contents of the vial into her drink. "Go ahead, it won't hurt you. I took a swig and haven't keeled over yet. Actually, it's pretty good."

143

At first she was hesitant, then shrugged her shoulders and took a sip. "Hey, this *is* tasty. Thanks. Best darn brew I've had in a long time. Wow, I feel so much better. Guess it's just what the doctor ordered."

"Darn hot coffee heated me up a bit." He exhaled and wiped tiny beads of sweat from his brow. "Well, I don't know about you, but I'd say the old conjurer's juice is a *huge* success."

"I certainly made a fool of myself last night with that ridiculous outburst." She sipped a bit more of the flavorful liquid. "I don't know what all the fuss was about. After all, Ios *is* just a big, dumb snake, and I totally blew the episode out of proportion. Not sure why I reacted as I did. I felt so scared, but for some strange reason, I don't feel that way now." She snickered and took another swallow.

Randy grinned. "Under the circumstances, you had a right to be a little upset, kiddo. It's sure a relief to see you back up to snuff again."

Meeley spilled a bit of the coffee as she set the half empty cup on the table. "Say y'all, why don't we freshen up and go grab a bite to eat. Maybe afterward, you can tag along with me to go see Knox. I really do have to check on him, and soon. He gets a tad anxious if I am gone long."

"Sounds like a terrific idea, Meeley. I think it's fair to say we're all a little curious about this *flying machine* of yours. I'll go get Jay. I'm sure he's starving by now. Meet you girls in about fifteen minutes. Uh, will that be enough time for you chicks to pretty yourselves, or do you need an hour or more?" Randy let off a hearty laugh and bolted for the door.

Meeley playfully slung a pillow at him as he ran, while the others mumbled a few humorous obscenities.

During breakfast, Randy informed the girls of the King's plan and said they would most likely leave later that afternoon for Durmeleigh.

Everyone agreed the training was an excellent idea and looked forward to seeing the fabled Elf city.

Kat pushed back her chair. "Well, we apparently have a few hours to goof off — any suggestions?"

Tippy gently laid a folded napkin on the golden dish in front of her. "I really would like to get back to my book, if no one objects. There's a cornucopia of information in those pages, and I'd like to examine it in greater detail."

"Good idea, Tip," Randy said. "From the way it sounds, I'd say we're gonna need all the help we can muster. We'll check in on you when we get back, okay?"

She nodded, gave a cheery wave then hastened off for the library.

The teeth-gritting sound of a wooden chair as it scraped against the sleek marble floor broke the silence. Jay looked around and began to laugh. "Sorry 'bout that, dudes. What say we three head on out with Meeley and look into this Knox thingy of hers."

"Are you guys *sure* about this now?" Meeley's eyes twinkled. "Well, don't say I didn't warn you. I know a little short cut we can take. Ready?"

They followed behind her and were led through a secluded rear door.

"You have Knox boarded at the stables?" Jay questioned as they walked along "Don't tell me all this whoopla has been about a little old green flying nag?"

Meeley let out one of her gregarious laughs. "Good gracious no. My Knox would terrify those poor critters.

145

Adera prepared a special place for him away from everyone and everything."

Their pace slowed to a near crawl as they drew near.

The enthusiastic guide brought the group to a halt. "Are you three positive you want to do this? Looks like you're getting a tiny bit nervous. Sure you want to go on?"

"Of course we do. We're as ready as can be, or at least I think we are." Jay chuckled even though a slight frown remained. "Come on, Meeley, why don't you just get it over with and tell us what the dickens we're gonna see. Although, I doubt anything could scare the likes of us."

"Is that so, Jay? I'll give you a little hint. Knox is slightly large, dark green, and the first time you see him can be a trifle scary." A sly grin appeared on her face. "Oh, come on, you chicken livers. He's in the big building over there." She pointed to an enormous blue-domed outbuilding that now came into view.

"Holy blazes," Randy exclaimed. "That thing of yours must be the size of a 747 to need such a structure."

Kat felt the hairs on her neck prickle. "Uh, Meeley, I'm not so sure I really want to know what's in there either, unless you tell us right now what it is."

"Don't worry, Kat. Knox would never hurt a buddy of mine. Of course, he might be hungry and does have a hearty appetite for those who are mean to me, *Jay*."

This remark caused the prankster to stop dead in his tracks.

Kat looked at Meeley, her eyes filled with worry. *Shoot. I wonder if this new friend of mine might be a little on the loco side. Maybe coming here was a bad idea.*

Meeley briskly walked to the old building, flung open the two massive iron doors, and yelled into the cavernous structure, "Hey Knox, get your big fat green butt out here. We have company."

Suddenly, two enormous yellow eyes emerged from the darkness, followed by a spine-chilling guttural growl. The thunderous vibration of pounding footsteps caused the ground to quake as the voluminous creature moved forward and began to unfold from his den.

"Oh crap!" Jay screamed like a girl, bolted for a clump of nearby trees, and tripped over his own feet several times as he fled.

Kat gasped and grabbed hold of Randy's hand as the pair backed away, their eyes wide with fright.

On the other hand, Meeley doubled over in side-splitting laughter.

"Is-is t-that wha-what I think it is?" stuttered an obviously shaken Randy.

"Yep, it sure as heck is. I cautioned you might not be ready for him. Not many are." She beamed as a hand was extended in presentation. "Ladies and gentleman, meet Knox, my dragon."

He slowly meandered out until the mountainous body towered high over his mistress. Without hesitation, he lowered his head into her waiting hand. "I swear its okay. Despite the fierce looks, he's really quite harmless. Knox is more like a big puppy dog than anything else. Come on over and meet him," Meeley said as she rubbed the monstrous scaly head.

"Yeah well, to say I'm feeling a bit unhinged is an understatement. A blimp-sized puppy dog is not something I care to encounter."

Kat started to giggle, amused by Randy's sudden cowardice. "Don't be such a sissy. Show a little backbone. Meeley said he wouldn't hurt us, and I'm sure she wouldn't lie about something so serious. Let's go check him out. You go first!" She nudged him forward and conveniently tucked in behind him.

"Are you out of your ever loving mind?" Randy bellowed as he pulled back. "Listen here girly, if you want to see him so bad, you go first."

"But Randy, I'm just a poor helpless woman who depends on your manly protection. It's only natural for you to take the lead."

"Dang it, you women sure know how to use your charms when it's convenient. Seems I have no choice but to act like a man and go first, thanks to that eloquent exclamation. Actually, I'm a little over the initial shock. Although, I have to admit it's *darn* little." Randy shook his head and reached out for his buddy. "Come on Jay, go with me. Jay? Where the blazes are you?"

"I'm over here, and I'm staying put. So leave me alone." He peered out from behind a large oak tree as his body quivered uncontrollably. "I have no desire whatsoever to get near that sucker — absolutely none at all. You two can act stupid and go get eaten, but not this old boy. Momma didn't raise no dang fool. Thanks for the invite, but no way, Jose. I'll be more than happy to inform Adera tonight at dinner you both died bravely. Sorry dudes, I don't particularly care to be that beast's main course. I like to fill my gut, not spill it."

Meeley stood in the shadow of her dragon's prodigious green body and was almost rolling on the ground in laughter. She regained composure and spoke in a soothing voice, "It's really okay, Jay. You're safe, I promise. He's a bit much to take in at first, but trust me, Knox is just a big mountain of love."

Kat eased up to Randy and took his hand. "Come on, I'll walk up with you. I do trust Meeley and know she wouldn't say it's okay if it wasn't. Ready?"

Slowly, and with great caution, the pair approached Knox who had now unfolded his enormous wings and stretched them high above his body. Inch by inch, they drew closer until they at last stood alongside Meeley.

Randy looked up at the lofty mass in front of him. "I hate to admit it, but once you conquer the fear, this guy's truly a beautiful sight to see."

The remarkable dragon stood a good forty foot high. Iridescent dark green scales covered the monstrous body and lengthy tail, while outsized shimmering scales of pearlescent gray sheathed a long graceful neck and bulging stomach.

Knox had rather short legs, gigantic feet with immense spiky white claws, and a mouth full of large dagger sharp teeth. Feathery plates of fire-red protruded from the sides of the classic dragon-shaped head crowned by two majestic ivory horns. Protruding from his sides were a pair of massive leathery bat-like wings of translucent green, which appeared more than adequate to propel the colossal beast into the air.

"Relax, he won't bite," Meeley cooed to the two shaky visitors who stood frozen before the gargantuan creature. "Knox, these are my new friends, Kat and Randy. Oh, and looking out from behind the tree over there is the yellow-bellied, tail-tuckin', jelly fish, Jay."

The gentle giant peered down at the newcomers then unhurriedly lowered his head until it rested on the ground directly in front of them.

Still clinging tight to each other, Randy and Kat stared into a face big enough to gulp them in one bite. All of a sudden, he began to purr.

"Is he … purring?" Kat was astonished this meek sound could come from an animal of such magnitude.

Meeley rubbed the scale-covered head. "Yep, he sure is. It's his way of saying he likes you. Knox hatched shortly after my arrival. Our wise Queen realized flying was my first love, and it would be the one thing missed more than any other. She was confident Knox and I would bond, and we did. He was only a baby when Adera gave him to me, but let me tell you, this was some baby — about the size of a Thunder Hoove. After I got over the shock of him, I fell in love with this big bundle of bliss. At first, he was too young to fly, but in just a few months he carried me back into the clouds."

"He's pretty neat, Meeley." Kat reached out tentatively to touch him. To her shock, she found the scales to be hard as iron yet buttery soft and warm to the touch. "Jay, come on over. Just look at how gentle he is. Oh, come on dingy, he's not going to eat you." Her light touch caused the dragon to close his platter-sized eyes and tilt the massive head in a playful gesture of wanting more.

Jay moved from behind the great oak and inched toward his friends. Meeley saw the terror in his eyes so walked over and offered a supportive hand.

"Do you really fly this bugger?" Kat asked.

"Sure as shoot do. I always thought piloting a plane was the ultimate adventure, but it can't hold a candle to Knox. Riding him is like soaring on the wings of an angel. He can turn on a dime and rocket up and down like a roller coaster. The Elves designed a special harness, somewhat similar to the ones made for the flying horses, and I have to say I'm mighty thankful. It's plumb uncomfortable sitting on those nodular scales." She laughed and gave him an affectionate pat on the neck. "It'd only take a second to get him ready for a flight, if you'd like."

In unison, Kat and Randy shook their heads no. Each politely told her they would take a rain check on that offer.

Jay stood guarded behind his friends. "It might be a fun thing to do, but this is about as close to that sucker as I intend to get. I'm perfectly content to keep these feet on the ground, as well as my body, thank you."

Meeley rolled her eyes. "I really do understand, y'all. He is a bit to take at first. Although quite docile, his fierce protective nature would surface instantly if anyone or anything he loved was threatened. You see, Knox is not only a beloved pet, but also appointed guardian of the realm. I've been told he is believed to be the last living dragon. Merlin said they were feared and killed off many centuries ago. Miraculously, his egg was found and saved by an Elf warrior who carried it with him to this realm."

"How long will he live, Meeley?" Randy's curiosity surfaced. "I don't know squat about a dragon. Until now, I believed them to be the mere fabrication of an overactive mind. Does he breathe fire, or is that another tall tale?"

"I don't think he actually has a life span," she replied. "They are more or less immortal and only die if they are killed, which is darn near impossible to do. The myth of breathing fire is very real. In fact, he's pretty close to that stage now."

"This land is sure going to take a lot of getting used to with its talking horses, Elves, Unicorns, and now a purring dragon." Kat sighed. "Yep, it's gonna take *a lot* of getting used to."

Jay looked straight-faced at her a second then broke out in laughter. "Kat, I couldn't have put it better. For once, I think we are all in complete agreement. There are things here beyond my feeble mind's capacity."

"Meeley, when you said you would join the others in this forthcoming conflict, did that mean you'd be flying Knox?" Randy wore a questioning expression.

"You got it, ace. He's fast as lightening, and I'm hoping he'll be spittin' fire by then. I've seen puffs of smoke come out of a hiccup lately, so I know he's about ready. I believe such a particular talent might inflict considerable damage. Wouldn't you agree?"

"Yeah, I suppose so," Kat replied. "Gee Meeley, I can't thank you enough for showing him to us. Although, I kinda doubt Jay will ever get those brown racing stripes out of his britches."

All three looked at Jay and burst out in a hearty laugh.

"I'm glad y'all think it's so dang funny," he sneered.

"Oh now, don't go bustin' a corset." Randy choked a bit as he struggled to compose himself. "There's no denying Kat and I were pretty scared. In fact, I'm not so sure I don't have some of those racing stripes myself."

"Well, now that you've met Knox, I think we should head back to the Castle. I'm taking this guy to Durmeleigh, so need to get ready and get my fanny in the air. I would almost bet Adera has arranged for you to ride the flying horses there. Other than Knox, they're about the only thing that can make the trip in under an hour or so."

Kat's eyes widened. "Wow, do you really think she might have us take the flying horses? Shoot. If we use those suckers, we're gonna have one heck of a problem on our hands — Tippy. She won't even get on a regular horse, let alone one that flies."

"You're right, kiddo," Randy exclaimed. "All things considered, I can understand why it's imperative to travel there as quickly as possible, but there's no way on this green earth we'll get Tip to ride with us. Let's pray Adera can come up with a solution."

"Ya know, dudes, I'm not so certain I want to ride one either," Jay announced. "I don't even like going up in a plane. Kinda prefer my horse's feet on the ground."

"Just zip it, Jay. You know how to ride, and ride well, so cool your jollies. We have enough problems right now." Randy grabbed Jay by the arm, turned, and started off.

The two girls strolled behind the guys and could hear the fairly-heated discussion continue as they walked.

"I wouldn't worry any, Kat. Adera will get Tippy to Durmeleigh. She's a pretty darn smart lady and doesn't miss a trick. Say, tell me a little about Jay. Is he, uh, taken or anything? I know I've seen him around Tippy most of the time and thought perhaps they were an item."

Kat giggled. "Nah, they're just good friends. Sorry, don't mean to dash your hopes, but I know for a fact he'll never get romantically involved. Jay loved, and still loves, his Mary — even more than life itself. He's told me more times than I can count that he looks forward to the day he can join her in heaven."

Meeley elbowed Kat playfully. "Hey, lighten up. I'm not in the market for a lifetime partner. Just thought he was a fun character and would enjoy spending time with him now and then. Course, he is a handsome bugger."

"Let me clue you in on a little something," Kat whispered. "I've noticed him glance at you every now and then. In fact, it was quite often last night. He really thinks you're a trip which is kind of a compliment coming from that clown. For now, let's keep this our little secret, okay?"

The walk back was enjoyable, and soon the group entered the Castle.

"Meeley, thanks again for taking us to meet Knox. It was a blast," Randy said.

Jay scowled. "Yeah, it was *real* fun, at least for some of you. Meeley sure as the dickens got my heart pumping big time when she let the *dog* out. In all honesty, I didn't know I could run so fast and don't even remember doing it. One minute I was alongside you guys, and the next thing I knew, I was behind that tree. All I can say is they better have some powerful soap in this joint 'cause I've got some seriously soiled undies."

The group's laughter ceased as they entered the library and saw Adera standing with Tippy.

A vexed expression showed on the Queen's face as she hurried toward them. "Thank the stars you are back." Her voice resonated anger. "I have been nearly out of my mind with worry. Jerome said he saw the four of you leave the Castle, but knew nothing of your destination."

"We just went with Meeley to see Knox. Is something wrong, Adera?" Randy stepped closer to her. "You said we were free to roam around the Castle and the grounds, so what's up?"

Their puzzled stares instantly exposed the overreaction. "I — I am sorry and did not mean to sound so aggressive. You *are* free to do as you wish. My permission is not needed. It seems the arising problems caused foolish and needless worry. Please forgive me."

"Under the circumstances, I would say you have every right to be angry," Randy replied. "We should have acted more responsibly and at least told someone where we were going. It was a stupid mistake on our part and should have thought before pulling such a childish stunt."

"The incident is passed. I am just thankful you are safe. Your welfare is the most important issue. I believe this has proven to be a lesson for each of us. Now, it shall be put to rest and spoken of no more. Lunch will be served in half an hour. If I am still welcome, I would like to join you."

Randy wrapped his broad arm around the Queen. "You are our friend, Adera. A little misunderstanding would *never* alter our feelings. In essence, we were the main cause of your distress."

Dynamic turquoise eyes danced. "You place me in a state of euphoria. I have never known the happiness of friendship, especially one as fervent as yours. It touches my heart in many ways."

At lunch, the tales of meeting Knox provided a bit of entertainment.

Charlie let out a whoop. "Don't say I didn't try to warn you. Sure wish I had tagged along. So, you liked old Knox, huh Jay? I have a spare pair of trousers in my room if you need them."

Jay cast a nasty glance. "You're just a monkey on a stick, Chucky boy."

After the carousing settled, Adera rose to make an announcement, "My friends, last evening King Merneos voiced his concern regarding the fighting abilities of our sprouting militia. With this in mind, he has offered the services of his finest warriors. Each has graciously agreed to instruct those desirous to fight for the realm. The Elves are proficient archers and accomplished swordsman. You will learn much from them. They will also provide armaments. Their craftsmen are legendary. Every weapon is forged from the finest materials and infused with a touch of *unique* magic. King Merneos and his people further extend their assistance by opening the Kingdom to all who wish to obtain training. It is a most rare and unexpected gesture."

The prospect of seeing this mysterious kingdom launched an energetic exchange between guests. An invitation to visit the fabled Elf community was an uncommon privilege. Very few outsiders had ever been granted passage into Durmeleigh.

Adera cleared her throat. "Because time is of the essence, the flying horses will be used to expedite the lengthy trip."

Randy, Jay, and Kat looked at each other, then at Tippy. Her face was pale and taut.

The Queen wore a quirky smile as she walked over to the group. "I shall also travel to Durmeleigh. Tippy, might I persuade you to accompany me in my personal carriage for the journey? Utilization of the fleet-footed Thunder Hooves shall allow us to arrive around the same time as the others. Will you join me?"

Tippy almost leaped into the arms of Adera. "I wholeheartedly accept, Your Highness. You have no idea how much I appreciate the offer."

Meeley nudged Kat and winked. "Told you she would come up with a solution. You can't pull the wool over those pretty eyes."

Kat felt uplifted with the knowledge Tippy would have a pleasant and acceptable means of travel.

"Hey guys, mind if I ride with you today?" Charlie beamed as he walked up. "Quite a few horses are being taken to Durmeleigh. It's not a good idea to have a bunch of those frisky critters in the air with 'rookies' on their backs, so most of my pals volunteered to fly them on ahead."

Randy gave him an easy pat on the back. "Certainly, we'd be thrilled to have you ride with us. In fact, you might be able to give us *rookies* a few pointers."

Overwhelming enthusiasm filled the air like static electricity. Even the dubious Jay stated he was growing anxious to climb aboard one of the great winged horses.

Adera interrupted all conversation, "Please return to your rooms. Gather the personal items you require. Return to the Great Hall in half an hour. At the stables, Merlin shall give you an expedient lesson on how to ride these magnificent creatures. They are tremendously spirited and a bit tricky to master. However, I believe you will find the experience exhilarating. There is much to be accomplished and little time in which to do it. Your stay with the Elves should prove to be not only beneficial, but also enjoyable. One half hour then."

The room emptied quickly as every guest rushed to gather their goods.

"Well, looks like it's about time for me to be off," Meeley said. "Going to go saddle Knox and take to the air. Guess I'll see you all in a few hours. Enjoy the ride. Sure you won't join me, Jay? Knox can easily carry more than one you know."

"Uh, thanks for the invitation, Meeley, but think I've dirtied enough underdrawers for one day," he replied.

After gathering necessities, the friends met together. Within moments, Bagi came for Tippy and escorted her off. Jerome entered and made a somber announcement that transportation to the stables awaited embarkation.

Randy dashed ahead of the others to the last carriage. Kat followed and plopped on the seat next to him, her face strained. "Something wrong, Kat? Are those old fears creeping back again?"

"Not really. Just wonder what became of Adera and Tippy. I more or less presumed they were going to accompany us to the stables."

"They're most likely on their way, Kat. Besides, what purpose would it serve to have them tag along?" Randy fidgeted. "This constant nagging is driving me nuts."

Charlie nestled alongside and cradled her hand in his. "No need to fret and wrinkle that pretty face. The Thunder Hooves might be fast, but trust me, they are no match for the winged horses. Understandably, Adera and Tippy headed out in order to gain a bit of a head start."

"Say Charlie, can you fill us in a little on these critters?" Randy scooted to the edge of the seat. "We don't know diddlysquat about them."

"Well, let's see now. Each are quite large, even more so than the Thunder Hooves, with a bodacious wingspan. They're super strong so you really have to struggle to rein them in at times. I suppose the most amazing thing about these animals is the fact they're telepathic."

Jay made a comical face. "Get real, dude. How can a horse be telepathic?"

"You have to understand, guys, they are far from being a *normal* horse. Don't ask me how it works because I truthfully don't know. Each has the mystical ability to

158

tap into a person's subconscious and react without you ever saying or doing anything."

"Oh great, just what I always wanted to ride … a mind reading horse." Jay let off a robust laugh. "Guess I'd better clean up my thoughts, or I might get thrown into orbit. Any idea why they're taking so many horses, Charlie?"

"Yeah, I do. Seems King Merneos wants his Elves schooled on them as well. Since this is a training expedition, they decided it was logical to just do everything in Durmeleigh."

The carriage gave a slight lurch as it began to move forward and at last pulled away from the Castle steps.

Kat and her friends were about to encounter romanticized creatures of myth and legend. In a few hours, they would experience the enlivened and remarkable adventure of a lifetime.

Chapter 11
Beneath Calm Waters

Two mermaids huddled close to each other beneath the wide branches of a massive Elkhorn. Their bodies trembled in unadulterated fear. They prayed the menacing shadow swimming above would not discover them.

The great shark glided through the blue water, slowly swinging the grotesque hammer shaped head from side to side. Vacant black eyes on each tip of the wing like structure scanned the reef below in search of his intended prey.

Every ocean predator had been cautioned by the sea witch, Nimue, not to kill the Princesses. However, she voiced no objections to the indulgence of an insignificant, non-fatal bite. This was all the incentive needed. Sharks, more than any other creature, savored the sweet delicate taste of Mer-flesh.

"I'm so scared, Nerissa. I wish Maris would hurry home to us," Romey, the youngest and smallest of the two sisters, whimpered.

"Quiet little one. We must not speak. He will hear us." Nerissa pulled the nervous child close.

It seemed as though time itself had paused as the frightened Princesses watched the massive fish continue to search, swimming within inches at times. At last, unable to locate the illusive sisters, he moved on and disappeared into the infinite darkness of the sea.

Romey wept as an immature body quivered. Although young, she looked to be an adult in appearance. Sight of the ferocious predator skulking above had unnerved her.

The pretty mermaid stroked the long red hair of her baby sister. "It's all right, my sweet Romey, don't cry. He's far away by now. For the moment, we're safe."

"Do you think Maris got a message to Adera, or do you suspect Nimue captured her before she reached shore? Oh Nerissa, what's going to happen to us if she didn't make it? I've only begun to live and don't want to die. I'm not brave like you and Maris. How could Father be so spineless and let this happen to us?"

Nerissa grabbed hold of the panicky child and shook her. "Romey, I never want to hear you speak of Father in such a manner again. Do you hear me?" *I can see the time has arrived for this little guppy to grow up and face the bitter facts.* "It was wrong for Maris and me to shield you from these atrocities. The truth must be told so you can understand why Father could not inhibit these happenings. He, like most Mermen, grew lonely after Mother's tragic death. During this delicate time of susceptibility, he encountered the venomous crone, Nimue. Upon entrance into the sea, the witch initially took on the shape of a shark. In time, our two paths crossed. It was then the contemptuous deception began."

"She transformed herself into the splendid Mer-creature you now know. Armed with alluring beauty and charms, the temptress seduced Father, bewitching his mind until he no longer possessed a will of his own. After they were wed, she was crowned Queen of the Sea. The evil plan now began to ripen."

The two mermaids folded fins and settled on the sandy floor as the tale continued.

161

"Maris and I repeatedly beseeched him to rid our waters of this malignancy, but our words fell on deaf ears."

"In an ardent moment of passion, the anticipated opportunity presented itself. Father was defenseless and could not forestall any of this, Romey. Talented as his powers may be, they are ineffectual against those of this deranged enchantress. What a strange turn of events this has become. In the beginning, Nimue imprisoned Father by seduction. Now, he is again her prisoner, locked in a dark and filthy cave. His life hangs by a sheer wisp of hope."

Nerissa lowered her eyes a moment before proceeding. "A terrible war is about to commence, and I fear many lives will be lost. However, I also believe there shall be no escape for Nimue. She will meet her destruction at the hands of the powerful Queen Adera. Peace will one day return to our kingdom and to the land above. As for Maris, my heart tells me she is well and shall return before long."

Romey remained motionless for several seconds, her face void of emotion. "Thank you, Nerissa. It grants me great relief to know the truth. Everything appeared to be in a state of confusion, but now I understand how and why these detestable events are occurring. You and Maris give me so little credit. I'm no longer a child." She giggled and gave her sister a kiss on the cheek.

"A difficult time will come to an end before you know it, Romey. Soon, we will once again swim in freedom." *Ha, my words might sound convincing, but in truth I worry our older sister will not return. I fear what approaches. How can I possibly keep us from harm? Maris has always been the leader. Unlike me, she would know precisely what to do.*

"I'm so hungry, Nerissa. Can't we venture out for just a moment to gather something to eat?"

Her words were valid. Mer-people required frequent nourishment due to an extremely high metabolism. The two had been deprived of food for several hours, and they were fast growing weak.

Nerissa glanced at her once beautiful fins, now shredded by the prickly spines of the coral. Vivid scales of iridescent green and yellow were dull and lifeless, faded from lack of food and light. "You are right, my sister, if we do not obtain sustenance soon, Nimue shall have only our withered bodies to retrieve. I'll see what I can find nearby. You must remain close to this coral head. It will keep you safe. Under no circumstance veer from this spot, do you understand?"

The adolescent mermaid nodded, moved close to the base, and tucked herself in tightly.

Nerissa peered around and carefully exited. She was in great danger as tattered fins impeded normal swiftness. A short distance from the reef, she spotted an exposed area of rich vegetation.

Driven by fiery hunger, Nerissa grabbed a handful of the nutritious grass and began to eat with ravenous aggression. Each salty blade tasted delicious. Until this moment, the extent of near starvation had not been realized.

A fervent craving at last appeased, the re-energized mermaid wrapped her body in the elongated, flowing tail and settled down on the white sandy ocean floor. Using her long golden hair as a makeshift container, she worked at a feverish pace to harvest the life saving morsels. It was imperative she finish and return to the sanctuary of the coral head.

After collecting a sufficient supply of sea-grass, Nerissa unwound her tail and ascended from the sea floor. It was essential she hasten back to the reef's protective cover. In the vastness of this open range, she was susceptible to attack. A jolt of panic shot through her body like a thousand volts of electricity as a dark silhouette moved toward her from behind. Liquid blue eyes darted around in desperate search of sanctuary. Exposed, the mermaid was in great peril. Paralyzed by fear, she waited motionless as the ominous shadow approached, until at last it settled directly behind her.

She drew on all inner courage and spun in the direction of the aggressor. As they came face to face, both let out a bloodcurdling scream. At first, a fatigued mind refused to accept the reality of the intruder, but soon recognized a familiar presence. "Maris, is it really you?"

Nerissa rushed into the arms of her older sister and the two embraced. Suddenly, she was pushed back, grabbed by the shoulders, and given a fierce shake.

"What in the name of Poseidon are you doing out here in the open like this? I could have been a predator and killed you. Are you that scatterbrained? What were you thinking, Nerissa?" Maris yelled.

"I — I'm sorry, Maris, but we were so desperate for something to eat. I decided to chance it and gather food. I suppose it was foolhardy of me."

A quick scan of the sibling's deteriorated condition validated the excuse. Sadness showed in her eyes as she reached down and gently ran her hand along Nerissa's tattered fins. "Oh my poor sweet sister, forgive me. I should not have chastised you as I did, but the sight of you so unprotected, frightened me. Where is Romey? Is she all right?"

Nerissa told her they had taken refuge under a large coral head. With every pass, the sharks drew closer. It would only be a matter of time before they were found.

"This has been a nightmarish ordeal to endure, but it will soon be over. Adera has arranged sanctuary for the three of us in a lovely salt-water lagoon behind the Castle where we are to remain until this has ended, together. Now hurry, Nerissa, we must return to Romey. Danger lurks in every corner."

As the two approached the giant Elkhorn, they glanced at each other and gave a sigh of relief. There, tucked in under the large structure, was Romey, safe and well hidden from vengeful eyes. The little mermaid leaped with joy at the sight of Maris and pearly tears trickled down a flawless cheek.

"Pay close attention to my words, dear sisters, for there is no time for lengthy explanations. Adera's carriage waits for us on the shore. Although a short distance away, the trek will be hazardous. Merlin has prepared additional amulets so you may both obtain legs."

Golden coin-like trinkets, engraved with peculiar writing, dangled from a pair of silver chains. Maris placed one around each of her sister's necks then handed them an individual vial.

"We must drink this elixir as we approach the breakers. It will provide our new limbs with a tremendous burst of speed and propel us through the white water onto the beach. Once the carriage is reached, we shall be free from harm."

"Maris, will it hurt to grow legs?" the youngest asked.

"No Romey, but you will find it to be a rather unusual sensation. Don't worry, there is nothing to fear, I will be beside you all the way. Now eat. You must gain strength.

Away from the reef's protection, the open waters will be dangerous. We must swim as fast as our fins will take us."

After a hearty meal, the two weakened mermaids announced they felt ready to leave as strength return to their bodies.

"The metamorphosis is instantaneous. Under no circumstances make use of these amulets until you feel the pull of the breakers. I don't mean to criticize, Romey, but you have a dreadful habit of not paying attention. It is imperative to take note — your very life depends on it."

The young mermaid rolled her eyes.

Maris swam close, her voice snappish, "Stop with the flippant attitude, Romey. This is serious. Do you want to be dinner for the sharks?"

"Of course I don't. What a horrible thing to say, Maris. You're beginning to scare me." Romey hung her head and eased back.

"Good, I'm glad you're frightened. Perhaps now you'll pay attention." Maris skimmed their faces before she continued. "When you hear the thunder of the surf, take the amulet in hand, and say *Mutatio*. Are my instructions clear?"

The younger pair nodded in agreement.

"You must drink the elixir when you feel the fin conversion begin. Do not attempt to do so earlier for the magical powers last but a few seconds. However, the added strength it provides will deliver the speed necessary for escape."

Maris went over the directions a second time. To insure absolute comprehension, she made the siblings repeat every word back to her.

Minutes later, the three mermaids began the treacherous escape. Great caution was employed as they darted from the reef's refuge.

Less than a hundred feet had been traveled when Nerissa caught sight of half a dozen black tips above them. "Oh no, we've been discovered."

"It's okay," Maris said. "The smaller sharks fear a confrontation with Mer-people. Our concern is for the larger, aggressive variety. I know your speed is hampered by shredded fins, but we must hurry."

Suddenly, Maris stopped and pointed up as the large conical shaped head of a Great White materialized out of nowhere. However, the slow unhurried approach told the wise mermaid he had not yet noticed them. "Nerissa, Romey, lie flat on the bottom, face up," she whispered. "Do not move a scale, or you will alert him."

They obeyed without a second of hesitation.

After a quick, fruitless search, the massive creature moved off and disappeared into the darkness of the cold, deep water.

All three heaved a sigh of relief as they rose from the ocean floor, and the journey resumed.

Finally, the distinct roar of breakers could be heard. In the race to attain safety, a grave mistake was made as dangerous surroundings went unobserved.

An unexpected rush of bubbles filled the sea with screams as the great hammerhead attacked. They had been found. Now the desperate flee for life would begin.

"Swim like never before, my sisters," Maris shrieked. "I will try to divert him so you may reach shore. When you are safe, I will follow. Now hurry — do as I say."

There was no time to stay and argue, so the twosome flipped their tails and sped off.

Maris turned and gave a taunting yell to the assailant, "Hey you big finned dope, lookin' for me? Wanna play some games big boy, or are you scared of a little old mermaid?"

The fourteen-foot long adversary spun around and raced toward her with mouth agape.

Like a talented Matador at play, the clever and agile Mermaid would lure him close then move aside at the last second. On the next pass, a well-aimed snap from her tailfin slashed across his eye which caused the shark to retreat.

Maris used the opportunity to peer ahead and watch as her sisters approached the breakers.

Now, mere seconds from safety, disaster struck. The violent force of a ferocious undercurrent rolled Romey and wrenched the precious amulet from her neck. She turned to look for it, but visibility was limited in the clouded silt-churned surf.

Nerissa, unaware of the incident, took hold of the amulet and muttered *Mutatio*. Her body began to convulse in reaction to a mild shock, which lasted only a few seconds. A quick glance revealed a pair of flesh covered appendages where a tail and fins had been. She opened the vial and downed the bitter tasting liquid. In an instant, the potion-fortified legs drove her through the waves. Exhausted, the blonde mermaid rested a moment on the powdery beach. Unable to control the inelegant new limbs, she tried to stand, but fell.

"Allow me to assist you, Princess."

Startled by an unexpected grip on her arm, and the sound of a mysterious deep voice, Nerissa screamed.

"Please, do not be alarmed. I am Relar, Queen Adera's personal coachman and a friend. Come, we shall go to the carriage. There you may rest and wait for the others."

Too weary to argue, the offer was accepted. However, sight of the elegant coach and great horses made her pull back in apprehension. Unlike Maris, she had never visited the world above the sea. This was all strange and frightening.

Without delay, Relar explained everything to ease any fears. He remained by her side as the two waited for the remaining sisters.

₧₧₧₧   ₧₧₧₧

"Maris, help me," Romey screamed. "I've lost my amulet. Maris. Where are you?"

"Oh no, this can't be happening. Don't panic, Romey, I'm coming." She could think of nothing other than getting the young one to safety. "Take my amulet, and do as I instructed. Hurry and go join Nerissa," she demanded. "I'll find your trinket and join you soon. There's no time to waste, Romey, *go*."

Without further hesitation, the little mermaid swam to the surf, held the amulet in her hand, and muttered the word.

Maris felt relieved as she watched the pair of delicate ivory legs disappear into the waves above. A noise from behind caused her to spin around and shriek in terror. The hammerhead, who had returned, was almost upon her. The nimble sea-maiden darted aside, but her reaction was too slow. She winced in agony as sandpaper skin brushed against her body, tearing scales and flesh. He whirled around and charged, this time taking a large savage bite from her tail's mid section as he passed. Blood

169

began to mix with water as intense pain from the lethal wound brought her to a state of semi-consciousness.

His prey incapacitated, the bloodthirsty hammerhead charged the stunned mermaid. Grisly teeth again tore into flesh. Several pieces of delicate meat now ignited a voracious appetite. The ambrosial scent of blood set fire to the water around them. Nimue's warning went unheeded by the shark as it turned and headed in for the kill.

Within inches of claiming his reward, a pulverizing thrust to the side knocked him off course. His body reacted and began to wrench from the injurious strike. Again, he was struck by another ferocious blow, followed by several more. Slick gray bodies darted about like silver lightning bolts as a group of large bottlenose Dolphin attacked. Blood began to ooze from his mouth and gills as internal organs ruptured from the force of the tremendous hits. At last, the villainous fish spiraled to the sea bottom, dead.

Maris felt the devoted dolphins bear her blood-drained, butchered body toward the pounding surf. As they neared the breakers, another swam close and dropped the missing amulet around her neck. It had been found nearby, dangling from the lacey skeleton of a large red sea fan. She tried to speak, to thank them for such boundless loyalty, but speech was difficult as life faded from the mutilated body. Determined not to die, Maris drew on every ounce of inner fortitude, clutched the magical talisman, and uttered *Mutatio*.

As strength dwindled, the courageous Princess slipped into unconsciousness. Clenched fingers fell limp and surrendered a precious vial.

Two faithful dolphins nuzzled under each arm of the listless mermaid and surged through white-capped waves. Using great care, the royal daughter was deposited on the beach, and the pair then wiggled back into the salty sea.

ಌ಄ಚಿ   ಌ಄ಚಿ

Nerissa noticed the commotion and yelled for Relar.

He made a dash for the surf, scooped Maris in his arms, and sprinted to the carriage. "Your sister has been savagely injured. She requires immediate attention. Place my shirt firmly against the wounds and hold tight, little ones." He leapt to his seat and gave the monstrous steeds a sharp crack of the whip. The carriage shook with ferocious intensity, and its passengers fought to remain seated as the horses bolted into a full gallop.

Tears began to fall as Nerissa embraced the blood-drenched body of her beloved sister. "Maris, don't leave us. Please, try to hold on. Relar, we must go faster. She's dying!"

Another snap of the whip caused the horses to gather more speed. Forest and trees became little more than a blur as the pace accelerated. Torrents of blood flooded the carriage floor and splattered the stony pathway. A short time later, the Castle came into view.

The grand vehicle sped across the planked drawbridge and entered the courtyard. Hooves slid on the sleek cobblestones as the winded horses were pulled to an abrupt halt.

Relar bounded from his seat, grabbed the dying mermaid, and yelled for help.

Jerome, Bagi, and several others ran out. They removed Maris from the coachman's arms, enveloped the maimed body in blankets, and carried her inside.

171

Relar returned to the carriage and spoke in a soft, soothing voice as he helped them down, "Worry no more, my little Princesses. You are all safe now."

The two shaky Mermaids made their way into the Great Hall. Wide-eyed, they huddled together. Tiny droplets of blood scattered across the sleek marble floor indicated Maris had been carried off to another place for treatment.

Suddenly, a side door thrust open and out rushed Cook. "Oh, me poor darlins. Tis such a horror ya suffered this day beneath those calm waters. Now don't ya be worryin. That sister of yours will be just fine. She's in good hands, if I must say so me self. Well, just look at the two wee bits of ya. Why ya must be near starvin to death I'm thinkin. You come along with old Cook. I'll take ya to me kitchen where I'll whip ya up a nice big plate of fresh prawns and cuttlefish."

Unsure of what else to do, Nerissa and Romey followed the plump, outlandish woman.

Margaret Mary sat the two girls down then dashed around to gather food. At first, they refused to eat, but the tantalizing smell of the fresh salty sea morsels quickly changed their minds.

"Madam Cook, can you please tell us where our sister is?" Nerissa asked.

"Now, now, me darlins, I told ya not to be worryin them pretty heads. She'll be gettin the grandest treatment possible and be mended like new in no time. We've had a lovely room prepared for the two of ya tonight. You'll be findin it offers a nice salt-water bath to make ya feel a bit at home. Tomorrow, you'll be seein your darlin sister I'm thinkin. For tonight now, ya need to be gettin a wee bit o' rest. Come me angels, let Cook take ya to your room and get ya tucked in."

Nerissa and Romey hobbled along on graceless legs behind the jolly woman to their sleeping quarters.

ଛାଠଷ   ଛାଠଷ

After showing them around the room, Margaret Mary bid good night. At the door, she turned back toward them and her heart broke with pity. The bewildered young Princesses clung to each other as their bodies trembled from head to foot. Cook ambled back over and wrapped her plump little arms around the quivering sisters. "Now, don't fret. No harm can befall ya within these walls."

Mournful sobs could be heard as the door was eased closed. Cook knew nothing more could be done for them tonight, and reluctantly walked off, leaving the two to their grief. She sniffled and wiped away her own tears as she made her way through the darkened corridors to the welcome seclusion of her room. As she hurried along, a silent prayer was said for Maris. She had seen the horrendous injuries and knew the loss of blood was life threatening. As talented and accomplished as the doctors were, she feared they would be at a loss to save the noble Mermaid Princess. Her fate was no longer in any of their hands.

A hushed stillness, unlike any she had ever known, fell upon the Castle this night. All had left earlier for Durmeleigh, leaving only her and a few staff members behind in the soundless structure. Margaret Mary slipped into bed, pulled the covers up over a shivering body, and closed her eyes as the chilling silence of night crept into the darkened room.

173

Chapter 12
Flight to Durmeleigh

I n a futile attempt to block the light, Kat buried her head deep in the lofty pillow. However, the brilliant morning beams were relentless and beckoned. She began to pull herself from the cradled comfort of the warm, cozy bed. *No. I don't feel like getting up yet.* Hands placed behind her head, she snuggled back down.

Darkness had obscured the room's beauty. Now, in the lucidity of daylight, she marveled at its unbelievable splendor.

White cotton draperies, hung from a wall of decorative ivory columns, billowed in a gentle, flowery-scent infused breeze. A sparse amount of elegant furnishings provided a comfortable and pleasant atmosphere. Several crystal statues and vases, purposely placed to refract the sunlight, painted the pastel walls in a kaleidoscope of rainbow colors.

Kat looked around at the fairylike quality. *Is this all real, or am I still asleep?*

The previous day had been extraordinary. It began with meeting Knox, and soon after came the incredible trip to the Elf Kingdom on the fabled flying horses. Her mind drifted, and a serene smile formed. How wondrous it had been to first lay eyes on the magnificent creatures.

A vision of the event began to appear.

As the carriage proceeded to the stables, Kat felt her stomach churn in nervous expectation. Information about these winged wonders was vague.

Merlin stood by the entrance of the horse's titanic shelter and shouted a cheerful greeting to the trainees as they exited the carriages. "Good day and welcome. You are about to meet the most unique and mystical animals placed on the earth. This way please." The patrician wizard extended a hand toward an arched opening.

Stationed inside both walls of the lengthy stable were thirty-foot square box stalls. The shadowed movements within indicated they were occupied.

"I suspected this first meeting might trigger a bit of nervousness. Therefore, we have retained the horses inside their cubicles. Only the stallions are used for flying. Although the mares can attain flight, their smaller wings are incapable of carrying additional weight. For this reason, as well as breeding purposes, they are left to pasture. Take a moment to walk about and view them. It is advantageous to choose your own personal mount. Once you have decided, let the grooms know, and they will ready your horse for flight. It is unfortunate the riding lesson is time limited. However, the trip will be brief, and what training I shall provide should be more than adequate."

Jay stood with hands on hips, his manner of speech sarcastic, "Well, this is just great. Tell me *adequate* is enough when I fall the heck off at thirty thousand feet."

"Will you knock it off, bonehead," Randy snapped. "Kat, Jay, let's go check out these buggers like Merlin suggested."

All three walked to the first stall, looked in, and gasped at the beguiling animal before them.

The statuesque brown and white pinto stallion stood at least a full hand higher than an over-sized Shire. Firm, sturdy legs supported the stocky body. From between

175

burly, rounded haunches, flowed a floor-length showy tail. Cascading from a thick, arched neck, down past its knees, was an incredible mane. Through the lengthy strands, large brown eyes watched the strangers' every move. Protruding from the broad shoulders were lustrous white-feathered wings, folded tight.

Randy blinked and gulped. "This has to be about the most phenomenal sight I have ever seen."

"Dude, I couldn't agree more," Jay replied. "You're sure quiet, missy. What's your take on this critter?"

Kat snickered. "If he's any indication of their size, Jay, I think we're all gonna need a *lot* of Epsom Salts tonight."

The droll remark caused the two guys to burst out in laughter.

Somewhat over the initial shock, they continued to look into each stall. Half an hour later, every horse had been viewed. This was not going to be an easy choice. Each animal was as magnificent as the next.

Charlie sprinted up to them. "Hey guys, been looking all over for ya. Sorry I ran off when we arrived, but couldn't wait to see my horse, Fudge." He noticed the blank faces. "Kind of hard to pick one, isn't it? I know it took me awhile to choose. One of the grooms gave me a helpful hint. He told me to gaze into the horse's eyes and concentrate. The stallion will make it known if he's the right one. Try it. Just walk up to the stall and look into those deep brown peepers. When you find the perfect one, trust me, you'll know."

"I've already made my decision, dude," Jay replied. "I like the brown and white pinto in the first stall. When I looked in at that big fella, something told me he was the perfect choice. It's hard to describe, sorta like a whisper in my head."

Charlie gave Jay a firm rap on the back. "Yep, that's it, pal. Kinda freaky the way it happens, but they make better mounts when you choose this way. Swell pick, Jay. He's actually one of the gentler stallions … fast bugger, too."

Randy took Charlie's advice, walked around, and soon settled on a handsome Bay.

Kat continued to search, but felt no psychological bond. She noticed most everyone else had chosen their steed. Unless she wished to be left behind, a prompt decision needed to be made. "This mental connection junk is stupid. I'm just going to pick one and be done with the whole thing."

Merlin tiptoed up behind her. "Is there a problem, my dear?"

She jumped and spun around. "Dang blast it, Merlin. You startled the living daylights out of me." Kat exhaled. "Charlie told us some bunk about connecting mentally with the horses. Sorry to say, I've looked at every one and don't feel a crummy thing. Guess I'm not as gullible as the others. All this talk is nothing more than a romanticized illusion."

The ancient sorcerer let out a robust laugh. "Your frustration is a tad amusing, young lady. In spite of what you believe, the spoken tale is true. Most times, the horses will choose a rider, but not always … as in your case. Perhaps the correct steed has not been viewed. Come with me, dear one. I may have the solution to this dilemma."

Somewhat annoyed, she wanted to tell him to drop the matter. At this point, any horse would suffice, but relented and complied with his request out of respect.

They walked outside to another nearby structure. It was smaller and only contained three stalls, two of which were occupied.

Eyes widened as Kat cast a quick glance inside the first stall. "Oh my stars, it's a chestnut." The striking equine's coppery coat glistened in the candescent light like a shiny new penny.

Merlin walked over, opened the door, and rubbed the great stallion's neck. "This is my personal horse, Kiv. I made mention of him the first evening we met. However, this is *not* the one for you. I believe what you seek resides over there." He pointed to the other occupied stall and gave a mirthful wink.

Intrigued, Kat meandered over and peered in through the bars. The exquisite palomino turned, nickered, and cautiously walked toward her. She froze in awe, captivated by his astounding beauty.

Illuminated by sunlight, the horse's brilliant golden coat burst with color. A gentle gust of air tousled the illustrious silky white mane around an elegant head. Entranced, Kat stared into his dark eyes. Without warning, a strange euphoric sensation began to overtake her. At last, the fabled union was established.

Long black robes fluttered as Merlin rushed to her side. "This is a most pleasurable moment. I believe he has waited these many years for *you,* mistress Kat. Meet Junar, Kiv's brother."

"His brother?" she replied. "I think perhaps I owe you and Charlie a huge apology. It's just as described. You can in fact hear them speak inside your head. I've never experienced a phenomenon like this before."

"Nor will you ever again, my dear. Until now, Junar has connected to no other."

"Whoa, hold on a minute, Merlin. Are you telling me he's never been ridden?"

"You fear him wild and unbroken, but rest easy. He is one of my most well-mannered horses. I stated he has never *connected* with anyone prior. Now your two minds are linked and physical commands are no longer required."

Kat looked back at Junar, her eyes alive with excitement. She turned to the great wizard and gave him a hug. "Oh Merlin, he's absolutely amazing. I can't wait to take him out for a ride."

A wave of Merlin's hands brought two grooms running. Moments later, Junar and Kiv were led from the comfort of their stalls and prepared for riding.

The spirited creatures were a handful for the patient aides who applied great skill to ready them. Unique bridles, made from woven strands of gold, had a spellbinding affect on the mighty steeds. Once placed, the fiery animals became as docile as lambs. The saddles were little more than over-padded seats of thick woolen material with golden stirrups added for balance.

Once all the horses had been readied, they remained calm as the riders received instruction. Now and then, one would stretch his wings as though anxious to take flight.

Merlin began the brief training. "Please, pay close attention for I shall not repeat myself. To mount is rather tricky. The wings present a cumbersome obstacle. Our grooms will assist everyone this first time. I suggest you take heed of the proper method. The superlative manes are functional and used as a precautionary measure. Observe the long braid. It will be tied securely around one wrist, much like a safety line. Should a rider accidentally, uh, dismount, the horse will react and land post-haste to prevent injury to his charge. Further, a generous chunk of mane should be wrapped and held tight in the same hand. It will act as an additional stabilizer, much like the horn of a saddle. The wings help hold you in place, but it is imperative to keep your legs snug to the body for balance. These animals are not only fast, but turn with unbelievable quickness. Maneuverability is much like that of any other horse. However, the mental ties allow them to anticipate what is wanted, and trust me, they *will* react appropriately. Be cautious of all thoughts, or you might find yourself launched into the stratosphere." A glance at the solemn faces told him the humorous statement was not appreciated. "You have now completed all the training I feel necessary. Grooms, if you will assist our new riders upon their mounts, the journey shall begin. It looks to be a glorious day for a sensational ride among the clouds, wouldn't you agree, Charlie my lad?"

"Yep, sure looks that way, Merlin." Charlie grabbed a hunk of mane and swung up on the back of Fudge. "Can't say when I've seen a nicer day for a flight."

Mounting was indeed awkward, but once seated the breadth of the horses felt rather comfortable. The grooms walked around and checked to insure everyone had done as instructed and all were secured in place.

Kat could feel the exorbitant muscular strength of the animal beneath her as the stallion grew restless.

Randy yelled over, his tone a bit mocking, "Where'd ya come up with your nag, Kat? Glad I didn't get stuck on that yellow beast. You know how I just *love* Palomino's. Sorry you had to get the leftovers." He chuckled and cast a wink at Jay.

"Yeah, yeah, yeah, I know all about it, ding-bat. Well smarty, if truth be known, looks like I got the *best* of them, and stop calling my horse a beast. You can be such a cynical brat at times." Kat reached down and gave the golden stallion a loving pat on the neck. "Pay no attention to him, Junar. He's just a witless jerk."

The two guys continued to tease Kat until at last Merlin announced it was time to depart.

"Well, looks like the moment we've been waiting for is here," Jay said. "I don't know about you dudes, but my heart's about to pop out of my chest."

Randy and Kat shot a quick glance at him, nodded in agreement, and tightened their legs to the horse's sides as directed.

"We are going to do a slow ascent," Merlin announced. "This means we shall begin at a walk. When I motion, we will break into a trot, followed by an easy canter. At that time, you will notice the wings begin to stretch outward. Soon after, liftoff will occur. Once we are airborne, groups of three are to ride in a wide V formation behind me. This is to insure no wings touch and cause an unnecessary accident. Although we will be moving at a rather swift clip, I believe you shall find the ride to be enjoyable and smooth. Are there any questions?"

Not a word was spoken. The only sound heard was the rapid breathing of the impatient horses.

Merlin smiled as he loosened the reins and took the lead. The magical moment had arrived.

They had not quite begun and already Kat was fighting to hold Junar back. She looked at Randy and Jay who were having the same problem with their mounts. Suddenly, she understood what was wrong. "Guys, stop thinking about going airborne. It's obvious the horses are picking up our thoughts. Clear your heads, hurry."

As soon as all three altered their state of consciousness, the horses relaxed and became easier to control.

Kat took a deep gulp. *Wow. That was close. We really do need to monitor our minds with these buggers.*

The group followed pace as Merlin urged Kiv into a trot, then an easy canter. As predicted, the wings began to unfold from their sides and spread. At last, with one mighty whoosh, the adventure began.

"WAHOO," Kat had never felt such exhilaration and let out a squeal as the ground swiftly disappeared.

Within seconds, the rhythmic beat of the massive wings carried the riders high above the treetops.

Junar continued the ascent as wisps of misty clouds brushed her cheeks. Now, high above the great forest's canopy of green, the majesty of this vast and beautiful land could be realized. Kat took a firm grip of mane as the golden stallion banked to the right and headed toward the lavender shaded mountain range. *Someone pinch me … this can't be real. As a kid, I often imagined such a feat, but thought it impossible. Now, I'm in the clouds, atop a remarkable creature of legend.*

"Hey Kat, how ya doing over there, kid," Randy yelled. "Really is something, isn't it? I believe I could get addicted to this."

"Boy, you aren't kidding," she replied. "Yo Jay, ya hangin' in there?"

He looked over and grinned from ear to ear. "Oh yeah, baby. No more land-locked horses for this country boy. Merlin said my horse wasn't named, so I've decided to call him Big Mike. Dude seems to like it, too."

Randy chuckled. "Sounds good, Jay. What's he gonna call you? Big Bonehead?"

Jay scowled, but the thinness of the atmosphere made it somewhat difficult to speak, so the balance of the ride was more or less quiet.

All too soon, the phenomenal flight ended as they began a swift decent into the mysterious kingdom of Durmeleigh.

A secluded valley obscured the celebrated empire from prying outside eyes. Ornate complexes, wrought with extravagantly carved gingerbread trim, speckled several lavish plateaus. Magnificent waterfalls tumbled into the river below, as a haunting mist provided an evocative quality to the Elf compound. Colorful flowers dotted an opulent forest floor, while exquisite birds darted about in untroubled play. Few humans had ever witnessed such an incomprehensible sight.

Merlin signaled the group to set down and led them to a clearing near the edge of the forest. One by one, the horses made an effortless landing. The intoxicating journey was over.

After dismounting, Jay stroked the head of Big Mike. "Thanks for a fabulous ride, fella. We'll do this again, and soon. I promise."

"You best believe it, Jay." Randy walked up and patted the pinto. "Sorta makes riding a normal horse seem like taking a trip on a merry-go-round, doesn't it?"

Kat gave Junar a tender hug before an Elf groom arrived. He gently took the reins from her hand and led the lively palomino off to be unsaddled and given a well earned reward of tasty grains and hay.

BOOM!

The chunky, oversized bedroom door slammed against the wall and interrupted Kat's spellbinding daydream.

Tippy charged in. "Hey you, move those lazy bones. We have things to see and places to go." She ran over and plopped down on the bed.

"Oh Tip, wait 'til I tell you about our flight here. It was awesome." Kat proceeded with the story and left no detail uncovered. "Okay, now you've heard all the skinny about my trip. Tell me about yours."

"Well, I suppose it was pretty uneventful in comparison." Tippy giggled. "It was the first opportunity I've had to hold an in-depth conversation with Adera. She really is a great person. As we traveled along, she and I flipped through the pages of my book. Kat, some bodacious findings surfaced. Adera went to King Merneos as soon as we arrived to begin their implementation."

"That's great news, Tip. I always thought your studious nature would come in handy someday. Have you seen the guys yet?" She climbed out of bed and stretched.

"Shoot Kat, those two have been up for hours. They're prowling around somewhere. Girl, this place is amazing."

"Well, what the heck are we waiting for? Let's go check it out." Kat darted behind the corner screen and dressed. Seconds later, the two friends were out the door.

As they walked along, a loud wolf whistle caught their attention.

"Yo girls," Randy yelled. "We've been looking all over for y'all. Where ya been?"

"Just taking in the sights," Kat replied. "I almost feel like Alice, and I've arrived in Wonderland."

The four continued the stroll together, each open-mouthed, mesmerized by the sheer beauty of the ancient city. In time, they met up with Charlie and Meeley.

"Have you all heard about what happened at the Castle last night?" Meeley exclaimed as she ran up. "Maris, the Mermaid we saw the other evening, was badly injured. They say she might die. Adera, King Merneos, Merlin, and Nirage left for the Castle before daybreak. They hope their combined talents might give her a fighting chance."

Randy gnashed his teeth. "Don't even tell me. It was caused by Nimue."

"Yep, it sure was. She had the shark traitors hunt down those poor things. When Maris went to retrieve her sisters, she was attacked. It was darn savage from what I've heard."

Kat shook her head in disgust. "That witch. The very mention of Nimue fills me with such pronounced hatred. None of us are looking forward to this war, but when I hear stuff like this it almost makes me feel anxious for it to start. I'd love a chance to take a shot at that shrew."

"You got it, Kat. I'm with you." Jay slammed a fist into his hand. "The more I hear of Nimue, the more I want to wring her darlin' little neck."

"The opportunity shall come sooner than anticipated, my lad."

A strange voice from behind caused the friends to spin around. The handsome Elf walked closer to the stunned group. "I apologize for the impromptu approach. My name is Horace. I have been appointed to train you. Wise King Merneos decided it would be advantageous to teach in small groups, rather than one large gathering."

Horace, a tall stately-looking Elf, was blonde and fair like a number of the others they had seen. He possessed a distinct aloof mannerism, which made it difficult for them to ascertain whether they were liked or disliked.

By unanimous vote, Randy was elected to speak for the entire group. "It's very nice to meet you, Horace. Sure hope we won't be too much of a burden. None of us are what you would call 'battle ready'."

The Elf warrior turned his vivid blue eyes to Randy, his voice icy, "Your shortcomings shall not be problematic. We have been briefed regarding your lack in the necessary skills of war. Our exceptional weapons shall accommodate most needs. Combined with *my* unsurpassed talent, I guarantee you six will be made ready to fight."

"Well, that's encouraging," Jay muttered under his breath, the tone clearly sarcastic.

Randy gave him a quick nudge to the side and cast a warning glance.

"Today, you will learn to become proficient with the bow. I believe you shall find the lesson stimulating." The Elf looked into each face. "I see by the expressions, you are uneasy around me. We have little contact with humans and are somewhat unfamiliar in your ways, as you are with ours. What may I do to rectify this situation?"

"Well for one, you could try to lighten up a little," Charlie said.

"Ah, you perceive my personality to border on arrogance. I assure you, it is far from the truth. It appears my lack of lengthy conversation reinforces this opinion. We Elves speak little, but what is said is without reservation and of great importance. I shall try, as you have voiced so eloquently, to 'lighten up' a bit." A subtle curl of the lip formed.

Randy spoke up and moved closer, but backed away when the Elf raised an eyebrow. "Horace, humans often look at things in a somewhat different light. We're a bit more laid-back. What you and your people are doing for us is more than appreciated. Despite our casual mannerisms, I want to assure you we will be diligent students."

"These words are wise, Randy. I believe we shall work well together," Horace replied. "Now, if you would follow me to the archery field, training will begin."

Tippy walked up beside Horace. "I always wanted to gain knowledge of the bow. My husband, Jim, is a rather skilled hunter. Oh by the way, I'm Tippy."

"Mistress, I am aware of your names."

The pompous reply arrested her exuberance.

"You shall find our bows far superior than those in your human world. Our craftsmen are masters at their trade. Every weapon is unique, made as *only* an Elf can. The strings are effortless to pull. Our arrows, infused with elfin magic, are incredibly accurate. Even a human, such as you, would not miss."

"Sounds pretty amazing, Horace." Kat hoped to pull his attention away from her timid friend. "I'm afraid I'll need every ounce of help you can muster." She looked at Meeley and winked.

Untouched by the conversation, he walked on. Soon, they came to an open glen. Several other groups had already begun to shoot. Horace presented each member with a bow and a brown leather quiver of arrows. The lesson started with a thorough explanation of the archery equipment and its proper use. He then had each load their bows. In mere minutes, the students found themselves able to shoot at, and hit, the intended target with surprising accuracy.

"Kat, this is fantastic. I can't wait to get home and show Jim what I can do. In fact, I might even go hunting with him. Of course, he might not appreciate the fact I'm a better shot." Tippy began to giggle.

"I hate to be the bearer of bad news, Tip, but don't you remember what Adera said about returning? You won't have any recollection of this place, or of using a bow, or anything else. When you go back, you'll be as you were, not young like now. Besides, Jim seldom hunts anymore after his heart attack."

A saddened expression replaced excitement. "Gee Kat, you're right. It'll be much different when we return. Darn shame we won't be allowed to retain these memories, but I do understand why."

"I know, Tip, it doesn't seem fair in a way. Unfortunately, if they don't erase our minds, we might slip up at some point and jeopardize the entire realm. Well, let's just make the best of it for now and be good little soldiers."

Kat knew this was not the appropriate moment to say anything, but she did not intend to forget this place. If they lived through the battle, this would become her permanent home. The raven-haired girl grasped the opportunity to watch her friends. Tippy stood with the beauty, grace, and elegance of a great huntress. Jay and Randy goofed around like two handsome schoolboys. They began to shoot in competition with each other and seemed to be thoroughly enjoying the moment.

Sadness crept into her heart. Soon, they would be gone from her life. In the other time, all three would grow old until their very existence became nothing more than a memory. Tears began to form.

"Your sadness will pass, as all things do," Horace whispered in her ear. "We each walk a different path. No two are alike. Your destiny is far different from theirs, painful as it may seem."

Kat looked into impassive, cryptic eyes, somewhat unnerved by the fact he knew precisely what she had been thinking.

He smiled, touched her shoulder, and for a brief moment, allowed his great veil of indifference to fall.

She nodded in acknowledgement of the statement, drew a deep breath, and resumed training. For the present time, all thoughts were put to rest.

Chapter 13
<u>Skills of War</u>

The sun hung low in the flawless sky as the cavalier Elf wrapped up the archery instruction.

Kat hurried to gather her equipment, anxious to depart from the field.

"The balance of the afternoon is to be solely used for enjoyment and relaxation," Horace announced. "Our kingdom has much to offer. If you would allow me the opportunity, I would be delighted to escort you around."

"If y'all don't mind, I'll take a rain check. I should go visit Knox. He gets a bit touchy when he doesn't see me after a few hours. I'll catch up with everyone later." Meeley turned and trotted off.

"I hate to mimic Meeley, but promised the guys I'd meet them after practice," Charlie said. "We wanna go over some new maneuvers. Sorry. See you all at dinner."

Jay stepped up and rubbed his belly. "I don't know about you dudes, but my stomach thinks my mouth's been sewn shut. When do we eat around this joint?"

"I swear there's a hole in that bottomless garbage disposal of yours." Randy gave Jay a light-hearted shove.

At first, Horace wore a puzzled look. Suddenly, his eyes widened. "Forgive my foolish inconsideration. Elves require sparse nourishment, but I, more than most others, should have realized your famishment since my human mother has similar needs. We shall go to a nearby dining area at once."

Kat stopped dead in her tracks, astonished by this jolting declaration. "Hold it just a doggone second, Horace. Did you say your mother is *human*? I thought Elves were forbidden to marry outside of their race. How's this possible?"

"In the other world, it was forbidden, but in this realm, where all creatures are immortal, such marriages are permitted. Unfortunately, many who wish to maintain the purity of our species continue to frown upon these unions, which are and remain few."

"You certainly know how to shock the daylights out of us, Horace. This kind of explains your human name," Kat said.

"Helen, my Mother, gave me her father's name. My Elvin title is Netho, but out of admiration and love for my Mother, I answer to Horace."

The five arrived at an outside café of sorts. Within seconds, a scrumptious meal was placed before them. As the four friends indulged in a welcomed bite to eat, they began to bombard the warrior with a flood of questions.

Randy took a sip of water and cleared his throat. "Horace, do you know who, or what, we'll fight in this impending battle? It might be advantageous to know a little about the bad guys."

The Elf glanced at each of them before he answered — his demeanor clearly cautious. "Your question shall be answered tomorrow. Schooling is scheduled to continue with the bow for another day. However, I give fair warning … the afternoon targets will be a trifle *different*. It is unfortunate, but you may find the session distressing by human standards. Please understand, what shall transpire is necessary. Do not inquire further for I will speak of it no more today. Since your meal is complete, let us leave and allow me to show you our land."

Spectacular sights soon left the troubling incident far behind. The proud Elf explained places of interest as he led the foursome around the legendary Kingdom.

At dinner, they got together with Meeley, Charlie, and a few of the other flyers. Horace's unsettling remark was the main subject of conversation.

Meeley scratched her head. "Jeepers, I can't begin to imagine what he's hinting at."

A jolt of terror struck Kat. "Randy, you don't suppose they're going to use live animals for targets? You know how I am about killing any living creature. I couldn't, and wouldn't, do it."

Charlie reached over and patted her hand. "Nah, don't fret about it, Kat. I don't believe they would resort to such cruel measures. Elves are one with the earth and possess a great respect for life. They'd never intentionally harm any living thing."

Tippy leaned up to the table. "I hope you're right, Charlie, 'cause I'm not shooting any live critters either."

"Let's calm down a bit. This is all idle speculation. We could be blowing things way out of proportion and getting ourselves worked up over nothing. I don't know about the rest of you, but it's late, and I'm bushed. Think I'll turn in for the night." Randy stretched his arms and yawned. "We're just gonna have to wait and see what happens tomorrow."

Everyone agreed they *were* acting somewhat childish. A good night's rest was needed. One by one, each bid the other sweet dreams and headed off to their rooms.

Kat was up before dawn and strolled out onto the terrace. The peaceful tranquility of twilight appeared to intensify the beauty of this incredible place. Thousands of tiny lightning bugs illuminated a shadowed landscape with the twinkling of their golden light. *How could anything horrible possibly happen in such an enchanting world as this? We're all letting our imaginations run amuck.*

Soon, radiant beams of sunlight appeared on the horizon and signaled the dawn of a new day as the kingdom of Durmeleigh awoke.

After a hearty breakfast, the dynamic group made their way to the archery range. They were greeted by Horace, who stood on the edge of the field tapping his foot.

The uneventful morning exercise progressed well. Randy, Charlie, and Jay held a private competition to determine the best bowman. Tippy squealed with excitement whenever she pierced the bull's-eye, thrilled with her new found talent. Kat and Meeley laughed at each other's mishaps, content to just hit the target. By noon, the group's skills showed a vast improvement. Each had perfected their aim, and the arrows struck dead center nearly every time.

"I am impressed with your performance today," announced their instructor. "Perhaps you might be of some use in battle after all."

"Well, slap me on the behind and call me Robin Hood," Jay exclaimed. His jest caused everyone, except Horace, to roar in laughter. "Uh, Sir Elf, isn't it about time for this band of Merry Men and Ladies to go grab some grub? I'm starving."

Horace kept a somber face and looked off to the side. "I suppose if you must eat, you may all be dismissed. Be back in precisely one hour and not a second after. The afternoon session will commence at that time. Do not provoke my anger and be late."

193

The atmosphere throughout lunch remained cheerful and the group continued their merriment. However, the revelry came to a screeching halt upon their return to the shooting range. All other groups were noticeably absent. The hay targets had been removed and replaced with sturdy four-foot high wooden posts.

Eyes widened with obvious trepidation.

"Say, where's our illustrious leader?" Jay asked. "That dude told us to get our rear ends back here in one hour. Now *he's* a no show. What's going on?"

Charlie grabbed hold of Jay's arm. "I don't know, pal, but here he comes. Wonder what's in that box he's toting?"

Horace approached, set the rectangular container on the ground, and opened it … his voice icy, "Your current arrows are to be set aside. These will be used in their stead. As you can see, they are quite different. The tips have been forged from the purest silver. You inquired yesterday what enemy we are to face in battle. Alas, you will confront two abominations. One is the Helons, a tribe of odious Water Leapers. The others are Shankquas, a vile breed of sea goblin. Although both are fiendish creatures, you must fear the Shankquas most. They have been resurrected from the very bowels of Hell."

"I cautioned this afternoon's session would be disturbing. It shall be that and more. Each of you has become proficient in the use of the bow. Until now, the targets have been of mere paper and hay. Yesterday, a small band of our warriors captured several Shankquas. Today, you will learn what it is like to destroy them."

"What?" Kat exclaimed loudly. "You can't be serious and expect us to use these creatures for target practice? What sort of barbarians are you?"

194

The rest of the group chimed in and voiced their objections to such a horrific act.

The hardened instructor remained reserved, his eyes cold and emotionless. Finally, he held up a hand and brought them to abrupt silence. "I relate to your feelings, but you must also try to comprehend our reasoning. Not one of you has engaged in battle nor inflicted death upon another. If this brutality is not now experienced, you will hesitate in the midst of war, and rest assure, you will indeed perish. Do not perceive these creatures as a form of cattle or sheep. They are far from achieving the illustrious status of an animal. Each is a mindless devil whose only purpose is to kill and consume their prey."

Charlie stepped forward. "Hang on a second guys, I kinda understand what Horace is getting at. Believe me, I don't approve of these killings, but what he said holds a great deal of merit. During the war, we were conditioned to destroy our enemies. Sadly, they weren't manufactured demons, but fellow human beings. Although the task was repulsive, if any one of us wavered on the battlefield, they faced the imminent threat of death. It was kill or be killed. I believe it's going to be the same way here. I think we should pay attention, and as nightmarish as it seems, do as he asks."

Randy and Jay both shrugged in agreement.

The horrified expressions worn by the three girls indicated this murderous task was going to be difficult for them, if not next to impossible.

Horace motioned to several nearby Elf warriors. Seconds later, six small hooded figures were brought out. Each twisted and growled as they were led to the posts. The creatures stood around three feet tall. Smooth, putrid bluish-green skin covered a skeletal frame. Abnormally long arms hung below their knees, while sharp claw-like nails protruded from both hands and feet. Once safely secured, the coverings were removed to reveal a grotesque head. Demonic eyes glowed like fire as they canvassed the surroundings. Elongated green ears sprouted from the sides of a malformed skull. The nose was little more than two raised slits. A thin-lipped mouth, filled with rows of hellish fangs, snapped ferociously at their captors.

"Only the tip of your arrows may destroy these inhuman beasts. Their evil bodies cannot withstand the holy purity of silver." Horace paced back and forth in front of the dumfounded group. "It matters little where the arrow strikes. Once the skin is pierced, they will perish. Now, decide which of you shall take the initial shot."

Several moments passed in indescribable silence.

"I'll go first." Charlie stepped forward. Fingers trembled as he drew a silver-tipped arrow, took aim, and pulled back on the taunt bowstring. Kat and Tippy screamed and turned away as he launched the deadly projectile toward the intended victim's chest.

The creature let out a pig-like squeal, twitched, and fell silent. It then disintegrated into a pile of black odiferous dirt.

Randy did a double take. "Did you see that? The thing's gone. There's no body or blood. All that remains is a lurid heap of dirt. I guess what Horace says about these creatures is true. Okay, I'll give it a shot." He stepped up, drew a deep breath, and fired, destroying another.

Moments later, Jay proceeded to take out one more. Meeley shot next, followed by Tippy, who immediately whirled on her heels and vomited as the creature turned to dust.

One archer had yet to shoot.

Randy walked over next to Kat. Her eyes darted about in panic. "Listen kiddo, I don't like it anymore than you, but I do understand where they're going. Our survival depends on this exercise. Upsetting as it may seem, you have to do it. Look out on the field, Kat. All that remains from the ones we've shot are filthy mounds of stinking rubbish. You've got to grab the bull by the tail and face the situation."

"No. I'm not gonna kill it." Tears shot from her eyes. "I won't take part in this butchery. I can't believe you're condoning such depraved insanity."

Randy looked over at the noble Elf. "It's no use. Trying to reason with her now is like arguing with a fence post. Sorry."

The agitated instructor growled, "I see I have little choice. Unless action is taken, I will forever live knowing this life shall end on the battlefield because of my inability to train her properly." He guilefully walked up behind her, reached around, and grabbed hold of her arms.

"Get your filthy paws off of me. I won't kill it. Let go of me you pompous half-breed!" Overpowered, she screamed and struggled to get loose.

Horace placed his hands on hers, loaded an arrow, and pulled back on the string. He paused and cast a glance at Randy. "Forgive me, but I do what I must."

Randy nodded and lowered his eyes. "I know it's for the best."

"You *must* look at the beast, Kat. You must witness its destruction," Horace bellowed, his tone forceful and demanding. "Look at it, I said. *Do it now!*" The second he saw her head rise, he released the arrow. As with the others, the creature squealed as the silver-tipped projectile pierced its chest, then fell silent and vanished.

Kat dropped to her knees and sobbed uncontrollably. Her body convulsed in rage.

Jay knelt down alongside, placed an arm around her shoulder, and spoke softly, "Take a gander out there, Kat. Do you see any blood or dead body? We aren't actually killing these hellish things, because in reality they're not alive. For all intents and purposes, the Shankquas are nothing more than animated dirt. Horace is right. As despicable as it seems, without this preparation, we would refuse to kill them on the battlefield, but by the looks of it, those devils wouldn't fail to kill us. Come on, knucklehead, up you go." He extended a hand and helped her rise. "Try to look at it this way, Kat. Every one of those suckers we destroy today will be one less we'll have to do battle with later."

"You're right," she admitted. "I'm acting like a big ninny, but the sight of these creatures being led out for slaughter is almost more than I can bear. This isn't a training field — it's an execution ring. For your benefit, and *only* yours, I'll make an effort to comply with Horace's condescending demands. I suppose he's just trying to insure our safety, although I feel these bloodthirsty methods are a tad uncivilized for someone who considers his race to be so *superior*." The sarcastic comment was directed at the Elf warrior as amber eyes flashed with hatred and disgust.

After a brief recess, the systematic annihilation of several more goblins resumed.

Kat agreed to continue the repulsive session, and by day's end admitted to feeling less distressed.

"The six of you have accomplished a great deal today. This was not an easy assignment for human or elf. Each has performed beyond my expectations, especially you mistress, Kat. It is plain to see your heart overflows with boundless compassion. Even though you perceive me to be heartless, in truth, I identify with your mind-set."

"I'm afraid I might have overacted, Horace, and presumed you incapable of benevolence." Kat's voice resumed a more demure tone, "You were right. My first reaction would have been to show reluctance on the battlefield. I suppose it doesn't matter where or when you kill, it all leads to the death of another. It's seems unfair this war has to even take place. So many lives will be lost ... evil or otherwise. I am sorry for how I acted. Because of your fortitude, I can now help restore peace to this land. If we hadn't trained as we did today, I know I'd be unable to meet that requirement."

The Elf acknowledged her gratitude, then turned, and gazed into the sky. "I see King Merneos and the others draw near."

All eyes watched as the flying horses and riders approached.

Kat felt an enormous sense of relief knowing Adera had returned and wondered if the trip had been successful.

"I must leave you now, for there is much to do," Horace said. "Your next lesson shall teach you how to properly wield a sword. Rest easy, my students. Henceforth, there will be no living targets. I shall rejoin you in the morning." He gave a faint smile, bowed, and hurried off.

"So, tomorrow we're going to learn how to fence, huh," Jay beamed. "First we play Robin Hood, and now we get to play pirate. Well me 'earties, you may now address me as Captain Crook."

"That's *Cook* you idiot." Randy gave him a playful jab to the arm and chuckled. "You know, I might actually enjoy our next endeavor. I've always wanted to try my hand at this sport."

"I sure hope I'm not as lousy with the sword as I am with the bow," Kat replied. "Tip, you surprised the dickens out of me with this hidden talent of yours. I'd say you're quite an accomplished archer. Are you positive you never shot before?"

Tippy's bland expression turned radiant. "No Kat, I've never so much as picked up a bow 'til today. Say lady, you weren't so bad yourself. I watched you shoot a few times, and it was darn good. In fact, I think we were all pretty good."

As they walked from the field, Jay declared he was famished. By unanimous vote, it was decided they go directly to eat or suffer little peace.

"If y'all don't mind, think I'll just go to my room and turn in. I'm not very hungry. Afraid today's drained me a bit." Kat's face was taut, her eyes misty.

"Not a problem, kiddo, think we all understand. Go get some rest. We'll see you bright and early tomorrow." Randy rubbed her arm. "Sleep tight, and don't let the bed bugs bite."

Kat returned to the peaceful seclusion of her room and dashed to the bed as torrents of pent up emotions were released. After a well deserved cry, she readied herself for a welcome night's rest. Unfortunately, the comfort of the luxuriant mattress offered little solace as the day's events plagued a jaded mind.

"May I come in?"

Startled, Kat jumped and turned toward the familiar voice. "Adera," she exclaimed. "Oh yes, please come in." Tears of frustration began to flow again.

The Queen rushed over, sat alongside, and cradled a trembling body.

"I'm sorry to act like such a big baby, Adera. So much has happened while you were away, terrible things. They made us perform an unspeakable, atrocious act today. It was horrible."

"Yes sweet one, I am aware of what has occurred. I knew the grief it would deliver and came as soon as possible. There has been so little opportunity for us to converse, but tonight we shall take the time. I understand your distress, Kat, and shall try to alleviate the pain. Horace explained all that transpired. Although the tactics may seem morbidly unconventional, I assure you they were more than justified with their actions."

"Justified? Adera, they tied those poor little things to a post and made us slaughter them. How can you say anything like that is justified? It was nothing more than unadulterated murder."

She brushed the ebony wisps of hair back from Kat's brow. "I said I would ease your pain and so I shall. The Shankquas are unlike any creature you have ever encountered. Each is an unemotional, mindless shell of undiluted evil. That is why the bodies disintegrate when pierced by the hallowed arrows of silver. These fiends, designed only to kill, possess neither heart, nor soul, nor conscience. Did you not notice the lack of compassion as their comrades were destroyed?"

"They *did* react, Adera. I saw them turn toward every one of the slaughtered companions and fight with the ropes in order to help the one who had been shot."

201

"No, Kat. It was not an effort to assist, as you perceive. They smelled death and reacted as designed. What you witnessed was an attempt to break loose their bonds so they might devour the body matter of the fallen peer. You see, Kat, they are not only vicious toward others, but cannibalistic. Each will feast on the black dirt of one of their own as easily as they would on the flesh of any other creature."

Kat stared at Adera, her mind refusing to understand the morbid sacrifice.

"I see a hint of doubt remains in your eyes. Allow me to relieve these concerns. The Shankquas are goblins, evil spirits. The bodies are nothing more than enlivened mutations, formed from the fetid decay of Hades. Two days ago, several Elf warriors witnessed a band of Shankquas attack and devour an entire human family. These vermin swarm in groups, ripping the flesh from their prey's bones in seconds, much like a Piranha.

Our archers killed a number of the beasts and foiled the assault. Unfortunately, the valiant effort proved ineffectual to save any member of the family. They watched in helpless horror as a group of these demons ripped a small child to pieces then consumed him alive."

Kat winced and pulled back, appalled by the Queen's violent disclosure.

"Ah, you cringe and find the tale repugnant. I am glad. Perhaps now you will begin to understand why these loathsome beings need to be eradicated and why we show them no mercy.

A few Elves buried what pieces were left of the innocent victims while others collected the surviving Shankquas. The decision was then made to exterminate these monsters in Durmeleigh. You did not commit an act of slaughter as believed. It was the Shankquas who carried out such a sickening deed upon that harmless family. Had you not annihilated those vicious killers, the Elves would have gladly done so. Many seasoned warriors wept as they heard the agonizing and piteous screams of that poor child."

The gentle girl sat back a moment to let it all sink in. "I believe you've made your point, Adera. Why didn't the Elves tell us about the attack? It would have made the despicable task sensible. In fact, it would have almost been a pleasure to release the arrows."

"It was an imprudent mistake — one seldom made by our noble friends. Only your best interest was at heart. Has any of what I have told you removed a touch of your pain?"

"Duh, I'll say it has. I don't feel an ounce of regret now and believe I fully understand everything." Kat paused a moment. "Man, I owe Horace a whopping big apology. To say I was plain rude to him is an understatement. I was outright nasty."

"There shall be no need to apologize. Horace will not harbor ill feelings. Instead, he will hold enormous respect for your reluctance to kill."

Kat let out a huge sigh. "I felt so relieved when I saw you and the others return. Strange as this might sound, I feel insecure without you near."

"What kind words, sweet one. Now, I shall return the compliment and say I missed you equally. Although our time together has been brief, I have grown quite fond of you and your friends."

"I think most of those feelings might be more directed at Randy, wouldn't you say?" Heat began to rise in her face from the bold statement.

Turquoise eyes darted about as a slight tinge of pink rose in flawless cheeks. "I shall not deny he appeals to me, but for the moment I ask it remain our little secret."

Kat winked. "You got it. I won't breathe a word. By the way, how is Maris? Was your trip successful?"

Adera's expression turned sullen. "I am afraid the injuries are lethal. Her existence is no longer ours to determine. All that can be done for her has been tried. Only the will of the great heavenly force shall know what the outcome is to be."

"I don't understand how anyone could want to harm a being as sweet as Maris. Is her attack a sign the war is about to begin?"

"Yes, I regret to say it draws very near. The Shankquas vile raid exposes Nimue's growing impatience. We anticipate a full assault in but a few days."

A cheerless expression fell upon Kat's face. She rose from the bed, strolled across the room, and stood in thoughtful silence. A deep breath was drawn before she whirled around to face Adera. Eyes flashed with hate, and her voice resonated anger, "Good, I hope it starts soon. I'm sick of just sitting around waiting for it to begin. The anticipation is more nerve-racking than the war itself, and it's starting to wear us all down. To be honest, I can't wait to take a pot shot at Nimue."

The Queen grabbed hold of Kat's arms and squeezed. "I want you to understand here and now, the fate of Nimue resides *solely* in the hands of Merlin or me. No other can destroy her wickedness. Do I make myself clear?"

"Yeah sure," Kat replied, startled by her royal friend's forceful tone. "I didn't mean to upset you."

Adera gentled her firm grip. "Please forgive my irate outburst. You have said nothing to cause me distress. It is the thought of Nimue that burdens my mind. She has grown more powerful than believed possible. There now is but one way she may be destroyed. Her heart must be punctured by the dagger that killed Ganieda and Tanas."

"No way. Hand-to-hand combat is far too risky. You could get killed."

"Do not worry. Merlin and I have had many years to prepare for this moment," Adera replied. "Nimue's heartless act extinguished those we loved. Now, we shall eliminate what she holds most precious — her life!"

"I wish that witch would just go away and leave us all alone. This war is senseless and serves no purpose except to cause the death of so many blameless residents."

"Your people have experienced war many times in your world, where brother fought against brother, man against man. Excuses were given to cloak their justification, but in reality, all were brought about by greed, jealously, and one's thirst for power. It is no different with Nimue."

The clatter of silverware and dishes from the patio caused an abrupt turn of heads.

"Ah, the food I ordered has at last arrived. Come. We have had enough talk of war and sadness for this day."

The two walked out, took a seat, and eagerly indulged in the sumptuous meal placed before them.

"Horace has told me the lesson for tomorrow will involve swords. I believe you will find this most appealing, Kat."

"Funny you said that. I'm sorta looking forward to it," she replied. "I only hope I don't make a complete fool of myself. Those things are heavy, and I'm not the strongest person in the world."

Adera began to giggle. "There is no need to worry about lifting this weapon. Swords made by the Elves are light as a feather. In truth, you may be surprised by your expertise."

"Are you serious? Did you forget you're talking about the world's biggest klutz? Me! I was awful with the bow. Sure hope I can do better with a sword."

"Something tells me you shall, Kat. In fact, I am *certain* of it."

Kat winced a bit. "Adera, when are you going to tell me about this monster, Ios? I know nothing of him except the fact he's a big snake."

"Upon our return to the Castle, I will explain all you need to know about this Titan. Until then, there shall be no more mention of him."

"Guess you know what's best," Kat shrugged her shoulders. "Wow, I almost forgot … I need help with McLachen."

"McLachen? I do not understand. You and he possess a close fellowship. Is there a problem?"

"Uh, yeah, and it's kind of a big one. Adera, he intends to serve as my mount in the upcoming battle, and this can't be allowed. I love that horse so much and could never forgive myself if anything happened to him because of me. If McLachen is there, all I'll do is worry and not focus on Ios as I should. This distraction could prove disastrous."

"Your concern is valid. I shall speak to him when we return."

The active conversation continued for a while until both grew weary and decided it was time to rest.

As Kat snuggled deep into the warm down-filled mattress, the faint melodic sound of a harp crept into the hush of night. *Gosh, I wonder who's playing that haunting tune. It's unlike anything I've ever heard before — beautiful, yet agonizingly sad.*

Chapter 14
Preparation

Nimue assumed a comfortable position on the opulent chaise and looked around. The elegant underwater Palace of King Legar now belonged to her. Although the coral encrusted mansion overflowed with every possible luxury available beneath the sea, the evil sorceress longed to walk again in the land above.

She glanced at her loathsome tail and winced in disgust at the sight of it. For a mermaid, she was quite beautiful. Iridescent orange, gold, and turquoise scales covered the fish like appendage in colors that complimented wavy, waist-long, ebony hair and evoking green eyes. Bountiful strands of pearls modestly covered a shapely upper torso. Coiled around the soft, ivory skin of each arm was a juvenile black and white speckled moray eel.

The dark coldness of the aquatic surroundings was unbearable. She longed for the warmth of the sun upon her face and the cushiony feel of grass under her feet. Nimue, now Queen of all the oceans, controlled the boundless creatures living within. However, this kingdom was not the one she desired. *Soon, revenge will be mine. I will celebrate the day when I sit upon your throne, Adera, and you lay dead at my feet.*

The ghoul trembled as he approached the melancholy enchantress. He had been warned failure was unacceptable.

Nimue's eyes blazed as the fearful creature knelt in submission before her. "The very sight of you fills me with disgust. Your incompetent leadership has caused the death of many Shankquas. It was an insignificant undertaking I commanded, yet received catastrophic failure. What am I to do with you?"

He begged for exoneration in a low guttural voice, "Please, my Queen, grant me forgiveness. We successfully annihilated one family, but were attacked by a great band of Elves before we could proceed to another."

"I see," she replied in a waspish voice. "Explain to me how *you* alone survived when the entire battalion was either captured or destroyed. Could it be you abandoned faithful warriors and fled in order to save your miserable life?"

"There was nothing I could do, my Queen. We were overpowered by their numbers," he pleaded.

She rose from her platform and slowly circled around him, her eyes filled with ire. "OVERPOWERED?" she screeched. "I know for a fact, my Shankquas outnumbered the Elves. It appears you are not only a coward, but a liar as well. I question your fidelity toward my quest."

"Majesty, I am your most devoted servant. The incident was unavoidable. Please, have mercy. I will not fail you a second time, my beautiful Sovereign."

Nimue cackled, "Indeed you will not." She raised the powerful Trident and drove it deep into his chest. Bubbles surged from the limp body as the three-pronged spear was withdrawn. She spun around to face the trembling staff. "Dispose of this garbage. It disgusts me. Send in Ahren."

The large, muscular goblin entered the thrown room and bowed.

"I believe you need no explanation why I have summoned you?" Nimue said coldly to the vile being as he approached. "Heed my words well, Ahren. I will no longer tolerate these deplorable failures. Should you also prove unsuccessful, you will be terminated just as quickly. Do I make myself clear?"

The goblin nodded and pompously smirked, as his predecessor's remains were carried off. Unlike the former creature, Ahren was a fearless and lethal warrior, completely dedicated to Nimue. "Where others fail, I will triumph, Highness. Your army will be victorious, and the desired results realized."

Frustrated, the sea Queen swam anxiously back and forth. "I have grown intolerant of this watery tomb." She drew close to Ahren, her lip curled in rage. "Two days hence the land above will run red with blood. We shall meet the enemy head on and eradicate all who dare oppose me. My spies say Adera remains unsuspecting of so rapid an advance. This provides a valued element of surprise. Shortly, she will endure her subject's cries of death. Do not fail me, Ahren. You shall conquer, or you shall die. The choice is yours."

Black drool oozed from the corners of the goblin warrior's hideous mouth as he watched the sea hag Queen speed away.

Convinced a triumphant victory would be obtained in the forthcoming battle, Nimue hurried to the cave where King Legar and the Mer-people were imprisoned. She glided back and forth before him, flipping her nimble tail tauntingly. "You should know, my darling husband, the war is forthwith. Adera's life, and reign as Queen, shall soon end. It appears your dear friend Merneos sides with her. How tragic. After we defeat those meddling Elves, the Shankquas can have their way with him."

She paused then eased up to the bars. "I feel immeasurably generous today and offer your people a means to obtain salvation. If all bow and worship me as their Queen, I shall absolve them from death. The Shankquas may take who they wish as servants. Those who do not choose this path will be offered to the sharks."

"Then it seems the sharks are to have the benefit of a large feast, Nimue. My people will never surrender to such a tyrant. They would relish death before serving such an abomination of wickedness." Legar's eyes saddened. "I once adored you, made you my Queen, and offered unconditional love. Now, all I feel for you is pity and disgust. You will *never* defeat Adera. My greatest wish is to see her rid your body of that unholy heart."

Nimue convulsed in a shockwave of anger, incensed by his unanticipated words. "You will pay for such insolence, Legar. Be assured my threats are genuine. Perhaps it is time to feed my pets." She instructed several goblins to extract six Mer-people from their prison.

In moments, three Mermen, an adult Mermaid, and two small children were positioned before her. They struggled to get free and groveled for mercy. "Please, harm us if you must, but spare the small ones. They have committed no crime against you."

Their plea's fell upon deaf ears. The sea witch raised the Trident and beckoned forth a school of ferocious blue tips.

211

The hungry sharks began to circle, spiraling lower and lower toward the ill-fated victims. As they drew closer, the pace intensified.

Terror streamed from the eyes of the defenseless adults as they formed a ring around the children.

Nimue let out a shriek of delight as she thrust the razor sharp Trident at them. It effectively slashed their tails and caused torrents of blood to gush forth. The enticing aroma began to fill the area, inciting the sharks into a feeding frenzy.

"No, Nimue. Do not do this," King Legar screamed at his heartless wife. "It is I who should be punished. They are blameless. Spare them. I beg you." His appeal was answered by her unfeeling cackle as the sharks dashed in for their reward.

Within moments, the water exploded with the horrific wail of the prey as the onslaught began. At first, the adult Merpeople lashed out at the attackers, but weakened by loss of blood, the plucky endeavor became ineffective. The force of the shark's snouts penetrated the defensive circle. A macabre cloud of crimson quickly began to form as the sufferers were mercilessly torn to shreds. Soon, the sea fell silent.

Tiny scavenger fish darted in and out of the unholy creation and feverishly consumed any significant morsel of fin and flesh that remained.

Nimue swam to the cave entrance and clapped her hands in delight as the sharks departed. "What a *splendid* performance. I found it rather amusing and cannot wait for the next act. Perhaps an all-children's matinee might provide a more rapturous form of entertainment." Her webbed hand reached out to stroke the King's cheek, but the arrogant action caused him to recoil. "How interesting, my dear husband. All of a sudden, I no longer appeal to you. Well, I have long suffered such nauseating feelings. How could anyone of my distinguished stature love such a being? You are nothing more than a malodorous, slime covered common fish. I despised every second I was forced to endure your presence." She drew up close to the bars and spit in his face. "*This* is what I think of you."

The Mer-King hung his head as tears mixed with the salty water. He dropped to the sea floor, alone and helpless in the dark obscurity of his prison.

ഇ൦രു   ഇ൦രു

Kat could not believe her proficiency with the sword and felt strangely familiar with the deadly instrument.

A resounding clank of metal against metal signaled the early commencement of training. In place of practice targets, the group had been divided into pairs and would engage in somewhat harmless combat. Protective garments were provided and sword blades purposely dulled for further protection. Instruction on the proper use of shields added even more fortification from the advancing blades.

"Ouch," Randy yelled as Kat playfully gave him a pop on the derriere with the side of her blade. "I'm gonna quit if you keep this crap up. That really stings!"

"Oh Randy, you're such a big sissy. Your fat butt could get whacked by a 747 and not feel it."

"Okay, you miserable little brat, let's just see who's the best swordsman out here." He chuckled then unexpectedly lunged at her.

The action caused Kat to stumble as she leaped out of the way. He came in for the kill, but she tripped him with her foot, then pinned him to the ground, her sword at his

213

throat. "Looks like I have the upper hand after all, blubber gut. I believe you owe me an apology, or do I need to whip your chubby little fanny one more time?"

From behind them came an airy laugh causing both to look up.

Alongside Horace stood Adera with arms folded — a huge smile on her face. "It seems you have both mastered the art of sword play, and I use the term *play* liberally."

"Well, perhaps you didn't notice, but I wasn't exactly proficient," Randy announced. "Kat's the one going crazy out here. So far, all I've mastered is the ground."

Horace snickered, which made all three turn and look at him. Until this very moment, he had not shown a single sign of emotion.

"I don't believe it," Kat exclaimed. "Could we have finally broken through that iron exterior of yours?"

"It may appear to be so, but rest assured, I am in complete control of my faculties. I merely cleared my throat." The normal aloof composure returned at once. "Adera remarked favorably on the accelerated development of your new found prowess, which of course is the untarnished product of my expert tutelage."

Kat fought to hold back a giggle. "Oh, I see. I'll admit you are a bit hard to get along with, but appear to be a fairly-decent instructor. By the way, Horace, I'm sure there's nothing to worry about with your throat, but you might want to have it checked out."

The noble Elf maintained a condescending posture, cast an indignant glance, and ceased further eye contact.

Randy choked back a laugh and turned his attention to Adera. "Think a change of subject is in order. This unexpected visit's a welcome delight, Your Highness."

Her jovial expression disappeared. "I was curious to see if any headway was made in your training. Nothing more."

Kat's eyes traveled back and forth between the two, puzzled by the Sovereign's unusual reaction to Randy. *What is going on? I know she's super fond of him, so why the cold and indifferent act all of a sudden? Something's radically wrong with this picture.*

"I see you are indeed gifted with the sword as I presumed you might be, Kat." Adera's comment broke the frigid atmosphere.

"Yeah, it's kinda blowing my mind a little," Kat's voice rang with pride. "I'm not very good with the bow, but this feels great."

Heads turned as Jay let out a bloodcurdling screech, "*Ye-oow.*" He was on the ground clutching his foot.

Charlie stood nearby, arms wrapped around his sides, roaring in laughter.

Jay's face reddened as the hysterical friend helped him to his feet. "It's okay, nothing for y'all to get your drawers in a bind about. I was just goofing off as usual and accidentally jabbed the dang sword into the top of my foot. Thought they dulled these suckers?"

"I believe this is quite enough for now." It was clear Horace was not amused by the revelry. "Lay down your weapons and go to lunch. Perhaps a full stomach will bring more civility. I must apologize regarding my student's lack of restrain and unpolished exterior, Your Highness."

"Do not be concerned, Horace. At times, I actually find their antics entertaining. Your patience and expertise is most appreciated. You have performed a slight miracle with this group and molded them into outstanding combatants. Tomorrow, we shall return to the Castle, where their lessons will continue to hone the skills you have taught."

Tippy, alerted by Jay's outburst, walked up in time to hear Adera's comment. "I'm so happy we're going back tomorrow. I actually feel homesick for Bowlandria."

Adera's expression altered. "Things may look a bit different, dear Tippy. Much has taken place within and around the Castle. Preparation for the arrival of the Elves, and many others, has begun. Our royal structure will act as a fortress of sorts. It shall become our troops' temporary home for the duration of the war, which I pray will not be lengthy." The Queen paused, sighed, and continued, "In honor of all those dedicated to the cause, a grand feast will be held tonight. The Elves refer to such an event as a gathering. Now, I must attend to more pertinent matters and shall see you again this evening. Horace, will you walk with me? A few significant issues require further discussion."

The Elf gave a polite bow and offered his arm.

"Are you going to the Castle as well, Meeley?" Tippy asked. A strong attachment had evolved between the two girls.

"Merlin asked me to gather a few items from home, but then I'll be on my way to join you all. Knox and I are going to stay at the Castle until this has ended. I know my poor dragon will be homesick, but it can't be helped. He's just going to have to learn to live with it like the rest of us."

After lunch, training continued for three more hours. At that point, Horace ended the session.

As the group strolled from the field, Tippy grabbed Kat's arm. "You are really something else with that sword. Meeley and I stopped and watched you for a bit. I swear, your skills are remarkable, even better than those of Horace. Where on earth did you ever learn to do that?"

Kat cocked an eyebrow. "I don't have a clue, Tip. It seems to come natural. I'm finding it just as astonishing as you."

"Yeah and my rosy red buttocks are genuine proof of those talents." Randy rubbed his backside and snickered.

The three girls began to giggle at his antics.

Kat walked up beside him. "Sorry if I hurt your *'pride'*, but you deserved every whack."

Teasing continued as the six friends strolled along. At last, the boys separated from the girls as they proceeded to their quarters.

"Kat, did you notice the nippy reception Adera gave Randy this morning?" Meeley asked. "I've never seen her act like that toward anyone before. What do you suppose is up?"

"It sure as heck beats me. At first, she seemed thrilled to see him, but then did a one eighty and acted like he was poison ivy. I'm positive he hasn't said or done anything to offend her. Maybe we can corner her tonight and find out what's going on." She looked at Meeley then Tippy who each nodded in agreement.

The girls quickly dressed, met up with one another, and headed for the designed garden. It was quite large and could easily accommodate a sizeable crowd. Although they arrived early, a notable throng had already begun to gather. The melodious sound of entrancing music filled the cool night air. Thousands of aromatic candles cast a soft, golden light around the area, giving it an aura of captivating enchantment.

As the three friends wove their way through the masses, they would stop, introduce themselves, and talk briefly.

"Hey gals, over here," Charlie yelled. He stood with a group of unfamiliar guys and motioned for them to come over. "I want you three to meet my pals. These are all members of my original flight squadron." One by one, he introduced them and gave a brief description of their flying abilities.

Kat scanned the area, fascinated by the Elves' behavior. Their aloof and distant mannerisms seemed a trifle more animated this evening. Each casually strolled around and talked openly to everyone. The sound of someone approaching from behind made her spin around.

Obviously proud of the attractive, strawberry-blonde who accompanied him, Horace sauntered up. "Pardon the interruption, Kat. May I have a moment? I would like you to meet my mother, Helen."

"A pleasant good evening to you, Kat," she said softly. "My son has mentioned your name often. I am pleased we should at last meet. Have you enjoyed your stay in Durmeleigh?"

Kat eased away from the group. "I'm thrilled beyond words to meet you as well. This kingdom is extraordinary, and I have enjoyed *most* of my stay. Thanks for asking."

Helen was not only a physically pretty woman, but appeared charming, sweet, and kind. "I hope my son hasn't been too harsh. Beneath the rough elfin exterior beats a human heart full of thoughtfulness and compassion. Sadly, he seldom allows these emotions to surface. He is a valiant warrior and a marvelous instructor, but has been known to push his students to boundless extremes in order to help them attain full potential."

"Uh, yeah, he certainly can do that," Kat replied and gave a playful wink. "It took a while, but we've come to appreciate all he's done for each of us. In only a few days he's taken a bunch of awkward bumpkins and turned us into diligent warriors. I only hope his human heart can know how grateful we are and that he means a great deal to us."

Horace stared at Kat with a perplexed frown. He then smiled, bowed his head, and placed a fist on his heart in acknowledgement of the compliment. Moments later, an Elf child strolled up and took hold of the stately warrior's hand.

"Kat, this is my brother, Enal," Horace announced. "Unlike me, he possesses great intelligence and shall be a brilliant asset to our people in the years to come."

"You must be very proud of Horace, Enal, and righteously so." Kat bent down and extended a hand. "How do you do, young sir?"

The child let out a high-pitched shriek and cowered behind his big brother.

Helen laughed at the skittish child as soft hazel eyes sparkled with adoration and pride. "Forgive my youngest son's temporary apprehensiveness. He is not used to strangers, especially human ones. We see so few in this Kingdom. Now, if you will excuse us, there are several others to greet. It has been a great pleasure meeting you."

As they walked off, Kat could see the tremendous bond of love between the three and smiled. She could not help feel a little guilty about yesterday's outburst and how badly she misjudged Horace. Her thoughts were interrupted as Randy rushed up.

"Kat, I've been looking all over for you. We need to speak, *now*."

"Sure, what's up?" She took his hand and led him far away from the group.

"That's my question. What's up — with Adera? I've tried to talk to her several times tonight, but get the cold shoulder treatment. She acts like I've committed murder or something."

Engrossed with the evening activities, Kat forgot about the incident earlier and had not talked to Adera about the odd behavior. It was plain to see Randy was upset by the Queen's uncustomary actions toward him. *I don't understand what's happening either, but I have to try to appease his frustration.*

"I don't believe there's anything wrong, Randy. That lady's under a great deal of stress these days and definitely not herself. Shoot, I haven't even said so much as hello to her tonight, and I know none of the others have either. I wouldn't worry about it. I'm sure there's nothing to be concerned about. All this war crap has everyone on edge."

Randy nodded. "Yeah, think you're right. Guess I'm acting like a lovesick schoolboy. Sorry, kiddo."

They walked back and joined the others who were engrossed in deep conversation.

Kat inconspicuously peeked around and spotted Adera talking to King Merneos and Merlin. In her heart, she knew something was wrong, but it would be impossible to ask about it tonight. *When we return to the Castle, I'll try to find out why the Queen is acting so strange. Perhaps it's nothing more than our stupid imaginations.*

It was a welcomed evening event. Both elf and human grasped this rare opportunity to meet and converse. Soon, these strangers would become partners and fight side-by-side on a cruel and vicious battlefield.

The following morning, Durmeleigh was a hustle and bustle of movement. Adera decided to fly back on a winged horse. Tippy, who had already left, traveled alone in the royal coach.

Kat, Randy, and Jay sprinted to the pasture where the celestial horses were being kept, anxious to return to the air on them once again. Charlie had arrived much earlier and already saddled Fudge. Within minutes, the spirited animals were made ready, and soon they would again soar into the heavens.

A sudden whoosh of mighty wings just above their heads startled everyone. The great stallions snorted, reared, and spread their feathered limbs in fright while the riders fought to maintain control of the powerful animals.

All faces turned skyward to witness Knox and Meeley streak through the air. An overly energetic pilot laughed and waved as the duo disappeared into the horizon.

"Darn you, Meeley. I swear you got a hole in your bag of marbles," Jay yelled as he struggled with his frightened Pinto. "Whoa, it's okay, big boy. Easy now, Mike, they're gone. I swear if brains were leather, that dame wouldn't have enough to saddle a junebug."

Although Kat and Randy fought to hold their horses in check, they roared at Meeley's little fly by number, especially when they saw how flustered it made Jay.

As soon as everyone calmed their horses and mounted, they ascended into the awaiting heavens. The intense azure-blue sky was unblemished — not a white cloud in sight. As before, Merlin took the lead, flanked by Adera, who was astride a magnificent white stallion, and King Merneos, on a gorgeous Bay similar to Randy's mount. This time, they did not go as high as before, but flew at a much faster rate of speed. It was a euphoric return ride. They zoomed over the mountain tops, across vast green meadows, and scattered herds of lazily grazing sheep that fled in terror from the ominous shadows of the great horses' wings.

Kat found Junar hard to hold back. Like most horses, he was obviously anxious to return home. She squealed in delight and found this flight even more exhilarating than its predecessor. All too soon, the great Castle turrets came into view. She felt a touch of sadness as they approached and began the decent, ending the adventure.

"Wow, that was totally awesome," Randy exclaimed. He dismounted and ran over to join Kat and Jay. "I can't ever remember having such a ball, but my arms are killing me right now. That frisky bugger wanted to move out … took every thing I had to hold him back."

Jay rubbed his biceps. "Yeah, you're not kidding. Mike fought me tooth and nail. I wanted to open him up to see what he could do, but thought Merlin might not appreciate it. We were really booking along, yet Mike barely broke a sweat. How fast do you suppose these guys can fly?"

"I don't know, Jay," Randy replied. "But until I build up some added strength, I don't think I care to find out."

Charlie joined the trio who laughed and talked about the stimulating flight as they walked to the Castle. Once inside the Great Hall, they found Tippy snuggled in a bronze velvet chair immersed in her book.

Jerome and the house staff greeted the returnees.

Margaret Mary rushed to Jay and threw her chubby arms around him. "Tis a sight for sore eyes ya are to me, Master Jay. Saints preserve us, what have they done to ya me darlin lad? Why tis little more than skin and bones you are. Well, I'll be seein you get somethin to put in that cavernous belly of yours straightaway."

Randy laughed as Jay grunted from her energized embrace. "Cook, you should know by now this eating machine was hungry one minute after we left breakfast. Trust me. He ate while in Durmeleigh."

"Hey everybody, forget about me?" Meeley gave off an enthusiastic yell as she entered, brushing the dust from her clothes.

Jay broke loose from Cook's grasp and stomped over to Meeley. "You warped dragon flyer, pilot, thingy. What kind of idiotic, cockamamie, harebrained stunt was that you pulled earlier? It darn near got us killed. I swear you are about two sandwiches shy of a picnic."

Everyone, including Meeley, began to laugh at Jay's frustrating outburst. This caused his ire to melt and in seconds reduce the act to a comical memory.

Adera walked up to the group who were huddled in robust conversation. At first, she greeted Randy with a broad smile, but quickly turned her eyes away and focused on the others. "What a marvelous day we had for such an enjoyable ride. I have not taken to the air in some time and almost forgotten how pleasurable it can be."

Randy took a step closer to the Queen. "We thought it was wonderful as well. I hope after this war we might do it again before we return to our time. By the way Adera, your horse was magnificent, although his beauty was somewhat shadowed by the loveliness of his rider."

Adera blushed as turquoise eyes fused with those of the handsome man standing before her. There was an immediate alteration of her expression and a frosty reply, "Thank you, Randy, but the compliment is unnecessary.

Now, I am sure you would all like to rest before dinner as would I." She hurried off without another word.

Silent, Kat alternated her stare between Randy and Adera. This confusing behavior was *not* imaginary.

Tippy placed a hand on Kat's shoulder, breaking the trance. "Think it's about time we went to our rooms. I sure missed Hoki and Meon and can't wait to see them. Come join us, Meeley. We have loads of gossip to catch up on."

As the three girls walked off, Kat shot a glance back at Randy. He had evidently brushed off the rejection and was engaged in vigorous banter with Charlie, Jay, and a couple of the other pilots.

Kat entered her room and closed the door, shutting out the world. It felt as thought she were returning from an extended visit abroad. The spacious boudoir provided tranquil solitude, something desperately desired.

"I could sure use a cool breath of fresh air to clear my warped brain — the garden beckons." She strolled out to the stone wall and peered across the meadow. The flamboyant sunset was nearly overwhelming. Footsteps off to the side shattered the moment. "McLachen!" Kat ran to him and threw her arms around his majestic neck. "I've missed you so much."

"I have missed you as well, My Lady. The trip was enjoyable I trust?"

"Most of it was great, but some not so good." Kat sat on the wall and told him every detail of her trip to Durmeleigh, including the incident with the Shankquas.

"It is regrettable you endured such a troubling experience, My Lady, but I believe it was for the best. You are now fully briefed on this demon's destructive ways."

Kat curled a strand of silky mane around her fingers as she spoke, "I still don't like killing them, but at least I understand why it must be done."

His voice was soft, relaxing, "Let us change the subject. Tell me of your adventure on the winged horses. Are they not incredible?"

"They're super, and the flight on them was like a dream come true. Still, not a single one can hold a candle to you, McLachen."

He raised his head and whinnied. "You flatter me, My Lady, and I fondly accept the compliment. Now, I believe several friends await your arrival."

"Oh dang it, I forgot all about dinner. Thanks, McLachen. I promise to spend some time with you tomorrow. I've missed you more than I can say. We still have loads to talk about. Good night."

"Good night, My Lady. Sleep well."

෪෬ ෪෬

Deep in the icy depths of the ocean, a ghoulish army prepared for war. The new commander was relentless in his training.

In the land above, legions of Elves progressed toward the Castle grounds. A multitude of humans packed and departed their homes, each proceeding to the designated encampment area.

Soon, these armies of good and evil would meet in battle, and the outcome would determine the fate of many. One path would lead to destruction — the other to peace. Even the most gifted clairvoyant would be unable to predict how this war was to end. That particular knowledge was known only to destiny.

Chapter 15
Adera's Deception

Kat leaped from her bed, abruptly awakened by the boisterous clamor outside. "What in the sam-hill is going on?" She pulled on a robe and grabbed her watch. It was quarter to eleven. "Holy crackers, I can't believe I've slept in so late — again." A walk outside revealed an unexpected sight.

A great number of troops had arrived and were setting up camp. Hundreds of tents were being erected, as the expansive meadow was transformed into a boundless field of chaos. Hordes of people scurried about the lush breadth of land as far as the eye could see. Horses had been placed in makeshift corrals while soldiers unloaded supply wagons.

She dressed and rushed into the darkened corridor, only to discover the Castle void of occupants. Now and then, the flustered girl would encounter a staff member who bid good-day then hurried off. Unsure what to do, she headed for the kitchen. However, it too seemed to be in a mortified state of havoc. A hodgepodge of strangers scurried about in complete disarray as the earsplitting clash of pots and pans permeated the air.

Cook looked up and saw the perplexed girl stationed in the doorway. "There ya are me darlin' Kat. We've been waitin to see ya."

"What in the world's going on, Cook? Who are all these people?"

"Oh, tis nothin ya need worry your pretty little head about now. Come join me in a wee cup of fresh coffee. I have just the place to sit. Follow me."

Kat obediently fell in close behind Cook who hastened to a small table nestled in a secluded corner.

"Ah, it feels good to rest me weary toes it does," Margaret Mary declared as she plopped into a chair.

A quick sip of the welcome beverage warmed her throat. "I hate to sound like a broken record, Cook, but who are all these people? Some appear to be Elves."

"Aye, that they are. King Merneos brought several ladies ta help out. Tis a large army we have ta feed. Several humans joined the cause as well. Seems ta be enough for now."

The sound of dishes crashing to the floor brought the blustery Irish woman to her feet. "Merciful Saints preserve us! I better be gettin back to me kitchen before I have none left ta cook in at all. Now, don't ya be frettin about all this me darlin. Once I get things a bit organized, twill all be better I'm thinkin."

"Cook, do you have any idea where my friends are? I can't seem to locate them anywhere."

"I believe you'll be findin Randy and Jay at the stables helpin the Elves round up our lovely horses from their sweet pastures. Tippy and mistress Meeley went off with Merlin, but ta where, only heaven itself knows." As Cook bent over to pick up the pieces of several broken dishes, the sound of shattered glass came from another part of the gigantic kitchen. "Oh me dear Lord in Heaven, what have they done now." There was distinct anger in the jolly woman's voice.

"Uh, thanks for everything, Cook. I think it's time I got out of your hair. See ya later." Kat wandered around a

227

bit more before she caught a glimpse of the red-headed nymph rushing down a corridor. "Bagi wait, I need some help."

"Yes madam, how may I assist you?"

"Can you tell me where to find Adera? I must speak to her."

Kat received a cool reply, "I am sorry, but cannot disclose the location. She asked to be left alone for the moment."

"Please Bagi, this is very important. I understand the dedication to Adera, but it's an urgent matter. True, you hardly know me, and can I understand your hesitancy, but I beg you to trust me on this. Please."

The pretty nymph eyed Kat with suspicion. "Very well … Her Highness is alone in her study."

"Thank you, Bagi. I promise not to betray your trust." She sprinted up the spiral staircase to the distant tower room. Winded, she paused at the ornate door and noticed it ajar. On tiptoes, Kat peered inside and saw the royal Monarch positioned at the window.

Ancient hinges creaked as the door opened "I'm sorry to intrude, Adera, but I must speak to you."

The Queen did not turn around, but raised her head and stood in silence with her back to Kat.

"It's about, Randy!"

Adera's body straightened before rotating to face the impatient girl. She strolled to the desk and gingerly placed an object near a jumble of papers. "Please, come in. Has something happened?"

Kat stood her ground. She felt perturbed by the Queen's lack of consideration for him. Anger and frustration shot out like a fireball. "Yeah, you might say so. What's up with the heartless attitude toward Randy all of a sudden? One minute you act like you care and the next treat him like dirt under your feet. What the blazes gives? That poor guy's worried sick. He fears he's done something offensive and honestly thinks you hate him."

Her body trembled in rage, and she paused a second to get escalating emotions under control. "Let me clue you in on something, your *Royal Highness*. Randy's never given *anyone* else so much as a second glance since Sandy died. Now he's come here, against his will I might add, and opened a broken heart, only to have it crushed into a thousand pieces. How callous can you be, especially when we're about to go into battle. A certain *Queen* has consumed all thoughts, and that lack of concentration might cause his death. Unlike *you*, I happen to give a hoot and don't care to see him slaughtered because of irrational thoughtlessness. Even your attitude about me is questionable. What kind of manipulative person are you?"

"Please Kat, let us sit. I shall offer an explanation." Adera motioned to a pair of nearby chairs. "What you claim is true. I have been unreasonably harsh with Randy and prayed it would not escalate to this level. My intention is not to cause pain, but to spare his life."

"What? That makes no sense. How could breaking his heart save his life?"

The Queen leaned forward and took hold of Kat's hand. "What is uttered in this room must not pass beyond these walls. Do I make myself clear? Vow to me no words of this will be spoken to anyone. Randy's life shall depend on it."

"All right, I'll bite. I *vow* not to breathe a word to anyone o*r anything*," Kat replied with sarcasm.

"I apologize if my actions caused any apprehension ... they are most sincere. As for Randy, the love I feel for

229

him blossoms more each day. It flourishes even as we speak. If Nimue suspected a romantic involvement, she would make a concerted effort to capture and kill him out of vengeance, just as she did with Tanas. To guarantee his protection, I have tried to cleanse my thoughts, but I am failing. It is impossible to suppress these intense emotions when he is near. I would rather suffer a thousand deaths than see him murdered by the hands of that evil creature. To treat my dearest as I am forced to do, burdens my heart more than you can know."

Kat eased back in the chair, dumbfounded by the tortuous divulgence. Empathy now replaced anger. "Dang Adera, talk about jerking a knot in your tail. Why didn't you explain this the other night? Perhaps together, we could have devised a plan to soothe his pain and make your life a little easier in the process. I thought I was your friend? In our world, friends don't let each other suffer alone."

Eyes began to fill. "Oh Kat, I truly pray we are friends. I have never known someone as dear to me as you. My mind swims with confusion. If only there was another solution, but think as I might, I cannot conceive one."

Shrouded in silence, Kat tried to sort through paralyzing thoughts. There had to be some way to appease Randy and not divulge Adera's true feelings. "I think I've got it." She edged forward in the chair. "Look, I'm not saying it's gonna be easy, but believe this might just do the trick."

"I will try anything, Kat, anything to spare his heart a second of pain. My love for him was unforeseen, and I did not realize how intense his feelings had evolved."

"Let's get something straight. I don't approve of telling lies, but this particular case calls for a tiny bit of deception. It often bothers him that we're so informal around you. He's even suggested we address you as *Your Highness* in mixed company. We need to fabricate a story about how imperative it is you maintain a royal status charade while so many visitors are here. I'll tell Randy we spoke, and you're not the least bit angry. Although you are super fond on him, during this time of turmoil, it is imperative to portray the part of Bowlandria's Queen. If any affection were shown, even in the slightest degree, there's a possibility it might be misconstrued as a sign of weakness and allegiance's severed. After all, Merneos demands kingly respect from his subjects and would insist you receive nothing less."

Hope began to rise in Adera's face. "It is brilliant, Kat, and may work. I detest pulling such chicanery, but if it would mean preserving his safety, I am more than willing to comply with this devious deception."

"Whoa, hold on to those royal britches. We still have a few things left to iron out so our underhanded ploy will go off without a hitch. For example, the next time you two meet, pitch him a demure smile and wink. I know it sounds ridiculous, but that stupid little gesture will imply I've told the truth. It's simply part of the cover up. I'll set the stage and tell him your amorous thoughts make it difficult to remain in control when he's around. That's the reason you're avoiding him."

"Oh Kat, what would I ever do without you." She leaned over and hugged her.

They continued to fill in the blanks, until the web of deceit was tightly woven.

Curious to see what Adera had set on the spacious desk, Kat rose and casually strolled over to it. There, on

231

the engraved leather surface, was an exquisite jeweled dagger. "Is this the weapon used on Ganieda and Tanas?"

"Yes, it is the very piece that took their lives."

Kat ran a finger over the gemstone-infused golden handle. "Strange how an item so devastatingly sinister is surprisingly beautiful." A frown formed as amber eyes drifted to the sharp nine-inch blade.

Adera picked it up. "Have you noticed the metal is tainted? It holds the blood of Tanas and Ganieda, which was never wiped away. The spirit of their innocence is the only destructive force capable of destroying Nimue."

"No one should be made to suffer as you've done all these years, Adera. It's impossible to imagine the horror of witnessing a loved one killed in such a manner. Now, that witch is causing your heart unwarranted pain once again. The more I hear about Nimue, the more I loathe that woman."

"My heart indeed weighs heavy with revenge, but it shall soon be appeased. This may appear a bit forward, but tell me of your one true love."

Kat was somewhat taken aback by the unexpected inquiry. "Wow, I didn't see this coming. Well, although I deeply loved my husband, another tugs at my heartstrings."

"Perhaps a day will come when you and he are reunited. It is said true love always finds its way home to the heart."

Kat chuckled. "I'm sorry to say, that relationship ended a long time ago and not on the best of terms. Shoot, I don't even know if he's still alive. Besides, I'm afraid Tom will remain far from me forever. You see, if I make it through this war, I've decided to stay in Bowlandria, if that's okay?"

"This difficult decision delights me beyond words. I believe the time has come to show you a very special weapon." She walked to a large mahogany cabinet, opened the doors, and removed a beautiful ornate sword.

"Now *that's* a sword," Kat exclaimed. "Is it my imagination, or does the blade sparkle?"

Adera laughed. "It is not your imagination. The metal has been magically infused with diamond dust. You will find its strength incredible — strong enough to pierce the head of Ios."

"Okay, back it up a bit, lady. You just said *pierce his head*? Are you serious? Is *that* how I have to kill him — from above? How the thunder can I possibly do such a thing?"

"Do not worry. When the opportunity presents itself, you will react in the appropriate manner. Here, feel how light it is."

Before the eager girl could get a firm grip on the weapon, a strange sensation, similar to a mild shock, pulsed up her arm and into her body. Startled, she tossed it to the floor.

"Ah, I see the sword's magic flows into you. You are beyond doubt the chosen one, for only she can bring forth the power it possesses."

Kat reached down, picked up the weapon, and studied it. "I swear I've seen this somewhere before. Wait a second. The girl in the tapestry has a similar piece."

"How observant, Kat. I am impressed. The sword in the tapestry is the same as the one in your hand. There is none similar in existence. Guard it well — your life will depend on it."

"Isn't it about time you filled me in on Ios, Your Highness?"

233

"Yes, it *is* time. Ios is a sea serpent, and although similar in appearance to a common reptile, he is *not* in the same category."

"Okay, I get the snake thing, but how does all this apply to me?" Kat drew a long slow breath.

"For centuries, seaman have seen and feared such beasts. Most were harmless and merely surfaced out of curiosity of the passing ships. Ios, however, is far different. His thirst for blood grew as rapid as his body. He attacked many vessels and devoured all on board. In time, he even attacked and killed the other serpents. Now, he alone remains.

King Legar detested the senseless carnage. One day, he used the power of his Trident to imprison Ios. The beast was to remain in an eternal sleep, secured in a cave just beyond the boundaries of our realm. When Nimue obtained the Trident, she released Ios, who is now bound in servitude."

"So, what does this big jerk look like? Can't be all that bad, can he?"

"I will not lie to you, Kat. Ios is a hideous creature. Grayish snake-like skin covers his body, which is perhaps eighty-feet in length and big around as a great oak. The head, similar to that of a dragon, is crowned with a waving mass of unshapely lavender wisps that continue down his back all the way to the tip of the tail. Enormous red eyes are reptilian. From the upper jaw protrudes a pair of fangs thick as the handle of a broomstick. Putrid saliva drips from the corners of his mouth and permeates the air with the stench of decay. Small translucent fins act as stabilizers and allow an undulating body to move swiftly through the water. Although he resides in the sea, this

Titan has the ability to move about on land. Ios is every bit as quick and lethal on solid soil as in the liquid ocean."

Kat shook her head and slapped both hands together. "Well, I asked for it, and you sure delivered. I just *had* to know what this monster looked like didn't I? How on earth am I supposed to attack and kill something so large when I'm so small?"

"I have observed several training sessions. You have tremendous skills and remarkable dexterity. Ios can be easily out maneuvered by such agility. He has one enormous flaw. Although great in size, the creature lacks intelligence and reacts on sheer instinct. Keep this information in your mind at all times. Always allow this inner strength and intellect to act as a guide. They will be your greatest defense. Patience is the key, for Ios is most vulnerable when he strikes. It takes a few moments to raise the monstrous head and recoil his mammoth body. That will be the prime time for you to react."

"So in essence, I'm going up against a big, stupid, snake and need to hit him when he's down," Kat replied.

Adera began to laugh. "Well, yes, I suppose that is about the gist of it."

Kat sighed. "There's still one looming question that bothers me. Ios slipped through the portal in the depths of the sea, but how did that evil witch Nimue get in? Why didn't the force keep her out?"

"Nimue fears death more than anything else. When she fled to our realm for refuge, that intense dread cloaked all vile thoughts, and thus access was granted. The erroneous flaw has since been corrected, and no other like her shall *ever* again enter our world. Now, let us lighten the conversation. We have spoken of enough terror today. It is far too glorious of an afternoon to remain inside. Would you care to join me in a walk? I should like to visit with Maris and her sisters. They reside in a lovely lagoon on the far side of the grounds."

"Maris," Kat exclaimed. "Then she's all right?"

"She is doing well and should recover, but it shall be a painful and slow process. The wound was most severe. For the remainder of her life, this sea child will bear a horrific scar. A large portion of tail had to be removed. It will leave her partially disabled and in need of constant care. Sweet Maris unselfishly sacrificed herself to save her sisters, her Father, and her kingdom. This Mermaid showed great loyalty and devotion to me as well, and I shall remain forever indebted. I believe you shall enjoy meeting the three Princesses. Their aquatic form is rather beautiful. Come, we shall leave through a secret passage."

Once outside, they followed the winding stone path through a delightful garden. Off to the side, Kat saw an impressive white marble tomb. It bore the name *TANAS*. She also noticed Adera ignore its presence. *The sight of this tomb must bring back a ton of painful memories to her. I think it best to just keep my mouth shut for now.*

All three Mermaids were stretched out atop a cluster of boulders basking in the warm sun. The sound of approaching footsteps caused them to panic and escape to the safety of the tepid water.

"Do not fear. It is I, Queen Adera. I have come to visit and brought a friend."

Upon hearing Adera's mellow voice, the timid mermaids surfaced and resumed their prior stance on the rocks, their faces aglow.

Maris was positioned in the middle. Long dark hair dripped like a silken waterfall down her back. The horrendous wound had been artfully wrapped in bandages and concealed the disfiguring laceration on her royal-blue and aqua tail.

Their torsos were very human like in appearance. Flawless, pale bisque skin had the soft luster of pearls. In place legs and feet, they possessed magnificent fish like tails with extremely long, broad, wispy fins. Similar appendages were affixed to their arms from the elbow to the wrist. Resplendent tresses cloaked most of their bodice, which was modestly covered with pearl imbedded shells. The configuration of their tails was identical, but varied in color. Perhaps the most outstanding feature of the trio was their striking white-blue eyes.

Nerissa was blonde with vivid green and gold scales. Romey, the youngest, had vibrant auburn hair and brilliant red and orange scales.

Adera and Kat nestled down alongside the lagoon's edge. The conversation was light and enjoyable as the Mer-Princesses enthusiastically told Kat about their fabulous underwater kingdom.

After a good hour or more, Adera announced it was time they return to the Castle.

As the pair rose to leave, Maris suddenly eased from the rocks. The immobilizing wound caused awkward movement and would forever hinder former nimbleness. "It is said you are the chosen one, Kat, destined to face Ios. Take care. He is a resourceful, vile creature. I pray with all my heart you will safely defeat him."

"Thanks, Maris. I have never been more touched than I am by your heroic and unconditional sacrifice. It oddly infuses me with a great courage I've not felt until now. I'll do whatever it takes to eradicate this monster and make your home safe once more." Kat felt on the verge of tears. "I promise not to let you down."

The easygoing stroll back to the Castle was the perfect ending to a blissful afternoon.

"I have enjoyed our day together, Kat, but must attend to pressing obligations. The oncoming war leaves little time for leisurely recreation. I shall see you this evening at dinner. Hopefully, we will be able to implement our devious plan." Before she walked off, the dignified Queen gave a practice wink.

₧₧ ₧₧

Ahren had been relentless and drilled his forces fervently, determined to obtain some form of perfection. The Shankquas required little training. However, the Water Leapers remained a far cry from the crushing warriors Nimue desired. She had come to review the troops, and he hoped this loathsome army would pass inspection. Little emotion crossed his face as the vengeful sea witch eyed the unholy assemblage. He puffed out his chest, confident the great sorceress would reward him after viewing such a remarkable achievement.

She darted up to him — her face only inches away. "You call this a well prepared army, Ahren? I have seen a school of mackerel perform better. If you do not wish to feel my wrath, I suggest the instruction be a bit more diligent. These troops must be ready by tomorrow. I will wait no longer. My patience wears thin. I *will not* tolerate failure. Do you understand?"

Eyes lowered. "Do not worry, my Queen. Every warrior will give you an undeniable victory."

Nimue paused a moment, then eased away from him. "Tomorrow, I shall once again stroll in the sunlight. This thought causes me to feel a trifle benevolent, Ahren, so I shall graciously provide a bit of assistance."

238

She spun around and sped to the coral encrusted dwelling occupied by Ios. "Come out, my sweet pet. I have a pleasurable chore for you."

Large eyes opened and glowed like a pair of burning embers as the monstrous serpent came forth.

A webbed hand stroked the horrific head. "At the edge of the sea forest, you will find a small village of humans. I want you to attack tonight. Destroy every man, woman, and child. To substantiate your success, bring me five bodies, living or dead, it makes no difference. They shall serve as a welcome treat for my sharks. Do what you want with the rest. Their lives are meaningless to me. Now go, my precious. Serve me well."

The giant serpent swam off and disappeared into the dark water.

Nimue headed for the prison cave to gloat before the husband she despised. Her voice resonated glee as she approached the confined King, "I want you to know, my darling, Legar, Ios has been sent to a nearby village. Tonight, Adera shall not rest. The wail of her beloved people will thunder throughout the kingdom. Tomorrow, I will transform and regain my glorious human body. At long last, I shall tread upon solid land. After this night, you shall never again enjoy my delightful company."

"Enjoy your company, Nimue? The mere sight of you sours my stomach. As for walking on solid land, you know as well as I, Adera has condemned you to the sea. As long as she lives, your feet can never again touch soil."

"You underestimate my cleverness. I have created slippers of shell. The soles of my feet shall be immersed in sea water. They will not contaminate her *precious* soil. Mercifully, the discomfort of wearing these appalling contraptions will not be long suffered. Adera shall soon

239

lie dead, and I will have no further need of them. Now I bid you good night, Legar my sweet, or should I say *good bye!*" Nimue cackled as she swam off, delighted her plans would soon lead to the death of the one she hated most — Adera.

ഔരു ഔരു

Kat wandered around a while longer and soon spotted Randy and Jay. Anxious to see what they had been up to, footsteps quickened. "Wow, you guys are a filthy mess."

Randy pursed his lips and gave a quirky look. "Nice to see you too, Kat." A cloud of dust rose as he brushed his jeans. "We've been out wrangling horses. Took a while, but we got them rounded up and secured in the paddocks."

"I'm telling you girl, we were busier than a one-eyed cat watchin' nine rat holes." Jay draped his arm over Randy's shoulder. "I swear we chased those suckers a thousand miles, but what a ride it was. As soon as I catch my breath, I'm ready to go again."

"Jay, you ain't right. I'm so darn tired I don't know whether to scratch my watch or wind my butt." Randy's comment brought a chuckle from all three.

"Why did you two guys have to gather up the horses in the first place, Randy? There's plenty at the stable already."

"We really had no choice, Kat. Although the Elves brought every mount they had, there wasn't enough for everyone. A decision was made this morning to go out and collect our entire herd, but I still don't believe it's gonna be an adequate amount. So, what have you been up to, missy?"

"Not much really. I spent most of the day with *Adera*." She tried not to laugh as his head snapped around like the tail end of a whip.

"Adera? Uh, what did you and Her Grace talk about, if I might ask?"

Kat replied in a slow, teasing manner. "Oh, just a little of this, and a bit of that — and you."

"Say Jay, why don't you head on back to your room? We can hook up in a bit. I need to talk to Kat a minute."

Jay made a face at Randy. "Fine, if you two don't want to share the royal skinny with me, so be it. Actually, I feel the urge for some food. Think I'll mosey on by the kitchen and see what Cook has lying around."

Kat started to offer a word of warning, but figured why waste her breath. He would only ignore it and go anyhow.

Randy pulled her over to a nearby seat. "Okay, spill the beans. What was said about me? Is she mad?"

What a golden opportunity. Now, I can set our plan in motion. She took her time and carefully explained Adera's dilemma in precise detail.

He squeezed her hand as a look of relief flowed across the handsome, tanned face. "Is *that* all that's been wrong? Why didn't she just tell me? I would have understood. She knows I've always respected her title. So, the royal *looker* really likes me, huh?"

Kat frowned at the comment then continued, "Yeah, she sure does. Promise to keep all this under your hat, Randy, and don't dare breathe a word to anyone. Adera has a lot of people around her now … King Merneos for example. If you truly care, leave her alone and try not to make things more difficult. You'll have plenty of time to get together after all this is over."

241

"Trust me, I'll make every effort to steer clear of Adera and allow her to perform those Queenly duties. Thanks, kiddo. You're the greatest."

Kat sighed. So far, the deception was working. All that remained was for Adera to finish him off with a coy little wink. A miraculous change in Randy's persona took place almost instantly. He appeared to be in high spirits and unworried about the relationship with Adera. This transformation would easily allow the Queen to hide all feelings from probing eyes.

That evening, Kat joined up with Tippy and Meeley.

"Hey girlfriend, you won't believe what's happened." Tippy gushed with excitement. "The two of us spent the entire day with Merlin. He asked Meeley to stop by her home on the way back from Durmeleigh to gather a large sack of scales Knox had shed over the past few months. I found this formula in my book, and Merlin knew exactly how to prepare it. You take the old scales, grind them into a fine powder, and combine them with a bit of pine tar to make a paste. Once applied to our armor, the pieces become virtually impenetrable."

Tippy paused to catch her breath. "You won't believe how strong our shields are now. Merlin tried to pierce one with a sword and bent the blade. Tomorrow, we're gonna brew a potion that will give everyone a little added strength and agility. Kat, I'm starting to believe we might win this war and open the doorway home. Isn't it the best news you've heard all day?"

Kat nodded, but changed the subject to avoid any further talk of going home. *I know they won't approve of me staying, but I'm not gonna return. With a bit of luck, the romance between Randy and Adera might hold him here as well.*

As the three girls entered the enlivened dining hall, Jay looked up and motioned to them. "Well, it's about time you babes decided to join the living. Did ya get lost or something?"

Meeley took his arm and batted her lashes impishly. "Now Jay, how could we allow ourselves to get lost knowing you handsome chaps were waiting?"

He laughed. "I swear you gals look prettier tonight than a glob of butter meltin' on a stack of wheat cakes. What say you and I go grab a cold one, Meeley?" Hand in hand they walked away.

Merlin beamed as he joined the group. "Good evening everyone. I trust you are enjoying this happy gathering?"

"I think we are," Kat answered. "You look mighty handsome tonight. I understand Tippy's book has been of tremendous help and might give us the edge we need to defeat Nimue."

"Yes indeed. We have been blessed by her timely discovery of it." The gallant wizard's eyes sparkled as he turned to the timid blonde. "May I be so bold as to state how beautiful you appear this evening?"

Tippy blushed and took a step back. "Uh, thank you for the lovely compliment, Merlin, but I think it should apply to all of us ladies."

The illustrious wizard was a bit on the flirtatious side, but lately his attention appeared keenly focused on Tippy. Although separated by two worlds, Kat knew her friend remained devoted to Jim and would never betray their love. "Merlin, I have a question about one of the maneuvers. Could you help me?" She took a firm grip on his arm, gave Tippy a coy grin, and led the flabbergasted wizard away from the group.

243

After dinner, the guests retired to the large drawing room. Kat was chatting with some staff members when she caught sight of Adera nervously approach Randy and the others. The moment of truth had arrived. Either the deception would work or fail miserably.

Adera directed most of the conversation at Randy. "It has been enjoyable, but now I must take my leave. There are many others who require my attention." She started to walk off then glanced back at Randy, smiled, and winked.

He gave a slight nod, turned his back, and continued with the previous discussion.

Kat was overjoyed. The ruse had worked and for the remainder of the evening Randy kept his distance from the Queen.

Jaws dropped when a familiar individual strutted into the room.

"Well knock me down and grease my butt with goose liver. I don't believe it," Jay shouted. "It's Horace. What do you suppose he's doing here?"

The whole group rushed over and greeted their former instructor.

As usual, his composure appeared standoffish. "I only came to watch over this motley horde since each knows so little of war. Should something unfortunate happen to one of you, it might cause Queen Adera a great deal of distress."

Randy grinned sheepishly. "Are you sure that's the *only* reason for this visit?" In reality, the two had developed a strong bond of friendship, and he knew the Elf's aloofness was nothing more than an act.

"Of course, what other reason could there be?"

"All joking aside, Horace, do you suppose there will be much of a battle?" We've gathered a lot of manpower and should have Nimue's ghouls well outnumbered," Randy's tone and manner turned humorless.

"Our observations indicate we may be outnumbered three to one," Horace replied. "It is of little concern for an Elf. In days past, we have defeated others whose numbers far exceeded these."

Randy, Charlie, and Jay looked at each other, shrugged their shoulders, and laughed. The girls, however, did not share the enthusiasm.

"Horace, three to one's not exactly what we had in mind," Meeley declared. "You're acting like it's a simple walk in the park."

The noble warrior showed little expression as he spoke, "Numbers are irrelevant. Elvin skills welcome such a challenge. You need not worry, mistress. I am to personally continue your training tomorrow. By days end, you should be almost as efficient as any Elf."

No one noticed Merlin rise from his seat and dash to the window. He angrily flung it open causing everyone to turn abruptly at the sound of breaking glass. Terror and panic gripped his face as he yelled, "Oh merciful stars!"

Chapter 16
Empathy for Innocence

"**M**erneos!"

The reserved wizard's outburst caused Kat to jump. "Wow, something sure has him riled up."

"My old friend, what causes such grief? I have never seen you react in such a manner," exclaimed the Elf King who rushed to Merlin's side.

There was a mixed tone of anger and dread in the ancient conjurer's voice, "The trees inform me the beast Ios has come ashore. He heads for the sea village and means to destroy it."

Adera hurled a crystal wine goblet to the floor. "Are you certain of this, Merlin?"

"Of course I am. Our woodland friends do not tell untruths."

King Merneos grasped the Queen's hand. "Time has not allowed us to evacuate that particular location. It was to take place tomorrow. We must gather warriors to ward off this onslaught without a moment's delay."

"Those residents are defenseless, Merneos," she screamed. "They will be slaughtered."

The wizard turned to the bemused crowd and announced what was about to transpire.

Several Elves dropped their tankards in haste as they stampeded from the room followed by Merlin, Adera, and King Merneos.

Randy's grip halted Horace. "Do you seriously think you're getting away without us? Sorry bunko, we're in this together. It's our fight as well."

"You are correct, my friend, and I welcome this joint union." Horace twisted around to face Kat. "I demand you remain within the Castle. Your time to enter the conflict will arrive soon, but it is not destined for this night."

She nodded and offered no protest.

Jay joked to Charlie as they scurried from the room behind Randy and Horace, "Well dude, looks like we won't have a training session tomorrow after all."

The three girls stood silent in disbelief as the men vacated the premises.

From behind, Nirage placed a hand on Kat's shoulder and whispered in her ear, "Do not despair. Harm will not befall your friends. Your impassioned strength is now needed in Queen Adera's absence. Look about. There are many frightened occupants. They require leadership and a great deal of appeasement."

Kat acknowledged the Elf's advice, spun around and shook Tippy, who stood frozen in dismay. "Snap out of it. We need to get away from the windows. I think the best place to go would be the music room. All the walls butt up against the inside courtyard and will provide protection. Tippy, Meeley, I can't do this alone and need your help."

The two girls emerged from their panicked fog and darted around to inform the other women of their plans. Soon, the small group, along with Cook and remaining staff, headed for the inner sanctuary — away from the dismal sounds of the men preparing for combat. The nervous assemblage silently awaited the outcome of this skirmish, unsure of what that might be.

෨ාᎠ   ෨ාᎠ

Randy and the men sprinted to the encampment, armed themselves, and hurried to saddle several horses. In a short span of time, the commanding band of warriors was mounted and ready to be under way.

Adera grabbed a shield and sword, then abruptly snatched a horse from one of the Elves and mounted.

King Merneos reined his steed over to her and yelled, "No Adera, leave this baneful confrontation to us. Remain here."

"These are *my* people, Merneos, not yours. I *will* go to them. Neither you nor anyone else shall tell me to stay behind, nor shall I comply." Before he could stop her, she whirled the spirited mount around, spurred it hard in the side, and galloped off.

He glanced over at Merlin, who shook his head in resignation, then motioned for the fellowship to expeditiously follow.

Beacons of light from the silvery full moon broke through the night clouds and illuminated a shadowy landscape. At the riders' beckoning, fleet-footed horses pounded the ground beneath them.

"Merneos, the trees advise me Ios has entered the village," Merlin bellowed. "We must hurry or I fear we will arrive too late."

The sharp crack of leather against the animals' sides prodded them on even faster as sturdy legs pumped like thunderous iron pistons.

As the array of warriors approached at breakneck speed, they could hear bloodcurdling screams.

248

Randy and Jay cast a quick glance at each other and drew their swords. There was no time for fear, only immediate action.

Within moments, they entered the settlement, but were greeted by a morbid quietness. The winded horses were brought to a walk as the brotherhood proceeded through the grisly debris left by the vicious attack. Mangled and mutilated bodies splattered the stony streets. Several human warriors retched at the gruesome sight. In the dark confusion of night, Ios had completely decimated the entire village in a sheer matter of minutes.

Jay heard the tortuous moan of a woman lying by the shattered side of a home, gravely wounded yet still alive. He leapt from his horse, rushed to the bleeding victim, and cradled her in his arms as the life force drained from a severely battered body. A lone tear crept from the corner of her eye and trickled down a bruised cheek as she looked up into his docile face. He perceived a faintly audible *thank you* before she fell limp.

Randy came over, leaped from his mount, and knelt alongside his sobbing friend. He looked around in the dimness and saw the shattered bodies of a man and little child lying nearby, horribly torn to pieces by the ferocity of the sadistic beast.

The silence was broken by Adera's chilling scream, "*No*, my poor people. Damn you to hell, Nimue, damn you to hell! I promise to avenge these innocent lives if it takes my last breath to do it."

Merlin drew up beside her. "I hoped to offer some form of consolation, my Queen, but unfortunately find myself ill with distress. I doubt there is one among us who does not feel empathy for these souls as they view the deplorable devastation."

Randy grimaced at the ghastly rubble Ios had left behind. A fury unlike any he had ever known began to build inside. The sound of a horse's footsteps from behind made him spin around and stare into the somber face of his Elf friend. Unable to contain the anger that gushed forth like a whirlwind, he picked up a piece of pulverized wood and slammed it hard against the ground, yelling in unadulterated rage.

Horace dismounted and placed a firm hand on Randy's shoulder. "Your anger is great, my friend. It is right to alleviate these feelings. No words can be spoken to ease the pain of this butchery. I beseech you to understand what I am about to say. My heart bears great sensitivity for the lost lives of so many harmless victims, but we must remain steadfast. It is time we tend to the grim task of burying the dead. What you witness is the overwhelming carnage of Nimue. Just as Ios has shown this night, the demon armies will grant no mercy to other innocents. There is nothing good to be said of war, but it is upon us, and you must remain strong." The stalwart Elf pulled a blanket from the debris. He walked over to Jay, pried the woman's broken body from his arms, and tenderly wrapped it in the makeshift shroud.

After a moment, Jay rose and made his way to Randy's side. They stood and looked around at the numerous corpses scattered about like foul garbage.

"Horace is right, Jay. The only thing left to do is give these people the dignified burial they deserve. We can't let them lay here like pieces of disposed trash."

"I know, Randy, but that poor woman tore my heart to shreds. She did nothing to deserve such a thoughtless death. I couldn't help think this could have been Kat or Meeley, or as far as that goes, one of us. Ios's demonic aggression came without warning as they slept. I'm not a violent person, but I can't wait to strike back on their behalf. The only reason I agreed to help Adera with her precious war was to return home. The motive for it meant nothing to me. Now, after observing this mindless butchery, it's become personal. I have a purpose to show these fiends no pity."

As they went about the bitter task of burying the dead, only the endless sound of shoveling dirt and an occasional sob broke the unholy stillness. Even the horses seemed to sense the appalling sadness that filled the air, and fell into an unnatural, revered silence.

The ride back was slow and speechless. Alas, thoughts of the senseless massacre would remain embedded in many minds for all eternity. Adera rode between Merlin and King Merneos, sobbing and totally inconsolable. At last, they reached the encampment where the mood remained gloomy. The weary horses were tended to, and the covey of exhausted militia made their way back to the Castle.

ഏരുക്ക   ഏരുക്ക

The door to the music room flew open and almost hit Kat as Jerome burst in. "The men have returned."

Everyone dashed to hail the returning warriors, but witnessed no cheers of jubilation, only a macabre silence and anguished faces.

Randy sauntered up to the three girls and spoke firmly, "Look, we've been to hell and back again tonight and don't care to speak much about it. I'll tell you what I feel is necessary and no more. When I'm finished, let it drop, or you might hear more than you bargained for. Got it?"

They nodded in agreement. It was obvious the men had undergone a nightmarish ordeal. There would be no additional questions.

"It's not necessary to go over all the barbaric and gory details. To be honest, I wish I could forget all I saw." Randy proceeded to explain what had been encountered.

Tippy gasped at the few atrocities he revealed. She turned ghostly white and collapsed into a chair.

Meeley winced, turned away from the group, and wept into cupped hands.

Kat remained silent, her expression unemotional. An intense resolve began to seethe and was about to burst forth. Finally, a tidal wave of emotions surfaced. "All of you stop blubbering and follow me. *Now.*" Without uttering another word, she bolted for the drawing room.

The friends sprinted after her, but screeched to a halt at the doorway.

In front of the notorious tapestry stood the raven-haired girl, face taut and drenched in tears. "Do you see the young woman in this?" Her voice was harsh and vicious. "It's no coincidence we look alike. I am she, and the devil beast is Ios. Let it be known here and now, I vow to avenge those villagers and put an end to that vile serpent's miserable life."

"Pardon the interruption." Merlin sauntered in holding a dusty old bottle. "I concocted this hearty brew many ages ago and have never had the pleasure of partaking in it. It appears tonight would be the perfect moment. I believe we may all benefit from its intoxicating properties."

The wise wizard had no sooner uncorked the bottle when Adera and King Merneos joined the uncommon assemblage. The Queen wavered and was guided to a nearby chair by the gallant ruler. Merlin promptly poured a goblet of the alcoholic beverage and handed it to her. Brows raised as the regal lady downed the liquid in one gulp.

Her soft voice cracked, "Thank you, dear Merlin, these spirits are truly welcome. The tragedy witnessed tonight reveals the sadistic treachery to be encountered. Together, we shall fight side-by-side in battle, and our staunch unison will rid the world of this malignancy."

Merlin held his glass high and shouted, "A toast to Adera and Bowlandria."

"To Adera and Bowlandria," replied the rest as they mimicked the gesture of honor.

"Our troops are ready. Tomorrow we march to the sea," King Merneos decreed. "We must keep the arena of conflict away from the villages and Castle grounds at all cost. Merlin, are the flying horses and your squadron primed for combat?"

The conjurer's dark eyes brightened. "They most definitely are. Charlie and his men, as well as your Elves, are well practiced. I am sorry to say, Randy, Jay, and Kat have much to learn. I would like to take them up in the morning for a tad more training."

Jay's voice was somber, "We're ready for whatever's deemed necessary, Merlin. Do you suppose we might shoot at a few targets from the horses to get a better grip on things?"

"That's really a swell idea, Merlin," Charlie interjected. "The men and I haven't actually shot from them either. It might be advantageous to have the entire squadron join this session."

"Good point, Charlie, my lad. Please notify the men. At daybreak, we meet and will take to the sky. By noon, everyone should be thoroughly polished and ready for the fast approaching war."

Adera set her empty cup on the table next to the chair. Legs quivered as she rose to her feet. "The hour grows late. We should all retire. Sleep well tonight, dear ones. I fear we may not have the luxury of a peaceful rest for several days to come. Let us pray this war will be brief and loss of life few."

Moments later, Merneos and Merlin bid good night.

Randy picked up the bottle of 'wizard's brew' left behind. "Jay, Charlie, I think it's time to get good and plastered. Excuse us ladies, but we have some serious drinking to do." The three left without another word.

Kat shook her head. "Wow! I've never seen Randy or Jay act like this before, Tip."

"No, I haven't either," she replied. "Something sure has set them off. Whatever it was, you can bet it was plumb horrible."

"I don't know Randy and Jay as well as you two," Meeley said. "But I do know Charlie. I'm positive the only reason they didn't talk more about the incident was to spare us from feeling as they are. Seems chivalry still exists. What say we turn in for the night and try to grab a little shut eye? We have a long day ahead of us tomorrow."

First light unveiled the grounds in a bustle of activity. Several targets stood in a nearby field waiting for the aerial bombardment from Merlin's Marauders.

Kat had a hard time keeping up with Randy, Jay, and Charlie as they made their way to the stables. She wanted to probe more about the previous night, but realized it was best to let it lay. Other than Jay complaining about a hangover, the guys appeared to be in fair spirits.

The unique telepathy of the stallions allowed the riders to maneuver hands free as they dived and darted about the sky. At first, the flyers found it difficult to hit the targets, but after a few passes all became remarkably accurate.

In the afternoon, the group met Adera and Horace at an area designated for ground training. All eyes fell on the beautiful sovereign who wielded a sword with astounding dexterity and skill, proving she was a masterful virtuoso of weaponry.

Before sunset, several legions would move out and head to the sea. Soon after, all would follow as the Kingdom prepared for war.

Horace gathered his students around. "I must enlighten you more about the enemy. This is necessary to ensure success. You know little of the Water Leapers. These ugly, toad-like beings possess a stubby reptilian tail and small bat-like wings. Like the Shankquas, each is cannibalistic, killing and devouring anything in sight. Use caution when you attack and do not fly too low. Although weak-winged and unable to attain flight, they are capable of leaping to great heights. Target only their large heads. No other place on their armored-skinned body can be pierced by your arrows. Unlike the Shankquas, silver will have no effect. You must aim well, and shoot with precise accuracy. "

"Don't worry, Horace. Those dudes have about as much a chance of beating us as a rubber-nosed woodpecker in a petrified forest. I for one don't intend to miss a single shot." Jay gave the Elf a friendly pat on the shoulder, but backed off when he received a chilly glance.

Randy rolled his eyes. "Sorry Horace, Jay can be one fish shy of a string at times."

"I can't help notice you haven't been in the air with us. Where will you be fighting?" Kat asked.

"There are not enough horses, either on land or in the air. I am to be part of a specialized division of our ground forces. It will be our job to lure the Shankquas and Helons out into the open and provide easy targets. I suggest you take out the Water Leapers first. They are fewer in number. Once they have been eliminated, the silver-tipped arrows will efficiently annihilate many Shankquas. If you dismount for any reason and must fight with your swords, do not fear. The blades have also been infused with silver. They will prove to be as deadly as your arrows. I see my company is about to embark. I must leave you for now."

Randy stepped in front of the Elf. "Hold on a second, Horace. This is a bit overdue, but on behalf of us all, we'd like to say thanks for everything you've done. Please, be careful and rest assured we're gonna keep a watchful eye on you from the air."

The noble warrior looked at them and uncharacteristically smiled. "Thank you, all of you, for this gratitude and concern. It touches my heart." He bowed then briskly left to join his battalion.

The gloom was broken by the sound of Jay's voice, "Think I'll take a quick jaunt up to the Castle and see what Cook is doing. Hey, don't look at me like I'm a pecan bar, dudes. Everyone deserves a last meal, and I don't intend to fight on an empty stomach. Besides, who knows when we'll get another bite to eat out there? Shoot, I might even have Cook make me up a doggie bag. Sure don't want to starve to death."

Randy chuckled. "I swear I don't know what we're going to do with you, buddy. Not even a dang war can keep you away from food. Well, don't fill that bottomless pit with too much chow, or your poor horse will never get off the ground."

"Oh hardy har har, you're just a bundle of jokes. Big Mike will be just fine, unlike that old plug you'll be on." Jay huffed and strutted off to the kitchen.

"Kat, have you seen Tippy?" Charlie looked around. "She was with us at training then suddenly disappeared."

"Adera wanted to speak to her alone," Kat replied. "The two of them are going to be together in this battle. Guess they will use a coach or something since Tippy is so fearful of horses. A group of Durmeleigh's best warriors are going to tag along as bodyguards for added protection. Adera suggested Tip stay behind, but she wouldn't hear of it. I'm telling you, our timid girl is turning into an avid soldier, and a talented one at that. It's kind of funny when you think about it. All of us look and feel young again, but in reality we've matured a great deal, mentally."

Talk continued as Meeley, Charlie, Randy, and Kat walked to the Castle and hastened to their rooms. Unsure how long they would be away, it was essential they gather a few necessities.

In her room, Kat found Meon and Hoki crying. They ran over and embraced her legs. "Oh mistress, we are so frightened. Please come back safely. The thought of never seeing you or mistress Tippy again is a heavy weight upon us."

"Listen, you two dingys, we're gonna be fine. I won't let any of us be harmed. Now, dry those tears and help me get ready. I have a lot to do in a little time."

Kat and Meeley met the guys in the Great Hall and proceeded out to the cobblestone courtyard. Oddly,

Tippy was nowhere to be found. It was surmised she had been taken to Adera's carriage, much like when they left for Durmeleigh, and all dismissed any real concern.

A great throng filled the open enclosure. The invigorating conversation was brought to a screeching halt when the revered Queen stepped out from the shadowed doorway.

She looked magnificent dressed in warrior-like attire. Her honey-gold hair had been pulled straight back and braided. Even the ungainly outfit could not deter such astonishing beauty. Bright turquoise eyes flashed as she faced the militia.

Kat noticed a glow on Randy's face as he caught sight of his beloved Queen. Ironically, Adera returned a similar glance to the handsome combatant.

Adera raised a hand and an eerie hush fell over the crowd. "The time grows near for us to depart. My heart overflows with love as I see you stand before me, willing to wage war against boundless evil. Such unfaltering devotion is beyond words. I bestow the blessings of my father upon you and beseech his powers to shelter all from harm. We shall reign victorious in this quest for peace and forever celebrate our forthcoming conquest. Evil will *not* succeed. Soon, you will face godless forces, but we shall emerge triumphant and send these vile beings back to the pits of hell. My dearest friends, I offer my soul as your shield."

A rousing cheer bellowed through the air. The uplifting words of encouragement touched the spirit of man and Elf as each left to join their appointed detachments.

Chapter 17
<u>To War!</u>

I n the darkened depths of the sea, Nimue gathered her forces. One last briefing was rendered prior to embarkation. The long awaited confrontation drew near. In a few short hours, the chance to engage and kill Adera and Merlin would come to pass. Her quest for Bowlandria's throne would be put off no longer.

The sea thundered as the devilish horde began its departure for the land above. Tiny fish scattered in terror from the oncoming force. If all went as planned, the soulless, demonic army would attack with swift ferocity and end the war within hours.

Nimue was giddy and could barely contain herself as the trek to the surface began. Next to her swam the loathsome Titan, Ios. Word of his successful assault upon the hapless village fortified the belief she would emerge victorious. "Do not worry, my pet," she cooed. "The chosen one shall be little threat. She is a mere human girl who possesses inferior skills. Kill her before you move on to feed. Be mindful, you are not to touch one hair on Adera's head. Her fate resides in *my* hands. I have endured much and waited many years to wreak my revenge."

The sun had begun to set when the vile army approached the shoreline. Nimue beckoned the troop leader. "Ahren, make camp near the forest's edge. We will attack the unwary enemy at first light, swarm the land like locusts, and consume all that lies in our wake."

A pulling undertow indicated nearness to the beach. Her magical moment had arrived as she entered shallow water. Minutes later, the shape-shifting enchantress began the complicated transformation from mermaid to human form. Shedding of the scaly tail for limbs was painful and brought a scream as the metamorphosis took place. Once completed, she fastened the shell slippers to her feet and stood erect for the first time in centuries. The sea Queen felt euphoric as she walked through moonlit waves and once again set foot on solid soil. "I had almost forgotten how beautiful the land is or how fresh the air smells. Never again shall I be forced to live in that wretched watery domain."

She glanced at the Trident clutched in her hand. "I have no further need of this tawdry piece of trash. Soon, I will hold a scepter befitting my royal status." Nimue indignantly hurled it back into the sea, turned, and headed toward the flickering fires of the fiendish encampment. Time would prove this arrogant gesture to be one of many mistakes she would make.

ℴℴℂℝ ℴℴℂℝ

Still imprisoned, King Legar looked up in total disbelief. Several devoted dolphins approached carrying their monarch's source of power, eager to return it to the rightful owner. It was the tool needed to provide escape. Once in his possession, he sent a powerful blast to the locks. They instantly fell to the ocean floor and released him and his people from their torturous captivity. With a mighty thrust, he raised the golden Trident high overhead and shrieked in anger, "I may be helpless to offer any assistance to the land above, Nimue, but if you, Ios, or any of your demons try to return to my waters, they will meet instant annihilation."

ℬℭ   ℬℭ

As the squadron of winged horses arrived, Kat caught sight of the massive war camp. King Merneos had taken several troops ahead to quadroon off the area and set up proper accommodations. Several scouts kept diligent watch around the perimeter. The glowing illumination in the sky signaled Nimue's army had come ashore. Sight of it sent an unnatural chill down her spine. *Looks like tomorrow's going to be one hectic day, and bring Ios one step closer — to me.*

Once all landed, Merlin directed the riders to tether the stallions. "Feed your mounts well tonight. In due time, they will need to muster every possible ounce of energy."

After the horses were settled in, Randy, Kat, and Jay excused themselves from Charlie and the others. Anxious to locate Tippy, they began to search the impressive encampment.

Jay came to an abrupt halt, pointed, and yelled, "Leapin' lizards. Take a gander at that."

Through the active throng, they saw Tippy coming toward them — on horseback.

Randy led the way as the three sprinted to her. "Tippy. What in blue blazes are you doing on a horse? How did this happen?"

She giggled like a young child and did a lady-like dismount. "Hah, Mr. Smarty Pants, afraid of a little horsey competition? Bet I can out do you ten to one." She caught her breath and put a hand on his shoulder. "Sorry, I sorta got carried away and shouldn't act so smug. It's just after all these years of teasing, I couldn't help brag."

Kat linked an arm through Tippy's. "You go right ahead and toot your horn, girl. These clowns deserve to get knocked down a peg or two. How did you overcome your fear? I'm baffled."

Around Tippy's neck dangled a decorative onyx amulet on a braided silver chain. She reached down and held up the round token. "Check this baby out. Adera and Merlin gave it to me earlier today. This is a magical talisman and allows me to ride as competently as any of you."

"Well knock me down with a feather," Jay teased. "Tippy can actually stay in the saddle now without the aid of super glue or a seat belt. I suppose the old saying is right. Miracles never do cease."

After a bit more banter and a few laughs, they headed for their designated campfire to join up with Meeley and Charlie.

Four additional members of the squadron joined in and helped energize the conversation. One of the flyers had actually flown in combat, although admitted to using a slightly more orthodox mode of transportation. "Ya know mates," Monte said in an obvious Australian accent. "War's an ugly mutt, and this one looks to be a bloody mess to boot. Might sound a bit odd to you fellas, but I'm feeling a slight bit excited in me gut and can't wait to dig into these blokes."

One of the original members of Charlie's squadron, Howell, spoke up, "Personally, I think we're gonna knock the crap outta these monsters. We've been well trained and are flying aces. If the ground forces successfully flush the beasts out, we should be able to inflict some serious damage from the air."

Charlie slapped his knee. "You bet we will, Howell. Don't forget, we also have the Elves on our side. They can be darn vicious when it comes to doing battle. Skilled and rather lethal warriors reside beneath that delicate exterior of theirs. I heard this isn't the first time humans and Elves have united to fight, and that skirmish turned out pretty successful."

After an hour or more, the weary group disbanded and retired to their tents for the evening.

Tippy, Meeley, and Kat shared one tent, while Randy, Jay, and Charlie shared another. Two thin blankets created a makeshift sleeping bag, but provided little padding from the hard ground. Lulled by a symphony of chirps from field crickets and pond frogs, the exhausted throng drifted off to sleep. However, it was short lived.

Roused by a loud commotion, everyone dashed from their tents. Several scouts sounded the alarm and yelled aggressively while shooting arrows into the thick underbrush of the nearby forest.

Kat burst through the canvas door flap, but was halted by the repugnant smell of rotting flesh. The air seemed to permeate with it. "Whoa! It sure *stinks* out here."

Randy dashed over. "Get your gear on, kiddo, and don't spare the gas. It's started. The scouts are already engaged in a skirmish at the wood's border."

"What's that terrible stench, Randy? Smells like something died around here. It's almost making me sick."

"That odor's from the Water Leapers, and if you don't get your tookus in motion, you're going to be that dead something. Now move it girl. Get to the horses." Randy gave her a sharp rap on the backside and hurried off.

Meeley pushed past Kat and pulled her boots on in mid stride. "I better get to Knox and fast. All this pandemonium is going to make him frantic, and I don't know what he might do. For his safety, and everyone else's, I need to get him into the air. Kat, I'll see you in the clouds. Tippy, please be careful." With those brief words she was off.

Tippy and Kat stood in a slight befuddled state. The two watched the encampment explode in turmoil as warriors hustled to prepare for an engagement. The time had come at an unexpected moment. War was now upon them.

"Well, looks like this is it. I'm heading out to Adera's tent. Think you better move your fanny." Tippy rushed to prepare herself. "Kat, go get your armor and sword. *Kat!*" She yelled once again, but received no sign of acknowledgement. "Sorry, but you leave me no other choice." She drew back and administered a firm slap to her friend's face.

The startling force of the blow instantly emerged Kat from the dazed state. "Thanks Tip, I needed that. Just do me a favor, and don't hit so hard next time. *That hurt.*" She chuckled then leapt into action and grabbed her armament. "Stay well, Tip. I'll keep an eye on you from the air."

Wheezing from the long jog, Kat approached the flying horse compound. Most of the squadron had already taken to the air. Frantic, she spun around, anxious to locate her mount. He was nowhere in sight.

Out of the darkness came a familiar voice, "Without more ado, my lady, we must go. The Leapers are near and could fatally wound the horses on the ground. We will be safe when we ascend into the sky." Merlin emerged from the shadows, holding the reins of Kiv and Junar.

Kat's mind raced. *I have to calm down. Breathe, Kat, breathe. Junar, I've got to get him in the air.* She took the reins of her nervous steed from Merlin and mounted.

Merlin swung up on Kiv. "There is no time for a slow ascent. Release your grip and give Junar his head. We must hurry to join the squadron." He whirled Kiv around and gave a kick to his sides. Without a moment of hesitation, the chestnut stallion spread his wings and shot into the heavens like a bolt of lightening.

"Okay Junar, let's go boy." She eased up on the reins and leaned forward. Sensing her intentions, the golden horse extended his ivory wings and bolted straight up with the swiftness of a rocket. As the ground disappeared, Kat looked down and caught her first glimpse of the Water Leapers.

The creatures were truly grotesque and reeked with the putrid stench of decomposing meat. Each had brownish green bodies with a massive deformed head that resembled a toad. Across the width of their faces was an enormous mouth, lined with prickly, needle-like teeth that snapped tauntingly at the circling flyers. They had large webbed feet, bulbous dark brown eyes, a long broad warty tail, and a fat reptilian-skinned body supported by thick scaly legs. In a futile effort to attack, many jumped toward the sky. Luckily, the small, thin leathery wings barely lifted the massive bodies much higher than twenty or thirty feet.

Kat watched as a unit of their men advanced toward the Leapers. Suddenly, she spotted a division of Shankquas hiding in the underbrush, visible only from her vantage point in the sky. "Randy, the Leapers are trying to lure our soldiers into that clearing. It's an ambush."

He looked to where she pointed and caught sight of the fiends. The unsuspicious troops were headed for impending doom. Randy maneuvered over to Jay and Charlie who circled nearby and pointed down. "We've got to warn them. They'll be slaughtered," he shouted.

"What?" Jay yelled. "I can't hear a dang thing over that commotion below."

"They can't hear me, Kat. If I don't do something quick, the men will die. Stay here." Randy reined his horse and dived downward. "Merneos, it's a trap. Pull back. They're waiting for you in the bush." He motioned in the direction of the hidden enemy. "Merneos, pull back."

Alerted by Randy's forceful outcry, the King peered at the woods and abruptly called a halt to unit's advancement. The skilled combat tactician divided the forces into three divisions. This now allowed him to strike from several directions. The center group inched forward, which allowed time for the others to circle around and get in position. Now, the tides were turned. *They* had the enemy surrounded.

A bombardment of arrows blackened the sky as the skilled Elvin archers shot into the trees. Hooves pounded, and the earth quivered as though struck by a massive earthquake. A heated battle cry jetted across the hillside — a sound so fierce it would corkscrew down the spine of most mortals.

Merlin signaled the squadron to attack the Leapers. "Hurry lads, get in formation."

As in practice, the horses' telepathy took over. With both hands freed, the riders were able to strike with amazing accuracy. One by one, the Helons began to fall as the aerial assault began.

Junar was flying at a tremendous speed, and often caused Kat to catch her breath as he dove for the creatures. She loaded her bow and fired. The arrow found its target and struck down the leader. She did not wait to see if it was dead, but reloaded, fired, and killed yet another.

The combined ground and airborne blitz lasted over an hour. At the battle's end, nearly all of the Helons lay dead or dying.

King Merneos and his soldiers managed to inflict severe damage to the Shankquas, who fled into the depths of the forest. Several members of his forces began to rummage through the carnage. Any creature who remained alive met death. None of these fiends were to be taken prisoner.

Kat joined the other flyers after they had brought the winded horses safely to the ground.

"Wow. That was exhilarating." Jay patted the brown and white pinto on the neck. "Nice going, Big Mike. We sure gave those buggers a run for the roses, and I'd say by the looks of things, we took quite a few out in the process. Killin' those beasts was as easy as sliding off a greasy log backwards. Nimue, be warned. The *Exterminator* has arrived. When me and 'ole Mike get through, she won't have an army."

The guys yelled and cheered as they gathered around the campfire, excited about their first victory in this detestable war.

Kat led Junar away, unsaddled him, and offered a welcomed drink of cool water.

Randy ran up, overflowing with excitement. "Hey Kat, why don't you come celebrate with us? Isn't like you to miss a bit of merriment. We sure whooped some bodacious monster butt today, kid."

She didn't look up or reply.

"Hey, it's me, Randy. What gives? This mopey faced girl isn't even a shadow of you. Something's wrong, so may as well spill your guts, kiddo, 'cause I won't let up 'til you do."

"You go carouse with the guys, Randy. I'm sorry, but don't feel much like partying."

He grabbed an arm and spun her around. "You've never turned away from a good time in your life. It has to be serious for you to act this way."

Amber eyes looked into his. "The skirmish we just fought only means I'm one step closer to confronting Ios. I'm so scared, Randy."

"Its okay, Kat, I understand." He put a muscular arm around her and gave a gentle hug. "Don't worry, kiddo, things will work out, you'll see. That cull doesn't stand a chance with us here to back you up. Come on. Let's head over to camp. Those silly nitwits will brighten this glum outlook."

"Thanks, Randy." She drew a deep breath and sighed. "I actually feel a little better now. Guess it's not good keeping my feelings hidden. Is Tip okay?"

"Yeah, she's fine. Both her and Meeley are as excited as a hen laying her first egg."

Rays of sunlight at last illuminated the darkened landscape.

Kat looked up and admired the celestial masterpiece. *May as well enjoy it while I can. That battle was too quick. I'm afraid once the enemy regroups, there will be another surge.* Ironically, her thoughts were almost prophetic.

Nimue screeched to the heavens in anger, enraged by her loss. She lambasted Ahren about the unacceptable defeat. "Gather your forces and make them ready for another onslaught. I will destroy any who fail this next scuffle, including you." The sea Queen was furious. Adera's knowledge of the premature assault had denied her the desired element of surprise. Emerald eyes blazed with hatred. She held a fist high and yelled into the infinite universe, "Enjoy your victory dance, Adera. Your demise grows near. I *will* have my revenge."

ଚ୬୯ଓ   ଚ୬୯ଓ

As though the wind personally delivered the threat, Adera turned and glowered in the direction of her nemesis. *Revenge will be had, but not by you, Nimue. A consecrated dagger seeks your impious heart.*

Merlin spoke softly as he strolled up to Adera, "I also heard her words, my Queen. They carry through the trees. Strange as this may sound, it pleases me. Nimue's overconfidence shall indeed be her downfall."

Adera looked at the handsome wizard and emitted a slight smile. "The hour for us to face each other is near, my old friend, and it will be the foul sorceress who shall perish this time. When we three meet, and it shall be soon, she will perish, either by my hand or yours."

Merlin nodded in agreement and glanced down at the tainted dagger secured in its sheath by her side. He knew all to well the death and destruction it was capable of inflicting.

Whether wielded by him, Adera, or Nimue, the renowned weapon would once again drip with the blood of its victim.

Chapter 18
Battle Into Hell

Morning revealed the scrimmage's tragic damage. Kat winced as she passed several cloth-covered bodies. A wagon was brought forth, and the lifeless warriors placed upon the wooden planks. They would travel to Durmeleigh and remain until time allowed them to be given a valiant soldier's burial in gratitude for their bravery.

"Horace, who is it we've lost?" Randy asked as he, Kat, and Jay walked up to the noble Elf.

"There are nine brave souls who have departed ... five Elves and four humans," he replied.

Sadness showed in Kat's eyes as she watched the wagon depart. "It was impossible to tell the extent of the destruction from the air. How are the rest of the troops?"

"Many are wounded, but the injuries have been properly cared for," he replied. "You should try to gather some nourishment. I believe we shall again engage in combat, soon. This time, I fear it will be on a much greater scale. Your performance today was admirable. I am impressed. However, do not become overconfident with this encounter. It was nothing more than a strike to test our capabilities."

"Well, I for one think we did a darn good job up there. We sure kicked some Leaper butt." Jay's eyes were wide with excitement. "Dudes, all this fighting has kinda left me a little hungry. Think I'll mosey on over to the old chow wagon and grab a snack."

Randy shook his head in disbelief. "Unlike my garbage disposal friend, I feel much as you do, Horace. There *is* something in the air — something that leads me to believe a far more intense battle is about to begin. I don't mean to sound as pompous as Jay, but we did manage to kill most of the Water Leapers and inflict considerable damage on the Shankquas. There can't be many more left."

The Elf warrior maintained a somber face. "We encountered only a small band of the Leapers. Several hundred remain. It is unfortunate, but they are now aware of your aerial forces and will be better prepared. As for the Shankquas, we shall meet several thousand more on the battlefield. I would say there will be around fifty-to-one. It is a rather satisfactory number."

Kat and Randy scowled at this nonchalant, brash revelation.

"What?" Kat exclaimed. "What the blazes happened to three-to-one?" Up to now, the true enormity of Nimue's army had not been revealed.

"We hoped to spare the humans unnecessary apprehension. It can only hinder your ability to perform. To an Elf, fifty-to-one is not an overwhelming figure. I see a tinge of trepidation in your eyes. Please sit, and allow me to explain my lack of concern."

His demeanor remained stoic. "Although we appear outnumbered, the Shankquas lack intelligence. It is a simple matter to draw them out from the protective cover of the underbrush. At that point, they become easy targets. Nimue had no way to envision an assault from the sky, especially by such a large group of well-armed and accomplished warriors. This in itself provides an enormous advantage — she is unprepared. In battles of

271

ages past, the Elves overcame even greater odds. We united with humans and formed a brotherhood, determined to achieve victory and peace. This event is no different. A bond of friendship exists, one far stronger than ever before. There shall be casualties … it cannot be avoided, but we will emerge triumphant."

"Well, you sure know how to build up one's confidence." Randy chuckled and glanced over at Kat who sat silent and looked somewhat detached.

Horace took her hand as cool blue eyes penetrated her soul. "To be frightened is understandable, but this emotion must be vanquished. It will only deliver disastrous results. Your time approaches. Remain diligent. Trust every instinct … focus *only* on Ios. Do not let *anything* distract you for even a second, or it shall be your last. Do you understand?"

"Yes, Horace. I'll be careful and do as you say. Thanks for the boost of encouragement. I promise to maintain a grasp on my haywire emotions and not allow them to control me as they have in the past. Believe it or not, I truly respect your wisdom and appreciate all you're doing to guide us through this mess."

In an Elvin gesture of good wishes, Horace bowed his head and placed an open palm to his heart.

Merlin struggled for breath as he dashed up to them. "Thank goodness I've found you. I have searched the entire camp. We must hurry to the horses and take to the air. Are you fools, or do you simply lack the intelligence to pay attention?" He pointed up. "Look at the sky!"

The three unwary friends whirled around and gasped in mortification. The heavens had grown thick with dust, a clear signal Nimue's army was on the march and very near.

272

"We can't take those horses up again in battle so soon, Merlin. It's only been a little more than an hour. They're exhausted," Kat yelled. "We'll kill them."

Merlin grabbed hold of her arm, his voice filled with anger, "They have rested enough. Flying horses recover much faster than their common cousins. Do not concern yourself with such trivial matters. Now hurry to them and depart for the heavens. Must I give you a blast from my wand to make you move?"

Randy looked at his two befuddled friends. "We better do as he says before he turns us into rocks or something. Horace, you take care of yourself. Just remember, I have your back and will keep watch over you from up there. Come on Kat, we better split."

Fearing reprisal from the great wizard, the three raced off.

Tippy and Meeley were on their way out of the tent and collided with Kat, almost knocking her to the ground as she darted in to grab her armor.

"Are you okay, Kat? I didn't mean to crash into you like that, but I'm kinda in a rush. Knox is going nuts, and I have to get to him fast. You better hurry to Junar as well. I'll see you up above. Knox and I will be participating in this skirmish. Me and him have a little gift for Nimue. Hope she likes it." Meeley let out one of her robust laughs.

Kat's voice was raspy, marked by a touch of fear, "I think this is going to be a big one, Tip. Promise me you'll remain out of harm's way. That goes for you as well, Meeley."

Emotionally overwrought, the three embraced, each wishing the other a safe return. With tear-filled eyes, they went their separate ways.

Kat dashed to Junar, and within minutes, he was saddled and ready to go. She leaped upon his back and the pair skyrocketed into the clouds. It felt peaceful soaring in the tranquil heavens, and at times seemed as though nothing were amiss. However, the idyllic daydream disappeared in a flash when she glanced down and caught sight of the titanic army advancing toward the encampment. "Oh my stars. How can we ever defeat so many?"

Randy heard her yell out and flew near. "Kat, don't go freaking out. Just remember what Horace told us. Their numbers are meaningless."

She looked over at him and felt her face drain of color. "I know what he *said*, but he's wrong. There is no way we can win against such odds. We'll be slaughtered like sheep. Look, over near the edge of the forest, it's Ios! Oh Randy, I thought I could do this, but I can't. I'm too scared. I've got to get out of here."

"Don't you *dare* quit on me, girl. That beast can't hurt you up here. Forget about him right now and concentrate on more important matters," he roared. "Last night, Adera filled me in on Nimue's plan. It appears she not only intends to take over this realm, but ours as well. She means to destroy it as heartlessly as this one. The war is no longer isolated to Bowlandria. One successful battle on our part could end this fiasco. Kat, you have to remain steadfast. Now get that stubborn head screwed back on, 'cause the show's about to begin. Merlin's signaling for us to fall into formation. Move that fanny of yours this instant, before I help it along with my foot."

Golden eyes grew wide with curiosity, and she edged Junar closer to him. "When did you talk to Adera? What about?"

"*Dang it, Kat. W*hat in the blue-blazes is wrong with you? I think we have more pressing matters to contend with, so focus and don't ask such stupid questions at a time like this. Let's go."

Not another word was spoken as she and Randy joined the other flyers. In silent anticipation, the squadron circled, ready for the opportunity to strike.

Meeley waved to the group as she and Knox hovered nearby.

Kat nodded at Merlin who was off to one side, alone as usual. The wizard bore an uncharacteristic expression and held no apparent fighting apparatus. *Holy smokes, I bet he's going to attack with his wand. None of us has ever seen him use it before. I wonder what mysterious powers it possesses. Could it be stronger than any of our weapons?*

The two ground forces briskly approached the other and would soon engage in battle. A small detachment of Elves were sent ahead to intercept the advancing army, but the noxious sea hag apparently anticipated the move. The entire group were ambushed, slaughtered, and consumed. A large mounted detachment witnessed the fatal skirmish and rushed in, but failed to notice a second division of Shankquas hidden in the underbrush. The demon attack was swift and considerable loss inflicted to the brave warriors. Bloodcurdling screams penetrated the air as the hideous devils pulled helpless victims into the scrub and began to devour them. Wounded horses squealed in pain as they fell.

Jay's eyes blazed. "Look at those stinking beasts. Somehow or the other we have to get those ghouls out into the open so we can take a shot. Dudes, we have to do something." Before anyone could stop him, Jay reined Big Mike toward the battle. They landed in a clearing not far from the demonic army. "Hey, you stinking goons. Try and get me." He raised his bow and taunted the enemy.

Hellish eyes fell upon him and the winged stallion. The creatures dropped their prey and charged the pair, but before they could strike, Big Mike bolted into the air.

Jay's valiant effort managed to lure the brigade of Shankquas and Helons out into the open. The celestial squadron now had the perfect opportunity to attack.

Merlin let out a commanding battle cry and held the carved wooden wand out in front of him like a great spear. He leaned forward and Kiv dived at the masses below. It was a magnificent sight to see as the copper-coated stallion tucked in his wings and plummeted downward. As the duo neared the Shankquas, Merlin yelled, *"Trucido."* A blast of multicolored sparks flew from the wand's tip and hit the enemy. The stalwart force of the magic annihilated a considerable mass of goblins.

Triggered by Merlin's blitz, the squadron followed suit and opened fire. A barrage of arrows rained upon the earth and impaled the intended targets. An enormous plume of black dust erupted from where the demons had been standing. Without hesitation, the squadron soared back into the clouds like fiery missiles, reformed, and prepared for a second assault.

Before the flyers could employ the offensive, a large detachment of Bowlandria's infantry rushed the enemy and engaged in hand-to-hand combat.

Merlin's Marauder's circled above, powerless to assist their comrades. Fearful of killing their own, they did not dare fire into the thick, black dust.

A colossal assemblage of archers flanked the battling infantry. They loaded their bows and made ready to shoot as the battered unit before them appeared to retreat. However, it was merely a ruse to lure the Shankquas farther into the open expanse of the battlefield. The ploy worked, and the archers fired. It looked like a torrential hailstorm of arrows descending from the angry heavens as they struck a deadly blow to the Shankquas, and inflicted substantial and demoralizing casualties.

A cluster of over two hundred Helons burst from the forest and sped in the direction of the archers. Fortunately, the imperceptible wind was sympathetic to the just. With one mighty gust, it dispersed the vile black canopy. The desired window of opportunity had been opened to the restless aerial squadron who instantaneously attacked with lethal precision.

Only three Leapers managed to evade the arrows of death and fled into the dense foliage, grunting in terror.

King Merneos, and his dynamic legion of horsemen, charged forward and engaged Nimue's militia in explosive combat. Two additional divisions of Shankquas, cloaked by the dense underbrush, approached from each side. Their apparent strategy was to encircle King Merneos and strike from all directions. If this group of noxious goblins were not decimated, the entire battalion of horse soldiers would be destroyed and the battle lost.

Merlin spotted the trickery and tried to warn the Elf King of the impending assault. Unfortunately, the noise on the battlefield was deafening … his words of alarm could not be heard.

The Shankquas now had the unwary cavalry surrounded and rushed in from all sides.

Kat let out a scream, "Merlin, allow us to attack. Merneos needs our help."

The great wizard motioned, and without a second of delay the aerial team maneuvered into position. He was just about to give the signal to charge when a green flash streaked past him toward the swarming horde of goblins. Startled, Kiv dove off to the side and darn near unseated the stupefied enchanter. "Zounds!"

"Guys, it's Meeley and Knox," Kat exclaimed. "Go get 'em girl."

The duo whizzed by at breakneck speed. Knox drew in a deep breath, which caused his sides to swell unnaturally. It was then the surprise Meeley had spoken of was sprung on the hideous creatures. The emerald dragon exhaled, and a monstrous bolt of flame erupted from his mouth. While he and Meeley darted above the enemy, the enraged dragon turned his head in all directions to spread the lethal fire about until he had incinerated the entire onslaught. King Merneos and his soldiers were safe.

"Holy fuming corn fritters, did you dudes see that firestorm?" Jay shouted. He gave a robust wave as the dragon and his pilot neared. "Way to go Meeley and Knox."

"Told you blokes I had a bit of a surprise in store for that witch. Nice to have a little flame thrower to help out, isn't it." She threw her head back and let out a yelp as they whizzed by, which brought a rousing whoop of approval from the entire squadron.

"Merlin," Charlie yelled. "Should we fly down and finish off the scum with a few arrows?"

"That will not be necessary, my lad. The flames come from a creature of magic and will efficiently eliminate the scoundrels. It appears our Knox has reached adulthood, and it couldn't have happened at a more favorable time."

The ominous battle raged on for several hours. Blows of devastation were delivered by both sides. Aided by an aerial assault, Bowlandria's ground forces would surge forward again and again. The combined effort proved to be most effective and soon eradicated the bulk of Nimue's army.

Kat looked down upon the blood-spattered battlefield. Bodies of man, Elf, and noble steed were strewn in every direction — all tragically slain. Even the most callous heart could not help feel remorse for those who had fallen. All of a sudden, out of the darkened shadows of the great oaks, emerged an attractive, willowy figure.

The wizard's blue-black eyes widened with evident anger. His voice boomed like thunder, "Pass the word. None are to follow me. Remain steadfast." Without a second of delay, he drew his wand and reined the copper chestnut toward the sorceress.

Obedient, the squadron watched in helpless awe.

Kiv performed with tremendous speed and agility. A kaleidoscope of sparks spewed from the wand's tip as Merlin bombarded Nimue with a violent flow of magic. Time after time, he attacked with little to no results. As predicted, she had gained unadulterated power. His magic now proved useless against her.

Sight of the evil sea Queen triggered Adera to separate from the battle and gallop toward Nimue at breakneck speed. However, a few yards from the intended target, her mount was felled by Ahren. The piteous animal squealed in pain then dropped to the ground, which caused the honey-haired Sovereign to take a nasty spill.

Randy let out an earsplitting shriek, "Adera."

Tippy, encircled by a group of nine Shankquas, aggressively slew the beasts. She then sped to the stunned

279

Queen, leaped from her horse, and helped Adera to her feet.

Horace and several infantrymen ran to protect Adera, but soon found themselves surrounded and in deadly peril. The sharp clash of metal against metal rang through the air as the band fought for their lives, many falling victim to the advances of the diabolical fiends.

Merlin sped to Adera and leaped to her side. "Go Kiv, my trusty friend. Fly to the safety of the clouds. You can do no more to help."

Jay yelled out, "Dudes, I can't sit here like a bump on a log and let them be slaughtered. Either follow me or stay behind. The choice is yours." He loaded his bow and reined Big Mike toward the fight.

Fellow riders let out a war cry and dove on the vile offenders like a swarm of killer bees.

Kat noticed Randy was flying foolishly close to the skirmish and screeched, "You're too low, Randy. Pull up."

A barrage of arrows shot into the air, and Randy's gallant bay grunted as several projectiles fatally struck its body. Mortally wounded, the horse instinctively tried to protect its rider and fought to maintain some form of stability. As they neared the ground, he let out a mournful whinny, folded his wings, and died.

༄༅ ༄༅

The violent force of the impact tumbled Randy end over end. Before he could regain full composure, several Shankquas descended upon the fallen rider. The undaunted warrior rolled to the side with sword drawn. Deflecting their aggression with his shield, the master swordsman mowed the demons down as easily as one

280

would cut grass. He boldly fought through the loathsome pack in an ambitious quest to reach his beloved.

Randy successfully eliminated all of the attackers and paused to catch his breath. Bent over, he could not see the massive goblin warrior bolt toward him.

Streams of sickening drool flowed from Ahren's mouth. With arm extended, the creature raised a weighty sword and prepared to strike this reviled adversary.

An iron-strong thrust to the side knocked Randy off his feet. He rolled to one knee just in time to see Horace wince in pain as Ahren's sword pierced his side. The brave Elf looked at Randy, gave a quirky smile, and collapsed in a bloody mound.

Kat, Charlie, and Jay witnessed the contemptible act from above. All three let out a scream as they watched their heroic newfound friend take the deathblow and save Randy's life. They plunged downward to the ghoulish warrior and sent a flurry of arrows in his direction.

At first, Ahren skillfully used his shield to avoid being hit by the cosmic deluge. Arms flailed at the incessant bombardment, as he dashed into the protection of the forest's thick canopy.

Randy's eyes filled with rage as he glanced at the crumpled body of Horace. He snatched the bow secured to the saddle of his fallen steed, loaded it, and took careful aim at the runaway monster. Upon release, the silver-tipped projectile flew through the air at the intended target with lightening speed, followed by the repugnant sound of skewered flesh.

Ahren halted and looked down at the arrow that protruded eerily from his stomach. He turned and cast a venomous stare at the handsome warrior, let out a hideous growl, and erupted into a hellish mound of black dirt.

A halfhearted victorious grin formed on Randy's face as he watched the goblin fall. A feeble moan caused him to spin around. "Horace." He started for his friend who remained motionless on the bloody battlefield, but was stopped by Tippy's spine-chilling scream. She, Adera, and Merlin were about to be overtaken by fifteen or more Shankquas. "Forgive me, Horace. I must attend to their needs." With great reluctance, he raced to the aid of the hapless three.

One of the Shankquas lunged at Adera, but her dragon-scale coated armor blocked penetration from the sharp blade.

Randy battled to his lady's side. "Someone told me there was a Queen in need of some assistance." He smiled and winked. "Now, what say the four of us finish off these degenerate beasts?"

A clash of swords ensued until the remaining enemy had been destroyed.

The quake of pounding hooves echoed across the meadow, as King Merneos and his Calvary pursued the residual Shankquas and Helons. The majority were slain, while the rest abandoned Nimue and fled to the sea. However, the water would grant no sanctuary. Further destruction would be met at the hands of King Legar and his people, who waited.

Adera tossed her sword to the ground and dashed into Randy's open arms. "My sweet darling, you are safe. The day has been good to us."

Merlin walked over and stood beside the couple. "Do not be so quick to rejoice, Adera. The war remains unfinished." His warning was stern. "She is here. Our time for restitution has at long last arrived."

Nimue strolled unconcerned from the edge of the forest, accompanied by the loathsome serpent Ios who slithered on the soft turf behind her. "How easily you cast aside my words, Adera. I see you have again taken heart with a filthy mortal. Such foolishness now seals his fate as it did with your former admirer. Neither you, nor Merlin, may enjoy the ecstasy of love while I exist," the Sorceress shouted as she entered the open savanna.

Adera turned away from the sea witch and stroked a dirt smudged face. "Please Randy, return to the safety of the air. Leave this task to Merlin and me. It is our destiny — not yours."

"Sorry my precious Queen, but it seems I couldn't escape now if I wanted to. You see, my horse was killed, and since I don't appear to have wings, it looks like I'm stuck right here beside you."

Merlin placed a firm grip on Randy's shoulder. "Now is not the moment for humor, my lad. It is imperative you and mistress Tippy return to the air. If you truly love Adera, honor her wishes. Your presence will hinder necessary concentration and perhaps bring about her demise."

Randy jumped as Kat draped an arm around her friend. "I see you're lettin' that old stupid pride of yours get in the way again. For once, do what is asked. Merlin holds more wisdom in his little finger than any of us combined. He knows what he's talking about. From the air, I saw the events unfold, including Nimue and Ios's unwelcome parade. Here, take Junar, grab Tippy, and get the dickens out of here. Leave this tussle to the three of us. I'm sure your heart pleads to remain, but you'll only be in the way. So scat. Get the blazes out of here, and take good care of my horse."

With reluctance, Randy took hold of the reins and planted a kiss on Kat's cheek. "Listen kiddo, the guys and me will be right overhead. We'll do whatever we can to assist all of you. Try to remain calm. Remember all you've been told. I promise to protect Junar, so don't worry that pretty little head. You just take care of business and stay safe. I love you, Kat."

Tippy cleared her throat. "Hey you two, forget I have a mouth? My feet are not gonna move one inch. I've put up with riding a land horse, but there's no way on this green earth I'm going to climb aboard some four-legged airplane."

Randy raised his voice, "Like it or not, Tippy, you *are* going with me on this horse."

She huffed at him and started to walk away.

"I'm sorry girl, but I don't have time for this nonsense." He scooped her up and physically placed her on Junar. "Scream all you want. It won't do a bit of good. Now hold on tight and stop squirming." He looked back at Kat and Adera then swung up behind Tippy.

Nimue was now only yards away. "So, your lover runs like a coward. He may be safe for the moment, Adera, but I assure you that will soon change. I wonder if his human blood will run as red as your beloved Tanas? Will you brush his cheek as you hold his bodiless head in your hands?"

Adera's voice was strained, "Hurry Randy. She speaks with sincerity."

Randy nudged the giant palomino stallion into action causing Tippy to let out a frightful squeal as he shot into the air. After they rejoined the rest of the squadron, he looked down as Ios and Nimue moved closer to the three waiting figures.

Jay glided close on Big Mike. "Welcome to my world, Tippy. Nice to see ya."

"Shut it, you moronic baboon. I'm not in the mood," she barked.

He smirked and looked down on the field below. "Dude, thought you were going to fight alongside the lady. What changed your mind?"

"It's a long story, Jay, and I don't have the time to explain. The three of them are in big trouble, and we have to try to help in whatever way we can. You with me?"

"Dang straight I am, and so are the others. Take a gander at Ios. That sucker has to be the size of a football field."

Randy paused and eyed up the situation. "There's not a lot of support we can offer Merlin or Adera, but we might be able to give Kat a leg-up. I'm pretty darn sure we can inflict some damage to that slithering beast from up here. I think he needs a little taste of Merlin's Marauders."

Word of the attack spread among the riders quickly. They regrouped and prepared an assault upon the giant sea serpent.

ഇൟഝ   ഇൟഝ

Kat's breathing was rapid and insides quivered as the horrific, snake-like Titan approached. Her heart raced so hard she thought it would virtually burst from her chest.

Suddenly, a shafted shower of devastation struck the serpent. It coiled and lashed out at the speeding horses, but his movements were cumbersome and could not halt the aggression.

The blitz continued for several minutes. Flyers darted around the beast's body, weaving their horses about like aces in a dogfight. A great abundance of arrows tore into the creature's flesh. Although the aerial attack could not destroy Ios, the enormous loss of blood from the wounds diminished his pace.

Undaunted, the beast continued to slither toward Kat. Slowly, it rose and towered over her like a great mountain as it prepared to strike.

Amber eyes darted about in fear while every bone in her body told her to run. *How on earth do they expect me to defeat this monster? It's impossible.* She took a gulp of air. *Buck up. You can do this. Stay cool. Let this jerk make the first move.*

Adera stood several feet away with Merlin at her side. "Kat, remember our conversation. You must move around quickly. Strike *only* when his head is down."

She took her focus off Ios for a brief moment and glanced at Nimue. Her beauty was almost mesmerizing. *Holy crackers! I expected to see an unshapely hag, but she's gorgeous. How on earth can someone so lovely be so evil?*

"Stand fast, Adera. Allow me the privilege to strike the first blow." Merlin drew his wand and moved closer to his tormentor. A crisp flick of the wrist sent a thunderbolt of magic at her.

Green eyes danced as she threw her head back and laughed. "Have you lost your touch, Merlin, or have I become more powerful than the great wizard himself?"

Undeterred by her taunting, he delivered blow after blow, only to have the spells bounce off like water from a duck. "It appears my sorcery is of no avail, Nimue, but my sword remains sharp." He threw down the ancient wand and charged.

In response, the sea Queen drew her weapon. The smile on her face changed to a wince as the tip of Merlin's sword drew first blood, and a thin red line trickled down an ivory arm. Furious, she spun around and lunged at him.

For several minutes, the peal of swords reverberated across the field like iron thunder. Merlin was indeed a master swordsman and was about to overpower her.

"Ios help me," she shrieked. "Get rid of this menace."

The obedient serpent veered from the intended prey. With the force of a massive whip, the creature snapped his tail at Merlin and flung the unwary wizard several yards away from his wicked mistress.

Nimue's upper lip curled as she viewed the wizard's stilled body. "You are as useless as ever, Merlin. It appears to be between you and me now, Adera. I have long desired this moment." With sword drawn, she stormed.

Foul drool oozed from the grotesque mouth as Ios whirled back around and fixed evil red eyes upon his quarry.

Kat cautiously watched every move and covertly slid the jeweled sword from its sheath. In the background, she could hear the clank of blades and knew the two Queens were tangled in a heated battle, but dared not look away.

Destabilized from the flyer's unbridled assault, Ios teetered as the massive body ascended.

For a moment, it was as if time were frozen — eerily hushed. Suddenly, the giant head lunged at the chosen one. Venomous tusks dripped saliva and thirsted for a fast kill.

At the very last second, Kat jumped aside, as ivory fangs sunk deep into the soft turf. Taking advantage of the mishap, she ran past Ios and swung her sword, opening a large gash in his side. Kat spun around and readied for another attack, which came almost immediately. Again, she avoided the beast like a mongoose would a cobra.

This lethal cat and mouse game went on for many minutes. The hideous Titan lunged time and again. Giant pockmarks formed over the meadow's green carpet as dagger-sharp teeth continued to miss the intended victim. With every attack, Kat effectively sliced away more flesh and the grass-green arena ran red with blood.

The brittle snap of a twig caused Kat to turn her head to look in that direction. Beneath a tall oak at the forest's edge stood the Unicorn stallion, Nalay.

Unfortunately, this haphazard distraction provided a prime opening for Ios. A harsh blow from the serpent's tail slammed the sidetracked girl to the ground.

She regained her wind and looked up just in time to see the monstrous head coming at her. With no more than a second to spare, she rolled aside as fangs struck only micro-inches from her legs. Knees quivered as the shaken girl struggled to her feet.

Crimson eyes widened with anticipation as he caught sight of the wobbly target. Ios recoiled and prepared to deliver a fatal blow.

Kat let out a scream when a sudden jolt from the side knocked her away from the looming strike. The violent fall battered her skull against a large rock, and a gusher of red, sticky fluid seeped from under raven hair. Her head throbbed in mind-boggling pain. *I have to remain conscious and get up. What on earth hit me?* With incredible fortitude, she stumbled to her feet and wiped the blood from puffed eyes. "No, McLachen!" As if in slow motion, Kat watched in horror as Ios struck her beloved horse. Vile fangs sunk deep into the Bayard's magnificent neck, and the ebony horse screamed in agony as deadly venom entered his bloodstream. The great stallion reeled then collapsed as the toxin took effect.

A hurricane of hatred erupted within Kat, eliminating all fear. She rushed at Ios, intent on his destruction. "Get away from him, you miserable piece of filth."

The titanic serpent rose, let out a strident hiss, and struck at her. As before, incisors missed flesh and lodged into the tainted earth.

Fear now completely removed, Kat dashed forward with lightning speed. She pounced upon the creature's head like a golden-eyed pather, lifted the diamond-coated sword high, and drove it deep into the bony skull. Before Ios could react, Kat placed both hands on the handle of the sparkling steel and pushed.

Ios roared as the enchanted blade pierced his evil brain and writhed in an agonizing death roll. The mighty leviathan had been defeated and at last lay dead.

Kat ran to McLachen. Oceans of scarlet surged from two massive neck punctures, and she could feel his paralyzed body grow cold as the life force drained. Tears mingled with her blood and clouded amber eyes. "Please, don't die, McLachen. Why didn't you do as I asked? I begged you to stay away from here. You can't die, I won't let you go!"

Randy and a few of the others landed nearby after witnessing the entire event from the sky. They found Kat flung across McLachen's neck, sobbing bitterly. Copious streams of blood poured from her head wound and spilled over the lifeless body of her beloved horse.

"Kat, we have to get you to the doctors, you're badly hurt." Randy reached down and attempted to pull her from the fallen stallion.

"No, I won't leave him," she screamed. "Randy, do something! Save him, please."

He looked down on the frozen body and spoke softly, "It's too late, kiddo. He's beyond our help. Come on, you need to get that wound treated. Kat, you have to let him go."

She suddenly grew quiet, stood up, and looked over at Ios. Her weakened body convulsed with uncontrollable rage. "I'm not finished here. This is for you, McLachen." She stumbled to the serpent's body, reclaimed her weapon, and thrust it once more into the bloody skull. Placing one foot on the dead beast's head, she pulled the sword out, held it high in the air, and released pent up emotion with a booming victory cry.

Tippy grabbed hold of Jay's arm. "I don't believe what I'm seeing. It's as though someone long ago took a picture of this exact moment and transferred it to that cloth. Jay, this is the scene on the drawing room tapestry!"

Kat tossed the rapier to the ground and staggered back to McLachen. She plopped down near his head, stroking it — overwrought with grief.

"Please, you have to come with me," Randy pleaded as he again reached for her. "That's a darn nasty head wound, and you're losing a tremendous amount of blood. You need medical treatment."

"Don't you understand? I don't want your help. Leave me alone," she sobbed. "If he can't be saved, then I want to die with him. Just get away from me."

Randy could see she was on the verge of collapse and pried her off McLachen's body.

She screamed and fought back, trying to break his hold, pleading to remain with McLachen. "I don't care about myself. Just leave me be. I won't let him die alone out here. If I can't save him then I'll die with him. Get away from me."

Randy yelled at Jay, "Help me get her away from here."

In desperation, she tried to fend off the two of them, kicking and screaming, "No, let go of me. I won't leave him. You bas —." Her words trailed off as she gracelessly collapsed into semi-consciousness.

Tippy led Junar over, and Jay helped Randy load Kat into his arms. "I know you're tired, Junar, but she'll die if we don't get to the Castle in time." As though understanding Randy's plea, the golden horse nickered and shot into the air.

ༀ☙☙   ༀ☙☙

Adera stunned Nimue with a brisk jab to the jaw with her shield. This provided a fleeting moment to observe the happenings. She saw Randy take to the air with Kat's limp body cradled in his arms. Her eyes then fell upon the blood-soaked ground surrounding the devoted black stallion. It became crystal clear what had transpired. Enraged, she rushed at Nimue, grabbed a handful of hair, and pulled the sorceress to her feet. "You and your kind have killed for the last time."

Drawing on all strength and skills, Adera fought feverishly with the depraved sea Queen.

"I expected more from you, Adera," Nimue taunted. "A child could fight better. I expected a more challenging opponent."

291

Adera glowered at Nimue for a moment, drew her fist tight, and delivered a well-placed punch to the jaw, knocking the witch to the ground. She leaped upon the dumfounded hag with lightening speed, straddled her, and peered into the evil green eyes she so hated. With one hand placed on Nimue's throat, the other pulled the consecrated dagger from its sheath.

Nimue spit blood into the Queen's face. "No one on this earth possesses powers strong enough to slay me. Only a fool would think a mere dagger could bring about my destruction. It is as pathetic as you."

Adera waved the blade in front of the sorceresses' battered face. "How unfortunate you do not recognize this weapon. The stain it bears comes from the blood of those innocents you butchered long ago. Its hallowed blade will indeed destroy you, for their virtuous essence gives it the power."

Nimue stared at the tainted metal, as eyes grew wide with fear. "It is not possible. This cannot be the weapon. It was destroyed."

"No witch, it was plucked from the body of my betrothed. I have held it safe these many years in hope it would serve a better purpose."

The villainous harpy began to squirm beneath Adera as she realized this was truly the very same weapon used on Tanas and Ganieda. It *could* deliver a fatal blow.

"Draw a breath, Nimue, for it shall be the last. Your stay on earth is finished. Go back to the bowels of Hades where you belong." Adera's face was red with rage. She raised the dagger and plunged it deep into the black heart of the foul enchantress.

The instant the holy blood of Tanas and Ganieda mingled with her own, Nimue let out a blood-curdling scream, twitched, and then slumped lifeless. Evil had been defeated.

Merlin, who had at last regained consciousness, held a piece of cloth to his lacerated head and staggered to Adera's side. He looked down on the inert body of his nemesis and spit upon it in disgust. A chivalrous hand reached for Adera. "Allow me to help you to your feet, Your Highness."

ഇരുന്നു   ഇരുന്നു

In short time, King Merneos returned with the troops and viewed the sickening death and destruction strewn about the vast battlefield. Medics attended the wounded while others performed the grim task of loading the dead into wagons.

Eyes, normally impassive, showed a glint of hatred as the King caught sight of Nimue's bloody corpse. Merneos dismounted, drew his sword, and separated head from body with one mighty blow. The gesture was then repeated on Ios. "Let no one bury this filth. Leave them to the maggots."

ഇരുന്നു   ഇരുന്നു

The war had ended, but the price paid for peace was dear. When everyone had at last retreated, and the land grew silent, Nalay strolled from the forest's obscurity and made his way to the motionless body of McLachen. He gazed down on the heroic horse as vivid blue eyes welled with tears. In reverence, he bent on one leg and rested his muzzle on the soft black coat of the fallen stallion.

The skies grew dark as a tremendous sadness blanketed the land. Never had the realm been so gloomy — never had there been such a tragedy. The great stallion lay still, motionless, his body growing cold as the black veil of death drifted over him.

293

Chapter 19
The Return

Randy's blood-soaked tunic stuck to his chest. He could feel Kat grow weaker by the second and urged Junar on in an attempt to save the life of his friend. *We gotta hurry. She's bleeding to death in my arms.*

Although near exhaustion, the giant palomino continued the trek at a furious speed. Sweat-lathered sides labored as the horse struggled for wind. Weary legs shook as he landed awkwardly in the cobblestone courtyard.

Unconscious, the valiant girl's head bobbled as Randy eased off Junar's back and carried her into the Castle. The sound of the massive wooden doors slamming against the walls brought Castle staff running.

"Oh merciful heaven, it's Kat," Margaret Mary exclaimed as she ran to the couple. "Hurry lad, we must get her help or by the looks of it, they'll be nothin left ta save."

A team of doctors met them at the infirmary, released the wounded chosen one from Randy, and disappeared behind an opaque glass door.

"Come now, darlin," Cook cooed as she clutched his hand. "The doctors need ta be doin what they must. Come along with ya, and don't be worryin. She's a strong bit of a thing, and twill be fine I'm thinkin."

Randy tried to mask a look of concern. "Sure hope you're right, Cook. She's lost a lot of blood. I suppose all we can do now is pray. Do you know if there are any more horses left at the stables? Poor Junar's spent, and I don't dare take him up again. When I left, Adera was in a heated battle with Nimue. I must return to her."

"There will be no need, Master Randy," Jerome said as he hastened up. "Everyone is returning. Queen Adera rides in front with Merlin and King Merneos. She appears to be well."

Cook slapped both hands together. "Praise be to Heaven. Perhaps tis good news and the cursed war is ended. Well, what the devil are ya standing here for? Get yer feet moving now lad, and go to your friends. I'll stay with Kat. Now get on with ya."

Excited, Randy started to dash off, but doubled back and planted a kiss on the jolly woman's cheek. Feet barely touched the steps as he bounded down the staircase.

The courtyard exploded with the clatter of hooves as it filled with weary troops.

Adera galloped up, leaped from the horse into his open arms, and ignited a flame in his heart with a rather passionate kiss.

"Whew. Now I'd say *that's* a reward worth fighting for," Jay shouted.

The sound of voices made the couple pull back from each other. Before them stood a throng of smiling faces which caused a blush to inch up the pair's dirt-smudged cheeks.

Tippy began to applaud the overwhelmed lovers, and soon everyone else followed suit. Deafening cheers ensued and ricocheted off the granite stone walls.

Randy clasped Adera's hand and held it high. The victorious gesture roused a louder ovation from the enthusiastic crowd.

Tippy sprung from her mount and bounded up the marble steps, trailed by Jay and Charlie. Euphoric, the happy group embraced one another.

ಔ಄ ಔ಄

Obscured by the courtyard's great fountain, a joyful wizard sat astride a sweat-drenched earth bound horse.

Beside him, the Elf King loosened the reins of his steed as it restlessly pawed the ground. "It appears we may have a wedding to plan before long, my old friend."

Merlin shifted his weight in the iron stirrups of the tattered leather saddle. "So it seems, Merneos, but one never knows what will be foretold. Remember, destiny never sleeps." He paused and glanced at the jubilant couple standing atop the marble steps. "The courageous foursome has successfully completed the appointed task. An opportunity to go home is *now* within their grasp. I am fearful this romance may be as doomed as our Queen's first. A life with Tanas was denied Adera at the jealous hand of Nimue. Sadly, Randy may choose to return to his world and once again leave her broken hearted. We must beseech the stars to bless this would-be union and keep him by her side."

King Merneos nodded then dismounted and joined the others on the graduated plateau. "It is with great pleasure I announce the war is ended and evil defeated. Together, Elf and man fought as one. Tonight, there will be a well-deserved gala unlike any Bowlandria has ever witnessed."

The royal Elf bent down on one knee in front of Randy, Tippy, and Jay. "It is with boundless gratitude we owe you the salvation of our realm. Your selfless fortitude restored peace to the paradise we love. By the

296

power of my Elf sovereignty, I bestow upon each of you the title of Knighthood."

Out of respect, Randy placed a hand on his heart and bowed to the King. "Speaking for all of us, we wholeheartedly thank you. However, the bravest of us all is not present … Kat."

The King rose and placed a firm hand on Randy's shoulder. "Fear not. When the lady is well, the highest honor of our land will be presented."

"How *is* Kat?" Tippy asked. "We've been worried sick about her. She looked so pale when you both left the battlefield on Junar."

"Doctor Magee believes she'll make a full recovery and be back to her old self in short time. Right now, she just needs a lot of bed rest," Randy replied. "If the trip had taken even a few more minutes, she wouldn't have survived. Junar nearly collapsed as we landed, but refused to miss a beat up there and brought us here in record time. That dang horse risked it all to save Kat. He's a winner in my book."

"Speaking of horses, Randy, we need to send someone to bring McLachen back and properly bury him," Jay said somberly. "You realize the minute Kat wakes up she's gonna want to know about him. If we tell her he was just left to rot, she'll not only be hysterical, but viciously angry as well."

"Your words are wise, Jay," Adera replied. "McLachen sacrificed his life to save our destined champion. We owe him a great deal of thankfulness." She beckoned a group of soldiers and instructed them to retrieve the stallion's remains. "A place of distinction will be found and a suitable monument placed on his grave."

King Merneos stepped forward. "I would be honored to have my craftsmen create a memorial in McLachen's magnificent likeness. It will be a fitting tribute to a most valiant warrior."

Everyone agreed and felt the suggested statue would, in some small manner, help ease Kat's grief over the loss of her friend and companion.

Moments later, the steps and courtyard were vacated, and the Castle erupted with activity as an overjoyed staff scurried in preparation for the celebratory jamboree.

Holding to her word, Adera stopped in to visit Kat. Meeley rushed home on Knox, but said she would return well before the merriment began. Everyone else retired to their rooms for a well-deserved rest.

€’€’ €’€’

Tippy's battle-bruised hand gently turned the green patina-hued copper doorknob to her serene quarters. Inside, she leaned against the closed door and drew a breath of relief. *I am so glad this horrific ordeal is over. Finally, we can go home.* Her thoughts were shattered by an unexpected squeal.

"Mistress Tippy," yelled Meon and Hoki. "You have returned — unharmed." The two Brownies scurried to her side. "We have visited mistress Kat several times, but remained invisible. Cook holds watch and would surely scold us. Please tell us about the battles. We know very little and wish to hear more." The two plopped down on a nearby cream satin settee.

A crescent smiled formed on Tippy's face. "Okay, let's see now. The launch of the Great War began in darkness. I was nervous as a kitten as I entered the camp on my trusty steed." She meticulously described the various conflicts and how so many on both sides had fallen. The two tiny beings would gasp and squeal as the vibrant tale continued, especially the part about Kat's courageous confrontation with Ios and her victory over the vile creature. The story ended with the battle of the two Queens.

"Now that all has been revealed about the blasted conflict, this dog-tired body could really use a nice hot bath. Do you think you could find something obscenely gorgeous for me to wear at the celebration tonight? I'll be leaving soon and won't have anything so elegant back in my world." Before another word could be spoken, the gurgling sound of water echoed in the spacious bathroom. Tattered and blood-stained clothes were gratefully discarded, and a weary body settled into the steamy tub. Aches obtained from the dire activities began to melt away. For the first time since their arrival, Tippy totally relaxed. After a long soak, she dried off, slipped into a pale pink robe, and re-entered the bedroom.

Draped across the black velvet spread was a magnificent gown of shimmering baby-blue and gold. Meon's masterful hands braided long golden locks. Hoki then wove delicate sprigs of white baby's breath and royal blue ribbons throughout the wavy tresses. After a few tiny touches of makeup, Tippy dressed and walked over to the ebony floor-mirror. "Wow. I can't believe this is me. Guess I better enjoy these looks now 'cause in a short time they sure will be gone."

Round, doe eyes peered up at her. "Mistress, you do not wish to remain with us?"

She bent down. "I've grown fond of everyone here, but am lost without my family around. I belong in the other time with them. Several grandchildren are surely heartsick. My son Billy Ray and his wife Debbie have three daughters. Diann is the oldest and will soon be a freshman in high school. The youngest, Myrtie, is just as precious as can be and such a sweet child, even when her older sister Judy torments her. Holley is the beautiful daughter of my other son, Harry and his wife Patricia. They have two sons, Nick and Chris, who can be little hellions at times and seem to get into everything. Try to understand, they are my flesh and blood … my family. I cannot be at true peace until I return to them."

"We understand, mistress, but we will miss you."

She hugged the two misty-eyed Brownies, then rose and prepared to leave. "Don't fret, my little friends, we won't be going back for several more days. The three of us will spend a few private moments together before I leave. I promise."

The delighted Brownies clapped their tiny hands together in glee then quickly vanished.

Tippy made her way through the Castle maze to the intended gathering room, overwhelmed with a confidence never before known. She stopped at the doorway of the opulent ballroom. "Holy smokes," she exclaimed.

Palatial chandeliers brightly lit the colossal room, which overflowed with sumptuous garlands of multicolored, perfumed flowers. Numerous tables were set with exquisite white china and silver. Aromatic platters and copious pitchers of vintage wine awaited the onslaught.

Many guests, including the three guys, had already arrived, and the sound of spirited music enlivened the air.

Jay boomed as Tippy neared, "Well get a gander at you, girl. I've never seen you look so dang good before."

Charlie yelled, "If you think she's something, Jay, check out Meeley."

Donned in a shape flattering kelly-green gown, heads turned as the spirited female pilot walked across the sleek marble floor. Until this evening, she had only been seen in somewhat masculine attire. Meeley's ashen curls were styled, and she wore just a hint of makeup, which enhanced delicate features. Hidden beneath a common exterior resided an attractive woman.

Divulgence of this feminine side of Meeley brought a smile to Charlie's face.

Energized by the victorious skirmishes fought earlier, the night's merriment was electrifying. Adrenaline rushed through the populous like dynamic floodwaters.

Merlin whirled around the dance floor like a human tornado and caused Tippy to giggle. *If that old wizard keeps this up, no lady in this room will have a sole left on her shoes.*

She scanned the animated chamber and couldn't help notice Adera and Randy slink into the darkness of an open balcony. A silvery halo of moonlight surrounded the couple as they nestled in each other's arms and lips met. Sight of the two dampened her thoughts. *Oh Randy, I haven't seen you this happy since Sandy passed away. It saddens me to know fate will once again deny you the lasting bliss of love. When we return to our time, her heart, and yours, will be torn to shreds and separated forever. It's so unfair.*

ꝏ ꝏ

Kat shielded sensitive amber eyes from the brilliant morning light that bounced off the stark white infirmary walls. Although painful, approaching footsteps caused her to turn an aching bandaged head.

"Say, what's the idea of sleeping in so late? What 'cha think this is, a resort or something?" Jay joked as he and the other friends entered the room. "You sure took a nasty hit to that noggin. Split the sucker wide open and scared us half to death. For a while, we thought you were a goner. 'Course, I hate to be the bearer of bad news, but the rock didn't survive."

Kat forced a smile. "Gee, sorry 'bout that. I can't say I feel like running a marathon, but should be back to normal in no time." Her voice was strained. Thoughts of McLachen tormented a fatigued mind.

"Good morning," Adera said as she entered the crowded room. "I am so pleased to see you awake this morning, Kat. We have been very concerned." A delicate finger stroked the velvety petal of a peach Cala Lily. "My goodness, I fear if our sweet little Pudge brings anymore flowers, there shall be no room left for you."

"I really don't mind, Adera. They're all so beautiful. That precious Gnome can bring all she wants. I'll make space somehow." Kat began to grow teary-eyed.

The Queen sat on the bed and cradled her hand. "I know what troubles you. We share this sorrow. McLachen was a cherished friend. Absence of our noble knight will be felt by the entire realm. When you are well, we shall have a royal burial for your heroic stallion."

Kat collapsed into the caressing arms of the Queen and wept. At last, she corralled rampant emotions and faced her friends. "I'm sorry to act like such a baby. Hope y'all will forgive me. I fear there's a hollowness inside me that will never be healed. I truly loved McLachen." She wiped her face and sat up straight. "What happened to Nimue? Please, tell me she's been destroyed."

Adera smiled. "The evil vixen shall never more walk the earth, nor will the beast Ios. You were successful, Kat, and our kingdom shall be forever grateful. You often questioned why I felt confident in your quest. I confess, the last line of the prophecy was purposely withheld."

302

Victorious she will stand
upon the great serpent's head;
Proclaiming to the land,
the evil lies dead.

Randy's placid expression darkened, and he jumped to his feet. "What? Why the blazes didn't you disclose this before now. It would've allowed Kat's mind to rest easier knowing she would defeat that beast."

"On the contrary, Randy, it may have led to her becoming overconfident and in turn altered the course of fate. This knowledge may have caused Kat to meet a death she was not destined to suffer. Merneos knew of this line and questioned my decision to withhold it, but when he realized my reason for doing such, he agreed wholeheartedly."

Kat's frown mellowed. "I think I understand. By not revealing my predestined success, you forced cloistered bravery to the surface. Knowledge of an imminent win might have brought about a lax attitude. Ios could, and probably would, have killed me. How strange it all seems now. Almost like waking up from a bad dream."

Eventually, the room grew noisy as an enthusiastic group engaged each other in dynamic conversation about the war. It had all began before daybreak, and by late afternoon the conflict was over. Not even the endowed seerer, Nirage, could have envisioned the swiftness with which it had ended.

A knock on the door brought numerous exclamations.

Out of the shadows emerged a stately figure. "May I enter? I would like to pay my respects to a most proficient student."

"HORACE!" Randy rushed over and greeted the Elf. "I don't understand. I thought you were dead."

303

"I do not believe I appear to be such, although the wound does cause a bit of discomfort at times."

"How is this possible?" Jay said. "We saw you push Randy aside and take Ahren's blade."

"That is true, my friend," Horace replied as he sauntered into the room. "It was a most unfortunate incident caused by a careless error. My armor became untied and allowed the blade to penetrate. I must admit, it was a rather painful moment. Luckily, the steel did not inflict severe damage to any vital organ thus allowing our gifted Elven doctors to quickly repair the injury. I do, however, thank you for the needless concern."

Everyone looked at one another, eyes wide in amazement as they stared at their mentor. One by one, hands joined in an impassioned round of applause.

Adera rose from the bedside. "It pleases me to see you well, Horace. I ask your visit be short, for it is time we all take our leave. This young lady requires rest."

The visitors bid their friend good day until the room emptied.

Although sad to see them leave, Kat welcomed the tranquility. She laid her head down on the lofty pillow and drifted off to sleep almost at once.

೮೦೧೪   ೮೦೧೪

In the corridor, Adera pulled the three friends aside. "Randy, Jay, and Tippy please come to my study for a private word. We have matters to talk about."

"Oh no, not another war," Jay whined as they followed her to the secluded tower room.

"Will you clam it, dummy. It's probably about us going home." Randy gave the joker a playful nudge to the side.

Once inside the spacious quarters, she bid them all to sit. "I have asked you here to discuss a chosen date for your return to the other world," Adera said bluntly. "Each has gallantly provided the means necessary to reverse the portal. When you are ready, I will make the appropriate preparations for departure."

"Adera, is there a time frame for this?" Tippy asked. "Kat's far from healed. We can't just up and leave without her."

Jay nodded. "Yeah, that sure would be a crappy thing to do. Besides, I wouldn't mind taking a couple days to just goof off. Maybe even enjoy another flight on Big Mike, if that's possible. I'm afraid my riding days will be over when we get home."

Adera smiled and spoke softly, "Take as long as you wish. There is no particular moment. However, all who shall return must leave together. The portal will not reverse a second time. Due to the war, you have been denied enjoyment of our realm. Now, peace has been restored, and it is again safe, so I beseech you to partake in whatever you desire."

The three huddled together. "We each agree and want to wait for Kat," Randy announced. "If you don't object, I would like to spend all my time with you, your Ladyship."

His bold statement brought a blush to Adera's face.

"Well, I'd like to take a ride to visit with Meeley and Knox one last time," Tippy said. "Especially since I can now stay glued to a saddle. Care to join me, Jay?"

"Sorry Tip, but there's no way I'm spending my last days here in the company of that nutcase and her green monster. I'm hanging with Charlie and the boys."

"Your decisions are pleasing," replied Adera. "Bowlandria and the realm are yours for as long as you choose to remain."

ഇൗരു   ഇൗരു

Time passed like a flash in the sky, and soon, Kat was back on her feet, eager to join her friends as they investigated the kingdom.

At last, the dreaded day of departure drew near. Tomorrow they would make the trek back to their own time.

The Queen gave the group one last briefing. "You will be returned within a few minutes of the original entrance through the portal. It saddens me to say, all will once again be as they were — old and frail, with no memory of this place, or anything that transpired."

Kat hoped the budding romance between Adera and Randy would entice him to remain and was a trifle upset when she learned of his decision to travel back with the others. "I don't understand, Adera," Kat said fiercely as they talked in private one afternoon. "He adores you. Why won't he stay? I understand Tippy's decision, and in part Jay's, but not Randy's. It doesn't make a lick of sense. There's nothing back there for him."

Adera strolled to the window and gazed out. "There are many forms of love, Kat. I cannot deny Randy and I have found true love of heart, but he also possesses a boundless devotion for his friend. This bond is why he has unselfishly chosen to return. When they re-enter the other world, Jay will no longer be the strapping young man you now see. Without Randy's companionship, he will soon perish. To save Jay's life, our love must be sacrificed."

"Well, for someone who's supposed to be so dang intelligent, that's kind of stupid isn't it? When Jay reverts, there's no telling how long he'll live. If something happens to him then Randy will be all alone. I just don't get it. Randy is making the wrong decision."

"It is the only choice he can make, Kat." A tear trickled down Adera's creamy cheek. "We have spoken at length of this moment and are in complete agreement. If we are blessed by the will of destiny, our true love will one day find its way home."

Deep in thought, Kat traveled at a snail's pace as she headed for the drawing room. She found Adera's true love proclamation perplexing since it was known the portal would not allow anyone to return a second time. Armed with the knowledge she would never enjoy the companionship of her friends again, she decided to put feelings aside and relish what little time they had left together. Tomorrow, her lifelong companions would vanish forever.

Morning arrived quicker than Kat hoped. A profound sadness tugged at her heart as she casually chatted with the three cherished peers during breakfast.

As they prepared to leave the dining room, Cook rushed out and put a bear hug on Jay. "Tis indeed a sad day. I'll be missin' the likes of ya, that's for sure. Me kitchen will not be the same without the presence of your smilin bright face, but perhaps me cupboards will stay a bit fuller now that himself won't be diggin in them."

"I've enjoyed our time together, Cook. You're the greatest." He planted a kiss on a plump, teary cheek, turned, and headed for the Great Hall with the others.

Meon and Hoki bawled like babies as a tearful Tippy bid farewell. She took one last glance around the Castle, walked out, and loaded into the carriage alongside Kat.

From the heavens came a booming voice, "Well I dare say it seems you were all going to leave without so much as telling me goodbye." Merlin hovered overhead on Big Mike.

"See ya, Merlin," Jay yelled. "Take good care of my horse now, ya hear? I'll sure miss you, Big Mike."

The trip to the sea was solemn. Relar kept a tight rein on the great Thunder Hooves and held them to a slow walk, thus allowing the group to spend a few more precious minutes together. As they approached the beach, all were amazed to see it speckled with an abundance of friends.

Charlie was almost in tears as Jay sauntered over. "It's been a swell time, pal. It won't seem the same flying around without you nearby."

"Positive you won't come back with us, Charlie?" Jay asked. "Adera said you could if you wanted."

"No," Charlie replied. "This is my home now. In that other time, most of the people I knew are long gone. There's really nothing for me to go back to. Besides, everything I care about is right here, especially a frisky little lady flier."

Jay chuckled and gripped his friend's hand for the last time.

Adera walked to the water's edge, placed a finger on the cool blue surface, and muttered an incantation in an unfamiliar language. Instantly, the liquid sea became solid, and in the distance, the rainbow gateway began to form.

Randy held Adera in his arms and shared a long and final kiss. At last, she tore herself from him and made her way to shore.

The three friends stepped onto the frozen sea and began to walk off. Tippy turned and saw Kat was not with them. "Hey girl, hurry it up, or you'll get left behind."

Salty droplets tumbled from amber eyes. "I'm … not gonna return with you. There's nothing for me back there — only lonely misery. Please, try to understand. I belong in this world, not the other. This has always been my destiny."

Randy raced back to her. "What in the blazes are you talking about? Stop clowning around, Kat. This isn't funny. Your home is with us, not here. You don't belong in this place any more than we do."

"Sorry Randy, but you're wrong. I've *never* belonged in that other time. I'm exactly where I should be. This *is* my home. For the first time in my life, I feel totally complete. Now, hurry off before the portal closes. I promise to never forget you."

His gaze alternated between Kat, Adera, and the looming rainbow. At last, the handsome head lowered, and he unenthusiastically joined Tippy and Jay on the slow trek out to sea. Just before entering the portal, Randy abruptly stopped and turned. "I'll always love you both. Part of my heart will forever remain in this land."

Seconds later, all three beloved companions disappeared into the multihued mist and vanished from sight. The luminous rainbow began to fade and the sea regained its liquid life.

Kat collapsed on the silvery sand and sobbed bitterly. She could not understand why they would want to go back and face death when they could remain in this world, young and healthy for all time. "What have I done? Perhaps I should have left with them."

Adera knelt alongside. "You acted as your heart directed, Kat. Many are delighted with this choice. Our hearts overflow with love and hope it will help ease a bit of the pain. Come, we should return to the Castle. There is only heartbreak to be found here."

"If you don't mind, Adera, I'd like to stay a bit longer. I really need some time alone."

"As you wish. I shall have Relar return in a short while."

Moments later, Kat found herself sitting in quiet seclusion on the pearly white sand. She stared aimlessly out to sea. *We shared so many memories over the years. How will I ever survive without you guys? It seems only yesterday we inadvertently entered this mysterious realm and clung to each other in fear and uncertainty. The four of us have always been together... in good times and bad. It feels as though you have perished and left me alone.*

Like a mother sooths a saddened child, a gentle ocean breeze fondled her face. The horror of watching as the giant serpent struck the valiant stallion flashed in her mind. *I loved you so much McLachen, but couldn't prevent your death. I've never been able to save anyone I ever loved — not you, Bill, mom, or dad. One by one, each has perished, no matter how hard I tried to fend off death. Now in that other world, the days will grow short, and my dearest friends will die.*

Emotions at last reached a boiling point and rushed to the surface like an erupting volcano. She cried out in anguish and wept into folded arms, "You stupid girl. You've really screwed things up this time." Overwrought with grief, she did not hear approaching hoof-steps.

"What has caused you to weep so, My Lady?"

Startled, Kat leaped up and stumbled in the soft sand. Swollen eyes caused blurred vision, but slowly a form began to unfold. "M-McLachen?

"Yes, My Lady, it is I," he replied. From beneath locks of a long black mane peered temperate brown eyes. The sleek coat glistened like polished ebony. There was no apparent sign of injury, yet she had witnessed the serpent strike and saw the blood gush from his neck as the fangs penetrated.

"Are, are y-you a spirit?" She took a step back.

"No, My Lady, I am flesh and blood."

"It's not possible. This can't be real. I know this land is magical, but even it can't bring one back from the dead."

McLachen nudged her hand with his head. "Allow the warmth of my breath to reassure my mortality."

Her mind was in a whirl. *This has to be a cruel hallucination.* It was all becoming too much for her weakened body, and she felt on the verge of collapse. "You're not McLachen. I watched him die and felt the life force leave his body."

"No, you saved me, My Lady. The venom began to drain all life from me, and I could feel the coldness of death approach. Your compassion brought forth Nalay."

Kat thought back to the battle. "I do recall seeing the Unicorn, but what has that to do with you being alive? I'm confused."

"Please, your legs are unsteady. Sit and rest while I explain."

Exhausted, both mentally and physically, Kat plopped onto the sandy beach.

311

The large horse then lowered himself down to rest alongside her and continued the story, "I lay on the battlefield, paralyzed from the attack. I could hear you, My Lady, but was unable to reply. Although injured, you vehemently refused to leave my side and placed your own life in jeopardy. Your only concern was for me. That gallant gesture and unselfish love moved the great heart of Nalay."

"A Unicorn has the unique power to render a poison, any poison, harmless with their tears. However, they do not shed them often. In fact, it is a rare occurrence. When Nalay witnessed your selfless compassion, it opened his heart and filled his blue eyes. After you were taken away, he knelt by my side and allowed the miraculous liquid to fall. Gleaming golden droplets, steeped with magic from the enchanted horn, trickled into the open wounds. I could feel my spirit return almost at once."

Kat reached over and hugged the thick neck. "Oh McLachen, it *is* you."

The great stallion whinnied, "I must apologize for my tardy return. Although healed, I lingered in a weakened state. For days, I slept in the forest and grazed in the nearby meadow until strong again. Nalay also returned home to rest. To mend in such a manner inflicts great strain upon a Unicorn. He was somewhat weakened by the experience."

"Will he be all right?"

"Indeed. He has fully recovered and rejoined Adel and Wister."

Kat snuggled close and felt reassured he was alive by the heat that emulated from his body. The tears now ceased, and all sad thoughts started to vanish.

"I — I understand our friends returned today."

There was a brief pause before she replied, "Yeah, they've gone. I think what bothers me most is not being able to know what will happen to them. If only I could watch them live out their lives, but I know such a thing is impossible. I'll just have to learn to deal with it."

"One never knows what can happen. In this land, the impossible often becomes possible."

She thought the comment odd, but then brushed it aside and looked out to sea. "You would have been proud of them, McLachen. They fought with such courage and helped rid our land of that inconceivable evil."

A velvety muzzle rubbed her hand. "It seems unfair your companions shall have no memory of their noble feat. How will they explain their absence?"

"Adera said it would look as though there was a boating accident, and I was lost at sea, my body never to be found. They won't remember Bowlandria, us, or anything that transpired."

"It is more important *we* remember. It grows late, and we should return home. Allow me to transport you."

"Home … what a wonderful sound. Are you strong enough to carry my weight though? I can walk if need be."

"I am right as rain, My Lady. We shall converse more and enjoy the long ride."

Kat pulled herself up and eased onto his back. He rose carefully so she wouldn't fall and headed off in the direction of the Castle. The sun was drifting below the horizon when the pair entered the cobblestone courtyard.

"Thanks, McLachen. You can't imagine how happy I am. I thought I'd lost you forever. Something tells me we're going to share many wonderful adventures together and build a great deal of our own memories."

313

"I predict we shall build *many* memories. One never quite knows what path destiny has prepared for us. Good night, My Lady."

"Good night, McLachen." She gave him a gentle pat to the neck. "I'll see you tomorrow."

Kat bounded up the steps and hurried to her room where she was enthusiastically greeted by the two devoted Brownies. "Our hearts have been sad. We thought you left us. Is mistress Tippy coming back as well?"

"No, I'm sorry to say she will not. However, I'm here to stay and want you to know I will always be near."

The excited pair leaped into her arms and smothered a tear stained face with kisses.

At last, exhaustion took hold, and she sprawled across the opulent bed to rest. A smile crossed her face as she drifted off to sleep and entered into that mysterious world of twilight illusions. The nightmare of a life so hated had at last concluded. For the present moment, she would know only the harmony of peaceful dreams.

Chapter 20
Clatter of Friendship

Kat stirred, aroused by the aroma of fresh brewed coffee. She pulled herself from the bed's comfort, walked to the small round marble table, and poured a cup. "Hmmm, I wonder who set this here." She smiled at the sound of two childlike giggles that echoed from behind a nearby chair. "Thank you, Meon and Hoki."

Cup in hand, she meandered through the double glass doors into the courtyard garden. A soft, tepid breeze whispered through lofty tree boughs and tantalized the senses with the fragrance of wild flowers. The sound of footsteps pulled her from an entranced state and brightened golden eyes.

"Good morning, My Lady. I trust you slept well." Outside the stone wall stood McLachen, his mate, Darcy, and their frisky offspring, Chendar.

This was the first time Kat had actually seen the noble Bayard's family and was astounded by their splendor.

Darcy, a striking pale dapple-gray mare, had an elegant silver-white mane and tail. Chendar was a much deeper shade of gray with a cute little colt tail and budding white mane.

The empty cup rattled in the china saucer as Kat set it down and hopped up on the wall. "Well, good morning. I'm so happy McLachen has at last brought you to visit, Darcy. Hello, Chendar. How are you today?"

The young colt ceased the playful romping and cast an apprehensive stare. He then nestled in close to his father's side. After a moment, he replied in a quaint, child-like voice, "I am fine."

Kat began to giggle while her eyes danced with delight. "Oh McLachen, he's adorable."

The proud stallion gave a gentle nudge to the youngster. "It appears my son has his mother's beautiful looks and a bit of his father's talent. There are times I wonder if I will grow to appreciate this vocalization. He is downright headstrong and will voice his opinions, often when not wanted."

"I hate to be the bearer of bad news, McLachen, but that is part of being a child and the pitfall of being a parent."

"If you do not object, My Lady, I would like to introduce my family to the other horses and also take them on a tour of the grounds. We would stay longer, but it is rather difficult to restrain Chendar's exuberance for an extended length of time."

"I understand," Kat replied. "In fact, I should be going myself." She watched them walk off and giggled at the little colt as he frolicked around on long spindly legs. Soon, they were out of sight. "Guess I better get dressed and head out. I'm sure Adera is waiting."

Arrival at the unoccupied dining room stirred saddened emotions. "I can't sit in here and have breakfast. It's too darn painful without my friends around. Maybe Cook wouldn't mind me visiting with her." She pushed back her chair and made for the kitchen. The heavy oak door creaked as she peeked in.

Cook bounded over and gave a robust hug. "Oh ya poor wee thing. Why ya must be near starvin? Come, lass. Let me fix ya a bite to eat."

Kat entered the large cozy kitchen and sat at the informal corner table. Before she could blink twice, a heaping dish of hot oatmeal was placed in front of her.

"If ya don't be mindin, I think I'll join ya and rest me weary feet a while." The jolly woman plopped down across from Kat and sipped on a cup of hot black tea. "Well get on with it girl — eat before it grows cold. Ya need ta be gettin your strength back."

A spoonful of the hot porridge brought a smile. "Cook, this is so good. You're right. My body is still a bit weak from the accident. Gee, guess I must have missed Adera?"

"No lass, she's not been down as yet. I'm sure the poor dear is catchin some needed rest. Sleep tis a good healer they say and yesterday was a tad tryin on the two wee bits of ya."

A light rap on the door brought their conversation to an abrupt halt. They looked over and saw Adera standing in the doorway.

"Well Saint's preserve us, if it isn't herself." Cook shot from the chunky wooden chair and rushed to the Queen. "Will ya be wantin breakfast served, Your Highness?"

"I am famished, Margaret Mary, but if there is no objection, I would prefer to join you and Kat in here this morning. It may take some time to get accustomed to the quietness of the Castle once again." She took a seat alongside Kat.

Cook hurried to prepare a dish and placed it on the table.

The presence of the Queen brought comfort to Kat. "I was afraid I'd missed you this morning, Adera. Did you sleep well?"

"It was difficult, but some rest was obtained. My heart is grateful you chose to eat in this location, Kat. The coziness does ease the unpleasant stillness of the Castle."

"I went to the dining room, but didn't like the icy atmosphere," Kat replied. "This is such an enormous place, and without the boisterous clatter from the others, it seems almost lifeless now. I don't know how you've stood being alone like this for so long."

"Until your arrival, I never realized how unpleasant it was. I thank the stars you have decided to reside within these walls. Together, we shall overcome the emptiness. Have you made plans for today?"

"Really hadn't given it much thought. Without Randy, Tippy, and Jay around, I kinda feel lost. It's only been a matter of hours since they returned to the other world, but I miss those idiots already. My greatest regret is the fact I'll never see them again."

Adera reached across and took hold of Kat's hand. "How foolish of me to forget, and I do apologize. Late last evening, Merlin brought you a gift. I believe you will find it to be a most welcomed treasure. Come. Let us go to my tower room."

The two thanked Cook for such pleasant hospitality and hurried off.

In the spacious quarters, Kat nestled into one of the plush chairs and smiled as Adera handed her a small neatly wrapped package. Anxious to see what Merlin had brought, she tore into the unexpected gift with great vigor. Inside was an elegant egg-shaped crystal orb with a sparkling blue and gold flower center. "Oh Adera, it's beautiful and so unusual. I'll certainly make a trip to the stables to thank him. What a wonderful and thoughtful present."

Adera smiled. "The item is truly a masterpiece, but the appearance is not what makes it so special. It is magical and possesses a rather unique, enchanting feature. Gaze *deep* into it, dear one, and ask to see your friends."

Kat cradled it in her hands and stared into the mysterious sphere. "Okay globe, I wish to see … Randy." At once, the internal shape started to spin until it became little more than a blur. Soon, a form began to take its place. She gasped in amazement as the image sharpened. "Randy. Oh my gosh, Adera, it's really him. Randy, it's Kat. Can you hear me?"

"I regret to say, he can neither hear nor see you. Communication is not possible."

"That's a shame, but at least this will give me some peace of mind. Seeing them is almost like being together again. In a way, it's sad to witness the completed age reversion and also know they have no memory of this place." Kat continued to watch as tears formed.

Randy sat alone in a hotel room. Dark eyes, dulled by time, stared down at something in his shaky, wrinkled hand. A knock at the door broke the trance. "Come on in, the door's open."

Tippy entered — all traces of youth now erased. "Morning, Randy. Feel any better today?" She walked over and peered into his line crossed palm. "Where the dickens did you get that?"

"I found it stuffed inside my jacket pocket a few minutes ago, Tip. Pretty little thing, isn't it? Looks old and might even be valuable. I've been trying to figure out where the blazes it came from." He held up the item.

Dangling from a shiny serpentine chain was an elegant golden locket. It was in the shape of half a heart with a delicate hand crossing the face. Embedded around the entire perimeter were brilliant diamonds.

"You dang well better believe it's an expensive piece. This sucker is pure gold and these aren't fake stones. Have you opened it yet to see what's inside?"

"Nope, haven't done anything except look at it," he replied. "I have no idea who it belongs to and didn't want to pry."

"You can be such an idiot at times, Randy. The darn thing was in *your* pocket. You have every right to open it. Besides, it could shed a clue to the owner."

His arthritic fingers groped at the piece and located the latch. It flipped open, activated the tiny music box inside, and immediately began to play. "What a beautiful song. I've never listened to anything quite like it before."

Tippy wore a puzzled expression. "Have you gone and lost your marbles or something, old man."

Randy held it to her ear. "*Now* do you hear it?"

She shook her head no.

His lips grew taut and he slammed it shut. "Aw, forget it."

Kat paused from the vision and looked up. "I recognize that piece of music, Adera. We were in Durmeleigh, and it was being played on a harp late one evening. Hold on a minute, just where in the blue blazes did he get that locket?"

"I must confess it was I who placed it in his wrap before he left yesterday." Adera blushed. "The arrangement was composed by me specifically for Randy. Thanks to a bit of magical assistance from the Elves, the music box locket was created. In addition, Merlin placed a spell on it which allows only Randy to perceive the tune in that other time. Eventually, the melody will restore his memory of Bowlandria. He shall recall everything that transpired, but be unable to speak of it to anyone. There is also a snippet of my hair discreetly hidden under the faceplate. I have the other side of the piece. It contains a few small strands of his hair, secretly obtained for me by his Brownies. This magic shall unite us for as long as the two heart pendants are in our possession."

Astonished by this revelation, Kat blinked. She then noticed the companion half of the locket hanging on a delicate golden chain around the Queen's neck. "Well, I'll be doggone. Aren't you the sneaky clever one?"

"Unfortunately, the others shall continue to believe you perished in the boating accident," the Queen said. "He alone will know the truth and be granted peace."

"Oh, they're gone," Kat exclaimed as the crystal returned to its original state. "Can I see them again, or is this a one shot deal?"

"You may visit your friends whenever desired. This gift was the least we could do for such a valiant sacrifice."

"Adera, this Castle is too darn quiet. It feels so friendless. What do you think about asking Meeley and Charlie to move in here with us?"

Raised brows crinkled the Sovereign's forehead. "I had not conceived of such an idea. Neither of them desired to reside within these walls initially, but the company would be a welcome pleasure."

Kat touched Adera's shoulder. "That was a long time ago. Things have radically changed since then. I'll bet a dime to a dollar they'll jump at the opportunity. We've all changed a great deal, including you. Meeley and Charlie are no longer mere subjects. They're friends."

"For one so young, these words hold great wisdom." The Queen paused. "There are no pressing matters this day. The land is at last free of strife. Would you care to take a pleasant ride in the countryside? Perhaps, we might travel to see Meeley and present our request."

Kat sprung up. "You dang well better believe I would like to go. Just give me five minutes to get ready." She started to burst from the room, but stopped at the door, ran back, and gave Adera a robust hug. The bleak outlook felt earlier was disappearing. *Maybe the decision to stay here will turn out okay after all. I really do love Bowlandria.*

Within half an hour, horses were made ready, and the pair sped off. After a vigorous gallop across several sprawling meadows, they arrived at Meeley's residence.

As they approached the quaint thatched-roof house, the tall, mousey-blonde pilot threw open the door. "What a welcome surprise. I was just sitting here thinking about you two. Come on in."

Kat couldn't restrain her enthusiasm. "Meeley, Adera and I wondered if you'd consider moving into the Castle with us. Without the others around, it's so dreary. Besides, we miss your company." A nervous foot tapped the worn wooden planks of the floor.

The perky flyer paced back and forth for several minutes, then stopped, turned, and rubbed her chin. "I have to admit, I'm a bit lonely myself. Residing in that big place with the two of you would be a blessing. So yes — I accept the offer."

"Happy days are back," Kat shrieked. She rushed to Meeley and hugged her so hard the poor girl grunted.

"If you would care to stay in Tippy's old room, I can make the arrangements. That way, you and Kat will be close enough to chat anytime you wish."

"I think it's a keen idea, Adera, and know Tippy would have approved." Meeley exhaled and looked around. "Gosh, I have so much to do here and don't even know where to start."

"Don't sweat the small stuff, Meeley. If Adera doesn't mind, I'll stay and help you pack."

"Thanks for the offer, Kat ... sure could use some help loading up all this junk. Wish I could go right now, but priority number one is to find a place for Knox."

Adera began to giggle. "You both are such a delight and have introduced me to the contagious pleasure of real friendship. I no longer covet long days of solitude. Meeley, it *is* possible to come back with us today. Knox may reside in the structure he used prior to the war. It has since been cleaned and freshly prepared. I am sure it will meet his needs. Gather a travel bag with items of necessity, and fly Knox to the Castle. Tomorrow, I will dispatch a group to collect what personal belongings you desire."

Grey-blue eyes twinkled. "Hold on to your hat, ladies 'cause this gal's movin in. Knox is gonna be happy as a clam in that oversized barn. Gee Kat, this might allow us some time to fly together, that is, if you still do want to go up on Junar?"

"Are you serious? Of course I do. Well, on second thought, maybe I should give my thick skull a little more time to heal." She laughed and rubbed the side of her head. "Who knows, I might even be a bit more adventurous and try taking a little jaunt with you on Knox."

"That's a deal, lady, and I won't let you forget it either." Meeley rushed around like a whirlwind and gathered a few items. A short time later, she had Knox ready and took to the air.

The Queen and Kat mounted their horses and raced for the Castle.

Kat pointed upward. "Look, isn't that Charlie on Fudge?" A small band of mounted flyers soared above.

Charlie spotted them through the misty clouds, waved, then promptly landed nearby. "Hey you two, where's the fire?"

Obviously excited, the dignified monarch blurted a series of uninhibited sentences. "Would you consider moving to the Castle? Privacy is not an issue. There is an abundance of room. Since the departure of our friends, the isolation is intolerable. Meeley has agreed to relocate and is on her way. What say you?"

Charlie threw his head back and chortled. "*Slow down*, Your Grace, give me a second to breath." He let out a long sigh. "I kinda miss that bunch too, especially Jay. Things are way too quiet without that prankster around. Maybe *my* entertaining presence can bring back a little comic spark to that massive palace. Sure beats bunking in with the guys. Ladies, looks like you've got another boarder. When do you want me to move in?"

Adera clapped her hands. "You can move in immediately. Perhaps you will honor Jay by residing in his former quarters. As with Meeley, who plans to occupy Tippy's suite, all the necessary arrangements will be provided."

"Well, I certainly can't be outdone by Meeley. I accept your offer of Jay's room. Uh, does that mean I'm invited for dinner tonight?" A broad smile formed on the squadron leader's face.

Kat did a double take. "Can you believe this, Adera? He already *sounds* like Jay."

"Guess I better go get Fudge settled in and grab a few changes of clothes. See everyone in a bit … hope Cook has something tasty on the menu tonight. My stomach's rattlin' already." He gave off a spirited whoop, leaped on the handsome mount, and shot into the sky.

"It seems everything is settled, Kat, and I could not be happier. Oh my goodness, we better alert Margaret Mary there will be a few extra mouths to feed this evening." A shadow on the ground caught her eye. "I see Knox and Meeley have arrived. If you would like to go greet her, I will tend to matters at home."

Kat galloped to the big barn and watched while Meeley settled Knox in for the night. "This is going to be your new home, big boy. Isn't it great? I won't be far away and will back first thing in the morning." The gentle giant sauntered into the cavernous building and nestled his monstrous body into the fresh sweet hay. "Listen, Kat, he's purring. Whew, makes me feel better to know he's comfortable with this new arrangement."

Later that evening, the boisterous sounds of cheerfulness once again echoed throughout the Castle, and the atmosphere swarmed with gaiety.

After feasting on a hearty meal, Adera tapped the side of a crystal goblet with a silver teaspoon. "I have been restricted by so-called Queenly duties far too long. I now wish to enjoy life as an equal — and a friend. With your assistance, I will try to relax my formal mannerisms, that is, when protocol allows." An uncharacteristic yawn burst forth. "Oh, please forgive my discourtesy."

Kat laughed. "Looks like you're beginning to drop the good manners already."

Adera's lashes fluttered. "So it seems. Perhaps we should retire. It *has* been a long day. I wish you pleasant dreams."

The Castle was once again alive with activity, and the four spent many wonderful days in the company of each other.

The Royal Lady stuck to her word and relaxed courtly characteristics. She developed a tight bond of friendship with the new house guests, and for the first time, enjoyed life.

Kat often took the enchanted orb to the Queen's study. Once activated, the two would huddle together and watch. *Wow, when Randy comes into view, veiled passion certainly ignites in those turquoise eyes. Even his aged appearance hasn't dimed her attentive love. Kinda makes me sad to know they'll never be together.*

Chapter 21
Locket of Love

Randy's aged knees popped as he ambled down the brick steps of the old farmhouse and headed for the winding path that led to Kat's abandoned home. The decision was made — it was time for disposal. For several months after her disappearance at sea, the dreaded task had been put off. He opened the door, walked in, and stood frozen at the sight of her personal belongings. The scent of lilac perfume drifted across the room from her favorite pale-blue overstuffed recliner. "I can't do this." Eyes began to well as pent up emotions surfaced. "I've got to get a grip on things. She's gone, and tears won't bring her back."

On the mantel was a black and white photo of him and Kat taken at his and Sandy's wedding. The sight of his best friend, youthful and happy, triggered a dormant memory. A great fog began to lift from a distressed mind. "You're not dead, you stinker, but alive in that other time … in *Bowlandria*. Holy blazes, I seem to remember a great deal — including a very special lady named Adera. Wait 'til I tell Jay and Tippy."

He rushed home and arrived just as his friend pulled into the drive. "Hey buddy, you aren't gonna believe this, but Kat is uh … well she's uh …"

"Is what? Dead?" Jay huffed. "Darn it, Randy, you know she's passed on. Let it drop, and stop all this muttering nonsense. Are you going totally mental on me?"

"No. I'm as sane as you, which actually isn't saying much. It's the strangest thing, but for some reason the words just won't come out." Randy felt perplexed by the inability to speak of his earth-shattering discovery.

"Well, whatever it was certainly couldn't have been very important, could it? What's for dinner, dude. I'm starvin'." Crippled with arthritis, Jay shuffled into the house.

That night, Randy lay in bed and stared at the ceiling — his mind tormented by the day's macabre experience. He picked up the locket, opened it, and listened. As the haunting melody began to play, thoughts were transported back to Bowlandria, Kat, and his beautiful Adera.

₧₧₧   ₧₧₧

Having served in the Navy nearly half a century, the sea had always been the old man's love. Now widowed, Tom decided to take a long overdue cruise. Cathy, his wife, had been ill for several years and unable to travel. Ignoring objections from his two sons, Carsten and Connor, he made reservations for a lengthy voyage on the elegant Imperial Maiden.

Two weeks later, he flew to South Florida, boarded the mammoth luxury liner, and settled in as the great ship left port. Within hours, they were far out at sea. The calm, clear weather was ideal for ocean travel, and the mighty vessel steamed effortlessly toward its intended destination … one Tom would not reach.

After dinner, having no luck at slots, he decided to relax in the elaborate first class cabin. With drink in hand, he strolled out onto the balcony to enjoy the vivid sunset. The aged sailor leaned against the weathered rail and looked down into blue infinity. *I wonder how different life would have been if I'd stayed in South Carolina with Kat? It seems kinda odd to be thinking of her now after all these years.* He snickered. *Who do you think you're kidding, bunko? She's always been in this mind — and heart.*

Tom had been a devoted husband and adoring father. Although he loved Cathy and the marriage was strong, a part of his life always felt incomplete. Out of respect, all thoughts of Kat were laid to rest.

A vision began to play out in a worn-out mind as it recalled the last night spent with Kat. It was never his intention to hurt her, and yet that is what happened. The departure was violent and cruel. Tom had allowed foolish pride to get in the way of their happiness. Many times over the years, he placed a call to apologize, but always hung up before the first ring.

The sound of waves slapping playfully against the gigantic hull snapped him out of the daydream. As he peered into the multihued horizon, an unnatural greenish light caught his eye. It emanated from inside a mysterious cloud formation, which glowed eerily as the specter glided across the top of the water toward the ship. "What the sam hill is that?" The sinister vapor continued to draw closer. "In all my years at sea, I've never seen anything like this before."

Panic grabbed hold. He turned to flee, but found himself unable to move. It felt as though his feet and torso was bound in heavy chains. A bizarre, unseen force prevented any motion. Eyes widened as the alarming groan of distressed metal resonated in his ears. A sharp crack broke the air, and the sturdy iron railing gave way releasing Tom's feeble body. A half empty cocktail glass shattered upon the deck as the old man plummeted helplessly to the awaiting sea and vanished into the ghoulish mist.

ꕥ ꕥ

Kat rushed into Adera's study. "Jerome said you needed to see me immediately. It was a matter of great importance. What's happened?"

"Do not be alarmed. All is well within the realm. It seems a new visitor will arrive this evening. I would like you to greet this guest. McLachen will transport you to the sea."

"I don't understand, Adera. It's always been Bagi's job. Why on earth do you suddenly want *me* to do this? Say, how come I'm taking McLachen instead of your carriage?"

"Bagi is away at the moment, and someone must attend to this matter. I feel you are the perfect candidate. Would you rather I send someone like Cook or Jerome in your stead?" She snickered into a cupped hand. "As for use of my carriage — it is unnecessary. The one entering is an accomplished rider. McLachen can easily carry the additional weight and safely maneuver in the diminished light."

Kat felt irritated by this unprecedented request. "I'll do it, but don't blame me if something goes wrong. I'm not *Bagi* and can't guarantee the results."

"I have enormous faith in your abilities and confident the assignment will be handled appropriately," Adera replied. "You may want to depart at this time. They draw near. Thank you, my sweet girl. I shall wait for your return."

"Well, this is sure going to be one screwed up mess," Kat grumbled and belligerently tromped down the grand

330

staircase. Outside, she found McLachen. Once mounted, the pair galloped to the sea.

As they approached the beach, Kat looked into the darkening expanse of water and could see a figure emerge from the glowing dense mist. "Gee, McLachen, that looks like it might be a man. I know this is going to sound bonkers, but there's something familiar about his walk."

"Could he be someone you know, My Lady? Perhaps this is the reason our Queen has asked you to come."

"It would be nice to know who the blast it is, but dum-dum me forgot to ask. Uh, McLachen, *maybe* it'd be best for you not to speak straight off. I'm not sure how to handle things as it is and a talking horse might not help matters."

"That is a wise decision, My Lady, and I will gladly comply. We do not want to frighten this visitor more than he already must be."

As the man drew closer, clouds parted to reveal a handsome face.

She gasped. "His eyes, I know those eyes, but it can't be him. It's not possible."

The new arrival waved and picked up pace as he made for shore.

Kat stood motionless alongside McLachen as a soft sea breeze blended her long black locks with the stallion's mane.

Only yards away he stopped. "Kat?"

She tried to answer, but was unable to utter a sound.

Tom stepped forward, reached out, and warm fingers clasped a trembling hand.

She drew near, and once again stared into gentle hush-puppy eyes. "Tom, it *is* you — it really, really is."

331

Arms encircled each other, and lips met for the first time in many years. After what felt like an eternity, they walked hand-in-hand along the sandy beach.

"Kat … are we ghosts?"

To reaffirm their existence, she squeezed his hand. "No, we're quite alive. It's somewhat complex to explain, but I'll try. Just give me a second to catch my breath. I'm having a hard time believing you're here and find myself a bit speechless."

He began to laugh. "Now I *know* this is all make-believe. You've *never* been short of words in your life."

The sound of his voice caused a jittery stomach, and she could feel the radiance of love rebound in her heart. *Calm down, Kat, calm down.* She drew a deep breath before speaking, "You've entered another time dimension, Tom — a completely different world. Welcome, to the Kingdom of Bowlandria. You won't believe this place. Some things are beyond your wildest dreams."

"The only dream I personally care to have right now is the one standing directly in front of me."

Amber eyes lowered and cheeks blushed. "Dang it, Tom, pay attention or I won't tell you another thing."

"Fine, doesn't bother me, shortcake. I don't give a hoot how I got here or where we are. I only know I have you back, Kat, and I'm never going to let you get away from me again, ever." He lifted a bemused face to his and delivered a loving and passionate kiss.

A torrent of tears saturated his shoulder as she wept. "I've missed you so much, Tom. I'm sorry I hurt you."

Gentle fingers wiped a moistened cheek. "Don't cry, Kat. I never could bear to see you weep. It's me who needs to apologize, not you. My arrogance ripped us apart and destroyed our love. My entire life I've felt a void in my heart and never realized it was because you weren't there to fill it. I love you, Kat. Always have and always will. Can you ever forgive me for the pain I've caused?"

Her mind was in overload. There was so much to ask and tell, but maturity had made her wiser. She knew not to prod … to simply let things take their natural course. "The past is long behind us, Tom. We were both young and stupid back then. Now, let's have no more talk of it. For whatever reason, destiny has brought us together again and offered a second chance for the future." He teetered, and she grabbed his arm. "Whoa, you look a bit unsteady. Think we better sit you down."

He nodded and dropped to the soft sand. "Sorry Kat. This excitement is a little much for the old ticker."

"I understand, but it's not because you're aged. Look at your hands, Tom. Do they appear to be those of an old man? This weakness is due from the ordeal of entering through the portal. We all felt much the same. It tends to drain you of all energy for awhile."

He touched his face. Leathered, wrinkled flesh had been replaced with soft firm skin. "What's going on? How can this be?" He leaped to his feet.

The antics caused her to giggle. She gave a brief explanation of the miraculous gift, including their immortality. "Tom, this is a beautiful and magical land filled with all kinds of legendary creatures. McLachen is one of them."

"Your horse? He's magnificent, but what makes him so special?"

"Well," she said tentatively. "You see, he's a Bayard. They have the unique ability to speak."

The handsome young man looked at her and cocked an eyebrow. "Okay, what's the joke? You know as well as I do there's no such thing as a talking horse."

McLachen snorted. "I beg your pardon, young master. What My Lady says is truth."

The stallion's verbalization caused Tom to stumble backwards and fall. "Whoa, did he actually speak, or have you become a ventriloquist?"

Kat laughed so hard she thought her sides would burst. "Think I had better explain a *lot* more things before you have a heart attack."

He listened wide-eyed while she told him of the Queen, the Brownies, and some of the other creatures.

"We should be leaving for the Castle, My Lady," McLachen announced. "The hour grows late. If you will both mount up, I shall transport you home."

Tom walked to the elegant stallion and gently stroked an ebony neck. "You certainly are exquisite. I've never met a talking horse before, and it kinda threw me for a loop. Hope you'll forgive my tactless manners."

McLachen nickered, "It was understandable and forgiven. Would you be so kind to assist My Lady aboard?"

Tom scooped Kat into his arms, which brought a girlish squeal. He then placed her gently on the noble stallion's back, and flung himself up behind her. Moments later, they began the long trip to the Castle.

When the impressive residence at last came into sight, Tom gasped at the elegance and magnitude of the giant structure. McLachen halted to allow the awestruck new visitor a moment to take it all in.

To spare Tom a great deal of unnecessary stress, Kat explained as much as possible about the royal structure and the realm. "I'm sure Adera will arrange for you to have Randy's room. It's just across the hall from mine and opens into a wonderful little garden. I've never met the two Brownies who took care of Randy and Jay, but know they did an excellent job. I sure hope this will help you adjust a little easier. It was one continuous shock after another for the four of us. The biggest one was when we met Knox."

"Knox? Who's that?"

She snickered. "Well, if you think for one darn minute I'm gonna let you off the hook and tell you everything, you have another think coming. You'll meet him soon enough. All I'll say is hold on to your britches, or he might just scare them off you."

Tom threw his head back and laughed. "I always loved your down-to-earth sense of humor." He gave her a squeeze and a little peck on the cheek.

Beacons of crystal moonlight illuminated the spacious courtyard as they entered. After dismounting, they both thanked McLachen, who in turn bid them a gracious good night and walked off to join his family.

Kat pushed open the massive wooden doors and tried to conceal her laughter as she watched Tom turn in a slow circle, spellbound by the grandeur of the Great Hall.

"Good evening, Tom. My name is Adera. I am Queen of Bowlandria and a friend of Kat's. I trust your arrival went well?"

He stood silent with mouth agape. Flushed, he struggled to speak, "I — I must say, Kat's description was far from accurate. Your beauty and grace is beyond compare, Your Highness. I'm still somewhat confused, but am adjusting. It seems I tumbled off that ship right

335

into Kat's arms. This palace is remarkable, and I thoroughly approve of its occupants."

Adera beamed. "Thank you, Tom. I hope you shall consider it your home, as we all do. Will you join me in the drawing room? Dinner was served several hours ago. I hope our meager buffet will ease your hunger. Meeley and Charlie are waiting and anxious to meet you."

As they walked into the room, Kat tugged at Adera's sleeve and whispered, "It seems you knew *precisely* who was entering today, didn't you, my devious Queen. This was a down right sneaky trick. Jay would've approved wholeheartedly." She laughed, took the Queen's arm, and strolled in.

With pride, Kat introduced Tom to Meeley and Charlie, who, like Adera, fell in love with the charismatic young man almost right away. After some refreshments, and a great deal of camaraderie, the evening was brought to an end.

As predicted, Randy's old room had been made ready for the new visitor.

Later, the reunited couple met in the small garden. "I swear you're even more beautiful then I remember, Kat, especially these spellbinding amber eyes. Nothing could have prepared me for this moment. In fact, I dread going to sleep for fear I might wake up to find it all a dream." He pulled her close and kissed the waiting lips.

After years apart, the two were blissfully complete, exactly as 'destiny' had planned all along.

Days faded into months, each full of rapturous love and adventure.

Meeley and Charlie developed a romantic relationship. The pair was often seen soaring across the heavens together, alternating use of the flying horses and Knox.

Merlin had suggested Tom try Big Mike. Since Jay's departure, the stallion was somewhat depressed and allowed no other rider. Cheers of delight were sounded when the great pinto joined minds with this handsome new arrival. After that miraculous day, Kat and Tom joined in the fun and took wing alongside their companions.

The first encounter with Knox went just about the way Kat had envisioned. Everyone laughed hysterically as Tom fell flat on his backside when Knox strolled out of his barn.

Adera occupied a great deal of her time in the company of Merlin and King Merneos. Many times, the Queen would join the couples in flight on her unrivaled white winged-stallion, Pegasus.

Horace made numerous trips to Bowlandria and quickly grew fond of Tom. A brotherhood, similar to the one between him and Randy, developed.

One lazy afternoon, Kat enjoyed a peaceful moment alone with Adera. "It doesn't seem fair for all of us to be so happy while you suffer without your love. I feel guilty at times and wish there was something we could do to alleviate this anguish."

"Thank you for the kind thoughts, Kat, but do not concern yourself. Randy is never more than a heartbeat away. My soul finds pleasure knowing you are content and in the arms of the one always desired. I have often said true love will always find its way home to the heart. Be assured, it *always* does."

Months later, in a wedding ceremony fit for a princess, Kat and Tom were united in marriage, followed soon after by the unexpected joining of Meeley and Charlie.

The couples chose to make the Castle their permanent residence — a decision the Queen found gratifying. The four offered tremendous solace to the lonely Sovereign, and all shared a wealth of carefree moments. At last, the cold, lifeless structure had become a Palace of happiness.

One day, Kat began to notice an odd change in the Queen. She appeared to be in an almost euphoric state. *I wonder what the dickens has caused her to act this way.*

During breakfast, she asked the others if they had noticed the unusual behavior.

Meeley leaned up to the table. "I sure as heck have, Kat. If I didn't know better I'd swear she was head over heels in love. What else could make her as giddy as a schoolgirl?"

Kat nodded in agreement. "Sure seems that way, doesn't it. Maybe she's finally over Randy. After all, he's a long way from here and won't be coming back. Could she have found someone else we aren't aware of?"

"I'll bet it's Merlin. They do seem to spend a lot of time together." Charlie's statement brought several frowns. "Hey, don't look at me like that. It *is* possible you know."

Tom chuckled. "Yeah, it's possible, Charlie, but I don't believe it's him or anyone else we know. One thing's for sure, someone, or something, has our Queen in a thither. I've never seen her quite so buoyant. She's almost like a little girl in a doll factory."

That night, Charlie and Tom went to check on some colts recently born to the flying horses. Meeley tagged along to check on Knox who resided nearby.

It had been several months since Kat last checked on her friends back home. *Think I'll take advantage of this isolation, get my orb, and see what the old gang is up to.* They were well up in age now. Knowing their clandestine date with death would eventually arrive, she worried about them.

As the magical sphere cleared, she saw Randy kneeling on the ground in front of an engraved granite tombstone. The heading said ... LANDERS, Mary and Jay. "Oh no." Distressed by the unhappy spectacle, Kat tossed the delicate crystal egg on the bed, refusing to watch any further.

⁂Ȣ   ⁂Ȣ

As Randy wiped away a tear, Tippy hobbled up alongside the aging man and placed a liver-spotted, wrinkled hand on his shoulder. "Seems like one by one we're all heading for that big pasture in the sky. Eight years ago we lost Kat. Now, Jay. Things sure aren't going to be the same without our joker around. I've been thinking about you living alone in that big old house. It's going to get kinda lonely without Jay around. Maybe you would consider moving in with Jim and me. We'd be thrilled to have you."

Slowly, and painfully, Randy rose to his feet. "I appreciate the offer, Tip, but think I'm gonna ask my niece Donna and her husband Ken to move in. They're struggling a bit right now, and such a proposition would benefit us all. Donna has always adored the farm, and both love horses. After they get settled, I'm off to Miami. A while back, I purchased a boat and am planning to take it out on a short run to the Islands soon. When I return, I'll have Ken fly down and bring her back to South Carolina."

Tippy threw up her arms. "What? Have you lost your brains somewhere? You are seventy-six years old, Randy. That's too dang old to pull such a cockamamic stunt as

339

this. Those waters are dangerous. What on earth has gotten into you?"

He wrapped one arm in hers and strolled from the gravesite. "Let's just say I have my reasons for going, Tip, and leave it at that. You might remember the boat — the Charger?"

She stood by the car with hand on hip, her tone angry, "This isn't funny, Randy. That stupid boat caused Kat's death and darn near got us killed in the process. It's evil. Have you gone completely bats? The blasted thing needs to be taken out to sea and burned."

"Calm down mamma bear, before you bust a gut string. Ever since the accident, I've searched for the Charger. It's not some kind of nefarious entity, Tip. It's a beautiful vessel, nothing more. What happened was simply a tragic accident. A broker notified me a little over a year ago. Said the boat was in bad shape, but had potential. I flew down to meet with the owner who let it go for a song. I then sent the old vessel to the boatyard for a complete refitting. Three weeks ago, the exhausting task was completed, and the Charger's ready to go." He opened the car door and helped ease her tired body down.

"Ken's a darn good boat captain, but the charter business isn't very profitable unless you have your own vessel. I figured what the heck, why not give him and Donna the opportunity to make some money and have a go at life. They're coming over for dinner tonight, and I'm gonna propose my idea. Pretty darn sure they'll accept. Shoot Tip, everything will be left to them when I'm gone anyhow. Why not go ahead and give them a head start now."

Faded blue eyes filled with concern. "Look, I know you're upset about losing Jay, but this is nuts. You're not thinking straight."

"Nothing has ever been clearer, dear lady." He smiled and kissed her on the cheek. "Of course I'm sad to lose Jay, but you know as well as I do this is what he's always wanted. Since Mary's death, he couldn't wait to join her. Now they're together and he's finally at peace."

Donna and Ken arrived for dinner around six. During the meal, Randy divulged his plan. As predicted, the couple were overjoyed and accepted without hesitation. "Ken, I'm headin' to Miami in a couple weeks and gonna take the Charger over to the Bahamas. When I get back to port, I'll give a yell. You can then fly on down and bring this classic lady home. Every nut and bolt has been redone. The Charger looks exactly like she did the day they first put her in the water. Trust me. You won't have an ounce of trouble chartering her."

Ken sighed. "Are you positive you want to take this trip alone, Uncle Randy? You know those waters can be darn tricky at times. I'll be more than happy to go with you if you'd like."

"I appreciate the concern, Ken, but this is something I have to do for myself. Don't worry. There's still a bit of life left in this frail old body. I'd like for you and Donna to move in as soon as possible. Why waste any more of your money on rent."

Within a week, the relocation transpired. Donna happily positioned their personal things around the spacious farmhouse, while Ken tended to the horses and outside work.

Randy was scheduled to leave the following day for South Florida. That afternoon, he saddled one of his

341

favorite horses and took a long ride around the property. Kat's old house had long been removed. All that remained was an overgrown foundation. He stopped a moment and stared at the decaying mass, then smiled serenely and continued the ride. Later that night, he walked out on the elaborate portico, scanned the star-studded landscape, and filled his lungs with the sweet fragrance of the blooming Carolina Jessamine.

Early the next morning, Ken drove him to the airport. "Please Uncle Randy, let me tag along. I'm really worried. This is foolish."

An aged hand patted the tall lad on the back. "I'll be fine. Relax and grant this ol' geezer one last pleasure. You mean well, but I have to go alone."

Ken watched as the feeble, elderly man boarded the plane.

Dull eyes brightened as Randy caught sight of the Charger. She looked as grand and new as the day he first saw her. The boatyard had virtually performed a miracle and brought the deteriorating vessel back to its former glory. He slowly climbed to the fly bridge and turned the key. Two powerful new diesels sprung to life.

A dockhand threw off the lines, and the boat eased from the slip.

"Well pretty girl, it's just the two of us now. Let's see what you've got." He pushed the throttles down and the engines swiftly responded. The sleek bow of the Charger cut through the waves as though they were invisible. As before, once they entered the Gulf Stream, Randy set the autopilot and eased back in the thick-padded helm chair, both feet propped on the console.

Once out of sight of land, Randy reached in his pocket and removed the enchanted trinket. A smile formed as the music began to play, and his mind drifted to Bowlandria. On the horizon, he saw a familiar formation. "Looks like it's time to go."

The engines were shut down and a call placed to the Coast Guard giving the coordinates. Hands shook as he fumbled to inflate the small Zodiac. A letter to Ken and Donna was placed inside the cabin. Moments later, a farewell was bid to the Charger, and the aged skipper climbed into the raft. Unable to paddle with any vigor, he struggled to reach the awaiting arches. Tired, and near death, Randy laid back as the rubber vessel drifted into the welcome darkness.

ℂℂCQ ℂCQ

Kat and Tom were breathless as they bounded into the Queen's study. "You sent for us, Adera?"

There was an intense glow surrounding her like a halo. "Will the two of you accompany me to the sea? Someone special is entering today, and I desire your company."

"Who's coming?" Kat asked. "Isn't it rather odd for you to personally greet them? I've never known you to do such a thing."

"Yes, it is indeed unusual for me to perform such a task. However, this arrival requires my *individual* attention." Adera trembled and wrung her hands as though overly anxious. "Relar is waiting. We should be on our way."

When Kat and Tom caught sight of the royal carriage, they both looked at each other in amazement. Garlands of deep red roses were draped over its ornate white body and more trimmed the shiny black leather harness of the four white horses.

"Holy crickets," Kat exclaimed. "This must *really* be someone important."

343

The three climbed in, and with a crack from Relar's whip, they were under way.

Her Royal Highness looked more beautiful than ever. A gown of glittering pale lilac accented vivid turquoise eyes, which literally danced with life. Her hair fell softly to one side like lustrous waves of spun gold and had been adorned with a multitude of tiny purple violets.

Kat fidgeted as curiosity surfaced. "Okay, when do you propose to tell us who's arriving?"

Tom nudged her in the side and gave a nasty glare.

Adera giggled. "I shall tell you … it is … *Randy*."

Overwhelmed with excitement, Kat yelled out, "Are you serious? He's gonna come back? I don't understand. How's this possible?"

"My beloved should be entering at any time. One day I will explain how this came to be, Kat, but not today. It is rather complicated. However, there is one small request. I know you are justifiably anxious to see your friend, but please give us the first few moments alone."

"Don't say another word, Adera," Tom replied. "I *guarantee* she's going to stay right here in this carriage until you bring him back to us, even if I have to sit on her to do it."

Kat gave him a dirty look. "I had no intentions of interfering, Mr. Know-It-All."

Tom snickered. "Yeah, well tell it to someone who doesn't know you. You're gonna stay right here with me."

Soon, they arrived and could see Randy making his way to shore.

Adera jumped from the carriage before it had completely stopped and dashed to the water's edge.

Restored youthful legs allowed Randy to break into a brisk run and sprint forward.

The Queen, unable to restrain the anxiety, stepped onto the glassy blue surface and raced toward her love. Seconds later, they embraced as tears of joy overflowed.

He held her face in his hands, stared into alluring eyes then kissed her tenderly. "I believe, my Queen, you misplaced something? Does this belong to you?" Randy dangled the golden locket.

"I believe it does." She took the trinket from his hand and placed it next to hers. As the two halves touched, they were united by magic, and a single locket formed. "Now my broken heart is made whole once more."

After several moments and many words, Randy and Adera sauntered onto the silvery beach.

Kat could stand it no longer, broke from Tom's grasp, leaped down, and ran to her friend.

He grunted from a voracious hug. "Whoa kiddo, you're crushing my lungs."

With his beloved Adera on one arm, and Kat on the other, they walked to the carriage. "Holy smokes — Tom. How the heck — when the heck — did you get here? Talk about a surprise." The longtime friends gave each other a masculine welcome. "Wow, it just doesn't get any better than this. Life is absolutely perfect."

The two couples sat across from each other and snuggled contentedly.

Relar snapped the whip, and the spirited horses lurched forward, only to be reined in and brought to a slow walk. "Easy lads, we're in no hurry today." He cast a discreet glance back at the enraptured passengers and let out a hearty baritone laugh. "No, we're not in hurry at all."

The magic of the locket, and true love, had allowed destiny to fulfill its intended design. Happiness would

345

now resound throughout the land. That is … for the present moment.

ഔരു ഔരു

Four hundred and twenty miles to the north, in the desolate kingdom of Mantalac, the sunless sky shrouded the titanic structure with great despondency. A forlorn blackness of the Castle blanketed the land with boundless oppression, and happiness could not be found in even the smallest corner or within the humblest being.

The sound of cloven hooves reverberated throughout the dungeon as Cianest paced the cold hard stone floor within the confines of her prison walls. For many centuries, she desired freedom and lusted for the taste of fresh warm blood. However, all pleas fell upon the deaf ears of a heartless master.

She whirled around in the direction of approaching, and all too familiar, footsteps. Red eyes were set ablaze with hatred, and words of repulsion hissed as *he* neared.

Glossary of Characters and Terms

Adera (ah-deer-ra)-Appointed Queen of Bowlandria-blonde-turquoise eyes-strikingly beautiful-immortal-lives alone in Castle built by the Ancients-has never been married-Fiancé Tanas was killed by jealous sorceress.

Ahren (a-ren)-Demonic warrior appointed by Nimue to train and lead her troops-vicious-has no conscience-larger then other Shankquas-extremely muscular-hates Randy.

Bagi (Badge-gee)-A nymph-long curly red hair-emerald green eyes-beautiful-aloof-dedicated to Adera.

Bayard (bay-erd)-Mythological horses-can speak and carry great weight.

Bowlandria (Bow-land-dree-ah)-First occupied and the most important kingdom in other realm-gateway through the portal-beautiful-peaceful-medieval in appearance-no modern features.

Durmeleigh (derm-ma-lee)-An Elf kingdom-secluded-built in mountain valley-enchanting-private.

Ganieda (Ga-nay-dah)-Magically talented sister of Merlin who entered with him-kind-gentle-beautiful-killed by sorceress Nimue.

Helons (he-lons)-Goblin warriors resurrected by Nimue to fight Adera-toad like appearance-small bat-like wings will not let them achieve flight, but can leap twenty to thirty feet off the ground-cannibalistic-odorous.

Hoki (ho-kee)-Female Castle Brownie who cares for Kat-about two feet high-sharp pointed ears-large light brown eyes-pretty-pixie-like-short cropped light brown hair-delicate frame-shy and most times invisible-loyal.

Horace-Elf name is **Netho** (nee-tho)-tall-handsome-muscular-has strong features-blue eyes-part human-immortal-highly aloof-one of Durmeleigh's best warriors-keeps his gentle heart secret-Elf father is deceased-juvenile brother is Enal-(ee-nall).

Ios (eye-os)-Last of the sea Titans-an eighty foot sea serpent who can travel on land as well as in the sea-vicious-lust's for blood-imprisoned by King Legar for vile deeds-freed by Nimue and is now her servant.

Junar (ju-nar)-Kat's personal flying horse-brother to Kiv-a golden palomino with white mane, tail and wings.

King Legar- (lee-gar)- King of the me-people-handsome-long white hair and beard-icy blue eyes-widowed-has three daughters-meets Nimue in mermaid form, is seduced by her and they soon marry-he and his people become imprisoned by his Sea Queen to be used as slaves—or food for her pet sharks.

King Merneos-(mer-nee-os)-Elf King of Durmeleigh-entered when the Elves time among mankind had ended-aloof-kind-generous-tall-long platinum-blonde hair-penetrating blue eyes-pointed ears-pale skin-mannerly-intelligent-immortal-great warrior-close to Adera and Merlin-bestowed gift of youth and immortality to all who enter realm-detests violence, but will fight when necessary-has close relationship with Nirage.

Kiv (Keeve)-Merlin's personal flying horse-brilliant copper-coated chestnut with same colored wings.

Knox (nocks)-Meeley's dragon-enormous yellow eyes-large, leathery bat-like wings of translucent green- around forty feet high-iridescent green scaled body-short legs with long claws-immense sharp white teeth-dragon type head topped with ivory horns-harmless to friends, but protective of realm and those he loves-purr's when happy-fly's at tremendous speed-can breath fire-hatched shortly before Meeley arrived and given to her by Adera.

Maris (maa-rus)-Oldest of the three Mer-Princesses- name is Latin for Of the Sea-waist long dark brown hair-blue eyes-long, wispy flowing tail and fins-scales of blue and aqua-familiar with land above-wise.

McLachen (mick-latch-in)-A magnificent black stallion-the last Bayard-has the ability to speak-is exceptionally close to Kat.

Meeley (meal-lee)-Female pilot who entered realm in late thirty's-has whispery Kansas drawl-tall-gray eyes-somewhat attractive-hearty laugh-takes to the air on her "little green flying machine"-lives in a distant cottage with pet, Knox.

Meon (me-onn)-Female Castle Brownie who cares for Tippy. Appearance is similar to Hoki.

Nalay (nal-lay)-Unicorn stallion-white with exceptionally long curly mane and tail-penetrating blue eyes-magical-intelligent-has brilliant golden horn-tears can render any poison harmless-capable of great speed-gentle-lives with mate Adel-(ah-dell) and baby colt Wister-(wist-ter) at Unicorn Lagoon-shy and secretive-friend to Adera-very close to McLachen-fascinated with Kat.

Nerissa (ner-ris-ah)-Middle Mer-Princess-name is Latin for Daughter of the Sea-waist long blonde hair-blue eyes-and has green and yellow scales-impetuous at times.

Nimue (nim-u-ay)-Wicked sorceress who entered with Merlin-hates Adera-shape shifter-beautiful-long curly black hair-brilliant green eyes-shapely-murders Ganieda and Tanas then flees into the sea to escape the wrath of Adera-happens across Mer-people-transforms into a mermaid-enchants and marries King Legar to become Queen of the sea-possesses his Trident-builds demon army-longs to control all of earth, including other realm-control's Ios.

Nirage (near-raj)-Hauntingly beautiful-Elvin sorceress-tall-immortal-slim-mysterious-long white hair-icy blue eyes-has gift of clairvoyance-is very old-wise-magical.

Pegasus (pay-ga-sus)-Legendary horse and personal flying mount for Queen Adera- pure white body and wings-is the original stallion brought to Bowlandria by the ancients.

Relar (ree-lar)-Adera's personal coach driver-dark skinned-medium height-strong masculine features-handsome-deep brown eyes-short black hair-very regal looking and acting-has baritone voice with slight Jamaican accent-easily controls the Thunder Hooves-compassionate-extremely intelligent.

Romey (rah-mee)-youngest Mer-Princess-acts much like a young teenager-name is Latin for Sea Dew-waist long red hair-has orange and gold scales-very immature and disobedient.

Shankquas (Shank-qwas)-Horrific water goblins raised up from the bowels of Hell by Nimue to fight Adera-three feet high-donkey like ears-putrid green skin color-cannibalistic-deadly-grotesque-somewhat human in body shape-dagger like teeth-sharp claws-like finger tips-emotionless-soulless.

Tanas (tan-nas)-Friend and protégé of Merlin-handsome-fearless-falls in love with Adera and becomes her fiancé-killed at Adera's feet by Nimue.